ARCTIC MENACE

"[Amber Dawn] is a great action-packed novel. It lets you in on the complexities of the United States intelligence community in our war on terrorism. The author obviously knows his way around the territory!"

Robert Miller, former Navy intelligence officer

"Intrigue, action, terrorist plots, political maneuvering. *Amber Dawn* has it all. Ken Andrus weaves an intricate, complicated web as this tale winds toward its exciting climax."

George Wallace, author of *Warshot*

"A great read. Don't start *Flash Point* unless you have the time to finish it in one sitting. Andrus knows the region, the politics, the militaries and the importance of the South China Sea area. Today's news headlines mirror the "fiction" he began writing several years ago."

Adm. R.J. "Zap" Zlatoper, USN (Ret)

"*Flash Point*…will make your day."

All Reading World

ARCTIC MENACE

KENNETH ANDRUS

On the 20th anniversary of 9/11, I am honored to dedicate this novel to those who have served our country in the armed forces, protecting our liberty, freedom, and way of life.

There are no extraordinary men, just extraordinary circumstances that ordinary men are forced to deal with.

William "Bull" Halsey, Fleet Admiral, US Navy

Prologue

THE CHUKCHI SEA
CAPE LISBURNE, ALASKA
MONDAY 30 OCTOBER

Li Tsang reached his decision to return to their mother ship, yet he remained unsettled. What was it about this desolate void that refused to release him from its cold, dark embrace?

He gave a push to his wire-rim glasses with his index finger, adjusted his woolen watch cap, and peered through the *Flying Fish's* viewport, studying the barren, olive-gray mud flats of the Chukchi Sea's abyssal plane. An ancient Chinese proverb came to mind prompting him to flip the toggle for the mini-sub's exterior floodlights. *Better to light a candle than to curse the darkness.* Something caught his eye at the far edge of the beam's light.

"*Zhè bù kěnéng!*" He gasped in disbelief, the piercing sound amplified within the *Flying Fish's* cramped personnel sphere. Surely his eyes deceived him. He clutched the mini-sub's joystick, peering through the vessel's viewport. "This can't be," he repeated.

He switched his focus to the 3-D feed from the sub's external cameras and toggled the zoom for a better look. Clusters of crystalline-shaped rocks blanketed the sea floor.

He knew what they were at a glance: polymetallic nodules. He'd seen them before, surrounding the hydrothermal vents spewing basaltic debris in the deep-sea trenches of the mid-Pacific and Indian Oceans. But these were huge, unheard of. He'd read the isolated reports, hearsay really, a fool's dream: monazite and bastnasite. A trillion-dollars' worth of rare-earth minerals. Were the reports true? Geologically, his discovery made no sense. Would anyone even believe him? *But if they were real and we could secure the mining rights?* The implications stunned him. China would rule the world. And me....? *I would be awarded the Order of the Heroic Exemplar, our nation's highest honor.*

He activated the video record and shot a glance at his co-pilot wedged into the seat beside him. At first, he mistook the quizzical expression on Chenglei's face for mutual disbelief at what they'd observed on the ocean floor. Then Chenglei turned to him, his eyes widened with alarm.

"Do you smell something?"

Tsang sniffed the scrubbed air and jerked back from the video display. His nostrils flared at the faint acrid odor of burning insulation. A paralyzing chill raced down his spine, dread replacing the euphoria of discovery. *There must be a short in one of their electrical systems—or something worse.*

He fought the suffocating fear that gripped his chest, forcing himself to scan the vessel's bank of computer monitors and service panels. An electrical fault, however minor, could burst into life-threatening fire. Did he detect a hint of smoke coming from one of the circulation vents?

Tsang fixed his eyes on the readout of the electrical supply system. The amperage of their lithium-ion battery stacks indicated an unexpected drain. He'd already noted a loss of charge from the stacks earlier in their mission. He'd presumed the batteries were depleted supplying power to push the *Flying Fish* through the strong offshore currents of the Bering Strait.

An ominous silence and the eerie red glow from the sub's interior lighting reinforced his unease. He held the back of his hand to one of the vents. Nothing. *What would cause that? Are the ventilation fans down?* Without the fans, their scrubbers wouldn't function properly. The cabin's carbon dioxide levels....

They had to return to their support ship or risk being trapped under the advancing ice pack, slowly poisoned by the cabin's foul air. But he couldn't return. Not yet.

He twisted toward Chenglei. His co-pilot's pupils were dilated in terror, the color drained from his face. "Check our operating voltage and discharge current."

Chenglei's head snapped toward the incandescent green of a touchscreen mounted to his right. He tapped his index finger on the battery icon and studied the readouts: Temperature, discharge rate, operating voltage, remaining capacity. His eyes remained fixed on the monitors. "What's our position?"

He looked at the real-time navigation display and grunted before double-checking their track. A black dot marked their current position ten miles off the Alaskan coast west-northwest of a point named Cape Lisburne—well within American territorial waters. His pre-deployment brief included a side note that Cape Lisburne, the site of an old cold-war defense radar base, was being evaluated for re-activation.

He hissed a curse. *Wáng bā!* He'd been too distracted by his unexpected finding to notice the extent of the incursion. He'd taken the submersible to the depths of the Mariana Trench, but faced an entirely different proposition navigating the shallow waters of the U.S. continental shelf. His orders directed him to collect bathometric data of the seafloor and document the peculiar convergence zones of the different currents, cascading isothermal layers, and salt gradients for the Navy's submarine force.

And now? Few, if any ships ventured this far north in late

October. No one dared being trapped by an unexpected storm, their hull crushed by tons of ice. He read out the results. "68°52 North, 166°35 West."

Chenglei tapped *Flying Fish's* touch-screen power control and life support icons. He cast a worried look at Tsang. "Our oxygen level is acceptable, but the cabin's carbon dioxide level is increasing."

"And if we——?"

Chenglei cut off his commander. "We must power down all unnecessary systems and return to the *Kexue* immediately."

He exhaled through pursed lips, willing himself to remain calm. The expletive had unnerved his companion. "Yes. Power down the systems. We must continue on this track a bit longer."

"But——"

"Patience."

He eased the *Flying Fish* forward at three knots, adjusting their course to follow several dark-gray streaks from a recent mudflow. The bottom topography changed to a mix of light-gray and black pebbles swept from the limestone cliffs of Cape Lisburne. A ghost-white bottom fish drifted through the thin beam of light emanating from a string of LED lights set along the vessel's sampling arm. "There."

"Where?" Chenglei echoed. "What do you see?"

"A subduction zone. It's a fault line from an ancient seismic event." He sorted through the possibilities, seeking refuge from his stress with scientific exactitude. *The nodules may be metamorphic rocks from a pre-Cambrian Age uplift volcano, an extension of the Alaskan Brooks Range.* He voiced his conclusion. "That might explain it."

"Explain what?"

He ignored the question and the fear in Chenglei's voice. There must be no room for error, no room for second-guessing. "We must collect samples for mineralogical and geochemical analysis."

"But, Li, our batteries and power control. We—"

"I understand that." Tsang collected himself. It would serve no purpose to snap at Chenglei. "I will notify our superiors on the *Kexue*."

They were six hours into their mission at the edge of their effective communication range of twenty-five kilometers. He must try. He reached for the microphone, then dropped his hand. No, a text would be better. There would be no voice distortion from unexpected electromagnetic interference or from sending his signal through the thick surface ice. His fingers moved over the keyboard. *Unexpected finding.* He waited for the acknowledgement from their support ship. The cryptic response: *Unersto. Ice ridges forming.* He dismissed the operator's typos in the garbled message but the message was clear. They must return.

He maneuvered the *Flying Fish* toward the nearest scattering of rocks relying on the vessel's auxiliary power unit to power the thrusters. The submersible's forward beams cast their light for thirty meters through the clear water. He selected his first target. Turbulence buffeted the sub.

"What was that?"

He glanced at Chenglei. Sweat dotted his crewman's forehead despite the chill permeating the sub's cabin. He turned back to the viewport. Microalgae and suspended particulate matter illuminated by the sub's lights undulated in the current. Beyond that, a black void. He sought to calm Chenglei and give him something to occupy his mind. "Must be a pycnocline. Fresh water from the shoreline. Take a sample and note our position."

He triggered the sub's thrusters to compensate for the turbulence and activated their vessel's hydraulic grappling arm while maintaining position over a prospective target. "Here we go."

A dirty-gray cloud of billowing detritus and glacial silt deposited over the eons obscured his vision. He backed off, slowly lowered the sampling arm, grasped the rock, and dropped it in the sample basket. He added several more, one a red-brown, another with a hint of yellow suggesting a high sulfur content. "Okay, let's go home."

Only nineteen meters separated him from the surface and the rapidly forming ice extending from the Alaskan coast. A polar low with gale force winds drove the flows with their ice keels that descended toward his vessel like so many daggers. They were barely making headway near the forward margin of the ice. Would his comrades be able to maintain station?

The eleven-centimeter thick titanium sphere of the *Flying Fish's* personnel compartment could survive a collision. The damage to the rest of his craft would cripple them. He chanced another look through the viewport dreading what he might see. Nobody had ever planned for or studied the implications of operating the submersible in the Arctic.

Questions flooded his mind. Would he be able to break through the surface ice or would they ram into an ice keel extending down from the bottom of the ice pack that would rip their craft open like a mere sardine can? Would there be a catastrophic failure of his electrical systems? And, even with perfect conditions, he would still have to affect the rendezvous with the *Kexue* in complete darkness.

So, what if we are to perish? His wife and children would be provided for. *And me?* He resigned himself to his fate, pushing his concerns to the back of his mind. There were no other options. He sent another text to the *Kexue* informing them of his intent to return. That task completed, he entered a reciprocal course into the navigation system to the last known position of his support ship.

Time slowed, the basso thrumming of the *Flying Fish's* twin propellers dulling the turmoil raging in his mind. He tried to shut out the sound of tons of ice being crushed, driven into ridges, then torn apart by the winds of the approaching polar front. Deep rumbles like thunder; screeching, sharp cracks like those made by a splintering tree. Chirps and whistles echoed within the personnel sphere. The ice seemed alive, speaking to him, filling him with dread. He'd heard a name coined by the early Arctic explorers for the sounds: The Devil's Symphony.

He closed his eyes and fingered the jade amulet around his neck offering a silent prayer to Mazu, the Chinese goddess and patroness of the sea. There was nothing more to do. He pulled his woolen sweater tight across his shoulders. Only a few of the sub's critical systems were functioning and the sphere's temperature continued to fall. Despite shutting down all non-essential systems, they were now dependent on what little power remained in their emergency batteries.

He debated over-pressurizing the sphere to increase the cabin's temperature, but that would require releasing their reserves of pressurized oxygen. He discarded the idea, focusing on the more immediate threat. If they didn't reach the *Kexue* soon, they'd be unable to maneuver—helpless, driven northeast by the offshore Alaskan current surging through the Bering Strait. Their power would be drained before their oxygen supply ran out, but by then …?

The auspicious dates of his birth chart as prescribed by The Four Pillars of Destiny had predetermined his fate. *But didn't the precepts of Hòu Tiān also state that his fate could be affected by chance, risk, and trust and those aspects of life that he could control and achieve with effort?* Perhaps fate had reserved another path for him, intertwined with that of another person?

He keyed his microphone and sent a voice message to the *Kexue,* Nothing. He tried sending a text. His hands fumbled over the keyboard *earinm ladt knooow posijin. Rewuesr.* He stopped, concentrating, using his index finger to tap out the message. *Nearing last known position. Request instructions.*

His reply arrived within seconds: *Repeat your last.*

He repeated his message.

The answer crackled over the overhead speaker. He leaned

forward, straining to understand their directions. Were their communications being jammed?

Have you on sonar. Activate your homing beacon. Will guide you in.

Several more garbled messages followed. His mind benumbed, he was unable to decipher most of what the support ship had transmitted. Had the support crew managed to expand an open area in the ice near the ship, a polynyas? If so, clearance to surface would come soon. Convulsive shivers wracked his body. *So tired … must wake Chenglei.*

"Shhehlei?" The engineer didn't respond to his slurred name. He reached over and shook his arm. "Shhehlei."

A shrill alarm pierced his ears. The capsule plunged into darkness. Several emergency lamps clicked on. They began to drift, widening their distance to the *Kexue*. He must surface or they would be lost. He managed to flip open the safety cover for the sub's emergency ballast system and pressed the red button enabling the relay switch. *Will it even work?*

The sub gave a small lurch as the vessel's electromagnets released their grip on the steel brackets holding the vessel's ballast. The 450-kilogram weights fell away and the *Flying Fish* began to ascend. Twenty meters, ten, five … He focused on the depth gauge.

Was that to the surface or to the bottom of the ice?

The answer came with a grinding crunch, the noise deafening within the confined sphere. He could only guess at the damage. Would the sample basket be dislodged and his specimens lost?

He felt movement. Were they in open water? Ice screeched against *Flying Fish's* hull. He dared not open the escape hatch—even if he could. A text: *Nearing your position. Hold on.*

A thin veneer of ice covered his computer screens, moisture, condensed from his breath, frozen to his instruments. *Odd, I'm no longer shivering.* How long had they been waiting? It didn't matter. Nothing did. His mind numbed beyond caring.

A voice? No, a new sound. Metal clanging on metal.

He stared upward, trying to locate the sound. The dog lever on the hatch moved. Then stopped. The clanging intensified. The hand-wheel gave way, spinning, and the hatch flung open. Several chunks of ice cascaded through the opening, pummeling his head and shoulders. He barely felt them.

"Tsang!"

He tried to answer. Silence. He tried again. A whisper escaped. "My specimens."

Hands reached down, grabbing his shoulders, pulling him up through the hatch onto the deck. A blast of freezing wind staggered him. He fell to his knees. Ghostly apparitions approached, their movements backlit by the eerie electric blue and green colors of the aurora borealis swirling above the horizon. Someone pulled a fleece ski hood over his head. Another wrapped a thermal blanket around his shoulders, guiding him toward the *Kexue*'s Zodiac.

He lunged toward the bow of the *Flying Fish* intent on diving into the icy water to retrieve the specimen basket. A hand pulled him back to safety.

"He will retrieve them."

His eyes followed his rescuer's arm toward another clad in an orange full-emersion suit. "Chenglei?"

"We must return to the ship."

He stumbled around a hummock of ice. Two crewmen grasped his arms and dragged him forward. He would survive. *But Chenglei? What of him? Dead? And his Flying Fish?* She would be abandoned, a captive of the merciless Arctic.

Chapter One

CREEKSIDE CONDOMINIUMS
ANNANDALE, VIRGINA
TUESDAY 13 NOVEMBER

Nick Parkos closed his eyes, pondering what had happened to his life or even if the answer even mattered. He fingered his last OxyContin tablet before popping it into his mouth and washing it down with a swallow of *Wild Turkey* bourbon.

His hand found its way to the angry two-inch scar etched on the left side of his chest. He traced the outline of the recent wound, then the star-burst shaped scar from the chest tube. The memory of that horrific day flashed back, intruding into his dulled consciousness. The surgeon in Miami who'd treated the gunshot had given him a prescription for sixty of the painkillers. He used them to deaden the pain from another wound—the one to his mind.

The empty whiskey bottle slipped from his grasp, landing with a dull thud on the stained carpet next to his recliner. He fumbled for his TV's remote and pressed 'mute.' There was nothing left to do but wait for the mind-numbing combination of narcotic and alcohol to take effect, to suppress the memories, the ghosts that haunted him.

Michelle had dropped him at his one-bedroom condo in Annandale but he couldn't recall his girlfriend leaving. She probed and he'd snapped. Both his ex-wife, Marty, and Michelle were alarmed at what had happened to the gentle man they'd known, but he refused to let them penetrate his protective shell of denial. He glanced at the black screen of his iPad, another reminder of his toxic mood swings, his capricious behavior, of good intentions never acted upon. He couldn't remember the last time he'd shared Facetime with his seven-year old daughter, Emma.

He fell asleep in a drug-induced stupor, the wordless late-night show flickering on the TV, the host's biting jokes so much meaningless pantomime. The iPad slipped from his hands, joining the empty whiskey bottle. He woke with a gasp, soaked in sweat, heart pounding, jarred awake by another nightmare.

The dreams from the horrors he'd experienced in Somalia rarely varied. The vultures picking the flesh off the face of the dead terrorist, the lipless grin mocking him. The snake slithering out of the corpse's mouth, striking. Blood oozing from the two puncture wounds on his forearm. Dying, unable to save his daughter.

Denied sleep, he drove the ten miles to his office at the National Counterterrorism Center in McClean. Perhaps he would find the key to drive away the demons.

———

NATIONAL COUNTERTERRORISM CENTER
   LIBERTY CROSSING
   MCLEAN, VIRGINIA

. . .

Nick settled into his chair and powered up his computer, intent on reviewing his encrypted email. He reached for his cup of Starbucks coffee as the short list of message headers appeared. The cup never made it to his lips. "What the…?" He clicked on the message.

He stared at the three words that flashed on the screen. *It's Not Over.*

Intended or not, the three words sent his mind reeling to a place, to a time he'd suppressed. *This has to be a prank.* His middle finger paused above the delete key. He couldn't summon the will to erase the message.

For some reason those three words haunted him. But then, his life haunted him. What he'd done haunted him, hardly the hero many professed him to be. He stared at the dull image of his face in the computer's screen. *Maybe I'm being paranoid and someone is playing a joke on me?* After all, he did have an overdue analysis on a little known transnational crime organization in the Balkans. His head throbbed.

He ran his hand through his hair, stopping to massage his temples. He'd become a recluse, running from the shadows, closing himself off from family and friends fearing what he'd become, afraid to admit who he might really be.

Nick, please let me help you. He tore his eyes away from the screen. The sound of Michelle's voice lingered. Like the questions, the doubts running ceaselessly around his mind.

He'd achieved a certain degree of notoriety within the Center by tracking down and eliminating the Chechen terrorist, Bashir al-Khultyer in a search that spanned three continents. Even his partner in the operation, Navy SEAL and National Security Council staff member, Captain Mike Rohrbaugh, declared him a warrior for saving his life in the attack on the terrorist base in Somalia. But …

"Hey, Nick. Up before the sun again?"

He sighed, lifted his left hand from the keyboard, and rubbed his fingers over the scruff of a two-day beard. He turned to the newest member of the department's analytic team, Austin Mack. With his name, square-jawed good looks, and deep baritone voice, Austin should have been wearing faded denim jeans and cowboy boots, belting out a country western song. Nope. Austin hailed from a small town in northern Wisconsin. Eagle River. His family raised goats, not longhorns, and crafted their own artisanal chèvre cheese. Austin knew a lot about cheese. *So much for stereotypes.* "Morning, Austin."

"Have a minute? I'd like to run something by you."

Nick gazed into the void over Austin's right shoulder, wary of what the '*something*' might be. "I'm right in the middle of analyzing a data run. Can I catch you later?"

"Sure thing. I'm heading to the canteen. Get you a refill?"

Nick tapped the side of his embossed cup of stale *Starbucks* coffee. "I'm good. Thanks." He turned back to the keyboard, more to hide his guilt than to do anything useful. Austin had good intentions and seemed to be truly impressed by his work on the last operation but Nick shunned the adulation.

"Great job," his colleagues had said, showering him with accolades, crediting him with … what had one said? Perspicacity. *Not so much.* Even his notoriety came with an asterisk. *Didn't it?* Something few knew. His mind returned to the cryptic note, *It's Not Over.*"

When he'd confronted the terrorist, al-Khultyer, on the second-floor concourse of Miami's cruise terminal, he had frozen, unable to shoot. The FBI's Chief of Station had to take out al-Khultyer before the terrorist could press his thumb to the detonator of a dirty bomb. Nick tried to explain but was cut off by agent's stinging retort: "Yeah, it's always complicated with you guys."

That was his problem, wasn't it? The complications. His thoughts drifted to Taylor Ferguson. The CIA operative had been one of his contacts, even providing the lead to finding al-Khultyer in the Somali terrorist camp. But with the death of the terrorist, the agency considered the matter closed. *Yeah, but.* Something still didn't smell right. Something new and that three word message? "Crap."

He returned to the immediate problem. He couldn't identify the smell's source. He began with what he knew—which was precious little. He tried to ignore the cryptic email but the statement remained fixed in his mind. *It's Not Over.* Is there another terrorist cell he hadn't discovered or is there something entirely different going on? Something only remotely tied to the original operation?

His eyes fell on his *Dilbert* cartoon desk calendar. The 20th. Last Friday. He read the panel: *This week I achieved unprecedented levels of unverifiable productivity.* He tore off four pages, crumpled them into a ball, and tossed it at the trashcan. The wad bounced off the rim and rolled across the floor. He didn't bother to pick it up, instead looking at the calendar. Tuesday, the 24th: *What fantasy will I use today to stave off madness?* He grabbed the calendar, opened the bottom drawer of his desk, dropped it in, and slammed the drawer closed.

"Hey, Parkos. You okay?"

He started at the sharp edge on his supervisor's voice, twisting his head toward the door. "Yeah." He read the skeptical look on Ned Strickland's face. "Sorry."

Strickland eyed the crumped paper ball lying by his feet. "Hell of a way to start your day."

"Just frustrated."

"You need to get your head screwed on."

He agreed, but kept the thought to himself.

Strickland looked as if he was about to say something. Instead, he gave a shake of his head and proceeded down the hallway.

He pondered their brief conversation as Strickland's footfalls faded. Another wake-up call. The Dilbert cartoons hit too close to home. If there only was a refresh key on his computer that he could press to recalibrate his attitude.

He reached for the cup of *Starbucks* and gulped down the cold remnant. A wave of nausea washed over him, his stomach revolting at the assault. Grimacing, he tossed the cup in the trash and waited for his stomach to forgive him. He waited another moment before snatching a blank piece of paper from the printer. He drew a Venn diagram, something he was known for within the Agency.

His professor of criminology at Ohio State had drilled into him the usefulness of this simple tool. By creating a series of interlocking circles and populating them with knowns, their intersecting arcs would ultimately lead to the answer. His professor also added a caveat to his lesson: "It isn't what you don't know that gets you in trouble, it's what you're sure of that does."

The good news at this point? He wasn't sure about much of anything.

Another wave of nausea hit. He gulped and bolted down the hall to the restroom, just managing to slam the door of the last stall before the remains of the coffee and the previous night's leftovers erupted into the commode.

He gripped the edge of the bowl, gasping, stomach emptied. A couple men entered the restroom. He recognized Austin's voice but not the other guy's. The other guy spoke first.

"They've got me on a damn wild goose chase running down some blip off the coast of Alaska. Whatever the hell is the source, it's broadcasting on a homing frequency used by the Chinese."

"Maybe some polar bear with a tracking collar?" Austin suggested.

"Could be. It's weak enough"

"Why would the Chinese be tracking wildlife in Alaska?"

"Beats the hell out of me. Maybe I'll just call the Wilderness Society and let them chase it down. They're always looking for some new cause to justify their existence."

Austin ignored the jibe. "Seems to me the Coast Guard would be a better bet."

"My bet is it's probably just some crab-trap buoy that went adrift. It can wait. There's a shitload of stuff piling up on my desk. The Chinese can take care of themselves."

Nick waited until he was sure they were gone, then wobbled out of the stall, rinsed his mouth, splashed some water on his face, and returned to his office. He found the bottle of extra-strength Tylenol in his desk drawer, swallowed a couple caplets, and set to work. His fingers froze on the keyboard.

Frowning, he grabbed a pen and tapped out a staccato rhythm on the desk top. Where to start? *Who sent that three-word email and why? What's not over?* The note appeared on his computer screen just after he'd logged on. There was no iden-tifiable originator. He typed out, "Who are you?" and hit the send key.

'Blocked: Unknown address.'

WTF? Who could do that? Or access his email account for that matter. The CIA, his own agency? *Why me?* What's the link?

He dropped his head back on the headrest and stared at the ceiling. He ran through the possibilities, grasping for elusive straws. After Miami, he returned to his old job investi-gating Transnational Organized Crime. Could the message refer to one of thos organizations, perhaps the Novorossiysk Business Group who'd provided the financial and logistical backing to al-Khultyer? He rocked forward. *Might as well start with the NIMD and DOMEX document and media exploitation data bases.*

The Novel Intelligence in Massive Data system, overseen by the National Media Exploitation Center, provided the National Intelligence Center access to a potential tsunami of raw data using advanced analytic programs to screen and compartmentalize documents, electronic media, video, and smart phones. Nick frequently tapped NMEX for the system's collection, processing, exploitation, dissemination, cataloging, and initial processing functions. NMEX also provided forensic analysis, but he passed on this service, preferring to trust his own instincts.

When the system came up, he accessed the Document and Media Exploitation program and searched Novorossiysk Business Group. In less than a minute, he had gigabytes of information processed from the DOMEX data cloud platform's tertiary storage system.

He scanned the report headers. A gaggle of Environmental Groups were raising hell with the Department of the Interior seeking to block any further exploitation of oil and mineral deposits north of the Arctic Circle. The organizations were well known: The Sierra Club, Greenpeace, The Wilderness Society, and The National Resources Defense Council. *What could any of these groups possibly have to do with the NBG?*

He scrolled through several more screens. The NBG appeared to be positioning itself to acquire a controlling interest in Newtech Resource Development, a Canadian company.

There was a precedent for such a move. A Russian company, allegedly helped by an insider at the Interior Department, had bought controlling interest in a Canadian mining company a few years back. With the acquisition, the Russians locked up a significant percent of the world's uranium supply and shut out the United States. Could the NBG be making a similar play? He freed his mind to explore the possibilities, to see what others couldn't.

What's so damn important in the Arctic besides oil and minerals ... and polar bears? He opened a new search to see where Newtech Resource Development fit. Within seconds, he had his answer. The company was a major player in mining operations extracting base metals from polymetallic shale deposits in the Canadian Northwest Territories. Exploratory talks were underway with an American company, Trident Metallurgics, to include them in a proposed consortium.

He no idea what base metals were. Another search ensued. Nickel, zinc, other precious metals. Rare-earth elements, the lanthanide group. He cocked his head, the words rare-earth catching his eye. He continued to read. Fourteen elements listed on the periodic chart from lanthanum to lutetium. Critical to the world's electronic and defense industries. REE's found in shale deposits were also used as markers in oil exploration.

Could this be the elusive key he sought? This information opened up a whole new set of probabilities. He picked up his pen and filled in the set of unknowns in his diagram: Shell companies, lobbyists, law firms, venture capitalists. The tension in his shoulder's lessened. This was the world he felt comfortable residing in.

He smiled at another thought. Strickland would conclude he was off on another one of his wild goose chases, or more likely, think that he was nuts. *Well, so be it. I probably am.* But his gut, no longer protesting, told him he was on to something. The problem? He still had no clue who sent the three-word message, what the short-term implications of his investigation would be, or where it would lead. Setting those questions aside, he set to work.

A pang of hunger broke his train of thought. He pushed himself out of his chair, glancing out the window. His office in building LX1 of the National Intelligence Center provided an uninspiring view across the Beltway still clogged with morning commuters. Slate-gray clouds hung low in the leaden sky, a harbinger of an approaching early winter storm. Snow flurries swirled by gusts of wind were already dusting the parking lot below his window.

He toiled through the remainder of the afternoon stopping only to grab a container of blueberry yogurt from the canteen. He flexed his fingers, pushed away from the desk, and crossed the room to look outside. Freezing rain carved ragged rivulets down the fogged window slicing up the dreary vista. *It'll be a mess getting home.* Fall faced a premature death as it succumbed to the early winter storm, dusk yielding to the night.

He turned away from the depressing sight and returned to the desk to continue his search for the elusive clue that would link the NBG to the two North American companies. His mind drifted to the conversation he'd overheard in the restroom. A crazy thought crossed his mind. Could Austin and that other guy have stumbled onto something?

The key to his questions came to him just after six o'clock. He'd focused on the Russians, but were the Chinese also players? He reviewed his scrawled notes from his research of rare earth elements. Neodymium—batteries, essential for computer spindle motors and voice coils. Monazite and bastnasite—critical elements for the defense industry. Electronic displays, guidance systems, GPS systems, lasers, radars…. My God, if the Russians…. And China? Beijing had a near monopoly on REE ore and refining. What would they do to maintain their stranglehold on these elements? He set the latter question aside and focused on the Russians.

Chapter Two

THE UPPER CRUST TAP AND GRILL
ARLINGTON, VIRGINA
TUESDAY 20 NOVEMBER

Nick tapped the brake of his worn Ford Escape, slowing for the Fort Meyer Road exit ramp. On a whim, he'd decided to try out a new bar he'd read about in *The Washington Post*'s "Lifestyle" section instead of going home to an empty refrigerator.

The repetitive *thunk* of the windshield wipers kept him company, the old blades tracking large smears across the windshield. He made a right turn and maneuvered down Wilson Lane, craning his neck forward searching for a parking space on the one-way street. He finally located one a block-and-a-half past his destination.

He gathered himself, preparing to face the elements while second-guessing his decision. *Man, this is just nasty.* Maybe I should have grabbed something at the McDonald's drive through and gone home. He dismissed the thought. *Nope.* Not another night spent eating alone in his recliner. "Let's do this," he said to the car.

His umbrella popped open in the gusting wind, several broken spines threatening to collapse the entire thing in an everted heap. Slashes of wind-driven rain drove through the feeble orange halos of the streetlamps, bouncing off the sidewalk, soaking his pant-legs. He picked up his pace, dodged the largest of the ice-skimmed puddles, and jogged across the empty street.

A swaying antique wood and brass sign suspended below a dripping green awning announced his destination. A poster to the right of the door featured a buffed, handsome dude clad in a black muscle shirt, 17th century captain hat, and white apron advertised "Hot Pilgrim Night" for the coming Saturday. He shook the rain off the tattered umbrella wondering about Pilgrim Night and pulled open the stained-glass door of The Upper Crust Tap and Grill.

He hesitated, surveying the interior: shaded table lamps, dark paneling, burgundy-colored faux leather chairs, a hint of wood smoke from a fireplace to his left. The place was also packed, a riot of voices and pounding pop music far from the quiet refuge he'd sought. In the far corner of the room a lone flat-screen appeared to be featuring a *Victoria Secrets* runway show. *No sports? Odd.*

The scene set him on edge. He turned to leave, then wavered when he spotted an open stool at the bar. Two women, a short-haired brunette dressed in an expensive jacket with a matching skirt and a blonde wearing a tailored dark-gray pantsuit occupied the chairs to the left. To the right, a man about his own age.

The guy wore a dark plaid sports coat, open-necked white shirt, and jeans. A loosely knotted cashmere scarf like those he'd seen men wearing in Paris hung around his neck. A pair of fashionable square-frame tortoiseshell glasses perched above a prominent nose set off his face. The man took a contemplative sip of his beer, apparently indifferent to what the other patrons might be thinking.

He worked his way through the gnarl of thirty-somethings jammed around the free-standing tables. The two women cast him a sideways glance. The brunette pulled her purse out of the way, but otherwise they ignored him.

He jerked out the counter-height stool, cringing at the accompanying screech of the legs across the hardwood floor. He slid into his seat, inadvertently catching the eye of the guy to his right who reeked of cigar smoke. The man appeared unfazed by the intrusion into his space, hefted his beer, and nodded a welcome.

"Tough crowd tonight," the man said over the noise. "Seem to be mostly lawyers and lobbyists." He aimed his chin vaguely in the direction of a corner table. "Couple congressional staffers over there with an Undersecretary from Interior. Humm, a lobbyist just joined them." His flight of observations continued. "Interesting hair on that one. Nice wave cut, but the highlights are seriously dated."

Nick grunted a non-committal, "Yeah," not the least bit interested in the group, stylish hair or not. He looked away intent on flagging down the bartender while debating whether he should change seats or just pack up and leave.

The bartender responded to his waving hand and approached with a smile. "What's on your mind?"

He pondered the open-ended question, deciding a safe bet would be to just order a drink. He ran his eyes over the white porcelain taps for a selection of exotic import beers before they settled on a bottle of Laphroaig 12-year Scotch whisky orphaned on the counter. "How about the Laphroaig?" He resisted saying more. The guy appeared to be swamped with orders and likely had no interest in what really happened to be on his mind.

"Neat?"

"Yeah."

"Sure thing."

"Could you make that a double?"

"Something to eat?" the bartender asked, holding out a menu.

He set the menu on the polished burl-wood counter and pushed it aside. "Maybe later."

The man sitting next to him popped a couple beer nuts into his mouth. "Rough day?"

"I've had better."

The guy held out his right hand. "Geoffrey Lange."

He gave Lange's hand a quick shake. The name seemed familiar, but he couldn't place it. Lange saved him the trouble.

"I'm an investigative journalist."

He pulled back, his eyes narrowing.

Lange laughed. "Sorry, I tend to have that effect on people."

"Guess it comes with the territory."

"I think I've seen you in here before. You work nearby?"

His answer slipped out before he could catch himself. "No, first time. I work in McClean."

"One of the three initial agencies?"

He scrutinized Mister Geoffrey Lange: Sharp jaw, intense gunmetal-blue eyes framed by his glasses, dark close-cropped hair, a dusting of gray at the temples, broad shoulders. Perhaps someone who'd spent some time in the military. Despite his easy demeanor, Lange had an understated tough-ness suggesting he wasn't somebody you'd want to cross. He detected a hint of a Midwestern accent. He'd have to run a profile on him.

"Don't worry. Your secret's safe with me," Lange said.

"*Secret? What secret?*" He pushed away from the bar intent on leaving. "I'm paid to worry. Now, if you'll excuse me."

Lange stopped Nick in his tracks. "I'd say they don't pay you enough."

"Oh? How's that?"

"You look like hell. You've got stress written all over you.

Clipped speech, two-day beard, bags under your eyes. And your clothes look like you've slept in them."

His fists tightened. He had no idea who this person was: Russian agent, CIA, FBI? His own agency trying to entrap him? Perhaps Lange could actually be an investigative reporter. It didn't matter, he'd heard enough.

Lange reached for Nick's arm. "Sorry, man. That was out of line. I've been cursed with lousy people skills. I'm pretty damn good at what I do for a living, but stink with the inter-personal stuff. I tend to irritate people with my acerbity." He waved his hand at the crowded tables. "Probably why I'm here at the bar. How about I buy that drink?"

"I'm not looking for a date."

Lange locked on Nick's eyes. "So, that was a misfire?"

He dropped back onto his stool. "Excuse me?"

"I take it you're not gay."

"Ah, no," he responded while struggling to figure out if he'd sent out some unknown pickup signal. *Was that the "secret" Lange referred to?* He gave the room a quick scan. Nothing seemed out of the ordinary. At least that he could see. There just weren't many women. *Crap, now what?*

Lange laughed. "You know this is a gay bar, right?" He paused for a response. "Oookay … so the answer to that is a 'No.' Well, not to worry, I'll give you a primer. For starters, guys don't mess around with the preliminaries. You size up your target and make your move."

"Like going into a store and picking out a pair of socks you like? I want that one."

"Exactly."

He was momentarily left with a rare loss-for-words at this latest revelation. Lange filled in the void.

"You can learn all sorts of things in this place."

His eyes flicked around the room. "Yeah, I guess."

"You can observe a lot by just watching."

Caught. He also recognized the quote. "Seriously, Yogi Berra?"

"A wise man, even if he did play for the Yankees." A wry smile formed on Lange's face. "Let's start with that couple sitting next to you."

He looked at the reflection of the two women in the bar's mirror.

"What do you see?"

"Two women having a drink unwinding after work."

"Epic fail." Lange laughed and popped another handful of beer nuts into his mouth. "How about their mannerisms, their dress, how they're interacting?"

"Seem normal enough. Maybe their makeup's a bit overdone."

"How about their Adam's apples?"

Damn. He resisted looking over his shoulder for a closer examination of his neighbors. The bartender saved him, arriving just in time with the scotch, setting it on the counter before he could comment—not that his comment would matter. His body language spoke to his discomfort. He unwrapped his arms that had worked their way around his chest and dropped his hands to his lap. He looked at Lange, then to the bartender. Hell, even that guy wore an amused expression.

"Got a novice," Lange said.

"Yeah, I'd say that's pretty obvious. He about to bolt?"

"Naw, he's safe. Why?"

The bartender motioned toward the end of the bar. "Couple guys got a bet going. Five minutes and he's out the door."

He just wanted to disappear. My *God, I've got 'Clueless' flashing across my forehead."*

Lange noted his discomfort. "I'm about to enlighten him. I figure he could benefit from learning a few basic survival skills."

"Good luck with that." The bartender chuckled and stepped away to serve another customer.

Lange nodded at the bartender's back. "That's Cam. Good guy. He's straight. So, what do you say we begin with your name?"

His hands were now clutching his drink. He released the right and offered it. "Nick Parkos."

Lange's eyebrows shot up in surprise. "No shit. Parkos. Somalia. The al-Khultyer incident? Weren't—"

He cut him off. "Past history."

"That's it?"

"I don't want to talk about it."

Lange cocked his head, then appeared to come to a conclusion. "Yeah, I've been there too. So, what would you like to talk about?"

He felt the tension in his shoulders lessen even though at the moment he didn't want to talk to this guy about anything. On a positive note, he sensed Lange understood or at least had enough sense to drop the subject of Somalia. He thought a moment about how to respond. Something Lange had said earlier worked its way into his consciousness. He looked toward the far corner of the room. "I'm interested in what you said about that table over there. The one with the guy from the Department of the Interior and the lobbyist talking with those Congressional staffers."

Lange swiveled around in his chair, a thoughtful look crossing his face. "Well, that is a bit odd."

"How so?"

"It's complicated."

"I do complicated," Nick said.

Lange leaned forward so his voice wouldn't carry. "What is it about those folks that interests you?"

He swirled his drink. "Something I've been working may touch on Interior."

"Care to elaborate?"

He remembered an old adage he'd learned the hard way: 'Never pass up the opportunity to keep your mouth shut.' By themselves, most of the pieces of his research to date were open source and non-classified, but strung together … "No."

Lange pulled out his wallet. He extracted his business card and handed it over while keeping his voice low. "Our interests may intersect." He dropped a twenty on the counter and stood, turning his back to the couple. "Stay in touch."

He shoved the card into a coat pocket without looking at it and watched Lange disappear into the crowd. Lost in his own thoughts, he barely noted the two transvestites settling their bill. He turned away when the brunette gave her,—or should it be his?,—partner a peck on the cheek and made for the door. He had no idea, but settled on 'her.'

No sooner had the brunette departed than the remaining member of the duo cast him a fetching look, sending a cloud of stale cologne his way. "You have such beautiful eyes. You live nearby?"

He recovered enough from the dual-edged assault to blurt, "Ah … thanks, but I'm taken." He grabbed the menu and busied himself making a selection.

"Such a pity, darling. He's a lucky man."

———

Distracted by the encounter, Nick didn't see the brunette reach inside her purse for her iPhone, lift it slightly above her waist, and snap off several pictures. She hoped her contact, sitting at the table with the Congressional staffers, would be pleased. Not only had she recorded Lange's conversation with the stranger, but she'd also managed to capture a picture of the guy he'd been talking to. She placed the iPhone back in her purse and wove toward the bathroom.

A moment later, the man with the wave-cut set down his beer and made his way across the room to join her.

Chapter Three

U.S. COAST GUARD MH-65E HELICOPTER, CALL-
SIGN: GOOSE 21
THE CHUKCHI SEA, ALASKA
WEDNESDAY 22 NOVEMBER

Lieutenant Sarah MacAuley, United States Coast Guard, scanned the ragged edge of the pack ice extending seaward from the desolate headlands of Cape Lisburne. *Nothing.* She toed the helicopter's anti-torque pedal and advanced the cyclic. The MH-65E Dolphin responded with a shallow turn and accelerated toward the dim orb of the setting sun.

The maneuver put the helicopter's starboard side to the gale force winds of a polar front roaring in from the northeast. She didn't appear to notice the wind buffeting the aircraft as she tracked the northern arc of the search zone. Her real concern was staying aloft much longer. They were miles from her ship, the *Midgett.* Maintaining station in the turbulent seas just south of the advancing ice pack, she knew the Legend-class Cutter's skipper would keep his vessel in position to recover her aircraft.

The new Cutter, named after iconic Coast Guardsman, CWO John Midgett, Jr., had replaced the venerable Cutter *Sherman*. Launched in 1968, the *Sherman* had served with distinction in the Vietnam war. And MacAuley? She'd graduated from the Coast Guard Academy in New London, Connecticut, class of 2008 before heading off to flight school.

———

The *Midgett* and her air detachment were deployed in support of operation Arctic Shield. Their expanded mission included fisheries enforcement and keeping a watchful eye on Chinese factory ships. These huge fishing boats were appearing with increasing frequency in the waters of the Bering Sea and desolating the native sea-life populations despite the best attempts of Greenpeace and Sea Shepherd to stop them.

The *Midgett* intercepted one such vessel the day before that was setting a high seas drift net in violation of international fisheries agreements. The Coast Guardsmen boarded the vessel, noting the extensive antennae array dotting the boat's superstructure before they began their search. The array far exceeded anything needed for the vessel's supposed function.

The boarding party soon discovered a compartment accessed through the pilothouse of the 191-foot *Yin Yuan* crammed with sophisticated communications equipment. This equipment almost certainly meant the vessel was part of Beijing's maritime paramilitary fleet involved in a covert surveillance operation. They'd made an initial assessment of the gear, but a cryptic message ordered them to abort their inspection and return to the *Midgett*.

They received another surprise as soon as they had secured the Cutter's rigid hull inflatable, the craft's name shortened, military style to RHI. The *Midgett* put on speed and swung across the bow of the *Yin Yaun* assuming a northerly course into the tempestuous waters of the Bering Strait. The boarding party understood the plan had been to escort the *Yin Yuan* to the south where they were supposed to rendezvous with the Chinese Coast Guard Cutter, *Haijing*. They had a new plan.

Dense gray water burst over the forecastle of the *Midgett* as she dug her bow deep into the northeast swell. The surprised boarding party clustered at the taffrail watching the *Yin Yuan* tossed about in the turbulent white-capped sea before it vanished beyond the haze-cloaked horizon. A metallic screech caused them to turn away from the mesmerizing vista.

The flight deck crew had opened one of the Cutter's two hangar doors preparing to position a helicopter for take-off. Several of the boarding party broke away and staggered across the open deck to lend a hand. MacAuley ducked around the helicopter's tail rotor and strode toward them. She cast a look at the ocean, her eyebrows knitting. Her preflight brief noted the sea state: Five on the Beaufort scale. The weather was forecast to deteriorate over the next several hours.

"What's up Lieutenant?" one of the crewmen yelled.

"SAR mission," MacAuley hollered over the mounting noise. "Skipper got a message to investigate an EPIRB. She didn't bother to translate the shorthand for Emergency Position Indicating Radio Beacon."

Her crewmate splayed his legs and grabbed for the nylon mesh of the safety netting to catch his balance on the pitching deck. Spray whipped off the wave tops towering behind him. "Good luck, ma'am. I sure wouldn't want to be going up in this weather to track down some emergency beacon."

She shifted her flight bag on her shoulder and tossed him an informal salute. "Yeah, tell me about it." She continued on while running a gut check. She'd never met a pilot who liked going up in this kind of weather, but there might be somebody stranded out there and there was only one person who had the final 'go,' 'no go' decision—the pilot. She would execute her mission come hell or high water. This was a matter of intense pride. It's what the Coast Guard did.

What she hadn't volunteered was the peculiar twist to her mission that she'd learned in the pre-flight brief that had put a different spin on her tasking. The 17th Coast Guard District headquartered in Juneau had received the request for her mission from Homeland Security via an alert passed from the National Intelligence Agency. On receipt of the new tasking, the *Midgett*'s commanding officer altered course and transited the Bering Strait to assume their current position in the southern Chukchi Sea. The cutter's rendezvous with the Chinese Coast Guard would have to wait. Something was up that had gotten the bigwig's attention and that, in turn, demanded her attention.

———

MacAuley pulled in more collective and nosed the aircraft over. Her margin for error was minimal but she'd committed to the mission and its inherent risks. If it were a Chinese vessel out there, maybe they'd score some points with Beijing even if she only recovered the bodies. She concentrated on the jumbled ice sheet below pockmarked with disconnected leads, flows, and polynyas. *If anybody—or anything—was caught in that, they're toast.*

"I've got something."

She faced her co-pilot, Lieutenant Junior Grade Brian Fields. "Where?"

"One o'clock. Three-hundred meters."

A faint black and white image on the Forward Looking Infrared Radar, the FLIR thermo-imaging display caught her eye. "Let's take a look. If we don't see anything, we'll head back to the barn."

"Roger that."

They'd been aloft for a little more than an hour and the

sun would soon set. She would have some visibility with nautical twilight, but the ambient light would still be of some benefit. She intended to use her automated flight control system to make her initial approach to the Cutter, then rely on the FLIR and her night vision goggles to close on the Cutter's flight deck if they had to stay aloft much longer.

A fist-full of ice pellets ricocheted off the cockpit window. The edge of the southern air mass they'd been skirting had collided with the cold front driving toward them from the northeast creating a condition known as advection fog. She frowned and activated the wipers. An opaque curtain of haze and rain obscured the horizon. The last thing she needed was freezing rain even with their new rotor blade deicing system.

"I have a contact," Fields said. "Something's hung up in the ice. Got an orange topside." He leaned over the console studying the object. "Well, damn. Take 'a look at that. We've got ourselves a mini-sub."

She slowed and pivoted the helicopter. The source of the faint heat signature lay on its port side, the stern thrust toward the sky exposing twin propellers and two pair of stabilizers.

"Looks bad." The forward hatch was flung open. No sign of the crew. She ran her eyes over the guppy-shaped mini-sub one more time and gave her head a defeated shake. If the crew was still on board, they'd be frozen solid. Their chances of surviving on the open ice sheet would be no better.

She put the Dolphin in a hover just lee of the sub. Large Chinese letters scribed in blue were visible along the sub's exposed side. "What's that doing here?"

"I'd say it's been abandoned for some time," Fields answered. "Those dorsal stabilizers look pretty beat up. No telling what happened. Looks like it collided with something."

"What's it doing so far north?"

"You'd figure with that open hatch, it should have sunk."

"You'd think. Unless it was abandoned after getting trapped in the ice."

"The guys at the Arctic Domain Awareness Center should be able to analyze the wind and current data and calculate the sub's probable start point," Fields said.

"Mark the coordinates."

Her crew chief's voice broke over the intercom. "Want me to go down and take a look? I could—"

Another blast of wind rocked the helicopter before he could finish. The aircraft's integrated weather radar system sounded a simultaneous warning.

"Too risky, Jamison. Grab some pics."

"On it."

"Make sure you get a close-up of those characters running along the hull. They should identify her."

Jamison responded a moment later. "Got 'em."

"Okay, let's head back." She spoke into her helmet's microphone to alert the Cutter of her intentions. "*Midgett*, Goose 21. How do you copy?"

"Got you Lima Charlie, Goose 21. How was the hunting?"

"We spotted a mini-sub hung up in the ice. Looks to be a Chinese research vessel."

"Any sign of life?"

"Negative. We're heading home."

"Copy that."

She ended the transmission and assumed a heading back to the *Midgett* maintaining an altitude of two-thousand feet. A couple hundred feet below her, the tops of an unending sea of angry-gray clouds. "Brian, we're going instrument meteorological conditions. I'll be shooting an instrument approach. Verify our target heading and watch the power settings."

"On it."

She skirted the cloud tops for another minute preparing herself for the spatial disorientation she'd experience when she dipped into the clouds and lost the horizon. "Okay, here we go."

The helicopter descended into the dense clouds, engulfed

in darkness. She focused her full attention on the attitude indicator, maintaining straight, level flight while fighting the momentary illusion she was pitching up. "Distance?"

"Five miles."

"If conditions allow, we'll switch to the automated flight control system."

———

The *Midgett*'s commanding officer came up on the circuit. He had to recover his aircraft and there were precious few minutes and fewer options for maneuvering his vessel. The evolution would be further complicated by the deteriorating sea state. Now registering as a nine, a severe gale, the storm's winds were gusting to forty-three knots. There was a real danger the winds would push white water over the flight deck. *And if a wave hit MacAuley's rotor blades …?* He turned to his XO. "Alert the rescue swimmers and position the RHI on the ramp ready to launch."

He swiveled his command chair around to look out the port bridge windows, judging the swell period and wave run-up to the flight deck. Visibility was one-thousand yards at best. If the copter went in the water, the chances of retrieving all of his flight crew were close to zero.

"Skipper, we have visual."

He turned to see MacAuley break through the clouds and begin her approach to the Cutter's port side. Less than two-hundred feet separated the helicopter from the base of the clouds and the turbulent sea. Precious little room for her to maneuver.

He shifted his attention to the live feed from the flight deck camera. In a pinch, he could order them to make for the gravel runway at the abandoned Long Range Radar Site at Cape Lisburne. His jaw tightened at the prospect. It would be cold as hell out there without shelter. *Still a better outcome than dead.*

The crests of the raging sea were now approaching seventeen feet. The *Midgett* heaved thirteen degrees and pitched into a deep trough, before rolling in a gut-churning yaw. The Cutter dug into another roller, the wave exploding over her bow. A wall of olive-green water roared over the forecastle, inundating the forward 57mm gun mount before slamming into the superstructure below the bridge. She shuddered at the impact, then recovered, saltwater cascading through the scuppers and down the side.

Another huge roller lifted the *Midgett's* bow, suspending the Cutter at its crest before releasing its hold. The Cutter plunged into a deep trough, the drop accompanied by a chorus of thumps, bangs, and curses from the crew in the chart house aft of the bridge.

He gave his head a wry shake, acknowledging all the chaos behind him. This storm had given a new, more literal meaning, to what had been planned as his Cutter's "shake-down" cruise to the Arctic.

"Skipper, we have an amber deck."

There was one variable he could minimize—the vessel's roll. "Port ten-degrees rudder."

The *Midgett* turned into the swell. He watched the compass. "Rudder amidships. Maintain course 035."

The bow lifted, paused at the peak of a roller, then she staggered forward, her bow digging into the next. The captain peered at the waves sweeping by the bridge, gauging the time between their ragged crests. *About five seconds. That's all MacAuley had.*

He shifted his attention back to the flight deck camera. The stern of his Cutter dropped into a trough with a savage corkscrewing motion. He caught a glimpse of MacAuley off the port side hovering twenty-feet above the deck, matching the Cutter's speed. His hands gripped the arms of his chair. "Okay, let's bring 'em in."

———

MacAuley rolled her neck to relieve the weight of her helmet pressing down on her shoulders. She switched off the automatic flight control system that had guided her to a stable hover over the flight deck. She would now rely on visual cues and those transmitted by the Cutter's Aircraft Ship Integrated Secure and Traverse System, ASIST. She side-slipped across the *Midgett*'s pitching flight deck.

The wind tore the top off a monstrous wave, whipping white-water across the deck. Her horizon tilted. The helicopter's advanced avionics would be of little use in these chaotic seas. Their approach and landing would require raw skill.

She loosened her grip on the cyclic. She needed to feel, to sense her aircraft's motion. She tapped the anti-torque pedal bringing the helicopter's nose around a few degrees and depressed the collective, descending several feet. A blinding silver-white cloud of spindrift burst from the cutter's bow. The cloud swirled down the *Midgett*'s side coating her windshield before being pushed aside by the wiper blades.

She flicked her eyes from the orange-vested Landing Deck Officer stationed in his glass-enclosed control station above the hangar doors, to her flight controls, and back to the flight deck. Her aim point: A white circle transected by the parallel curved tracks of the Cutter's ASIST system.

She was grateful for the open expanse of the Cutter's fifty x eighty-foot flight deck. *But,* she cautioned herself. *Yeah, hotshot, you've got a major "but" here.* Sweat poured from the leading edge of her helmet, running in rivulets down her face. Her tongue darted over the beads of sweat dotting her upper lip.

"Shit!" She pulled up the collective gaining altitude, then keyed her microphone. The system tracking the helicopter's position relative to the deck had just failed. "I've lost the RSD."

"Copy that, Goose 21. You've lost input from the RSD."

Two crewmen darted from the safety of the hanger to trouble shoot the device.

Her console monitor flashed back into operation with a new data stream. "I've got nominal input … Okay, system's back up."

"Roger that, Goose 21. We have an affirmative. Rapid Securing Device is operative."

She edged sideways back over the deck, hovering a mere twenty feet above the white centerline of the landing circle. The RSD was tracking fore and aft just as it should, matching her aircraft's movement.

She caught a quick look at the towering waves to her right. A rogue wave could lift the stern of the Cutter, thrusting the flight deck upwards into her undercarriage as she descended. The force of the collision would send them tumbling over the side or crashing into the superstructure. She murmured a brief prayer. *Please, God, get us home.*

Maintaining altitude over the rocking deck, she judged the timing of the *Midgett*'s heave, waiting for that brief moment when the Cutter was almost motionless, suspended above a crest, before it plunged back into a trough.

The LDO held his arms outstretched from his sides, grasping a pair of red-tipped flashlights. He braced his legs countering the Cutter's slanting deck, then lowered his left arm a tad indicating she was not quite parallel to the deck.

She adjusted. The LDO's arms shifted, confirming her correction, then he dropped them. *It's now or never, hotshot.* She tapped the rudder pedal, her left hand depressing the collective, her right, adjusting the cyclic, descending.

The wheels touched, then lifted off the non-skid surface as

the Cutter's stern dropped. The helicopter met the pitching deck, settling within the painted circle. The deck crew scrambled from their safe haven in the hanger to verify the aircraft's probe was securely attached to the RSD. The desk officer flashed her a thumbs-up.

She exhaled at his confirmation, shut down the engines, and activated the rotor head brakes to stop the spinning blades. Secured to the deck, she felt the tug of the landing assist system on her aircraft. They were beginning their traverse to the safety of the hangar. She pulled off her helmet. "Well, that was sporty."

"Yeah, tell me about it," Fields answered. "I wonder what other surprises they have in store for us?"

She gave her head a shake in response, voicing the Coast Guard's motto: "*Semper Paratus,* my friend. I figure if things begin to heat up in this neck of the woods, we'll have plenty of surprises."

"The Chinese?"

"Maybe. You never know where this minisub stuff will lead."

"The Law Of Unintended Consequences?"

"Yup."

"Think we should have left well enough alone and not risked our necks?" Fields asked.

"Maybe, but that's above my pay grade."

Chapter Four

3110 PROSPECT STREET, NW
GEORGETOWN, WASHINGTON, D.C.
WEDNESDAY 4 DECEMBER

Jia Lin-Wu Tai poured boiling water into a small Qing Dynasty era teapot then opened the sealed bag of Da Hong Pao oolong tea. He emptied the warmed vessel before extracting three teaspoons of curled dark-green leaves from the bag, pausing to savor their floral bouquet before dropping them into the pot. He emitted a satisfied grunt, checked the temperature of his heated water, then topped the leaves with four ounces. He replaced the lid and set the pot aside to steep for precisely one minute. No one else, not even Esteemed Mother, was permitted to make the tea.

The tea, grown in the Wuji Mountains near his family's ancestral home in Fujian Provence, was very rare and very expensive. The tea set alone appraised for $2,500. He prepared his tea with the same meticulous care that he applied to his job. Bureau 3 of the Ministry of State Security did not object to this one indulgence or to the purchase of the Federal Era house in Georgetown that he had insisted upon. The weathered mid-19th century brick home located at 3110 Prospect Street NW bordered a narrow alleyway that was ideal for his purposes. The property also included a detached carriage house with access to a forgotten root cellar.

His watch chimed. One minute. He lifted the lid and filtered the fragrant orange liquid into a delicate blue and white Lotus Leaf cup, then brought it to his lips. *Exquisite.* He smiled and made his way to the home's paneled library over-looking the Chesapeake and Ohio Canal National Park.

The room with its floor-to-ceiling oak bookshelves and red-silk wallpaper was artfully decorated, but sterile. There were no informal pictures, nothing to suggest a link with family or to his ancestors. The lone exception was the faded photograph of an aged gentleman attired in traditional peasant cloths set in a place of honor on his desk. His grand-father had fought beside Mao.

A frown crossed his face. He hadn't seen or heard from his mother or his sister in months and with the death of his father, he had a void in his life—something that his work with the MSS couldn't assuage. Even his family's ties to the homeland had been severed. The Ministry had arranged for his parents to 'immigrate' to the United States assuming false identities to establish his own cover as a deep agent, a supposed first-gener-ation American.

The MSS also couldn't fill the void that his belief in Taoism filled. While he didn't consider himself atavistic, he would still consult his seer, Qui-Hsing, for guidance whenever he felt threatened or before embarking on a new clandestine operation.

Qui-Hsing's readings were often uncannily accurate. The previous week, he foretold of menace. As often the case, the seer could not divine from where the threat originated. While Lin-Wu could not fully credit Qui-Hsing's reading, he could not choose to discount the warning either.

He crossed the room, a sense of unease clouding his mind

debating whether he should notify the Vice Chairman of the Central Military Commission, General Zi Zhao of his concerns. He stopped at the picture window, his eyes coming to rest on the remnants of the old C&O canal and the dulled waters of the Potomac River flowing listlessly just beyond. Isolated shards of sunlight pierced the dull low-lying clouds adding a rare hint of warmth to the dreary winter day.

A siren wailed in the distance, matched to a set of flashing blue lights moving east across the Francis Scott Key Bridge toward Arlington and the Pentagon. His mind touched on the date. In several days it would be the seventh. Pearl Harbor Day.

While the Washington establishment appeared to be distracted these past few months by petty differences, he knew better. If faced with an outside menace, these Americans would once again band together to confront the threat. But he had no intention of providing the Americans this opening. The stakes of his new operation were too high. His battles would be on the personal level, with no quarter given.

General Zi had made it abundantly clear that no nation would threaten the country's monopoly of rare-earth elements, a resource key to Beijing's long-term security and world dominance. He'd even hinted the Peoples Liberation Army would resort to '*drastic measures*' to ensure that no country, including the United States, interfered with these goals.

The American's aside, there were also the meddlesome Russians. He pondered what he must do to block them from obtaining a controlling interest in Trident Metallurgics. Perhaps it would serve his purpose to adapt the precepts of deception advocated by the sixth century military theorist and philosopher, Sun Tzu in his classic work, *The Art of War*.

"Excuse me, sir."

He didn't turn. "Yes?"

"The American is here."

"Very well." He took another sip of tea and studied the

reflection of his bodyguard in the window. Tao Yixing was a compact, dangerous man, with a large gold tooth he would flash with a peculiar crooked grimace. A master of the Chinese martial art, Wuslu, he would follow any order, seemingly without conscious thought.

He also understood Yixing's other job was to ensure he didn't defect. While no risk existed, despite the fact that he suspected his mother and sister had been silenced, he found the lack of trust disturbing. But then he knew it best to take a pragmatic view of his superiors' motives. Their constant vigilance was necessary to ensure his operations were not compromised and cause unnecessary embarrassment to General Zi and by extension to the Premier himself. He pushed the thought aside. His missions were progressing as planned despite the inquiries from that intrusive reporter who threatened to expose their clandestine roots. His lips tightened. *Yes, I must do something about Mr. Lange.*

He set his cup on the end table, removed his glasses, and strode through the kitchen toward the back door leading to the carriage house. Despite his reticence to expose his identity, the second member of his team, Lam Huifeng, had persuaded him that it was time to meet this American.

Behind him, almost unseen, he caught the shadow of his amah padding softly across the tiled kitchen floor on her way to remove the cup. He smiled at the sight of her hip-length hair braded in a traditional long queue swinging from side to side.

Esteemed Mother, as he called her, jealously guarded her position within the household as the overseer of its proper function and spirit. And despite his efforts to conceal them, she could read into his petulant moods, absorbing and cataloging them in her mind with measured serenity. She would have also assumed he'd removed his glasses and placed them in his shirt pocket, smiling at this small show of vanity on his part.

Lam Huifeng met him at the door of the carriage house. A specialist in the intricacies of covert international financial transactions and espionage, Huifeng belonged to the PLA General Staff's 3rd Branch, 61195 Division. He also reported to the Ministry of State Security's Enterprise Division. This Bureau held responsibility for the operation and management of the various front companies that were part of Lin-Wu's intricate plan. Those responsibilities were all well and good, but Huifeng's connection to the Enterprise Division required frequent trips to the embassy, a potential risk that could lead to unmasking his own identity. He addressed Huifeng.

"The American?"

"He is crude," Huifeng answered. "Arrogant with a misplaced sense of importance."

"Like many of his kind. We will soon know if he is to be of further use or must be eliminated. Do we have another asset to exploit?"

"Perhaps. We need to complete our validation."

"While it is best to be prepared, there is yet no imperative to have the second." He turned toward the door. "Shall we?"

He followed Huifeng into the carriage house, noting the lingering scent of cinnamon and sandalwood. Esteemed Mother had left a joss stick smoldering in her small apartment above the carriage house's main room. He motioned for Huifeng to stand to one side.

The American set down the book he'd been leafing through and slowly turned with feigned insouciance to face Lin-Wu. The man's eyes betrayed a hint of anxiety as did his clenched hands and the rigid lines around his mouth. Perhaps he'd been unnerved by the necessity of the blindfold and the use of the side entrance off the alley. Lin-Wu completed his assessment noting the man's hair and dress. Vain, yet no sense of style. Character flaws he could exploit. He motioned for the American to sit, not offering his hand. "We have much to discuss, Mr.?"

"Ellen."

"Presumably you have a first name."

"Glen."

"Of course." He struggled to suppress a laugh. Glen Ellen? He'd lifted the name from the small wine country town in Sonoma County. What a fool. He knew the American's real name, Jason Moore, as well as many details of his personal life. Moore was also a registered agent for the Federation of Mineral Development. All useful, but—

The American interrupted his thoughts. "And you, sir. What is your name?"

"'Nobody' is my name." His American friends knew him, though as James Wai, a first-generation Chinese-American from San Francisco. The cover and his degree in engineering from Georgetown University, had served him well.

"I see."

"You don't, but it is of no matter."

Moore stiffened. "I know more than you think, Mr. Tai."

He didn't respond to the taunt, keeping his face expressionless. "Perhaps you do, but if that is indeed the case, please enlighten me."

"I've heard that certain documents submitted by Consolidated Seabed Resources to the Interior Department were flawed."

"And where does the blame lay for such misfortune?"

"Wouldn't that be for you to figure out?" Moore settled into a large red-leather upholstered chair, leaned back, and crossed his legs.

"I would think you would have reviewed them."

"Not my job. Why would I? I don't know anything about this Seabed company. I've been working the Olympic bid for you."

"Don't you? Then perhaps we need to consider what, exactly, are your responsibilities."

Moore gave an indifferent shrug, adding a smug smile for

effect. "The Federal Acquisition Regulations for such submissions are quite complex, but I am open to negotiations. Perhaps an offer of another one-hundred-thousand dollars would suffice to persuade me to assist with this Seabed company and another fifty-thousand for value added if I were to assist with both submissions. I believe you have the number of my Swiss account."

He suppressed his growing irritation at Moore's impudence. "Like men, Mr. Ellen, money is always a problem." He extracted a photo from his coat pocket and thrust it toward the American. "What do you know of this man?"

Moore's mouth gaped open and closed several times mimicking a carp who'd just been yanked from the water by its lips. "How did—?"

"His name is Nick Parkos, his given name unlike yours, Mr. Ellen, or should I say, Mr. Moore?" He watched the Amercian's eyes widen, then dart toward Yixing who'd entered the room. Yixing stopped, planting himself menacingly between Moore and any chance of escape.

"Do you think us fools? Perhaps so, but I assure you that would be a grave mistake. It would be a shame to see any harm come to you or to your father's reputation at Amherst. I'm told that he is a tenured professor of history, a distinguished scholar with an impeccable reputation. But he too has his secrets, doesn't he? As all men do."

He paused. "Does your mother or the administration know of his ... shall we say, dalliance with several of his students ... or the parties? I understand there are shocking videos of young boys that—"

Moore lurched to his feet, his face contorted with rage. "You bast—"

Yixing's right arm shot out, palm forward, elbow bent, his left leg positioned in a reversed stance prepared to deliver a lethal blow to the American's neck.

"*Tìhng dài!*" Lin-Wu held up his hand to stop his bodyguard. "I believe violence at this point would not serve any useful purpose."

Moore stared at Yixing's empty, coal-black eyes. "Ah … I …"

"Certainly." His lips tightened in a thin smile. "Now that we understand each other, perhaps we may continue. Yes?"

Moore nodded dumbly, fidgeting with his cheap cufflinks.

"What if I were to say that Mr. Parkos is an analyst at the National Intelligence Center specializing in Transnational Organized Crime?"

Moore straightened and responded with a degree of renewed confidence. "He could cause complications."

"Indeed." His eyes narrowed. "There are always complications to consider, Mr. Moore, such as Parkos' meeting with a certain Geoffrey Lange two weeks ago. A meeting I believe you were privy to."

He studied Moore's face. "Ah, yes. I see you do remember. So, what do you know of these two men and their investigation of the Novorossiysk Business Group and their dealings with Newtech Resource Development and Trident Metallurgics?"

Moore shook his head, his face a blank.

"And what of their inquiries about our Alaskan enterprise, Consolidated Seabed Resources?"

Moore's jaw dropped. Ah, *perhaps Moore is ignorant of these events. Or could he really be that clever and playing us both?* That seemed improbable based on his assessment of the American. He proceeded on that assumption. "As I suspected. To spare you any further embarrassment, I will outline for you exactly what those complications are and what you will do."

Chapter Five

THE WHITE HOUSE
WASHINGTON, D.C.
FRIDAY 6 DECEMBER

President Randal Stuart dropped the red-jacketed intelligence report he'd just read onto the leather desk blotter. "What do I need to do?"

"With the Russians or Sylvester?" his Chief of Staff, Dan Lantis asked.

"Sylvester."

"He's become a liability."

Stuart spun his high-backed chair around and gazed through the Oval Office's nine-pane casement windows. A mixed swirl of snowflakes and mottled-brown leaves spun across the frozen lawn as he recalled a conversation two years earlier with Lantis.

Nothing really had changed, except now it was the Russians instead of the Chinese who were testing him. His lack of confidence in the Secretary of the Interior, Sylvester Poad, remained.

He spoke to the window. "I'll need options."

"Yes, sir."

A soft knock prompted Stuart to turn to the door leading from the executive secretary's office. "Yes, MaryAllus?"

"Excuse me, Mr. President. Deputy Secretary Oakes would like a moment before the meeting."

Lantis looked at his watch and offered an indifferent shrug.

He sighed. "Of course, please show her in."

Oakes stepped through the door and made for the paired couches in the center of the room, her face set.

He recognized the expression, another harbinger, and placed his hands flat on the blotter. "Good to see you again, Katherine."

"Thank you, sir. Richard sends his regrets. He's under the weather."

"What's on your mind, Kathrine?"

"Sylvester."

"Oh?" He glanced at Lantis, noting his Chief of Staff's lips tighten.

"May I speak freely, sir?"

He withdrew his hands from the blotter and grasped the edge of the desk no longer happy to see her, regretting his decision. The last thing he needed right now were more complications. "Of course."

Oakes paused, appearing to collect her thoughts. "We've known each other for a long time. I'm concerned."

"Could you be more specific?"

"Sylvester's not handling the stress very well."

He remained silent, waiting for her to elaborate.

Oakes glanced at her feet. "I'm just not sure how much longer he can hold out. I'll try to support him today."

She didn't elaborate. He studied her face, not sure what to make of her statement, stood, and made his way around the massive oak desk ending the impromptu meeting. "Thank you, Katherine. I'll see what I can do."

He slowed his pace, allowing Oakes to leave the office first, then followed Lantis across the corridor to the Roosevelt Room.

An off-key chorus led by Sheldon Payne, the Secretary of Defense, greeted him as he passed through the door of the conference room. "Good afternoon, Mr. President."

He glanced over Payne's shoulder at the iconic portrait of Colonel Teddy Roosevelt. Clad in his Rough Riders uniform, T.R. stood vigil over the fireplace at the far end of the room. The iconic portrait depicted the former President mounted on a wild-eyed horse, upright in the saddle leading the charge up San Juan Hill. A man in control when the wild beast of war needed reigning in. A good man to have.

He took his seat and picked up a thick briefing book. "Formulating A New Arctic Strategy; Key Geostrategic Issues." Five tabbed documents accounted for the weight of the packet. He picked one at random: "Implementation Plan for the National Strategy for the Arctic Region."

He closed the cover and poured himself a glass of water, thankful nobody expected him to actually read the references. Truth be told, though, he'd read several of them the day before. He'd found the contents sobering.

"We've got our work cut out for us," Payne said casting an eye at the briefing book. "Our current approach won't work."

Stuart nodded an acknowledgement. Leave it to Sheldon to cut through the BS. He had chosen him to lead the Department of Defense because of his reputation of designing and implementing major corporate mergers. Easing his way through the confirmation process and into the Pentagon bureaucracy was his six years of military service including a tour in Vietnam as an Army infantry platoon commander. Wounded in action, he'd been awarded the Silver Star. He was a proven entity, cool and tough under pressure. Like T.R.

He spotted an empty chair that should have been occupied by the Director of Homeland Security. "Where's Chuck?"

"His office called, sir,' Lantis answered. "He went home ill."

"Homeland needs to be at the table."

A voice cut in from behind his right shoulder. "You look like you just swallowed a raw oyster."

All three men turned toward the Chairman of the Joint Chiefs of Staff, Robert Mahan Lawson. Stuart grimaced. Lawson knew he hated raw oysters.

Admiral Lawson was the latest in a long line of Naval officers to serve his country and he enjoyed Stuart's full confidence. They were both Naval aviators and Lawson had taught the newly commissioned Ensign Randall Stuart how to fly years before at Naval Air Station Pensacola. They also shared something else—the memory of a momentous night at the Flora-Bama Lounge in Perdido Key following the ceremony where he'd received his "'Wings of Gold.'"

He erased the sour look on his face. It had taken his stomach days to recover from the dozens of raw oysters and unknown quantities of *Aviator Mad Beach* craft beer he'd consumed. At the time, it seemed to have been a good idea.

"Sheldon served up a bit of unsavory news," Stuart responded.

Lawson cast a skeptical eye at Payne. "Something happen I should know?"

"We need to rethink our strategy for the Arctic." Payne said before addressing the man seated across the table. "Bryce, what do you think?"

Payne's question seemed to startle the man which, in turn, earned a curious glance from Oakes.

Stuart gave an imperceptible shake of his head and studied his Director of National Intelligence searching for a hint of a response. No telling what he might say. Bryce Gilmore was the zealous guardian of the nation's secrets and the grand inquisitor of its enemies. The job required constant vigilance, monitoring and analyzing other country's motives and actions that impacted the United States.

Gilmore pushed his half-glasses down his prominent nose and peered over its tip at Payne as if sighting a rifle. He didn't like surprises. "Think about whose strategy? State's? DoD's? Homeland's?"

Stuart held up his hand before Payne could answer. There would be no sidebars that would further muddle the issue. His Arctic strategy was fragmented among multiple civilian agencies, let alone within the military. "Kathrine, why don't you lead off."

Oakes flipped open her briefing book. "Thank you, sir."

He settled back in his chair, curious as to how the dynamics in the room would play out. There was no question the geopolitical landscape in the Arctic had changed dramatically over the first two years of his presidency. He also understood there were multiple reasons for this, not the least of which was global warming.

He tilted his head, tuning out Oakes' voice, more interested in what was not said, versus what was voiced by those sitting around him. Those voids would tell him more of what he needed to know, what he would need to address.

He shifted his attention to the end of the table to study the Secretary of the Interior, Sylvester Poad. Sloping shoulders, thinning hair, a small, petulant mouth, eyes undercut by dark circles framed within 'seventies' style wire-rim spectacles. Hardly vulpine. He focused on Poad's eyes. Shiftless? *No, the wrong word. They were alert, missing nothing.*

But there was something else. Poad rarely smiled. Lantis had told him there may be good reason. There were rumors of marital difficulties, a domineering wife, financial problems. All red flags. He'd married into a wealthy family and hadn't met their, or his wife's, expectations despite being a cabinet officer. It seemed that whatever he did, it was never good enough.

He paused, cautioning himself about the gossip. He couldn't allow himself to rely on hearsay or innuendo to justify the decision he would soon have to make. On another level, those same rumors also exposed his own ambivalence about his choice to lead the Department of the Interior.

"...global warming..."

Those two words, captured from the middle of a sentence, filtered through his morose thoughts, bringing him back to the brief. That, and a skeptical "Harrumph" coming from his left. Gilmore was shaking his head at the mention of the contentious issue. The DNI wasn't a believer. At least not completely.

He flashed Gilmore a hard 'cease and desist' look.

Oakes continued, either unaware of the brief interplay or ignoring it. "Our collective strategies to address these geopolitical changes has not been adequate, particularly since they have been based on a stable, conflict-free Arctic. That said, we have made some inroads addressing the various threats to regional stability by leveraging what little advantage we have as chair of the seven-nation Arctic Council."

He cocked his head at her statement and the change in her voice. *Where was she going with this? The Council was Poad's responsibility. Surely, she wasn't going to undercut him after what she'd said in the Oval Office?* He injected himself back into the conversation. "Sylvester, would you care to comment?"

Poad set his pen down on the table, letting his hand rest on it a moment. "Yes, sir, I would. The 'National Strategy for the Arctic' lists three goals: Advancing our security interests, pursuing responsible stewardship of the region, and strengthening international co-operation. This guidance, as well as that provided in the other four enclosures in today's briefing packet, are all broad in scope but short on details. Absent a clearly defined, coordinated strategy, the Department of the Interior has chosen to advance a policy of Constructive Ambiguity. We—"

Gilmore almost sprung out his chair. "Constructive Ambiguity? What-in-hell does that mean?"

Poad appeared unfazed by the outburst. "Our policy recognizes cooperation, Bryce, not confrontation. This approach has provided us the flexibility to respond to unexpected challenges in a non-confrontational manner without appearing to be in conflict with our government's previously stated positions."

Gilmore rolled his eyes. "Good Lord, no won—"

"Excuse me," Oakes cut in with a nod to Poad. "There are valid reasons for assuming this position, with which I note, State concurs."

"I'd be cautious on where you and Sylvester place your faith, Kathrine," Payne commented.

"For example," Oakes continued, "while the debate of causation is ongoing, the implications of global warming are without doubt the most significant. One only has to look at the impact on international shipping through the Canadian waters of the Northwest Passage."

"Canadian?" Payne interrupted. "I beg to differ. Those are international waters. They are not any different from those of the South China Sea that the Chinese have been trying to claim. We've been through this."

"The Canadians would beg to differ," Oakes responded.

Gilmore leafed through his notes. "I have a report here that says Ottawa intends to submit a request to the International Seabed Authority to append jurisdiction of their offshore territorial waters. If approved, those claims would extend Canada's sovereignty two-hundred nautical miles touching the North Pole."

"That doesn't help. They're supposed to be our allies," Payne said.

Oakes squared her shoulders, bristling at the remark. "I'd say we didn't help our cause any at the G-7 by Commerce screwing around with USMCA."

Lawson injected himself into the conversation, his words defusing the rhetoric. "Perhaps we should look at where we stand within the context of an iceberg. Suppose we're only seeing an eighth of what's going on. That which is visible, not the seven-eighths that are submerged. What aren't we seeing?"

"Polar bears?" Gilmore offered.

Gilmore's comment elicited a few isolated chuckles but drew another nonverbal rebuke from Stuart that quieted the table.

"Bob, I trust you're not going to use the Titanic as an analogy for our policy?" Stuart asked, grateful Lawson had interceded.

"In part, sir. Frankly we're steaming around the Arctic without a clear sense of where we're going or the potential hazards we're facing."

"By 'we're,' I assume you're referring to the Navy?" Oakes asked.

"And the Coast Guard," Lawson answered. "We've been collaborating with our sister service in Operation Arctic Shield developing strategies for fisheries, mineral and resource protection, freedom of navigation, and domain awareness. Our two services are also conducting a joint-requirements review of command and control, assets, and infrastructure."

"Let me expand on that." Payne reached down for his briefcase and pulled out a document. "This is a quote from the Russian Federation's policy: "In a case of a competitive struggle for resources, it is not possible to discount that this very competition might be resolved by a decision to use military might."

"There's no ambiguity in their position," Gilmore said. "The Russians view their destiny as tied to the Arctic, a natural extension of their homeland. Framed within this context, I'd ask, where do the Chinese fit? They've made no secret of their intent to expand their sphere of influence into the region."

"The Chinese?" Payne gave his chin a thoughtful rub. "Maybe in Greenland, but I'm not interested in them. I'm focused on Alaska and what the Russians are up to."

Stuart turned toward Gilmore. "Bryce, you have anything more about that sub that pertains?"

Payne's eyebrows knitted in consternation. "What sub?"

"Two weeks ago, the Coast Guard discovered an abandoned Chinese deep-sea research sub hung-up in the ice off Alaska," Gilmore answered. "It fell off our radar until one of our analysts kept pestering us to investigate."

He noticed Poad reposition his glasses on his nose, a tic betraying his consternation. Something didn't feel right. He needed to piece all this information together. "Bryce, can you back up a minute?"

"Certainly."

"Who's the analyst?"

"Nick Parkos. He convinced us to go to the Coast Guard and run down an unusual homing signal coming from the ice shelf near Cape Lisburne."

"Never heard of the place. Where is it?" Oakes said.

"The Alaskan coast, just north of the Bering Strait. There's an abandoned Air Force radar site left over from the Cold War. We're taking a look at it to support the expansion of our missile defense system."

"Hardly a coincidence then?"

"We're looking into it," Payne said.

Stuart's jaw tightened at the non-answer, but before he could ask another question, Gilmore spoke.

"Parkos noted something else while cleaning up some loose ends from the al-Khultyer affair. I've looked over his preliminary report and found his analysis troubling. He says our old friends, the Novorossiysk Business Group—"

"Who are they?" Poad interrupted.

Gilmore appeared not to hear him. "The NBG has made overtures to several North American corporations to partner in mining operations in the Arctic and the western U.S." He paused to look through his notes. "One's a Canadian outfit, Newtech Resource Development. The other's an American firm, Trident Metallurgics."

Stuart caught Oakes and Poad exchanging a quick glance at the mention of the two companies before Poad lowered his head and typed something in his iPad. Oakes' face remained expressionless. *What was that all about? Shouldn't Sylvester know about this?* He redirected a question to Gilmore not yet willing to read more into the nonverbal exchange. "See what else Parkos has on those companies and get back to me."

Poad twisted in his chair. "Mr. President. I must insist that these discussions remain under the purview of the Arctic Forum."

He struggled to keep his annoyance at Poad's comment off his face. Payne saved him the trouble.

"That is all well and good, Sylvester," Payne said, "but I recall your council specifically eschews any discussions that pertain to military/national security issues in the Arctic."

"That's--"

Dan Lantis cut off whatever else Poad was going to say. "Excuse me. Sir?"

Stuart glanced at his Chief of Staff who pointed at his watch. "Okay, we need to wrap this up. Good brief, everyone."

He pushed away from the table and caught Lawson by the elbow as he headed for the door. "Bob, would you and Sheldon join me in the Oval Office? You too, Bryce. Dan, would you round up the NSA and Mike Rohrbaugh?"

<h1 style="text-align:center">Chapter Six</h1>

THE OVAL OFFICE
WASHINGTON, D.C.
FRIDAY 6 DECEMBER

President Stuart rounded the corner of his desk and tossed a wave of his hand toward the Oval Office's twin couches. "Make yourselves comfortable, gentlemen."

He caught sight of Bryce Gilmore taking a furtive glance at his watch before the DNI settled into his seat. "I don't intend to keep you long. The others should be here shortly."

"Sir, if I may," Sheldon Payne said.

"What's on your mind, Sheldon?"

"Just to be clear, I didn't want to go into the details about our plans for Cape Lisburne in front of the broader group. It wouldn't be wise to make our intentions common knowledge. I also felt it would be imprudent to bring up our discussions at the Arctic Security Forces Forum in Helsinki. There's been pushback."

"From where?"

"The Arctic Institute. They rebutted any suggestion that we use of any of their forums to address the military issues we're confronting in the Arctic. I recall their reasoning was 'there existed no clear and necessary function of the ASFF that overrode well-established forums.'"

He cradled his chin in his left hand giving it a thoughtful rub. If nothing else, The Arctic Institute's statement pointed out a painful truth. He re-focused his attention on Payne. "Yes, you're right. What I read into their rebuttal is the ongoing turf battle between those two organizations as well as a good degree of denial by the good folks of the Arctic Forum about the militarization of the region. The brief could have easily veered off course. Our—"

MaryAllus poked her head into the Oval Office before he could continue. "Captain Rohrbaugh and Mr. Lantis, sir."

"Ah, Mike," Stuart said. "Please come in. Is Justin joining us?"

"No, sir. The NSA is still off campus."

"Okay, pass on what we discuss. Find a seat. You too, Dan. Sheldon just touched on what I wanted to talk about."

"Shall I continue, sir?" Payne asked.

"No, I'll take it from here. Simply stated, I don't want … no, I won't tolerate the Chinese snooping around our coast. My gut tells me that destroyed submersible is a strong indicator that they've been there before. And Bryce, your man, Parkos, has also painted an alarming picture of Russian meddling."

"Yes, sir," Gilmore said, "I trust his instincts."

"That's why I want him, not anyone from State, Treasury, or Interior running point to chase down whatever in hell is going on up there." Stuart held up his hand. He had to confront a major fault in the country's approach to the threats to the country's security posed by Beijing and Moscow. "I know this is irregular but absent a clear lead agent for my Arctic policy, I want you four to design and implement a cogent plan."

He turned to his Chief of Staff. "Dan, assist with the coordination. I'll need an Executive Order with the particulars for my signature. And I want an endorsement of the ASFF. If we don't address the military issues in the Arctic, the Chinese will harbor no qualms about filling any vacuum we happen to leave by default. That said, Bob, what are your shortfalls?"

"Including the Coast Guard's input, new icebreakers, ice-hardened long-range patrol vessels, aviation assets, communication networks, infrastructure. But foremost, we have to have a clear command structure. Just look at the Navy. We have the 2nd, 3rd, and 5th Fleets all responsible for some aspect of the Arctic."

"Just about everything," Stuart replied. He turned to the Secretary of Defense. "Sheldon, put together a viable strategic plan to address these requirements and cost it out. And make sure Chuck at Homeland is in the loop. Bob, touch base with the CNO. I want his input on establishing an Arctic Command."

"I'll call him this afternoon."

"I also need a point paper outlining what we need to do to make the ASFF a viable forum. And make sure you include the Coast Guard and that it specifically defines their role. Questions?"

He noted Gilmore drop his jaw as if to pose one, but he apparently changed his mind. "No? Then I'll let you go. Whatever the Russians and Chinese are doing off our coast, I want them stopped."

Rohrbaugh made to follow the others out the door but halted at the sound of Stuart's voice. "Captain, would you stay a moment."

"Yes, sir."

He waited until the door closed, then softened his voice. "Mike, have you stayed in contact with Nick since he returned from Miami?"

"Yes, sir. We spoke the other night. Kate and I are planning to ask him to join us for dinner over the holidays."

"I've heard he's had some trouble adjusting. I don't want to push him over the edge with this assignment."

Mike looked down a moment, then raised his head. "May I speak freely?"

"Of course. You've both earned that right."

"Thank you, sir. Nick's tougher than he knows, but he isn't coping very well with what happened in Somalia and Miami. He's shut himself off. I suspect he's drinking too much."

"Can I do anything?"

"I'll reach out… I've been there too."

"We both have."

"Some handle it better than others, sir. The flashbacks, nightmares, the mood swings. We all experience them at one time or another. If someone says they're not, they're lying. But, worse? They're lying to themselves."

A heaviness washed over him. He had his own memories. *Nothing like some, though.* His eyes fell on the small glass case mounting his naval aviator wings. The carrier ops. Piloting an A-6 Intruder during the first Gulf War. The hair-raising night missions, following in the footsteps of his old mentor, Bob Lawson. He'd lost close friends over the years. All remnants from his sole combat tour before he left the Navy.

Mike filled the heavy void in the room. "He's got a girlfriend, sir. Michelle O'Brian. She's a crewmember on Air Force One."

"O'Brian?" He smiled in recognition. "I sensed something might be going on with those two."

"I've spoken with her."

"Good." He paused. "I know this is asking a lot, but I want you to be my go-between again. Can you reconcile that with your personal relationship?"

"If I can't, sir, I'll let you know."

"Thank you, Mike." He stood and offered his hand. "He'll be needing somebody to watch his back."

Chapter Seven

NATIONAL COUNTERINTELLIGENCE CENTER
MCLEAN, VIRGINA
MONDAY 10 DECEMBER

Nick pushed away from the keyboard, swiveling his chair to face the window and the dull mid-afternoon sun. He crossed his hands on his lap, pursing his lips before taking several deep breaths in a futile attempt to settle his thoughts about what he'd just uncovered.

He spun the chair back and extracted a Venn diagram from beneath the clutter of research papers stacked precariously on the right side of the desk. The interlocking circles of the diagram represented an enormous amount of data that needed to be collected and analyzed to identify the facilitators and the obfuscating network of semi-legitimate shell companies, venture capitalists, banks, and law firms that shielded criminal activity.

He pondered the data he would need to explicate and discover the full extent of Trident Metallurgics, Newtech Resource Development, and the Novorossiysk Business Group's intentions.

Were the companies actually doing anything illegal? Or could the oligarchs of the NBG be collu— He caught himself. *Colluding or conspiring?* He searched his mind for the correct word. *Was it an illegal act?* He didn't know for sure. He chose *conspiring* with the Russian government to corner the market on a strategic resource. The United States now imported most of its rare-earth elements, an unacceptable reality in the emerging world of international economic bribery. He'd also discovered that most of the ore mined in the American west was sent to China for processing. *Incredible.* Why would we do that? He found a partial answer a few minutes later.

The recent bankruptcy of the nation's largest rare-earth mine, the Emmons-Powell Mining Company, had only exacerbated the problem. Located in Mountain Pass, California, the company bordering the Nevada line, had succumbed to the dual impact of plunging profits and an adverse ruling by the Environmental Protection Agency. A ruling preceding Stuart's election. The company's processing of the mined ore had resulted in a toxic plume contaminating the adjacent groundwater. The environmentalists had raised hell, strategic implications to the nation's security notwithstanding.

He had to admit it made sense for Trident to want to fill the subsequent void in production by acquiring the assets of the bankrupt firm. But could a new startup have the resources to even consider pursuing a joint venture? Operating under that assumption, he considered who could facilitate a partnership between Trident, Newtech and the NBG. He grabbed a pen and began to scribble a note on his diagram. His hand stopped in mid-sentence. *That lobbyist Lange pointed out in the Upper Crust. Who's he representing?* He'd found a starting point, but not a name. Undeterred, he set to unraveling the web of those intent on undermining the security of his country.

He focused on this new lead. Any transaction involving a foreign business entity seeking a controlling interest in a strategic American company or resource would first have to seek approval for the venture from the Committee on Foreign Investment in the United States, CFIUS. Crime syndicates would hardly bother to obtain permission from the Federal Government to conduct their business, but a front company would presumably have to submit the required justification and documentation for their business venture. *Presumably? But not necessarily.* He tapped "CFIUS" into his search engine and scanned the resulting field.

CFIUS: A nine-member inter-agency committee with cabinet level representation chaired by the Secretary of the Treasury … Other offices also observe and, as appropriate, participate … National Security Council, OMB, Homeland …. Tasked to conduct a risk analysis of pending transactions by foreign companies for threat, vulnerability, and consequences …

He nodded, closed the tab, and re-focused. *Chaired by Treasury, not Interior.* Okay, then. But who did the grunt-work for the committee that underpinned the decision process? It hardly seemed likely that the various cabinet Secretaries would be dealing with the minutia. That would be left to their staffers— and they would be influenced by the huge cadre of lobbyists that inhabited the Beltway. Just like those individuals he'd caught a glimpse of at the Upper Crust.

He paused, tapping his pen on the notes he'd written on the diagram. His eyes stopped on the isolated circle in the upper margin where he'd scribbled: "Chinese submersible." *Am I focusing on the wrong players?* He shook his head and X'ed out the circle. He'd found no evidence of Chinese involvement despite his earlier suspicions.

His thoughts returned to the lobbyist he'd seen at the Upper Crust. What could he learn about him? Surveillance of an American citizen was out of the question since he had no solid evidence to obtain a court order under FISA, the Foreign Intelligence Surveillance Act. Hell, he didn't even have a clue who to approach to submit such a request. The Justice

Department? Perhaps he could ask Lange for a contact … No, perhaps later. He pivoted back to the computer and pulled up an old file. If he were to continue on this track, he'd need help.

His eyes scrolled down his list of contacts. Jessica Caudry: FBI, National Security Branch. Mark Arita: Treasury, Office of Terrorism and Financial Intelligence. He'd worked with Jessica on the al-Khultyer affair. And Arita? They went back a long ways on joint investigations even before he tapped him to be on the committee he formed to help chase down and stop the Chechen terrorist. He copied down their personal phone numbers confident he could count on both to be discrete. But for now, their input would have to be off the record.

He closed his eyes, massaging his forehead and temples with his fingertips. He needed to slow down. Irrespective of whom he reached out to, there could be no second guessing, no turning around. He shifted through the pile of written notes on his desk before his wandering thoughts drifted back to Geoffrey Lange's business card.

What he'd found on his background search of the reporter raised as many questions as answers. The basics were straight-forward enough: Grew up in a small town in central Indiana. That accounted for the accent. Dual sports star in high school. Graduated from the University of Indiana before joining the Navy and serving in the Second Gulf War. But this is where things got interesting. Lange had been a Lieutenant Comman-der, a SEAL, before leaving the Navy to pursue a master's degree in journalism at Northwestern.

"My, God." He jerked upright. *How did Lange know about my involvement with al-Khultyer? Few knew, and, as far as he knew, his name had never appeared in any news reports. That information shouldn't have been leaked. Especially to a reporter.* At a loss, his thoughts turned to another SEAL close to Lange's age, his friend Mike Rohrbaugh. They must have known each other. *Perhaps Mike*

…

The sound of a familiar tread echoing from the hallway prompted him to twist in his chair. He caught a glimpse of the person passing by. "Hey, Austin."

The footfalls stopped and Austin's head appeared in the door, a coffee cup suspended in his right hand, an inquiring look on his face. Nick hesitated, caught by a moment of self-doubt. His hand brushed across the raw scar of the bullet wound beneath his shirt. *Was it right to involve him? Could he even be trusted?* "Got a sec?"

"Sure do."

"I'm on to something. Have a seat." He lifted a stack of files cluttering the chair positioned by the desk, waited for Austin to set his coffee cup on the floor, but stopped him when he reached for his pen. "Sorry, no notes."

Austin's eyebrows shot up. "What's up?"

"I've been looking at a small startup, Trident Metallurgics based out of Provo, Utah. They're currently in negotiations with a Canadian group, Newtech Resource Development, whose corporate headquarters are in Montreal. Newtech is a big outfit with mining operations scattered all over the world, not just Canada. Trident ..."

He stopped, reading the curious look on Austin's face. "There appears to be a link with the Novorossiysk Business Group. The Russian outfit with links to transnational crime that we've investigated before."

"What do they have to do with the other two?"

"Rare-earth elements."

"I'm sorry, sir. You've lost me."

"Rare-earth elements are a strategic resource. My gut tells me the NBG may be fronting for the Russian government to gain access to the assets of a bankrupt U.S. firm, Emmons-Powell Mining."

He held up his hand to stop another question. "There's precedent. An incident some years back. The Russians gained control of a significant portion of our uranium supply by linking their shell company with a legitimate company in Canada."

"How they'd pull that off?"

"Piggy-backed onto an existing export license that had been approved for another consortium."

"A strategic resource? How could that happen?"

"The deal was approved through the Interior Department via a vague third party."

"They bypassed CFIUS?"

He suppressed his surprise at Mack's insight. "Appears so."

"What do you want me to do?"

"This time around it appears the bulk of the projected startup costs are coming from a Swiss investment fund named Innovel Venture Capital." He handed Austin the Venn diagram. "I don't know if they're legit or a shell company fronting for the NBG."

Austin studied the diagram, then set it on the desk. "You mentioned these companies are looking to acquire Emmons-Powel's assets."

"Yes? What about it?"

"I'd think the first step they'd need to take would be to gain approval from Emmons's Board of Directors or whomever else may have receivership for the bankruptcy proceedings. The board would likely approve any reasonable deal that would give them a short-term gain to offset their losses."

Nick spun his pen around his diagram. "What else?"

"The new owners will also need to acquire the mineral rights to restart the mining operation. We need to take a look at the commodity traders who could be in play and where they're incorporated."

"My, God. I didn't even think of that." *This kid is way ahead of me.* Chagrined, he jotted down 'Commodity Traders' and 'Board of Directors' in the margin of the cluttered diagram. "They'd likely be using shell companies."

"That'd be my guess."

The jarring ring of the desk phone startled both of them, stopping Nick before he could continue. He picked the receiver up before the second ring. "Parkos."

"You care to tell me what the hell is going on?"

He recognized the voice of his supervisor, Ned Strickland. And Strickland wasn't a happy camper. "Ah, I—"

"I just got a call from the DNI. What—"

He cradled the receiver against his shoulder and grabbed a pen, shot a glance at Austin, and lifted his hands in supplication, shaking his head. Austin nodded, eased himself out of the chair, and made for the door.

"I'm sorry, sir. I don't—"

"Off course you don't."

"Sir, what's this about?"

"That Chinese mini-sub and the NBG. Your report found its way to the President. Are the two related?"

"I don't think so. This is the first feedback I've received."

"Okay."

The tone of Strickland's voice indicated his supervisor was far from '*okay*.' He stiffened, bracing for the next verbal assault.

"The DNI wants to see you."

"I'll—"

"Today."

"Yes, sir."

"Keep me in the loop." The line went dead.

He remained motionless for a moment, dropped the receiver back in the cradle, pushed himself out of the chair, and made his way across the room. He stared outside, his fingertips resting on the narrow windowsill, his mind in turmoil. *Now what?*

———

Nick checked the time. 1510. Almost time to go. He had a general idea about what the DNI wanted to talk about. Strickland's cryptic call had mentioned his analysis of the possible intent of the Chinese submersible and the NBG had gone all the way to the Oval Office.

He stared at the characters on his keyboard, then logged off. The answers he sought would not be coming from one of his data bases. He pulled the access card from the slot on the keyboard and slid it into the plastic holder dangling from his neck. A quick scan of his office confirmed his sensitive documents were secured. *Okay, you got this. Nothing to worry about.* He locked the door and made his way to the seventh-floor office of the DNI not convinced he had anything but trouble in store.

He paused at the closed double doors leading to Gilmore's office, pulled out a comb, and ran it through the unruly tangles of his hair. *That's just going to have to do.* He took a deep breath and crossed the threshold to be greeted with a welcoming smile from Gilmore's executive secretary, Wendy. His reception was a one-eighty out from the first time he'd been summoned to see the DNI. On that occasion he'd been completely unnerved by her skeptical gaze.

"No Ohio State tie?" she asked.

"No excuse. Especially since my Buckeyes are in the national championship playoffs again."

"Let me see if Mr. Gilmore is free."

"Is that Parkos?" boomed a voice from the inner office. "Don't keep him waiting out there, Wendy. You guys can yak later."

"Guess I have my answer," Wendy said. "Go on."

Gilmore waved Nick to a chair across from his desk. "This won't take long."

"Yes, sir."

"I brought up your analysis during an NSC meeting we had on the Arctic last Wednesday. The president wants you to take the lead in figuring out what the Chinese are up to off Cape Lisburne. You'll have the details outlining the scope of your authority and what assets are available as soon as the NSC fleshes out the details and he signs the Executive Order. He also wants a full report on the links between the NBG, Trident Metallurgics, and that Canadian outfit. If they're making a play for Emmons-Powell, he wants them stopped."

Chinese? Nick stared out the window behind Gilmore, stunned by this latest turn of events, imagining the possibilities. He felt a trickle of sweat run down his inner arm. *What have I gotten myself into?*

"Nick?"

He refocused. "Sorry, sir."

"Anything going on that I need to know about?"

"No, sir. I was just thinking about the Chinese."

"As you should." Gilmore stood and thrust out his right hand. "Go forth and slay the dragon."

Chapter Eight

CREEKSIDE CONDOMINIUMS
ANNANDALE, VIRGINA
TUESDAY 11 DECEMBER

Nick pushed through the shirts hanging in the bedroom closet. *What-in-hell do you wear to a gay bar?* His hand stopped on an old golf shirt that looked like a relic from the 80's. Which, in point of fact, it was. He'd bought the gaudy shirt at the local Goodwill Store after an old high school friend's invitation to play a round of golf. He accepted even though he'd never swung a club in his life.

He smiled, remembering the name of the course. Bash. An appropriate name considering the ensuing round. He dropped his hand wondering what had happened to his friend. Another loose end.

Bill the Cat padded into the closet and brushed against his leg. He reached down and gave his pet a vigorous scratch behind the ears that elicited a grateful purr. He named the stray he'd adopted because of his resemblance to the frazzled character in the cartoon strips *Bloom County* and *Opus*. The character, known for his hairballs, vocalized "Acks" and

"Thptts," and free-basing Tender Vittles resonated with him. Far from deranged, though, Bill turned out to be a pretty good companion—except for the hairballs. If his nightmares didn't wake him, Bill could be counted on to fill in the gaps at night with his retching. Nick watched the cat saunter off for the kitchen in search of food and turned his attention back to the golf shirt. *Nope. Bad idea.*

His iPhone sang out from the bedside table deterring any further search. He backed out of the closet to answer the call he was expecting from his girlfriend, Michelle. A crew member of Air Force One, she said she'd check in after the aircraft landed in Dallas and the president and his staff were taken care of. He grabbed the phone and tensed at the sight of the caller ID: Unknown Caller. He hesitated, then against his better judgement answered. "Yes?"

"Change of plans …"

He recognized the voice. Lange.

"… 3136 M Street Northwest. Same time. Ask for me. Oh, and wear a sports coat."

He set the phone down and headed back to the closet. *Well, that takes care of what to wear.* Beyond that, he hadn't a clue what to expect.

————

THE NICHOLAS
  3136 M STREET, NW
  GEORGETOWN, WASHINGTON D.C.

Nick walked past the upscale shops lining M Street counting down the addresses before halting at 3136. He'd almost missed the small polished-brass numbers affixed to the brick wall beside the building's sage-colored wooden door. The entryway's ornate doorknocker was balanced by a pair of colonial-style columns and a matching crenelated pediment. A small wrought-iron sign next to the door identified the establishment: The Nicholas.

Good name, Nick thought. He spotted a small surveillance camera tucked under the corner of the sill and the push-pad for an electronic door lock. *What is this place?* He glanced up and down the street. Nothing suspicious. He reached for the doorknocker and gave it a couple sharp raps.

The door opened to reveal a formally attired doorman. "May I be of help, sir?"

"Ah, yes." He recovered enough from his surprise at the man's attire and Scottish accent to add, "Mr. Geoffrey Lange is expecting me."

The doorman responded by stepping aside "Certainly, sir."

He stepped through the door into another world, one completely removed from the Upper Crust Tap and Grill. He glanced over the doorman's shoulder. A beautiful carved-oak bar with four matching stools dominated the far wall beyond the parquet floor of the foyer. A stained-glass divider separated the bar's flanking columns on the left from a hallway presumably leading to a cloak room. On the right side of the epic structure, a framed picture mounted on the wall depicted a colonial-era tavern with two dandies sporting walking canes standing before it.

"May I take your overcoat, sir?"

He slipped off his coat and handed it over. Left to his own thoughts, his eyes ran over the labels of the bar's selection of scotch and gin. *Impressive.*

The doorman returned, and with a polite sweep of his arm indicated Nick should follow. "This way, please. Mr. Lange is in the upstairs drawing room."

He followed the man while muttering under his breath in a feigned English accent, "But, of course, my good man. Where else would he be?"

The stairs were just to the left of a well-stocked library with clusters of large red-leather armchairs. He detected the faint cherry scent of pipe smoke drifting from the room. Several men seated in the far corner didn't turn their heads at the intrusion, intent on keeping their own counsel.

He caught a glimpse of a large portrait on the far wall as he grasped the banister. The gentleman in the painting wore a Colonial era blue naval officer's coat with buffed-white facing and gold epaulets. *Nicholas?*

The stairs opened onto a comfortable room of subdued opulence. Old oils lined English-green walls set off by oak-wainscoting. A plume of cigar smoke swirled up from one of a pair of tufted wingback chairs set in front of a large fireplace, a warming fire dancing in its hearth. The thin column of smoke wisped across the front of a painting hung over the mantle depicting an eighteenth-century sea battle.

"Mr. Lange, your guest, sir."

Lange, attired in a maroon smoking jacket offset by black lapels, lifted himself from his place of repose. "Thank you, Edmund."

"Will there be anything else, sir?"

Lange faced Nick. "Care for a wee dram of scotch? I recall you drank Laphroaig the other night. We have a nice eighteen, but I'd recommend giving the McCallan Third Edition a try."

Caught off guard by the ambience of the club and the offer, he hesitated.

"Edmund, can you bring Mr. Parkos the McCallan?"

"Certainly, sir."

Lange followed Nick's eyes to a musket mounted on the far wall. "1766 French Charleville .69 caliber. The Continental Congress ordered them for the Marines." He gestured to the oil painting. "That would be them on the fighting top of the *Alliance*, America's first frigate. She was designed by William Hackett to carry thirty-two guns. Of course, she carried more. The club is named after Major Samuel Nicholas, first commandant of the Marine Corps. You might have seen the picture of Tun Tavern downstairs. That's wh—"

"Geoff, why am I here?" he said, tiring of the long history lesson.

"In a moment." Lange motioned for Nick to sit and opened the lid of an exquisite wood inlaid humidor. The motion exposed an ugly burn scar covering most his left hand and extended to several deformed digits.

He averted his eyes, but not fast enough. He hadn't noticed the injury at the Upper Crust. *Could the deformity be why he left the Navy?*

"Yeah, typing can be a challenge."

He had enough sense to not ask about the injury, just as Lange hadn't pried into his own past at the bar. Every man had his secrets. He'd learn about Lange's story in due time, when the reporter was ready to talk about what happened.

"Cigar?" Lange asked.

"I'll pass, thanks." He settled into his chair and tried another tact. "What's going on?"

"Turns out, a lot."

"Care to elaborate?"

Lange shifted his cigar, rolling the tip in the ashtray set on the table between them. He fixed Nick with his eyes. "I presume you checked me out."

He nodded an affirmation.

"Good, then I won't bother you with the details. Suffice it to say, I've come across information that might be of interest to you."

"I'm listening."

"That guy in the Upper Crust, the lobbyist with the bad hair? His name is Jason Moore. He's a registered agent for the Federation of Mineral Development with contacts in Interior and the State Department's Planning Office. A while back he approached Interior on behalf of a new start-up, Olympic Industries."

Well, that's interesting. He hadn't run across that firm. "What's this have to do with me?"

"The Chinese."

He equivocated. "I'm not looking at the Chinese."

Lange tilted his head in a none too subtle display of doubt. "Maybe not yet. But you have been looking into the Novorossiysk Business Group and their link with Trident Metallurgics and Newtech."

He worked to keep the surprise off his face. *How did Lange …?* A possible answer flashed into his consciousness. *That email on his computer: "It's Not Over."* His lips compressed, anger replacing surprise. "How do you know that?"

Lange took a long draw on his cigar, then slowly exhaled, the smoke cloaking his face in an acrid cloud. "I've got my sources."

"Who are they?"

"Can't say."

He gripped the arms of his chair, his knuckles blanching. "Damn it, don't play me. Tell me. Otherwise, this ends right now."

Lange set down the cigar and leaned forward to grab the fireplace poker. He gave the logs in the hearth a vigorous stir, sending a cascade of glowing embers up the flue. "It's for your own protection. We may be caught in the middle of a power play between the Chinese and the Russians."

"We?"

"The United States."

He struggled to string together the fragments of information that Lange had divulged. He had to regain control. "What's the end game?"

"Control of our supply of rare-earth elements."

The answer assuaged Nick's anger, at least to a point. "What's the connection?"

"Emmons-Powell Mining. There's another player besides Trident and Newtech.

"You got a name?"

"Olympic Industries."

"They're the Chinese connection?"

"That's my guess. Their operation is hidden behind a layer of shell companies and their financial backers. You know the mine company's history?"

He decided to not reveal what he knew and focused on pulling more information from Lange. "Some of it."

"Emmons-Powell went bankrupt for a number of reasons. They took a financial hit when Beijing relaxed their own export quotas for REEs, flooded the market and sent the cost of ore plummeting. Emmons's profits plummeted in turn. Couldn't meet production costs. They barely remained solvent. Then they were hammered with an eighty-million dollar fine by the EPA for wastewater contamination of the adjacent aquifer. They couldn't recover. Olympic wants to purchase the company and corner the market. They're also working to obtain the mineral rights so they can resume operations."

Olympic? Where did they come from? Lange now had his full attention. "Who's backing them?"

"I'm researching that," Lange replied. "Could be the Pan American Development Bank out of Seattle or a Swiss investment fund, Innovel Venture Capital.

"No, it's not Innovel. They're backing Trident. It's the link I've found to the NBG, the Russians. Is Olympic involved in any other ventures in the U.S.?"

"Not that I know of, but that's an interesting point," Lange said. "My contact at Interior mentioned another company recently submitted an unsolicited Request for Proposal to develop a prospective site off the Alaskan coast."

"Why the RFP?"

"Figure they're trying to bypass Interior's Mineral

Management Service review and approval process. Among other things, the MMS looks at proposals that impact the Outer Continental Shelf Lands Act and the National Environmental Protection Act. In this case, this company submitted an unsolicited application along with a site assessment plan written in such a way as to be designated a noncompetitive bid. From what I've heard, the submission was rejected."

"Back up a sec. What's the company's name?"

"Consolidated Seabed Resources."

He'd never heard of it. Nonetheless, he was intrigued by the possible link of between the OCSLA, Consolidated Seabed Resources, and the Chinese submersible. Maybe he'd been premature in X'ing out the circle representing the Chinese submersible on his Venn diagram. "Do you know any details on why the application was rejected?"

"Only that it was flawed."

Lange paused in his narrative as Edmund reappeared. He poured a generous portion of the McCallan from a crystal decanter into a tulip shaped Glencairn glass and set it on the polished end table to Nick's right. He finished his service by placing a small pitcher of water and a plate of snacks with a selection of prosciutto, brie, apple and pear wedges, almonds, and bread sticks beside the humidor. "Will there be anything else, sir?"

"No, that'll be all."

Lange waited for Edmund to descend the stairs. "I'd go with the brie. The fat content will hold the scotch's flavor." He added several drops of water from a glass-angel topped pipette into his own scotch to release the bouquet, swirled it around, then picked up an apple slice and took a bite. "Not these or the pears, though. They'll mask the McCallan's apple and pear notes."

He passed on the condiments and took a contemplative sip of the McCallan while he pondered the connection between

Consolidated Seabed Resources and the abandoned Chinese submersible discovered off Cape Lisburne. *Could the Chinese have found something up there?* He decided to withhold his information. "So, who's Moore's contact at Interior?"

"I've got some ideas."

"And your source?"

"Remember? Can't say. But I need your help. Do you have a reliable contact within the FBI's counter-intelligence office?"

He didn't answer.

"I need a pretext to pursue a hunch. Any information they have that pertains to racketeering, extortion, and conspiracy to commit money laundering."

"I know someone in their National Security Branch."

"How reliable is your source?"

"I've worked with her before. I've already reached out. I've also contacted a friend at Treasury's Office of Terrorism and Financial Intelligence."

"How'd you contact them?"

"My cell phone. I didn't want to use an official channel."

"Do you use one of the encryption services like WhatsApp or Telegram?"

"I'm an analysist, not a damn spook."

Lange held out his hand. "Give me your phone."

"What?"

"Just give it to me."

He handed it over and watched in astonishment as Lange opened the back and ripped out the SIM card.

"What-the-hell are you doing? Are you nuts?"

"We're dealing with dangerous people. It could be hacked. In fact, it probably is." Lange handed back the phone. "You need a clean phone. For starters, get a new iPhone for your personal use. I'll give you a burner to contact me. And when we meet, don't bring either one of them. I don't want anyone tracking their location."

When we meet? "You don't think you're being just a bit paranoid? I'll set it to airplane mode…if we meet."

"We'll meet. But that said, airplane mode won't work. You don't think that if Google can download and track everything you do, a government can't? You've heard Homeland Security has detected an uptick of anomalous activity from Stingrays?" Lange shot him an inquiring look. "Yes?"

In point of fact, he hadn't heard anything about the cellphone-site simulators. What little he did know was these devices, ubiquitous on the cell towers of foreign embassies, could locate a cellphone, lock on, and track the user's location. *And only God knew what else.*

A picture of his contact in the CIA, Taylor Ferguson, crossed his mind. He now worked at the Agency's Center for Cyber Intelligence. *Is that how he knew so much about what I was doing to chase down al-Khultyer? How could I be so damn stupid?* He erased the incipient frown from his face. "Is there a problem?"

"Could be." Lange prevaricated and changed tack. "Are you familiar with the Moscow Rules?"

"I've heard mention of them. Weren't they the name given a set of 'how-to' espionage guidelines used during the Cold War?"

"I'll give you one that pertains. 'Never travel directly to a meeting.'" Lange paused. "So, did you?"

He set his drink down and folded his arms. "Nobody's watching me."

"You sure of that?"

He glanced around the empty room.

"Yeah, that's what I figured. That brings me to rule number two: 'Assume nothing.' In your case, I'll lay even money you're being watched."

"Wha—"

"We're dealing with some bad actors."

"What exactly do you mean by '*We*' this time?"

"You met with me."

"I just happened to grab an empty chair at the bar," he remonstrated. "It had nothing to do with you."

"They don't know that."

They? He felt drawn into something he needed to avoid, but he also needed to know exactly where Lange was leading him. "All right, suppose I'm being watched. Who, exactly, are *They?*"

"Could be the Russians, or the Chinese, probably both."

He could understand his old Russian nemesis, the FSB, but Beijing? *Nope. I'm not even looking at them. Not possible.* "The Chinese?" he echoed.

Lange ignored him. "You know why you brought down al-Khultyer?" Lange didn't wait for a response. "I'll answer for you. You went with your gut. Right? Well, I've got a gut feeling."

He could only nod. He swirled the remaining McCallan in his glass, then finished it off, buying time to gather his thoughts.

"Refill?"

"I'm good."

"What can you tell me about that Chinese mini-sub?"

The question took him aback. *How could Lange possibly know about the sub?* He evaded the question. "Why are you doing this?"

"I've got some scores to settle."

A flurry of questions screamed through his mind, beginning with Lange's background check. What had he missed? Did it have anything to do with Lange's mangled hand?

Lange filled in part of the gap. "More to the point, I need to tap into your—"

He threw up his hands. "Stop. If you want me to become a rogue operator or one of your non-attributable sources, that's not happening."

"I need a partner," Lange replied. "Someone who can get

me access to the NSA's Tailored Access Operations Group and the CIA's Center for Cyber Intelligence."

Lange handed back the SIM card. "Someone who can run this for malware, find a digital trail, and pinpoint who's been tracking you." His eyes shifted to the SIM card Nick clutched. "I'd suggest you have someone check that."

He pocketed the card and stared at the flames rippling in the fireplace pondering the implications of Lange's request, weighing the information he'd learned from his brief meeting with Mr. Gilmore. Three points stood out from that encounter, the first being the president wanted a full report on the NBG's links to Trident Metallurgics, secondly, he didn't want anyone at Interior, Treasury, or State to take the lead in the investigation, and finally, the Chinese. And lead agent? At the time he'd thought that request odd. Not anymore.

But if Lange is right and I've already been compromised …? Could Lange be an asset, or should I cut him loose and have him placed under surveillance? He faced Lange and equivocated. "I'll sleep on it."

Chapter Nine

3110 PROSPECT STREET, NW
GEORGETOWN, WASHINGTON, D.C.
WEDNESDAY 12 DECEMBER

Lin-Wu unfolded the navigation chart of the North Aleutian Basin and spread it across the residence's rosewood dining room table. He had a general idea where the pilot of the submersible, *Flying Fish*, had found the polymetallic nodules, but he needed to fix the exact location in his mind. The vessel had been abandoned and presumably sank after being entrapped in the ice. Both the State Oceanic Administration and Second Institute of Oceanography choose not to authorize its retrieval and neither expressed concern that the vessel might be discovered by the Americans.

He smoothed out the creases in the chart, then ran his index finger along the longitude and latitude lines to the point where they intersected at the crew's reported rescue site, 68°52 North, 166°35 West. Overlapping the point were two superimposed blue lines running parallel to the coast labeled, Alaskan DEWIZ, and Alaskan ADIZ. He did a quick Google search on his iPhone: Alaskan Distant Early Warning Identification Zone and Air Defense Identification Zone.

The location of an abandoned U.S. Air Force early warning radar station just east of the jagged point of Cape Lisburne probably accounted for the lines. He made a mental note of the base's gravel runway edging the shoreline of the Chukchi Sea before shifting his attention to a more immediate problem.

On roughly the same latitude, but inland, was the huge Gray Wolf Mine. That established a precedent for approval of a mining operation. The problem he faced was the mineral deposits discovered by the submersible lay well within the American's twenty-four nautical mile contiguous zone extending from Alaska's continental shelf. Offshore mining permits were extremely difficult, if not impossible to obtain. This is where his new asset could come into play.

While he didn't know when, or even if, University of California, Berkley professor Ronald Hopkins would be brought into play, the cost of funneling several hundred thousand dollars to his environmental research projects was minimal. The professor was only one of many they were exploiting and he held no concerns about Lam's management of the rather laboriously titled National High-End Foreign Experts Recruitment Plan.

"Ah, yes," he said to the empty room as he recalled his puzzlement on Lam's use of the term "smurfing" until he'd learned of how Lam laundered the funds through a complicated web of transactions using multiple small organizations to avoid detection of their source. Hopkin's work for us, even if advertent, would be shielded.

He folded the chart, replacing it in the top drawer of the credenza where he kept several other documents pertaining to his operations, then made his way to the library. On his desk lay Lam Huifeng's background analysis and synopsis of the Federal Acquisition Regulation requirements as they pertained to Consolidated Seabed Resources. He permitted himself a fleeting smile at his clever choice of the folder's cover label: Operation Hoya Saxa. He'd lifted the name from his alma mater's Georgetown cheer, *Hoya Saxa*, Latin for "What Rocks."

The first tab of Lam's report summarized the salient information about the United Nations International Seabed Authority. To date, the ISA had approved twenty-nine oil and mineral exploration areas accounting for nearly 500,000 square miles of the Atlantic, Pacific, and Indian Oceans. Ventures from nineteen different countries had paid for the rights to develop these areas. Of the nineteen, China only held four ... *unacceptable*. He flipped to the next tab: Environmental Impact Assessment.

He skimmed over the basics before his eyes came to rest on a current operation in the Pacific. A Canadian mining company funded by its Russian and Omani owners, had begun mining operations off the coast of Papua New Guinea to extract the mineral deposits adjacent to deep-water hydrothermal vents. The initial reports of environmental damage caused by the company's excavator were not encouraging as they pertained to his Alaskan operation, but they were not unexpected.

He'd also been informed that the government's Ocean Mineral Research and Development division had tested a 250-ton excavator, benignly called a Seabed Mining Tool. To no one's surprise, the excavator bore a remarkable resemblance to the one the Canadians deployed off New Guinea. The Chinese behemoth, like its counterpart, measured 8x17x13 meters and was equipped with a two-meter diameter drum cutter/collecting device.

The Canadian company's excavator reportedly generated one-thousand tons of sediment per hour. The resultant toxic plume inundated over twelve kilometers of the nearshore ecosystem, smothering the coral formations and decimating the sea life communities adjacent to the destroyed thermal vents. A frown crossed his face. The Chinese machine would do no better, perhaps worse.

He didn't know what creatures inhabited Alaska's offshore community, but he understood the potential impact on the region's krill population and the creatures who consumed them, the humpback whales. That would not do. Starving the whales and their calves transiting the Chukchi Corridor migration route would most certainly incite the ire of the environmentalists who, in turn, would do their utmost to shut down his enterprise. That is, if they learned of the danger in time.

Not wishing to dwell on the foibles of these misguided people, he moved on to what he could do to mitigate the issue. The wrinkles soon lifted from his forehead. His actions would again be based on the writings of Sun Tzu. He would employ deception to manipulate and counter his adversaries. Sun Tzu's first three maxims pertained to the current situation:

When one is capable, give the appearance of being incapable;

When one is active, give the appearance of being inactive;

When one is near, give the appearance of being far.

To these he added subterfuge. His country should be able to take advantage of its observer status on the Arctic Council by leveraging several provisions of the United Nations Convention on the Law of the Sea. The Americans were a signatory to this agreement, but after years of debate, their Congress never ratified the treaty. That failure left them at a disadvantage.

He remained undecided on whether to exploit his nascent contact within the State Department's Policy Planning Office. He could, though, insist the reluctant Moore identify the flaw in their first unsolicited application and the site assessment plan submitted to the Department of the Interior. It remained an imperative to address the subsequent failure of the Mineral

Management Service to designate the submission as a non-competitive bid.

He considered several potential problems with the application. Could it have been something related to the Outer Continental Shelf Land Act? Or did it run afoul of some obscure provision of the National Environmental Protection Act? Or both? He concluded that since the OCSLA only pertained to waters three miles off the U.S. coastline, he would have Moore focus on NEPA.

Then there were the intelligence reports of a new Russian startup based in Vladivostok. There was no hiding Moscow's intentions to exploit their own oil and perhaps the Canadian's and American's mineral and oil deposits in the Arctic. Viewed within this context, his voiced concerns to the China Ocean Mineral Research and Development Association concerning the name of their own mining company, Consolidated Seabed Resources, had fallen on deaf ears.

The name, in and of itself, would be enough to alert the environmental jihadists that populated the Interior Department to a potential threat. Following the dismissal of his concerns by his superiors in Beijing, he'd then received a report from Hong Kong of an unsettling problem at the company fronting as Consolidated's financial backer, Oceanic Asset Management, Ltd. He spat out the Chinese curse. *"Nǐ yā tǐ de."*

He lay the report aside and closed his eyes. He slowed his breathing, feeling the muscles of his chest expand and contract, connecting one breath to the next, calming. Within the renewed stillness of his mind, the answer came. *Opportunities multiply as they are seized.* The words of Sun Tzu again. Rejuvenated, he summoned his Amah. "Esteemed Mother. Please find Huifeng and ask him to join me."

While he waited, he began to formulate a plan.

———

"Ah, Lam. Come join me," Lin-Wu said when Huifeng appeared in the doorway. "Tell me what you know of the Russians."

"Their threat to our goals in the Arctic region has grown more credible." Huifeng took a seat. "Vladimir Suslova, a Senior Presidential Advisor and NBG oligarch is the mastermind. He's garnered the support of the Arctic and Antarctic Research Institute to pursue exploration rights in the Bering Sea from the International Seabed Authority."

"Go on."

"We must blunt Moscow's efforts to acquire these rights."

"What do you suggest?"

"Sow seeds of distrust. The certainty of an environmental catastrophe if Moscow's request to the ISA were approved."

"A disinformation campaign," he said. "Leaks by certain confidants alluding to bribery, extortion, money laundering, and racketeering. These could all find their way to the American, Nick Parkos, and his investigation of the NBG's known links to transnational organized crime."

"Which effort would you prioritize?"

"Attend to the immediate problem. Moscow's attempt to acquire Emmons-Powell. Then we will deal with Cape Lisburne."

"Is there a weak link within Stuart's administration?" Lam asked. "Perhaps the Secretary of Interior, Sylvester Poad? I've heard that he has lost favor with Stuart."

He paused. He had a plan in place that Huifeng didn't know of, but he would only compromise the Cabinet member as a last resort. "In due time, Lam, but now I want to concentrate on our American contact. Do we have any further word from Mr. Moore?"

"He has passed on useful information about the bond holders of Emmons-Powell. They have become frustrated by escalating costs and have been bickering with Emmon's Board of Directors about debt refinancing."

"And the Trustees overseeing the Chapter 13 proceedings?"

"They have voiced their concern to the Board over the delay in approving a plan to liquidate Emmons-Powell's holdings. They have also sent formal notification to the Board addressing the continual drain of the funds set aside during the bankruptcy proceedings. These funds are being consumed by their efforts to prevent further ground water contamination adjacent to the open pit mine."

He only half-listened to Huifeng while pondering the usefulness of leaking rumors of malfeasance by Trident in order to derail the Russian's efforts. "Perhaps Mr. Moore has mended his ways and abandoned his insouciance."

"It appears so. Moore has proved useful in crafting our resubmissions for both Olympic Industries and Consolidated Seabed Resources to the Interior Department."

"Prompted no doubt by the transfer of certain funds to his Swiss account?"

"And the implied threat to his father's wellbeing," Huifeng added.

"Then we shall continue to play to both his avarice and to his fear."

"Moore will be the one to leak the rumors to the FBI and the Treasury Department?"

"Yes, but the Americans must not trace this activity back to us. They …" He stopped at the expression on Huifeng's face. "Is there something wrong?"

"No, just the opposite. I would suggest that the reporter, Lange, be Moore's conduit. Lange might be tempted to write an exposé or better yet, inform his partner Parkos."

"Very clever. What better way to entangle both Parkos and the reporter in a web of deceit. You will inform our contact in the Interior Department."

"Moore has also provided the name of an Emmons-Powell

board member that may be of use. This individual has been most vociferous in his support of Trident."

He worked through several possible ways to eliminate this 'problem' while Huifeng continued to elaborate. Direct action? Possibly. Employ an exotic nerve agent similar to the Russian's Novichok and lay the blame for the agonizing death at their feet?

But what of Moscow's botched attack on that FSB turncoat in London? Even if he accepted the international media scrutiny the assassination could spawn in the short-term, such an operation would require considerable lead time for planning, time he didn't have.

The short-term gain by the use of an exotic agent would ultimately end in defeat. Perhaps something more mundane like a mugging to eliminate the board member? A task he could contract to a third party. *Or would it be better to target another?* Perhaps a member of the Washington law firm, Duxtun, Luwan, and Merriman, representing the Russian venture in Utah. Or one of the bankers behind the project? *To kill one to terrorize ten thousand?* He voiced his conclusion in general terms. "We will take definitive action."

"And the threat from Parkos?" Huifeng asked.

"Parkos must be discredited after he has served his purpose."

"Then I have a plan."

"Excellent, Lam." A rare smile crossed his face as he recited an old proverb. "'Weeds cannot just simply be cut, they must be pulled out by the roots.'"

Chapter Ten

CREEKSIDE CONDOMINIUMS
ANNANDALE, VIRGINA
MONDAY 17 DECEMBER

Nick balanced the meager bag of groceries in his left arm, unlocked the door to his condo, and pushed it open with his knee. He took a step into the living room, kicked the door closed behind him, and froze. *Something's burning.*

He dropped the bag of groceries and took off for the unit's small kitchen. The smell intensified. He flipped on the overhead light and swung his head through an arc searching for the source. His search stopped on the counter by the refrigerator.

Damn. Did I really leave the coffee maker on this morning? He pulled the plug from the wall socket and lifted the pot, surveying the charred remnants of the special blend Michelle had given him fused to the bottom. He balanced the pot on the pile of encrusted dishes filling the sink. His hand froze on the faucet.

Where's Bill? He was always underfoot as soon as he came in the front door.

"Bill. Hey buddy, where are you?" He followed his calls with a couple whistles. Nothing. *Well, there's one thing that never fails to stir his interest.* He opened the pantry door and pulled out the bag of Bill's dry cat food. He gave the bag a vigorous shake. *That'll roust him.*

What the …? The bowl was full. That never happened. Bill never exercised restraint when it came to eating. The bag fell from his hand, sending the contents spilling across the floor.

His frantic search ended in the middle of the living room. He'd failed to find his missing pet. *Could he have slipped out the door this morning? I should have noticed.* "Why would he do that?" he asked the empty room.

He opened the front door and stepped into the cold. "Bill. Hey, Bill. Come here buddy."

Much too his surprise and great relief, Bill appeared from under the barren hedge at the far side the parking lot. "Come on, boy. Where-the-hell have you been?"

In way of an answer, Bill trotted across the lot, tail high in the air, apparently without a care in the world. Nick scooped him up and went back inside. "Damn, buddy. Don't do that to me. My day's been bad enough already." He dropped Bill who promptly disappeared into the kitchen in search of food.

He shook his head and refocused. Michelle would be over in a few minutes. She'd promised to go to the mall with him to help pick out a Christmas present for Emma. He'd hoped to get some time off to fly down to Florida to see her and his ex, Marty, but again, that didn't turn out. The best he could do now was get a package to FedEx first thing in the morning.

Adding to his guilt, he'd found the time to buy something for Michelle. It wasn't much, but then, the way things were going in his life at the moment, that also would have to do. He hoped she'd appreciate the gesture.

The first time he'd seen Michelle on the tarmac at Villa-coublay Air Force Base just outside metropolitan Paris, he'd been mesmerized by her green eyes, the scattering of freckles across her nose, and her flaming red hair cut short to meet military regulations but it was to her eyes he always returned and their mischievous glint whenever she teased him.

She'd been assigned to escort him aboard Air Force One for the trip back to Washington after al-Khultyer had detonated one of his dirty bombs in Paris. He'd remembered the date, the 13th of December. Almost one year ago to the day.

Their relationship had evolved, taking a direction he couldn't have possibly anticipated. They shared an easy platonic connection without forced expectations or demands.

He'd also discovered what he needed was a friend, not a lover and they could spend hours together simply talking. Nothing profound, just conversations that eased his troubled soul. Conversations that helped expiate the guilt he felt for what he'd seen and done. Not to say she hadn't pressed him to stop his drinking or voice her concern about his need to seek counseling for his capricious behavior.

A gentle knock on the front door broke into his thoughts. *Michelle*. He looked through the peephole and opened the door.

She swept by him into the living room and lifted a limp, purring Bill into her arms. "Hello, sweetie."

He understood the greeting wasn't meant for him, but …

Michelle set Bill down and cast him a quizzical look. "Are you all right?"

"I'm not sure."

"What's happened? Something at work?"

"No, work's fine. Just a bunch of weird stuff. I managed to leave the coffee pot on all day and Bill got out this morning. Scared the hell out of me."

"You sleep last night?"

He tensed at her implied question. "Yeah. As a matter of fact, I did."

"Nick … I didn't mean—"

His iPhone sang out, Metallica's "Unforgiven" ringtone stopping her. He looked at the caller ID. Mike Rohrbaugh.

"Hey, Mike. How you doing? … Oh, not bad. It's been an interesting day … Yeah, *interesting* does cover a lot of territory … Sure, that sounds great. Let me run it by the boss. She's standing right here." He faced her. "Mike and Kate want to know if we're free to meet them for dinner."

"After we buy Emma's present."

Chagrinned at his lapse, he replied into his cell. "Okay, we're on. Mav's Bistro … After we get Emma a Christmas present. They'll—"

He stopped and stared at the end-table by his recliner. "That's odd. I would have sworn I left my bank statement on the table— Oh, sorry, Mike. I gotta go." He walked over to his chair. "All this stuff is making me crazy."

"Maybe you put it away," Michelle offered.

"No. I was going to balance my checkbook." Disconcerted, he pulled open the table's drawer. His checkbook was right where he'd left it. He pushed around a small pile of bills and receipts. *Where are my bank statements?* He closed the door with a perplexed shake of his head.

"Anything else missing?"

"I don't think so but my bank—"

"You want to look around before we go? We've got time."

"No, that's okay. I'll look around later. I probably just misplaced them. It wouldn't be the first time. Right now, all I want to do is get Emma's present. He reached for his coat and flashed a smile. "I've got a couple ideas."

Chapter Eleven

3110 PROSPECT STREET, NW
GEORGETOWN, WASHINGTON, D.C.
FRIDAY 28 DECEMBER

Lin-Wu contemplated the traffic clogging the George Washington Parkway. The multitudes were heading home for the New Year's weekend. He held no doubt that many of these people, Federal employees stultified by their daily routines, would be professing illness and calling in sick on the following Tuesday. Then again, little, if any, work would be accomplished by those who did bother to show up.

The holiday held no interest for him. Nor, for that matter, did the upcoming Chinese New Year. The same could not be said for Esteemed Mother. Now she—

He turned from the library's picture window and his inconsequential musings at the sound of Lam Huifeng entering the room. He reached for the teapot Esteemed Mother had placed on the near coffee table. "Would you care for some tea?"

He didn't wait for a reply and filled a light-green celadon cup, its porcelain so thin as to be transparent A refusal would be unthinkable. He set the cup before Huifeng and waited for him to take a sip before handing him the morning's *Washington Post's* business section. "What do you know of Global Oil?"

Huifeng scanned the short article at the bottom right of the page titled: Global Oil Venture Fails. "I'm not surprised. A waste of several billion dollars. All the Russians have to show for their efforts is a dry well and more millions spent on legal fees."

"No doubt the environmental activists will be reveling in their victory."

"Perhaps they will let their guard down," Huifeng speculated. "Global's offshore drilling platform was only eighty miles from our proposed mining site."

"I wouldn't be overly optimistic. Our own venture's name, Consolidated Seabed Resources, could well raise their suspicions." He tempered his observation. "But then, Global may have bought us some more time, a point which brings me to the American, Parkos. Our gray operation is proceeding as planned. Yes?"

"Yes. Several members of Bureau 8's intelligence staff assigned to the embassy have kept Parkos' condo under continuous surveillance since the 18th. They report that he hasn't changed his routine. The operatives planted the incriminating evidence and now wish to further target his emotions, his sense of security. I've given them a provisional go-ahead for a second black-bag operation."

"And the cat?"

"They have no plans to harm the innocent feline."

He remained undecided. If Parkos' pet needed to be sacrificed, then so be it. "Will they plant a listening device?"

"There are no plans to do so. The risk from any blowback if the device is discovered would exceed any information that is collected."

He nodded in agreement. "Yes, a wise decision. We have

more effective means to compromise him. Proceed with the operation."

Huifeng set his empty teacup on the table. "I have also implemented Phase 2 of our plan."

"Excellent. Where are we?"

"The offshore account with Banco Investment and Trust, Ltd in the Cayman Islands was remotely opened via the internet. We simply supplied Parkos' personal information previously exploited from an American credit monitoring company. The process was remarkably easy. Banco's software is old and riddled with vulnerabilities. We also discovered the company's network architecture was unsecured and their email and web servers were not separated from their data base."

"How was this done?"

"A SQL code injection using a remote access Trojan inserted Parkos' data into Banco's contract management system."

"So, nobody will be the wiser?"

"No. The initial deposit of $10,000 has been verified and others will follow. I took the liberty of using our account for the first deposit, but—"

"Beijing will not hesitate to provide the additional funds."

"*Xiexie*," Huifeng responded simply, not wishing to appear effusive. "I have also programed the account to reflect that it was set up this past July. When it suits our purpose, we … that is, Banco, will submit a standard IRS Foreign Bank and Finance Report declaring the interest Parkos has earned on the account. All perfectly legal."

"The trap is set."

"I have also added another touch to our scheme. Certain documents including reference to an address in Wilmington, Delaware that implies Parkos is laundering illicit income."

"Delaware?"

"Yes. The State has, shall we say 'flexible' business laws and no corporate income tax."

"Something that would attract a man with Parkos' knowledge of transnational crime. What else?"

"A large sum of cash will be planted in his home to further implicate him. With his position within the American intelligence establishment, the IRS should alert the FBI's Criminal Investigation Unit. They will, in turn, work with the National Intelligence Center to conduct a damage assessment for a probable unauthorized disclosure of classified national intelligence."

"Should we implicate the Russians as the recipient of this intelligence?"

Huifeng paused. "That would be most clever."

He chuckled. "Imagine their consternation. And the denials Parkos will sputter when he is confronted by the FBI and his agency's internal affairs division. Most excellent, Huifeng. Does your operation have an appropriate code name?"

"We have not assigned one."

He closed his eyes, rubbing his chin in thought. "We will call it, CALAMUS, after the medicinal plant with the long, sharp leaves resembling swords."

Chapter Twelve

NATIONAL COUNTERINTELLIGENCE CENTER
MCLEAN, VIRGINA
TUESDAY 13 NOVEMBER

It's Not Over. Nick studied the words again. The meaning and the originator of the elusive message remained unknown, but he'd talked to Michelle and her recommendation was brilliant. "Take ownership of those words, Nick," she'd advised. "Post them above your desk. Let them motivate you."

He spun his chair around to study the corkboard that maintenance had installed the past Monday. He'd spent a good part of Tuesday pinning colored index cards to the board, linking their presumed connections together with lengths of string.

He screwed up the corner of his mouth. There were too many gaps in the sequences, too many unknowns. He was no closer to a definitive answer seven weeks after that mysterious message had appeared on his computer. The fundamental question continued to elude him. The answer to what, exactly? He felt like he was chasing ghosts. He turned back to his desk, Michelle's words echoing in his mind while he sorted through what he knew.

The play by the Russians and the Chinese for Emmons-Powell at least made some sense. His eyes fell on an isolated blue index card pinned to the upper left of the corkboard: "Cape Lisburne, Alaska" and the card pinned diagonally below it: "Consolidated Seabed Resources." The cards represented another "What." *What, if anything, was going on up there?* He turned back to his desk, tapping his index finger on the edge of the keyboard.

His frustration had lessened with Michelle's words, however he still was faced with the problem of ascertaining Beijing's and Moscow's probable actions. Acknowledging those mixed feeling, he understood that he still remained a spectator reacting to evolving events rather than driving a solution to prevent them. He turned his attention back to his cluttered desk.

Despite the appearance of the random piles of notepads, folders, and loose paper obscuring most of his desktop, he could find anything he needed in an instant, just like he could find his vegetable peeler in the clutter of utensils in his kitchen drawer or pull some obscure data point out of the clutter of data sequestered within his mind. His reached for the pile of papers stacked on the righthand corner in his desk and extracted the Venn diagram representing what he knew about the Chinese. Not nearly enough.

For the first time, the diagrams had failed him. While they were useful in defining the subsets of his inquiries, they hadn't provided him the broad view he sought to link the multiple factors in play. Accepting that gloomy assessment, he focused on what he had to do to understand these factors, their possible outcomes, and now to counter each before he met with Mike Rohrbaugh and the president's National Security Advisor on Friday. He'd also double checked to ensure that his supervisor, Ned Strickland, knew about the meeting. The last thing he needed was the appearance of going behind his back.

The necessity to prepare his brief and his concerns about Strickland weren't the only things that vexed him. His bank statement had mysteriously reappeared. He found it wedged between the chair cushion and the arm of the recliner. He would have sworn it wasn't there when he'd looked before, but there it was.

Finding the elusive statement remained one of the few positives in a very strange week. He gave his head an exasperated shake. *Hell, last week even the recliner kept getting stuck. Gremlins.*

"Gremlins?" He said aloud, jerking back from his desk. The conversation with Lange at The Nicholas. *My God, They cased my condo.*

"You ready for me?" Austin stood at the open door.

He looked over his shoulder, is eyes falling on the two coffee cups Austin held. "Sure am. Come on in."

"Here ya' go. Black. Figured you might need some." Austin stopped and peered at the new corkboard. "You've been busy."

"I'm not sure I've gotten any closer to figuring out how all the pieces fit together though. You having any luck?"

Austin pulled the plastic cap off his coffee and took a noisy slurp before settling into a chair. "Been peeling away layers of the onion. Your friend at Treasury, Mark Arita, has been great." He pointed his coffee cup at the corkboard. "A couple pieces we've worked fit with what you have up there. The Pan American Development Bank is Beijing's probable pass-through for Olympic Industry's efforts to purchase Emmons."

Austin's statement puzzled him. Hadn't Lange tied Pan American to Ocean Resource Development? *What's the connection?* He picked up a pen and placed question marks next to Pan American and Olympic on his diagram. He doubted the Chinese would be foolish enough to use the same front company to back two different ventures. There had to be another company backing Consolidated Seabed Resources.

"Something wrong?" Austin asked.

He looked up. "Just trying to understand the connections. What else you got?"

"Something new," Austin answered. "The Chinese have made their move to acquire the mineral rights for Emmons-Powell. A company called Pacific Commodity is fronting them. Pacific has links to Shanghai Venture Capital. They're likely funding the operation. One, probably both, are shells."

"The Russians can't be pleased Beijing is trying to elbow their way into what they thought was a done deal with Trident."

"Not much happier than us," Austin added.

"So, let's run with those assumptions." He pushed himself out of his chair and walked to the cork board. "The Chinese have to complete their acquisition of Emmons before Trident can close their deal. We should leverage this information to block both of them."

"Any ideas on how we go about doing that?"

"Not yet.

"Are there any American suitors?" Austin asked.

He shook his head. "None that I've come across."

"Too bad we don't have a government backed consortium we could put into play." Austin's eyes strayed to the corkboard. "Alaska's looking pretty isolated up there."

"Yeah," he confessed. "I haven't done much with it."

"I should have said several 'somethings' a bit ago, Austin said. "That Chinese mini-sub you asked about? There may be something entirely different going on."

"Oh, how's that?"

"Actually, there may be a number of things. The most likely is they were looking at the convergence zones of the Chukchi Sea's isothermal layers. Testing salinity gradients, recording thermoclines."

His face drew a blank at the foreign nomenclature.

"Temperature gradients," Austin clarified. "Submarines can hide under these different sonic layers."

"What else?" he replied, anxious to move on to something he could understand.

"There's an old radar site at Cape Lisburne. One of the sites that replaced the Distant Early Warning line back in the 80's. The Air Force is looking to reactivate the base to support the Ballistic Missile Early Warning System."

"Cape Lisburne is near where that submersible was found."

"Yeah. And as you'd suspect, the place is pretty much in the middle of nowhere. The nearest town is some twenty-five miles to the southwest. Point Hope. Population seven-hundred. Almost all native Americans. Beyond that, about the only notable thing about the area is it's part of the Alaskan Maritime National Wildlife Refuge that stretches down the length of the Aleutian Island chain."

He cocked his head at the mention of the refuge. "Intentional or not, that sub ventured into our territorial waters. We should assume the Pentagon is looking into the intrusion."

"I'd hope so." Austin paused, giving a thoughtful pull on the back of his neck. "I'm wondering. Could that sub have stumbled across something else? Something totally unexpected?"

"What else is off our coast that's so damned impor—?" He stopped as the answer came to him. "Lange's…"

"Who's that?"

He ignored Austin's question, not wanting to divulge his source. He also needed to protect Austin in case Lange wasn't legit. "Maybe that's why the environmentalists are so worked up," Nick thought out loud. "Oil, natural gas, minerals." He pointed to the cork board. "The key is Consolidated Seabed Resources."

"The Chinese company?"

"Correct." He tapped his pen on the desk. "We need to consider the unknowns, the gaps in my board: Who's driving this?"

"I'd be askin' who has the most to gain? And the corollary, who has the most to lose?"

"The National Resource Defense Council, Gree—"

"All the usual suspects," he interrupted. "But who are they going after?"

"Everyone," Austin answered. "Scattergun approach. Like a bunch of amateurs huntin' quail. Fire into the bush and see what you hit."

"Maybe, but that's shortchanging the environmentalists. Their approach has been way more sophisticated than that."

"You think they have someone at Interior?"

He started at Austin's observation. The kid had again displayed a surprising degree of profundity. "I'd be astonished if they didn't."

Could that person also be Lange's informant? And who's the Chinese connection? Nick pulled open a desk drawer and grabbed four index cards. "We're not going to get very far if I can't identify the mastermind behind the Chinese op. I've got to smoke him out."

"You?" Austin remonstrated. "Could be pretty dicey messing with those folks."

"I'll get help."

"But wha—?"

"Just a sec," he interrupted, penning a note on an index card. He pinned the card he'd labeled "Consolidated Seabed Resources," under the Cape Lisburne card. The three cards that followed matched three empty circles on his Venn diagram: Shell Company(s), Informant, and Mastermind. On the "Informant" card he'd scribed (Moore?), the beltway lobbyist Lange had pointed out at the Upper Crust.

His thumb paused over the tack pinning "Mastermind" to the board when another thought occurred to him, something transnational criminals were known to do. "Austin, you just might be on to something. I want to revisit your comment about a government sponsored consortium."

"You do?"

"Let me toss this out. What if we formed our own company?"

Austin's lips formed a silent, WOW.

He smiled at the response. "Five-million dollars will buy you a private foundation and a bogus front company: charter documents, officers and directors, bank accounts, a provision for authorizing signatures, neutral phones, FAX and phone numbers, addresses. The works."

Austin couldn't hide the incredulous look on his face. "Five million? You're saying we form our own company and submit a bid for Emmons?"

"Bingo." He returned to his desk. "We undercut both Beijing and Moscow. You said Emmons' creditors and bond holders are after the Board of Directors to unload the company and cut their losses, right?"

"Well…yes," Austin stuttered. "But, the money?" Who will——?"

"Not to worry. We won't go through a broker in Panama. We'll keep everything in house. Be a lot cheaper. I'll run a strawman by Strickland and the DNI. Our new company will submit a proposal to the Board suggesting they hand over the reins to our front company in exchange for writing off most of their debt. If they buy off on the idea, we set up our own holding company to handle the details."

"You think the trustees handling the bankruptcy proceedings will accept the deal?"

He reached into the drawer and grabbed a couple more index cards. "Who knows, but when the word hits the street, it'll definitely rattle the Chinese and Russians. No telling what will crawl out when we flip over the rock."

Austin tilted his head. "Rock?"

He stood, cards in hand, and strode back to the cork-board. "How about throwing out a couple names for our new company."

Austin flashed a toothy smile. "You're completely out of your mind."

Chapter Thirteen

EISENHOWER EXECUTIVE OFFICE BUILDING
WASHINGTON, D.C.
FRIDAY 4 JANUARY

Nick weaved through the narrow rows of parking stalls until he found an open spot on the third floor. He wedged his Ford Escape into the narrow space, squeezed out the door, and halted. "Damn!" He reached back into the car for a manila envelope he'd forgotten, then made his way to the exit on Pennsylvania Avenue. A blast of frigid wind greeted him.

He pulled up the zipper of his coat and stepped into the bone-chilling cold to begin the six-minute trek to 17th and State Place. Turning south on 17th, he skirted a pool of slush only to encounter a large crowd of tourists looming directly in his path. They were hemmed together in a disorganized knot by piles of snow mounded in dirty heaps on either side of the sidewalk. He stepped into the gutter to bypass the group, noting they appeared to be looking at his destination, the Eisenhower Executive Office Building.

The amount of camera gear, triangular yellow flag held

aloft by the presumed guide, and the attentive head bobs identified them. *Japanese*. Why they'd chosen to visit Washington in January escaped him.

He noted another man with Asian features make his way into the midst of the crowd while he watched the tourists. The guy snapped off a couple rapid pictures, slipped out the group, and hustled out of sight around the corner.

Odd. He dismissed the man before continuing on toward the visitors center. The drab, dark-gray building stood in stark contrast to the ornate granite and slate edifice of the EOB. He checked his watch, then crunched up the salted steps, grateful there wasn't a line of visitors waiting outside to be screened and made his way to an open window at the security counter.

"Name and Destination," the uniformed guard demanded.

"Nick Parkos. NSA. I'm scheduled to meet with Captain Mike Rohrbaugh in the EOB at eleven hundred."

"Two photo IDs, please."

He fumbled in his wallet and handed the agent his driver's license and National Intelligence Center ID. *Damn. My fingers are still numb.* He shoved his hands into his pockets to warm them while he waited for the guard to verify his name in a logbook. The security guard picked up the phone. *Is there a problem?*

The guard hung up. "Thank you, Mr. Parkos. Everything is in order. The agent over there will run you through the scanner and show you to the exit. Proceed directly to the South portico. Captain Rohrbaugh will meet you there."

He slipped his ID's back into his wallet, exited the building, and proceeded along the sidewalk bordering West Executive Drive. He strode past the visitor parking spaces he'd used on his previous visits to the West Wing to brief the president on the al-Khultyer affair. *Wonder if Mike can pull off another one of those special access passes?*

Mike met him at the entrance, holding open the door. "I see you survived your trek. How ya' doing?"

He was too cold to do more than grunt an unconvincing, "Fine."

Mike led him down the black and white marble tiled main corridor to an imposing set of stairs. *Impressive.* He'd never been in the EOB despite his many visits to the West Wing and craned his neck to look at the stained-glass rotunda while trailing Mike up the grand staircase to the second floor. "Must be nice."

"It's humble, but somebody has to use it," Mike observed when they entered his ornate office. "Pull up a chair. Coffee." Hefted a pot from the drip maker. "Black?"

"Black's fine, thanks."

Mike handed him a white porcelain mug embossed with the Navy SEAL crest. "The NSA's office called. He's delayed but wants us to get started."

"That's good, actually. Can I run something by you?"

"Sure. What's on your mind."

"Did you ever serve with Geoffrey Lange?"

Mike settled in behind his desk and took a sip of his coffee. "Yeah, we were in the same SEAL qualification training class. Crossed paths over the years. Why?"

He noted Mike's eyes, the hint of caution in his voice, and decided to hold back on his follow-up meeting with Lange at The Nicholas. "I bumped into him at a gay bar a couple weeks ago."

"That's it?" Mike leaned back in his chair. "You about to tell me you're coming out? Does Michelle know?"

"No, nothing like that." He felt his response jilted, too defensive, but that was the least of his problems. He had to level with Mike. "You know he's an investigative reporter."

"Geoff? Yeah, I've heard word from some of the guys. I didn't know he was in town."

"We got to talking." His hands tightened around the coffee

mug. "Some of the stuff touched on my investigation. He pointed out a guy at the bar, a lobbyist who might be helping the Chinese."

"No laws against that."

"We had a follow-up meeting. I don't know where Lange's getting his information, but it's equal to anything I've discovered. He even had a source in Interior. Maybe some others. I asked who they were, but he wouldn't give up their names."

"Doesn't surprise me. Journalistic ethos and all."

"One thing Lange did say, though, stuck with me. He said he had some scores to settle. Any idea what those might be?"

Mike looked at a picture on the wall with a bunch of tough, bearded guys in desert cammies, a far-away look on his face. "Could be a couple things. He came out of the closet. Not much tolerance back then. Still not."

"He has a nasty looking left forearm and hand. Looked like burns. Was he wounded?"

"That's just the part you can see. Geoff spent months in Bethesda. Intensive care, burn unit, rehab." Mike looked away from the picture. "It was a deep insert mission during the second Gulf War. His team was ambushed. A lot of his guys didn't make it. We learned later that they were set-up. A security leak somewhere tied to the Russians or the Iranians."

"Thanks, Mike. I know it's hard dredging this stuff up."

"Kind of a shitty bond we share."

He could only nod. Mike had also been on one of those deep insert missions. Wounded and awarded the Navy Cross. He'd read the citation. A true hero, unlike himself.

"You okay?" Mike asked.

"Define okay."

"All right, enough of this morose crap," Mike said derailing Nick's journey into self-pity. "What do you have that's so damn important?"

"This." He handed Mike a non-descript manila envelope.

"Not exactly secure, old buddy."

"Do I look like someone who's a threat to national security? Besides, I hid it in plain sight."

Mike read through the first page. "Anybody else know what's in this?"

"The DNI, Strickland, one of my co-workers. Jessica and Mark know some of the pieces."

"Can I hang on to it?

"Sure."

A knock on the door frame interrupted them. Both men stood for the National Security Advisor, Justin Brown. Nick noted Brown's bow tie, an old-school touch the NSA favored. He respected the man's independent flair. He also knew the old school touch concealed a tough, no nonsense persona.

Brown held a well-deserved reputation within the administration. A man of extraordinary intellect who never addressed any issue in half-measures. He'd earned his PhD at the Harvard College of International Relations before joining the State Department for a twenty-year career. After accepting a prestigious chair at Stanford University, the president lured him way from academia with an offer to join his cabinet.

"Sorry, I got tied up," Brown said. "Where are we?"

"Just got started, sir," Mike answered.

"Talking about old times?"

"In part," Mike admitted, handing over the envelope.

Brown set it on the floor and addressed Nick. "How about summarizing the salient points."

Brown listened without interruption while Nick spent the next several minutes reviewing his findings and analysis. "Intriguing. I'll speak to the DNI about your idea of forming our own company. If he concurs, I believe I can get the president to sign off on the op."

"I want to smoke out the Chinese mastermind."

"Could be dangerous," Brown observed.

He thought about his condo and Lange's warning. "Yes,

sir. I understand. The key may be that lobbyist for the Federation of Mineral Development that I mentioned."

"You're going to need help," Brown said.

"I've got a name."

"Don't tell me. I'll run the basics by the Attorney General. You may have enough to put this character under surveillance by the FBI if he's indeed the go-between. Should be straightforward enough to see if he's a registered foreign agent. Have you checked?"

His lips tightened, rebuking himself for his lapse. "No, sir."

"If he's not, we can obtain a FISA warrant," Mike ventured.

"I'd prefer to obtain the warrant from the 4th U.S. District," Brown answered. "It's tougher and we'd lose a layer of secrecy provided by FISA. The flip side is our case would be stronger. The court's approval will be based on the constitutional requirement for probable cause that surveillance will produce evidence of criminal behavior."

Brown picked up Nick's envelope signifying the meeting was drawing to a close. "Mike and I will see what we can do about pulling the right people together to give you an assist."

"Yes, sir."

Brown stood and waved the envelope. "What I need you to do right now is focus on Alaska. What you have in here is dynamite, particularly as it impacts our installation at Cape Lisburne and Chinese designs for the Arctic." He paused at the door. "Matter of fact, it wouldn't surprise me if the president says you two should take a trip up north."

Nick waited to speak until Brown had disappeared down the hall. "Oh, man. You know I hate the cold."

"You pining away for those hundred-degree days in Djibouti?"

"Hardly."

"Good. That said, I've got something else on my mind a hell-of-a-lot worse than Djibouti or the snow."

He gripped the sides of his chair, feeling an abrupt hollowness in the pit of his stomach. "What's going on, Mike? Is Kate okay?"

"Kate's fine. We're fine. It's not about us, Nick."

Questions spun through his mind. *What else could he be referring to? Something else he's working on? My, God ... Did Michelle tell them about the weird stuff going on in the condo? Wha—*

Mike broke into his thoughts. "Let's just say you need to tread very carefully, my friend."

He hesitated. "At dinner the other night did Michelle tell you about the weird stuff that's been happening?"

"What weird stuff? She didn't say a thing."

"In my condo. I don't know…" He held back, then made his decision. "You'll probably think I'm nuts."

"Try me."

He took a deep breath. "I didn't tell her everything. Geoff warned me, too. Hell, he even tore the SIM card out of my iPhone. Told me to get a burner to contact him. Said we're being watched."

Mike leaned forward. "I think you need to start at the top and tell me everything.

Chapter Fourteen

NATIONAL COUNTERINTELLIGENCE CENTER
MCLEAN, VIRGINA
THURSDAY 10 JANUARY

Nick's phone rang, jarring him from his research into the probable shell companies behind Consolidated Seabed Resources. He leaned across the desk and picked up. "Parkos."

"Pack your bags," Rohrbaugh announced.

Uh, oh. He grabbed a pen and note pad. "Okay, I'll bite. Where am I going?"

"For starters, we're both going."

He shifted the phone, jotting down a question mark. "Thanks for the clarification. Where are we both going?"

"Honolulu."

"Seriously?"

"Real deal. We're lined up for briefings at the University of Hawaii's School of Geology and Geophysics."

A suppressed memory intruded into his mind filling the void created by the words geology and geophysics. The last time he'd been to Honolulu was with his ex, Marty. A last attempt to salvage their marriage, and it had failed. He glanced at the picture of his daughter. Playing with Emma on Waikiki beach building sandcastles was the only positive he recalled from their time in the islands. He refocused. "You said *we*, Mike. What's going on?"

"Just looking after your welfare. I recall you saying something about hating the cold."

"How come I have a feeling that's not our last stop."

"It's our starting point."

"What exactly have you roped me into?"

"The NSA and I spent some more time discussing the information in your manila envelope. Among other things, that company, Consolidated Seabed Resources, caught our eye. The two of us have to get a whole lot smarter on a range of issues if we're going to level the playing field with the Chinese. In any event, after our stop in paradise, we'll swing up north to Juneau to meet with the Coast Guard."

"Juneau? That's cold."

"No doubt."

Nick sorted through the possibilities despite his reticence. "I just happened to be looking into Consolidated when you called. How about a visit to that old base at Cape Lisburne?"

"Perhaps. Our return date is open, but the extent of the winter ice will be the deciding factor. The Coast Guard is looking to see if we can link up with the *Healy*."

"The icebreaker?"

"Yup. All expenses paid Alaskan cruise. Just look at this as an opportunity to rack up some frequent flier miles."

"Yeah, great. Just what I need. So, when do we leave?"

"Saturday. The travel office secured reservations for us on United out of Dulles. Meet you at their check-in counter at 0630. Set your alarm."

DEPARTMENT OF GEOLOGY AND GEOPHYSICS

UNIVERSITY OF HAWAII, MANOA, O'AHU
MONDAY 14 JANUARY

Nick struggled to stay alert in the darkened room. His head bobbed again. He glanced at Mike who appeared to be wide awake, but then, SEALs weren't human. Their presenter, Dr. Willard Diekam, flashed his laser pointer at a new slide: Alaskan Ophiolites.

"This is a particularly interesting slide," Diekam said. "Here we have a cross-sectional representation of a typical mafic lava flow. A shear line representing the subsequent thrust toward the continental shelf..."

He suppressed a groan. So much for *Geology for Idiots*. And Mike's rather dubious idea for their cover? A couple of visiting scientists from NOAA? That was just plain nuts despite the fact that years before he'd taken "Rocks for Jocks" during summer school at Ohio State to satisfy some obscure graduation requirement.

He disassembled his pen, laying each of the seven parts out in a straight line mimicking an exploded-view mechanical drawing. He saw Mike glance at the pen's components, held up his index finger, and drew a graph in his notebook. He pushed the rendering across the table. On it, he'd labeled the ordinate and abscissa: "Pen Pieces" and "Attention Level." The line on the graph displayed his attention level decreasing as the number of pen pieces increased.

Mike shook his head at the inverse relationship and turned back to Diekam's presentation.

The professor waved his laser pointer around the slide before the red dot landed on a vertical cross-section of layered rock. "Our studies of these abduction and convergent plate boundaries suggest they are similar to those found in the Manus Trough off New Guinea. I should point out that a Canadian based mining consortium has recently begun deep water mining operations to extract rare-earth elements in this region. The resultant toxic plumes have confirmed our worst—"

Rare-earth elements? His stupor vanished. "Excuse me, Doctor. Could there be rare-earth deposits off the Alaskan coast?"

"Well, yes… I suppose so. Our studies of the lava fields of our own basaltic shield volcanos here in the islands are similar to those in Alaska. We've discovered these elements off the coast of the Big Island. Unlike the deposits off New Guinea, though, our findings come with a caveat."

He shot at glance at Mike, his eyebrows lifting to convey his sudden insight.

"May I digress?" Diekam asked.

"By all means," Nick answered striving to sound like he knew what-the-hell the professor was talking about.

"The range in concentration of the rare-earth elements of oceanic origin are quite wide. In point of fact, despite their name, these elements really aren't all that rare. The trick is finding them in concentrations that make their extraction economically feasible. Our Lapidary Facility here at UH has …"

He leaned toward Mike, cupping his left hand beside his mouth. "Mike."

"What?"

"That Chinese submersible we found off Cape Lisburne. I'm thinking that's our link to Oceanic. That sub may have found something up there."

Diekam waited for Nick's sidebar to conclude. "Excuse me, Doctor. You have a question?"

Doctor? He didn't immediately respond.

Mike answered for him. "Yes, please pardon our interruption. Dr. Miller and I have a specific interest in the geology of the northwest Alaskan coast."

"Completely understandable," Diekam said. "Indeed, at

the risk of repeating myself, the entire region has a rather complex geographic history. Folded shale, claystone, siltstone, sandstone, sedimentary rock, subduction zones, ophiolites, the Mesozoic sediments."

He gave a thoughtful nod.

Diekam became even more animated at the acknowledgement, selecting a new slide to project. "In point of fact, as far back as their joint '62 field season, the Coast Guard and the National Geodetic Survey conducted magnetometer studies over the Tigara uplift zone suggesting that the Brooks Range extends well across the Chukchi Sea. The…" Diekam froze, his laser pointer creating a small circle on the ceiling.

"Actually, come to think of it, Dr. Miller, the state of Alaska sponsored a symposium on rare-earth elements some years ago. I seem to recall in '88. Perhaps you've seen the report?"

The professor now had his full attention. He jotted a note to search for the publication. He tapped his pen on the desk in thought, then rephrased his earlier question. "Do you think there is a remote probability that rare-earth element deposits might be found off our continental shelf?"

Diekam scrolled through several slides and projected one depicting the ancient Panthalassa Ocean, the Paleo-Pacific sea that surrounded the supercontinent of Pangaea eons ago. "Remote? Perhaps. The geology of the region, the Caledonian age granite of the Precambrian and Paleozoic era supports the possibility. Might well be worth a look. There would need to be a complete mapping of the seafloor and collection of samples for mineralogical and geochemical analysis to confirm such a hypothesis."

"And if such a project were undertaken and these nodules were found in significant concentrations to warrant mining?" he asked.

"The ramifications of such a discovery could not be understated."

Chapter Fifteen

17TH COAST GUARD DISTRICT HEADQUARTERS
JUNEAU, ALASKA
WEDNESDAY 16 JANUARY

Captain James St. Clair, Chief of Staff for the 17th Coast Guard District, held out his hand. "Welcome to Juneau, Captain Rohrbaugh." He acknowledged Nick. "And you must be Dr. Parkos."

"Nick's just fine, Captain."

"Nick it is then." St. Clair pointed to a small table. "Either of you care for coffee before we get started?"

St. Clair topped off a couple mugs. "I'll forgo the command brief since we're operating on a shortened time-line." He led them back across the room to a worn conference table. "We've had to jump through a few hoops, but things are coming together."

Mike shifted in his seat. "I—"

He anticipated Rohrbaugh's reaction. "Comes with the territory up here, Mike. We're hardly the quiet backwater folks seem to think. That said, we've booked seats for you on the 1500 Alaskan Air flight to Nome this afternoon. We'll have to pull chocks no later than 1245 to get you to the airport. On arrival in Nome, you'll be escorted to the Cutter *Joseph Gerczak*. She'll get underway as soon as you embark to rendezvous with the *Healy*."

Nick hefted his coffee mug to make room for the worn navigation chart St. Clair unfolded.

"As I understand it," he continued, "you're interested in the immediate area around Cape Lisburne." His finger traced lines to several landmarks. "This would be the old Air Force radar site and a gravel runway we've used for emergency landings. Just inland of the base is the Inupiat village of Wevok. Point Hope, as the name implies, is situated on the tip of a narrow peninsula just to the southwest."

"Where was the Chinese submersible found?" Nick asked.

He tapped the chart. "Here. 68°79 North, 166°45 West. We gave the coordinates to the Arctic Domain Awareness Center. They factored in the wind and current data to estimate the sub's probable start point before it was disabled. That would be here."

"Well within our territorial waters," Mike said.

"We were tracking a Chinese research support ship, the *Kexue*, three weeks before we spotted the sub, but didn't connect the dots until we received the Center's input. The final piece of the puzzle was the Chinese characters on the sub's side that the *Midgett's* aircrew photographed. They translate to "Flying Fish," a known research vessel."

"Research?" Mike said.

"Had us puzzled too," St. Claire responded.

Mike leaned over the chart. "Any ideas about what it might have been doing?"

"Thing is, it's designed for deep sea exploration."

"Odd place for it to be."

"That's what had us scratching our heads. The best we could come up with was they had to be conducting oceanographic studies to support their submarine ops. They also may be interested in our plans to reactivate Cape Lisburne to support the Ballistic Missile Early Warning System."

"Makes sense," Mike said. "They haven't made a secret of their intent to expand their presence in the Arctic or their dislike of our ballistic missile defense shield."

"True enough. As a matter of fact, their newest icebreaker, the *Xuelong-2*, and the research ship, *Xheng He*, have just transited the Soya Strait."

"Where's that?" Nick asked.

"The gap between the northern Japanese island of Hokkaido and Russia's Sakhalin Island. The China Polar Research Institute claims their mission is to carry out oceanic, atmospheric, sea-ice, and marine research."

"Do you believe them?"

"To an extent. Their data will enhance their military's capability to project power into the region."

Mike ran his index finger over the Chinese ships' probable track. "Can we shadow them?"

"Not well. Satellite coverage is pretty iffy up north. The biggest factor, though, is we simply don't have the surface or air assets."

"How about us?" Nick asked.

"You mean the *Gerczak?* Depends on where the Chinese are going. She doesn't have an ice-hardened hull. In a pinch, she can make her way through the thinner stuff, but it'd still be a dicey operation with significant risk."

Nick dismissed the notion and refocused. "Can we get anywhere near Cape Lisburne?"

"Ordinarily the answer would be no, but this year is different. Unheard of, actually. The sea ice usually peaks in mid-March before receding, but a combination of this year's change in the jet stream coupled with warm southerly winds has created several areas of open water in the Chukchi Sea north of the Bering Strait. That said, close-pack ice twenty-four to forty-two inches thick still extends as far south as Nome."

Nick ran through several possible ways to complete his mission. A plausible one came to mind. "Does the *Healy* carry an Unmanned Underwater Vehicle?"

St. Claire placed his hands on the table and fixed Nick with a hard look. "Can I ask what you're looking for?"

Nick noted the edge in St. Clair's voice. "We have reason to believe that Chinese submersible may have stumbled across a field of rare-earth containing polymetallic nodules. I've been tasked to validate this presumption and if true, blunt any effort by the Chinese to exploit this resource."

"Under whose authority?"

Nick didn't want to have to play this card. He glanced at Mike before answering. "The president's."

"I see… So, to answer your question. Yes, she does. In point of fact, the *Healy* is ideally suited for your mission. A team from the National Science Foundation is on board conducting high resolution 3-D bathymetric surveys of the seafloor. They're operating a new twin hulled UUV equipped with an experimental Doppler and inertial navigation system. These provide the vehicle a degree of autonomous operation. The trick is maintaining the link to the *Healy* for the real-time optical. Transmitting signals through the ice has been a significant problem." He paused. "Captain?"

"This is a bit off-topic," Mike said, "but what about the Russians?"

"My personal cut? I'd say their actions in the region have been provocative, but they're not directly affecting our strategic interests. Their new Northern Fleet-Unified Strategic Command certainly warrants our attention, though. Within the context of your visit, I wouldn't go so far as to say we have a partnership with the Russians, but we do share a common interest in China's incursions into the Arctic."

"Interest or concern?" Nick asked.

"Both. The Russians are intent on protecting their Northern Sea Route from Murmansk to the Bering Sea. If I were in their shoes, I'd be harboring concerns that Beijing could seize the eastern end of this route as a means to out flank their forces and establish their own military presence in eastern Siberia and the Arctic."

"Why?"

"History. The Chinese still harbor considerable ill will for what they consider Imperial Russia's seizure of the southern portion of Siberia and the displacement of the region's ethnic Chinese in the 1800's. Furthermore, the Russians share our concern about the unregulated incursion of Chinese industrial fishing fleets plundering the resources of the Arctic. The other commonality we share with Moscow, and this touches on your visit, is the very real possibility of Beijing trying to exploit the oil and mineral resources within our respective territorial waters."

"We have to keep the Chinese away from our coast," Nick said.

Chapter Sixteen

USCG CUTTER *JOSEPH GERCZAK*, WPC-112
NOME, ALASKA
WEDNESDAY 16 JANUARY

Nick stepped aside, allowing Mike to proceed up the gangway of the Coast Guard Cutter *Joseph Gerczak*. The quarterdeck appeared at peace, shrouded in the diffused light of a brisk snowfall. The scene was at odds with the crew's frenetic activity on the pier preparing to get the ship underway on such short notice.

He shifted the duffle bag slung over his shoulder, grasped the railing, and carefully trod up the steps of the cutter's accommodation ladder. The last thing he needed was to make a spectacle of himself and fall flat on his ass.

He shifted his gaze back to the quarterdeck. One positive did occur to him about his sudden disappearance from the Washington beltway. A certain Chinese surveillance team wouldn't be happy. They might find a trail to Honolulu, but to Alaska? Not a chance.

The watch officer acknowledged Nick's safe arrival. "Welcome aboard the *Joseph Gerczak*, Mr. Parkos. Petty Officer

Gonzalez will escort you and Captain Rohrbaugh to your stateroom."

Gonzalez stepped forward. "Here, sir. Let me give you an assist with your gear."

Feeling the deck sway beneath his feet, he gladly relinquished the bulky duffle. *Gah, they weren't even underway yet.* He'd successfully made his way up the gangway but wasn't about to chance negotiating any steep ladders. No sense pressing his luck. He glanced at Mike who looked perfectly at home chatting with the watch officer.

———

Nick stood on the *Gerczak*'s bridge the next afternoon watching an endless procession of white-topped rollers fade away into the haze-shrouded horizon. He braced his legs against a sudden roll and turned away from the dreary vista of the dark-gray ocean dotted with patches of lighter-gray drift ice. Much to his surprise he wasn't hunched over a commode, green with sea-sickness.

The unrelenting darkness also surprised him. The sun hung suspended above the horizon about to succumb to the long Arctic night. What remained of its feeble light was filtered through a bank of low dark-gray clouds.

He pushed up his sleeve to check the time. Sunset would be in twenty-five minutes. Only five hours of daylight. *I'd go nuts up here.*

He turned to the watch officer, he'd learned was called the 'Officer of the Deck.' "Lieutenant, do you know when we'll rendezvous with the *Healy*?"

"Depends on the front that's approaching," the OOD replied. He pointed to a clutter of green-white images illuminated by the sweep on the ice radar screen. "We're operating close to a marginal ice zone."

He acknowledged the OOD's explanation having already

learned the radar's specialized design was crucial to identifying ice features such as high pressure ridges and open water polynyas.

"Those are ice ridges and hummocks to the northeast of us. Over the past day, the storm has driven them nearly nine miles toward our position."

He studied the turbulent sea. "Are we in danger?"

"We're in for a blow. I suspect the skipper will order us to reduce speed any time now to avoid colliding with any undetected growlers"

"Growlers?"

"Large blocks of drifting ice that can damage the hull. We'll maintain just enough headway to keep our bow into the waves, so we're not thrown around too much."

The OOD cast a skeptical eye at Nick. "I'd suggest you rig the safety bar for your rack tonight. Tuck your sheet and blanket in real tight, then crawl in from the top. It'll keep you from rolling around too much."

"That bad?"

"Could be."

The Cutter's bow plunged into a deep roller and corkscrewed over its crest, emphasizing the OOD's warning.

He staggered, caught himself, and clung to the stainless-steel bar mounted below the radar scope. *This is just great.*

The OOD spun toward the quartermaster manning the wheel. "Steady your helm."

He addressed Nick. "And, Parkos, don't even think about going out on the open deck tonight."

———

Nick jerked awake. The metallic sound of ice screeching down the hull of the Cutter seemed to be coming from right beside his head. The Cutter wasn't moving. A growler? A panicked vision of the Titanic flashed in his mind. *This can't be good.*

He wrestled free from his bedding and called out to the top tier of their bunk. "Mike?" Nothing. He dropped back onto the mattress. *Damn.*

He tried to calm himself. *Okay, there aren't any alarms going off. That's a positive. So, what's happening?* He struggled out of the rack, threw on some cloths, and made for the bridge.

———

"Over here," Mike called from the far corner of the bridge.

He gave his eyes a chance to adjust to the dark, then made his way over to join him. "What happened?"

"Ran into unexpected ice," Mike answered. "More like a thick slurry with large chunks mixed in. We're working the ice, maneuvering to get out of it."

He heard the captain give a string of commands and felt the cutter move aft, then stop. "Are we stuck?"

"Depends on your definition of *stuck*. Right now, we're oscillating fore and aft to keep open the polynya we're in."

He peered through the bridge windows. The beam of a searchlight cut through the darkness illuminating a patch ragged ice snarling the bow of the Cutter. "Polynya?"

"An open area in the ice. The crew's hanging fenders over the side to ward off the bigger chunks. The trick is to keep moving before that polar low smacks us. The helmsman told me the winds could force the ice under the hull fouling the rudder and damaging the propellers."

He heard a dull roar and swung toward the sound, grabbing the metal sill of the bridge window, stunned at what he saw. The *Gerczak*'s searchlight cut through the night, it's beam splayed across a rolling wall of fog racing toward them. "Oh, shit! Mike—"

A blast of wind rocked the Cutter. The fog followed, enveloping the ship in an icy embrace, extinguishing the stars. He gasped, the color draining from his face. "My God."

"All non-essential personnel clear the bridge," the OOD ordered.

Mike grabbed Nick's arm and pulled him toward the door. "That's us. We're going to be in the way."

———

The next morning, Nick shuffled after Mike making for the foredeck of the *Gerczac*. Fully encased in a "Gumby," as the Coast Guard called their cold-water immersion suits, he looked like a bright orange Stay Puft Marshmallow Man.

Off the port bow, a MH-65 helicopter from the Cutter *Midgett* hovered in the distance. Mike explained the extraction would be safer forward. Fewer obstructions.

Extraction? He studied the helicopter with doubtful eyes and frowned at the prospect of dangling from a rope being pulled up to a helicopter, fewer obstructions or not. *Yeah, right.*

He slid his left hand over the ice-encrusted railing for balance and glanced over the side. They were trapped. He looked up at the helicopter, the only option to reach the *Healy*. *This is just nuts.*

"You'll need to use the basket, sir."

He stared at the petty officer, then the tiny rescue basket festooned on either end with orange floats. He dropped his duffle and cast a dubious look at Mike.

Mike flashed a huge grin. "Trust me. For this evolution we won't use the term litter."

"Seriously?"

"As I recall, this whole Chinese thing was your idea."

"Harumph." He opened his mouth to add an embellishment, but a blast of downwash from the helicopter's rotors cut off his response.

"You wanna go first?" Mike hollered. "They can do a double lift."

"What's that?"

"The rescue swimmer from the helo can share the hoist and escort you up."

He thought about the offer. The visual image of clinging to the crewman was unacceptable. "Nah, I'll go up alone." He took a deep breath, grudgingly accepted assistance from the grinning petty officer, and climbed into the basket. He positioned himself and clutched the metal tubes of the basket's sides. *Oh, man, this is not good.*

"Keep your arms inside," the petty officer advised. "You may spin around, but don't let that spook you. We'll send your duffle up on another lift."

"Ah…"

The crewman addressed the helicopter's crew chief on his radio. "Prepare to take the load." He acknowledged the reply, completing his remarks with a 'thumbs up' as the hoist line tightened. He turned to his white-faced passenger. "Off you go."

He recalled what Mike said once about overcoming an obstacle. "The way out is through." *Well, in this case, it's up.*

His world slowly rotated around the axis of the cable as he cleared the deck. He resisted the temptation to close his eyes and chanced a look down at the Cutter. He caught a glimpse of Mike tossing him a salute. *Just great. I'm about to die and he's….*

A different pitch from the helicopter's engines cut short his thoughts. The basket swayed. He lagged behind, swinging in his basket like the bob of a pendulum. He grasped the basket's stainless steel tubing. The helicopter began to slide-slip, distancing itself from the ship. His horizon tilted. Mike disappeared from sight.

The wench continued to reel him in like a hooked fish until the basket bounced off the wheel of the helicopter's landing gear. He reached out to steady himself before the crew chief grabbed the basket and dragged it through the side door.

The crew chief notified the pilot, "Inside the cabin," then gave Nick a thumbs up and handed him a headset.

He pulled the set over his ears and adjusted the microphone.

"Welcome aboard, Mr. Parkos," announced the pilot, Lieutenant Sarah MacAuley. "Shouldn't be long until we have you aboard the *Healy*."

"Appreciate you not dropping me in the water."

"We really try not to do that."

The crew chief smiled, unclipped Nick's harness, and sent it back down to collect Mike. He cocked his head recalling that Mike once offered to teach him how to fast rope from a helicopter. *Ah, nope. I'll take a pass when we reach the Healy. They should have a real landing deck.*

Chapter Seventeen

USCG CUTTER *HEALY* WAGB-20
CAPE LISBURNE, ALASKA
MONDAY 21 JANUARY

Nick studied the open expanse of the Chukchi Sea from his vantage point on the 02 level of the Coast Guard Cutter *Healy*'s boxy superstructure. They had transited the Bering Strait the day before, five days and some five-hundred miles from the point of his and Mike's helicopter transfer from the *Gerczak*.

Hundreds of irregularly shaped white growlers flecked the surrounding waters. One of the NOAA scientists on board explained that the mini-icebergs were calved from the leading edge of an ice shelf looming just to the north. He shifted his gaze. Wisps of streaming clouds painted a bright-blue sky dotted by a flock of seagulls gliding along the icebreaker's side in search of an easy meal.

He turned from the mesmerizing sight at the sound of the stateroom's door opening.

Mike crossed the room and looked over Nick's shoulder. "Amazing, isn't it."

"Yeah. Sure is."

Mike handed him a brown government interoffice mailer. "Picked this up for you in the Comm center."

He unwound the red string securing the mailer and extracted a sealed white envelope. "Any idea what's in this?"

"Nope."

He ripped open the envelope and glanced at the first page. "It's an update from my co-worker, Austin Mack. The president approved our project to set up a false corporation, Eagle River, LLC."

"Sounds like a good name for this neck of the woods."

"We borrowed the name from Austin's hometown in Wisconsin. So far, he's completed a draft of the business plan, obtained a federal tax ID number, set up a bank account, solicited several venture capital funds, and created a website."

"Not bad for a couple weeks' work," Mike said.

"Yeah, darn impressive. Appears I need to keep out of his hair more often. He's even coordinated with the FBI to use a K-Street lobbyist on their payroll to push Eagle River's submission for mining rights to Interior. Austin thinks we might be able to use the lobbyist to smoke out the Chinese cell in D.C. He wants to see if any Chinese operatives approach the guy and try to turn him. Came up with the idea on his own."

"You got an intermediary for your lobbyist?"

"You mean a cut-out?"

Mike cocked his head at the use of the spy term. "Ah, who's your lobbyist working through?"

"It's complicated."

"That's it?"

He relented. "It's that lobbyist I mentioned a couple weeks back, Jason Moore."

"Does he know he's being used?"

"I doubt it, but that might depend on his level of involvement with the Chinese. At some point, he might be offered a plea deal and pressured to come clean. It would be great to smoke those guys out."

"I'd be careful what you wish for, my friend."

What he didn't offer was that Geoff Lange sent him a cryptic note stating that Moore had approached him with an offer to provide insider information for his investigation. Lange hadn't volunteered what that information might be or what Moore might want in return. He folded the report and opened the small safe on his desk to deposit the update. Just inside the safe were two airline minis of Seagram's Crown Royal he'd bought on the flight up. He moved his hand to block Mike's view, closed the door, and spun the dial. "Gotta go."

He walked across the room to don a heavy wool sweater, dark-blue watch cap, and the olive-gray parka that lay on his bed.

"Man, I gotta toughen you up," Mike said.

He ignored the jibe. "No rest for the weary. The NOAA and National Science Foundation guys said they'd be launching their UUV about now. You coming?"

"Yeah, maybe I will."

———

Nick and Mike made their way aft, stepping out on the starboard weather deck. They paused at the scene that greeted them. Looming over the eastern horizon were the rugged headlands of Cape Lisburne. He noted the look on Mike's face. "What's on your mind?"

"Thinking about what we may have to do."

He grasped the braided metal rope of the railing overwhelmed by an abrupt sense of foreboding. Emotionally disoriented, he shook his head to dislodge the negative thoughts swirling around inside.

Mike made his way past the cutter's rigid inflatable boat as he trailed behind, his eyes fixed on the black snow-streaked cliffs. A slash of indigo cut through the mountains where a small glacier had clawed its way to the sea. Thoughts on the enormity of what may lay ahead replaced those of the rugged vista. *Confirmation? Certainly. Danger? No doubt. What else?* He had no idea.

Mike stopped at the hatch of the National Science Foundation's twenty-foot ISO container positioned near the stern and pulled open the door. One of the two scientists inside nodded a distracted welcome and bent back over his instruments. The other, a Swedish-American named Sigge, waved him over. "Hey, Nick. Good to see ya'. We're just about done running our diagnostics. So far, so good. You been briefed?"

"Only on the basics."

"We've got several objectives based on spinoffs from last year's Marginal Ice Zone Project. They boil down to testing an array of advanced sensors, then modeling the data so we can better define the interactions of the ocean, bottom topography, and ice interfaces." With a nod to Mike he added, "Most of what we know about the bathymetry and hydrology of the Arctic comes from the Navy's submarine ops."

He recalled what Austin had said about convergence zones, temperature gradients, and isothermal layers. Submarines could hide under them. Made sense.

"The problem we're facing in the Arctic ocean is different from other bodies of water," Sigge continued. "Warm water on the bottom, cold on top interspersed with thin layers of freshwater melt-off. The resulting mix of temperature and salinity really screws up the buoyancy of the UUV and the propagation of its sonar and communication signals."

"Are comms the limiting factor?" Mike asked.

"Pretty much. We also lack reliable satellite links for anything above sixty-five degrees north latitude. Most of the communication satellites orbit at lower latitudes and can't cover the Arctic. We have to rely on the geostationary birds at the equator. The ship's comm gear is pointed just one degree of elevation above the horizon."

Mike understood the implications. "Even a small swell will disrupt your connection."

"On top of that, we have to deal with another peculiarity found in the high latitudes, the magnetic shifts caused by proximity to the North Pole. Despite a limited degree of autonomous operation, we're still pretty much reliant on a fiber-optic tether for commands and video feeds."

The other scientist looked up from his workstation. "Don't let that guy put you to sleep. If I were you, I'd head outside. All the action's on deck."

"Thanks, we'll do that," Mike said. "Catch you guys later."

He followed Mike out the door and crossed beneath the overhang of the flight deck. The yellow twin-hulled UUV was suspended beneath an "A" shaped gantry about to be swung out over the stern by the *Healy*'s articulated crane. Two deck-hands man-handled a pair of spring lines keeping it stationary in the gusting wind. Several others played out a long segment of the vessel's black tether from a huge spool.

A whirlwind of snow flurries sent a chilling wind down the back of his coat. He hated the cold. For some strange reason, his mind drifted back to his time in Somalia where the highs hovered near one-hundred and ten. He looked skyward. Clear, except the few wisps of high clouds. "Where the hell did the snow come from?"

"Beats me." Mike said, pulling him out of the weather and guiding him to the lee side of the superstructure where they watched the UUV until it slipped below the surface.

———

Sigge welcomed them back to the ISO. "Guess you guys aren't fans of the cold."

"Not much," Nick said, giving his arms a brisk rubbing before pointing to Mike. "He's okay with it, but then, he's nuts. You seeing anything?"

"Not yet, but we've got a few more minutes until we're over the seabed."

"Ever found any rare-earth elements up here?" he asked.

"Nothing earth shattering."

He groaned at the pun.

"Sorry about that. Anyway, we did detect traces in several core samples on our last expedition, but ..." He lurched forward, then adjusted the gain of the video monitor. "Holy crap. Hey, Nick. Come over here. This is amazing."

He stooped to examine the image of the seafloor illuminated by the UUV's forward beam. All he could see was a pile of silt-covered boards and a jumble of rocks scattered across the olive-gray mud. He caught a glimpse of a creature with orange tentacles and then a crab scuttling out of sight. "What am I looking at?"

Sigge pointed at the screen. "See all that stuff scattered across the sea floor?"

"Yeah?"

"That's got to be an old shipwreck. Those may be ballast stones. Look, there's a belaying pin and a tangle of rope. And the base of a mast. The preservation is incredible."

"Sigge's partner chimed in. "You don't think it could be the *Karluk*? That'd be crazy if we found her."

Sigge looked over his shoulder. "The *Karluk* was a Canadian two-mast brigantine. She sank in 1914 while on an Arctic scientific expedition. Crushed by the ice. Her crew made it to Wrangle Island, but half of them lost their lives. Quite a story."

His attention strayed from Sigge's story, his attention focused on the screen. He startled when he saw a different kind of rock appear on the ocean floor. "What are those?"

"Oh, those rocks that look a bit like giant crystals?"

He noted the disappointment in Sigge's voice. *The lost vessel was interesting, but...* "What are they?"

"Could be the polymetallic nodules you're looking for." Sigge pointed to the monitor. "There. Those crystalline looking reddish-brown ones. Those'd be a good bet."

He recalled what he'd read about monazite. That element was found in red-brown crystals...*and if the Chinese— ?* "Can they be mined?"

Sigge pulled on his chin. "Depends. We'd have to map this entire area. The deposits have to be in a concentration of at least ten kilograms per square meter to merit mining. From what we're seeing on the monitor, that'd be worth pursuing. I just don't know what they're doing here."

He studied the UUV's claw-shaped grasping device at the edge of the frame. "Can you snag one?"

"Sure can." Sigge turned to his workmate. "Hey, John. Can you fire up the sampling arm? I think we just stumbled across something besides the wreck that we can submit for publication."

"Ah, could you possibly not do that just yet?"

"Oh? Why not?"

"I can't get into the details. Let's just say we need to get those samples."

Chapter Eighteen

3100 PROSPECT STREET, NW
GEORGETOWN, WASHINGTON, D.C.
WEDNESDAY 21 JANUARY

Lin-Wu's right hand rested on an ivory-handled letter opener set atop a scattering of surveillance photos. He fixed his eyes on Tao Yixing's latest intelligence report, reading the concluding paragraph. Esteemed Mother slipped out of the library and closed the door behind her with a soft click. The two cups of fragrant black tea she'd poured remained untouched.

His eyes lifted from the intelligence report and locked them onto Yixing, pinning the man to his seat. "There is not a dog's fart of useful information here. It has been ten days." He set the letter opener aside, the gesture calculated, menacing. He gathered the photos into a pile. "When did you last see Parkos?"

Yixing hesitated, his attention drawn to curved four-inch blade of the knife. Several beads of sweat appeared on his forehead. "His condo... nearly three weeks ago."

"Where else?"

"The Old Executive Office Building."

He tapped his index finger on the top photo. "Yes, I have that in front of me. Do we know the nature of the meeting?"

Tao Yixing's mouth twisted into its peculiar grimace revealing his gold tooth. He prefaced his response with an annoying sucking sound through a gap in his front teeth. "There are many staffers there. We can only speculate."

He could detect no insouciance in Yixing's answer and decided to press him further. "Would you care to venture a thought?"

Yixing peered out the library's picture window as if thinking itself were a complex process.

"Perhaps he met with his old partner from the al-Khultyer affair," Yixing answered. "The Navy SEAL, Rohrbaugh. He remains on the staff of the National Security Council and has an office across the street from the White House."

He pondered this information. All pure conjecture, but involvement at that level of the government would represent a significant problem.

"They've apparently remained friends," Yixing added in the ensuing silence.

He reached for the letter opener. "And his condo?"

"There were no hints to indicate where he might have gone. His girlfriend took the cat and a bag of food."

"That suggests a long trip."

"Perhaps a vacation?" Yixing offered.

He circled the letter opener's point over the pictures. The gesture was not lost on Yixing who emitted another sucking sound that set his teeth on edge. "Have we tracked his iPhone?"

"We've had nothing for weeks."

All negatives. The threat to his mission from Parkos, more credible. He had even consulted, Qui Hsing, the day before seeking assurance. The seer's readings again foretold of danger. He set down the knife and took a deliberate sip of tea. "Parkos suspects. Nonetheless, review the transcripts of our prior intercepts. There may be something." He picked up the photos and placed them in a folder. "I will keep these. Find Huifeng. I want to speak with him."

———

Lin-Wu's mood lightened when Huifeng appeared. "Ah, Huifeng. We have much to discuss." He motioned to Yixing's untouched tea. "You should find the Oolong to your liking."

Huifeng seated himself and lifted the cup to his lips with both hands and took a small sip. "Excellent."

"Parkos has disappeared."

Huifeng set the cup down on its porcelain saucer with an audible CLINK. "That may portend serious difficulties. What do we know of his contact, Lange?"

He hadn't considered linking Parkos' whereabouts to the reporter. "Perhaps Jason Moore could provide a clue. Has he approached him?"

"Last week. Lange gave no indication that he knew of Parkos' whereabouts. As we directed, Moore dropped the name of our contact at Treasury, Devon Gant. He hinted to Lange that Gant could be approached as a source for information about Emmons-Powell and of possible malfeasance by Trident."

"The disinformation we planted?"

"Yes. Moore also suggested—"

He leaned forward intent on asking about Parkos but changed his mind and settled back in his chair. He needed to understand the interplay of the most recent developments impacting his two operations before acting to neutralize the American agent.

"Is something wrong?" Huifeng asked.

"No, please continue."

"Moore suggested we approach a certain K Street lobbyist, an associate of the firm, Creekside Consultants."

"Why is that important?"

"Eagle River."

His faced clouded at the mention of the new American start-up. "Your report states this company's goal is to compete with Consolidated Seabed Resources for the mining rights of the Cape Lisburne field."

"And Emmons-Powell."

He frowned at the new complication to his plan.

"However, we can block them."

Fascinated, he hefted the letter opener and spun it in his fingers. He knew Huifeng would not have come unprepared. "What do you propose?"

"I believe it is time to bring into play two of our assets within the American government. Kimberly Browning, who works at the Interior Department and Ashli Thompson, who holds a key position in the State Department."

"What are their roles?"

"Ms. Browning works in the department of Offshore Energy and Minerals Management. She will be persuaded to provide insider information for our counter proposal."

His mind leaped ahead, choosing not to ask how Browning would be *persuaded*. "I would expect Eagle River to fight us in turn, particularly if they happen to have their own collaborators within State or Interior."

"That too is my presumption. To that end, we have approached Ms. Thompson with certain financial incentives. She is a lawyer working in the State Department's planning office."

"How is she prepared to assist?"

"She is drafting a legal instrument that will classify the proposal as a protected document."

"I am not familiar with this instrument."

"In short, the classification of a document as *protected* prevents the details of that document from being released. Specifically, a Federal representative is prohibited from using non-public State Department information to benefit a private person or entity. In our case, Eagle River, LCC. If Eagle's corporate leadership has access to such an individual, we could identify that person and have him prosecuted."

He smiled. "Very clever. Using the Americans' own safeguards against them." He poured Huifeng more tea, then topped off his own cup. "And what of Mr. Moore's K Street lobbyist?"

"Darrell Nance."

"What do we know of him?"

"Just what we've found on social media. His biography states that he played an instrumental role in pushing the approval of the Gray Wolf Mine's business application through the Alaskan Department of Natural Resources."

He pondered this new development, placing the information within the context of his operations. "Is he on the published list of registered foreign agents?"

"No."

"Then, we'll presume he is not fronting for the Russians. That said, keep digging and put him under surveillance. We must know his vulnerabilities before we commit to turning him."

"And Moore?" Huifeng asked.

"He cannot be allowed to freelance." He ran his finger along the blade of the letter opener sorting through what he must do. There would be no need to dip further into his repertoire of intimidation tactics if Moore betrayed them. Moore would have signed his own death warrant. "If he strays, eliminate him."

Huifeng nodded his affirmation. "Do you wish to discuss the Russians?"

"Yes, then we address what we must do with Parkos."

"I will start with the Russians' bid for Emmons-Powell's assets. Trident Metallurgics, the firm based in Provo, Utah, has taken a more aggressive stance and have distanced themselves from Montreal's Newtech Resource Development. The Canadian company is receiving significant backing from the Novorossiysk Business Group. This is what caught the attention of the Americans."

"The Committee on Foreign Investment in the U.S.?"

"Correct. I believe the Russians realized they overplayed their hand. Their investment in Newtech amounted to a buyout. It's probable they've directed Trident's actions"

"Your use of *they* is vague. Have you identified the Russian leadership?"

"In Moscow, Economic Minister Dimitri Volkov. For the NBG, banker Sergey Nikolaev, a known facilitator for the oligarchs. In turn, Nikolaev is in bed with Vladimir Suslova, a Senior Presidential Advisor who we believe is the driver behind the takeover of Newtech."

"Very cozy."

"We've determined their pass-throughs for financing this venture are the Emerits Investment Authority and the Swiss investment fund, Innovel Venture Capital, Ltd."

"How much?"

"Sixty-million dollars have been traced to an account set up by Nikolaev."

He grunted. "Who is the Russian contact here?"

"Alexi Kuznetsov. He was assigned to their trade mission."

"Was?"

"He appears to have moved his activities to the embassy after the Americans closed their trade mission in Washington."

"Ah, yes. Part of the punitive measures for Moscow's meddling in the American's presidential elections."

"The move will work to our advantage."

His eyes narrowed at this new twist. "What do you have in mind?"

"Kuznetzov must be eliminated. Beyond the obvious benefit of taking him out of play, imagine Moscow's outrage at the murder of one of their diplomats." Huifeng paused for effect. "Now imagine what happens if certain information comes to the press' attention that pertains to his real mission."

He didn't hesitate. "See to it."

"There is another action I would suggest to keep the Russians off balance."

"Go ahead."

"We should target a senior partner in the law firm of Duxtun, Luwan, and Merriman to take them out of play."

"Do you have someone particular in mind?"

"Kuznetzov's contact, Dexter Merriman. Merriman and a junior partner have drafted the legal documents for Trident Metallurgics take-over bid of Emmons-Powell."

He took only a moment to make his decision. His conscience played no role. If Merriman must die, so be it. Men died all the time. "The act must not be traced back to us. It must be perceived by the police as a random event such as a mugging. Those are common enough in Washington."

"Do you have someone in mind?" Huifeng asked.

"Perhaps." He clasped his hands on the table and leaned back in his chair. There were no assurances the American investigators would conclude the loss of two lives were mere coincidence—especially Parkos. He would certainly link the two events. And if Moore .... There would be less risk by killing just one. At least for now. He opened his hands, placing them flat on the tabletop. "Target the lawyer. We will then decide Kuznetzov's fate. Now, tell me about Parkos."

"The third ten-thousand-dollar payment will be deposited in Parkos' offshore account next week. We also ensured there were sales of securities from the account that generated income. Banco Investment and Trust must report this income to the IRS."

"But that information wouldn't necessarily come to the attention of Parkos' supervisors."

"On its own, no. However, there is a separate reporting requirement mandated by the Foreign Account Tax Compliance Act. This information, contained in what's called a Suspicious Activities Report, is sent to Treasury's Financial Crimes Enforcement Department for investigation."

"And Parkos has no idea?"

"None. We are counting on the IRS to pick up the disconnect between the earnings report sent by Banko and the information Parkos submits on his income tax form."

"And the penalties?"

"Depending on the circumstances, civil or criminal charges could be filed. Parkos' failure to disclose will be deemed a willful attempt to hide income from an unknown source, presumably a foreign entity. He will certainly lose his security clearance, his job, and he will be investigated for espionage. I have no doubt he'll be imprisoned."

He made to respond, but Huifeng continued.

"I have also taken the liberty to add another measure to ensnare Parkos."

He suppressed his annoyance at this revelation. "What have you done?"

"We stole an unsolicited credit card application from his mailbox and opened an account in his name using the same personal information we used for Banko. Parkos has overspent the limit of this fraudulent card by thousands of dollars. Furthermore, he has not made any payments and, of course, has failed to respond to a debt collection agency's inquiries. That agency will soon notify his employer."

"Well done, Huifeng. Parkos will be ruined."

An ancient Chinese proverb, a dark premonition, wormed its way into his consciousness despite his outward show of support. *Yĭ luān tóu shí*, 'Try to smash a rock with an egg'. The saying's meaning? 'Overrate your strength and be defeated.' While improbable, Huifeng may have erred. He stared out the window and spoke to the gray sky. "Only time will tell if these actions are fatal." He paused. *But to whom?*

Chapter Nineteen

THE NICHOLAS
GEORGETOWN, WASHINGTON, D.C.
FRIDAY 25 JANUARY

Nick dashed from the sheltered bus stop near his parked car and scrambled into the back seat of his Uber ride. He slammed the door and twisted around to look out the rear window. *Nothing.*

Lange's call setting up their meeting and his insistence on subterfuge had unsettled him. The driver pulled away from the curb and made his way down Prospect Street. He shifted his gaze to the neighborhood's red-brick colonial homes and quaint shops festooned with colorful blue awnings and red shutters. So different from the white and blue-toned solitude of the Arctic he'd left behind a few days earlier.

He faced forward and confirmed his presumed destination, "3130 M Street," while examining the faces of the approaching pedestrians and a scattering of bicyclists. Most appeared to be of college age, their attire reflecting the sunny, but brisk January afternoon. None looked suspicious.

They skirted the old C&O canal, passing a small cluster of

people gathered in front of a bike shop's display window. Another group lined up outside an upscale coffee shop until they passed out of sight.

The car slowed and pulled over. He scanned the faces of the people walking along the sidewalk. *It could be anyone.* He gathered himself, exited the car unsure of what to expect, and made his way down the sidewalk stopping at the door of The Nicholas.

He glanced at the surveillance camera and gave the ornate door knocker a couple raps. He figured someone inside must be watching a monitor, a set-up that made him wonder who frequented this place. The door opened to reveal the formally attired doorman, Edmund.

"Good afternoon, Mr. Parkos." Edmund stood aside and guided Nick across the parquet floor toward the bar. "May I take your coat, sir?"

He reached for the belt of his new double-breasted trench coat. The action, or more likely, a reaction to the stress he felt, inexplicably triggered a vision of the *Pink Panther* and Inspector Clouseau. He shrugged out of the coat and handed it to Edmund who accepted it with a slight elevation of his right eyebrow.

He made to respond in a faux French accent but managed to hold his tongue. That didn't stop the line of dialog from one of the movies playing out in his head:

Would you please lead me to zee rheum?

The rheum, Monsieur? I do not know what a rheum is.

Zee lo-ca-shi-own where I am to meet Monsieur Lange.

Ah, a Rrruumm.

That eez what I said, a rheum. Are you deef?

He relented. Edmund looked confused by the long pause, his expression saying he wanted to be somewhere else. Anywhere else. "Where can I find Mr. Lange?"

"Mr. Lange is in the drawing room, sir. I believe you know the way."

He made for the stairs recalling another of his favorite Pink Panther movie lines. *My face! You've stolen my face! Give me back my face, you fiend!* He smiled, wondering how Edmund would have responded if he'd thrown those lines at him.

———

Lange turned from the casement window overlooking M street when Nick's blurred reflection appeared in the leaded glass panes. He took a long pull of his cigar and exhaled a plume of blue-white smoke, adding another masculine layer to the aroma of old books and leather in the paneled room. "I figure after your trip, you'd rather be with Michelle tonight, but what I have couldn't wait."

Nick stopped in midstride, any further thoughts of Clouseau wiped from his mind. He tried to cover his surprise at Lange's knowledge of his trip. "I'd say that's a good bet. She's bringing back my cat."

"I didn't peg you for a cat guy."

"Long story. He's a stray."

Lange's expression changed from non-committal to bemused. He pointed to a Glencairn glass set on the end table. "I took the liberty and ordered you a dram of Jura's Superstition. It has a unique character, quite different from the other single malt Scotches. What sets it apart are the ginger and cinnamon accents."

He took the glass and held it up to the light, then tilted the rim under his nose. He took a sip, rolling the whisky over his tongue, letting it rest a moment. The formality of the tasting gave him a moment to recover. Lange's actions had thrown him completely off balance. He took a second sip, feigning interest. "I like it. Great change of pace."

Lange motioned him toward the right-hand chair set in front of the fireplace, then settled in the other. His demeanor changed and his voice hardened. "Did anyone follow you?"

"No." The cryptic answer betrayed his uncertainty. He set the glass down on the polished tabletop and dropped into the other chair, intent on diverting any more questions. "So, what's so urgent?"

"Jason Moore."

The pronouncement puzzled him. While Moore held a place on one of the blue index cards pinned to the cork board in his office, he hadn't yet factored in as a major player in the investigation. That appeared about to change. "Moore's the lobbyist representing Pacific Commodities for the Chinese? Right?"

"He approached me at the Upper Crust just over a week ago. Suggested I contact a mid-level guy at Treasury named Devon Gant about possible malfeasance by Trident Metallurgics."

"Doesn't it strike you as odd that he thought you'd be interested?"

Lange looked into the crackling fire, then faced Nick. "Yeah, it does."

He felt on firmer ground having turned the tables but elected not to pursue his question. There wasn't a need—at least not yet. He'd discussed Moore's role with his assistant, Austin Mack, including their request to the FBI to put the lobbyist under surveillance. "Knowing what we already have on Trident's link to the Novorossiysk Business Group, possible malfeasance by the Russians doesn't surprise me. If Trident's takeover bid for Emmons-Powell takes a hit, I'll take that as a win for the good guys. Besides, Moore's in it for the money."

Lange tapped the ash off his cigar and studied the glowing tip. "All true, but doesn't that leave the field open to the Chinese?"

He nodded, acknowledging Lange's point.

"That brings me to another open question," Lange said. "Where does Gant fit in?"

"He's a conduit, but you can't rule out the possibility his

motives reflect a certain rectitude. All things considered, I'd be hesitant to give much credence to his offer."

"My guess is they want me to publish an exposé, but I don't intend to bite. I'd prefer to leave both of those guys dangling and see what they do next. One of the variables I'm considering is why Gant wouldn't keep whatever information he has on Trident in-house."

He massaged the stubble on his chin to mask an incipient frown. *An exposé? Could Lange have been the one to approach Moore? If so, what might he be hiding?* He decided to counter with a question of his own. "Could Gant have been fed misinformation?"

"By Moore, or somebody else?"

He equivocated. "Interesting question."

Lange removed his glasses and cocked an interrogative eyebrow. "How about you tell me."

"Could be either." He kept the tone of his voice matter of fact. "At this point, I'm not sure it makes any difference."

"It would if Gant could lead you to his source." Lange paused to contemplate his cigar. "So, with that in mind, did you reconsider getting me those points of contact in the FBI's counter-terrorism unit and the CIA's Center for Cyber Intelligence?"

His eyes clouded, the frost of his suspicion matching that etched on the windows. "Did Moore try to bribe you?"

"No," Lange said, his answer clipped by a flash of anger.

His arms tensed. He'd hit a nerve. *Interesting.* He backed off. "Look, Geoff, I've already told you. I can't get you access. I don't believe you're acting in bad faith, but there's no exigency. I've got a good handle on the Russians. What you can do is continue to work Moore and Gant. See if you can get them to tip their hands and lead me to the Chinese mastermind."

Lange acquiesced, the edge to his voice softening. "That's reasonable. But now everything we presume to know has to be circled back to what our working hypotheses are. We must determine if our premises are still valid."

Conspiracy theories whirled through his head. Were his presumptions wrong? "I agree, so let me throw this out. What if Moore decided to try his hand at freelancing and is working both sides?"

"Us and the Chinese?" Lange responded. "A dangerous move."

"Unless he wanted to feed us information about his client in case he ever needed to work a plea deal with the FBI."

"Does that mean you have something on him?"

"Nope. At least not yet." He didn't volunteer that the DNI had granted him access to the NSA's Tailored Access Operators group after they verified Nick's iPhone had been hacked. The TAO was part of the Signal Intelligence Directorate headquartered at Fort Meade and was linked operationally with the CIA's Center for Cyber Intelligence. The two groups were now working to identify who'd inserted the malware in his phone. A picture of his old nemesis from the CIA, Taylor Ferguson, who now worked at the CCI flashed from his subconscious. He despised the man's duplicity, but like during the al-Khultyer affair, he might need him.

Lange's eyes narrowed. "There something you're not telling me?"

"Nope."

Lange pushed himself out of his chair, his face reddening. "Then we're done."

He slammed hid glass down, stunned by Lange's acerbity and the turmoil roiling in his own mind. "Damn right, we are. I don't need this crap."

"What about your SIM card?"

"What?"

"Your SIM card," Lange repeated. "Hacked. What did they discover?"

He stood and moved to his left, placing the chair between

him and Lange. He clenched his jaw, debating what, if anything, he could divulge. For instance, that his contact at the FBI, Jessica Caudry, had already submitted the paperwork to the Fourth U.S. District Court to obtain a FISA warrant to put Moore under surveillance. He'd worked closely with Caudry on the al-Khultyer affair and trusted her. The fact she'd also been the one to identify the danger to his ex and his daughter from that damn terrorist went a long way.

"God damn it, Parkos, I'm on your side. If we're to get anywhere, we need access to Moore's iPhone and computers."

"We?" He gripped the back of the chair. He'd informed his supervisor, Ned Strickland, of the meeting with Lange. Strickland, in turn, cautioned him to listen to what Lange had to say, but not volunteer anything.

"You just used *we*. How can you presume *we* is even applicable? You lost your clearance when you left the Navy. Even if I was nuts enough to divulge what I know, I'd be breaking every rule in the book."

"Good point." Lange refilled Nick's glass. "Go ahead, sit down. We'll agree to disagree."

His jaw relaxed. "I'll see what I can do." He released his grip on the chair and sat back down resisting the temptation to wipe up the pool of scotch on the table. Instead, he took a long sip of what remained in his glass to buy time to think. Truth be told, he still didn't have much more than Lange. He considered, and then discarded telling Lange about the FBI's asset at Creekside Consultants, Darrell Nance. Who knows? Lange might even find out about Nance on his own. He decided to give up one piece of information. "Our Tailored Operations Access group is working my phone. They may have something."

"If they do, are they going to target the intruder's IPv4 and IPv6 networks?" Lange added an explanation. "Internet Protocol versions four and six that tag the user's IP addresses."

"I honestly can't say. I guess it depends on who they identify."

He knew his answers were completely accurate … to a point. What he couldn't divulge was what would happen as soon as Jessica's warrant was approved. The TAO had already accessed Moore's iPhone, Google and email accounts, and would soon unleash their full arsenal of code-named invasive tools on them. Nick counted on these measures to unearth Moore's links to the Chinese and lead him to the mastermind. *But if they used other methods to communicate… then what?*

Lange broke into Nick's thoughts. "You have something else you'd like to share?"

He focused on the fireplace. Flames danced angrily around the stacked logs. One gave way, blasting a shower of glowing embers up the flue. "Not now. Let's just leave it at that."

On a hunch, he decided to toss out the three-word phrase that had mysteriously appeared on his computer over two months ago. "It's not over." Nick focused on Lange's eyes. Nothing. *Either this guy's really good, or…*

"Far from it," Lange concurred. "So, I'll give you something. Run your data bases and identify anyone who shares a common link to the Chinese Ministry of State Security's Enterprise Division and the United Front Work Department, then match those names with their embassy staff and trade delegations in Washington."

"United Front?"

"A department of the Chinese Central Committee. Manages their students in the U.S., recruitment of agents, and clandestine ops among other things."

He pursued his lips. He hadn't thought of that angle. "You've done your homework. I don't suppose you already have a name?"

"As a matter of fact, I do. Lam Huifeng. It'd also be a good idea to take a look at the companies fronting for

Olympic. I wouldn't be surprised if his name or an alias doesn't pop up on your communication intercepts of Pacific Commodities and the Pan American Development Bank."

"How-the-hell do—?"

"You trust me?" Lange said

"You haven't exactly given me a lot of solid reasons to."

"Perhaps, but unless you do, we'll both go down."

"We?"

Lange stubbed out his cigar. "Let me know when you have your answers. Right now, I'd suggest you call Michelle and retrieve your cat."

<h1 style="text-align:center">Chapter Twenty</h1>

CREEKSIDE CONDOMINIUMS
ANNANDALE, VIRGINA
FRIDAY 25 JANUARY

Nick kicked a pile of dirty clothes into his closet and slid the door closed. The laundry taken care of, he hefted an empty cardboard box and made for the living room, intent on cleaning up almost a month's worth of accumulated flotsam that littered the condo. He checked his watch. Michelle would be here any minute, and still the kitchen to go.

He filled the box with an assortment of empty cans and bottles, old newspapers, and several dirty paper plates, grabbed the malodorous white-plastic trash bag from under the kitchen sink, mashed it into the box, and made for the dumpster. He almost made it.

Michelle was leaning through the open passenger door of her Navy-blue Prius that she'd parked in an open spot in front of his unit. She straightened and turned, a smile lighting her face. "Well, my wayward adventurer returns." She held up a cat carrier. "I've got your buddy."

"The door's unlocked. I'll be right there."

"Is it safe?"

"Sort of. I didn't get to the kitchen."

"Is the environmental hazard tape still up?"

"Jeez, it's not that bad. There's a bottle of chardonnay on the table. If you're hungry, there's cheese and some other stuff I picked up at the deli in the refrigerator."

Michelle looked in the cage, prompted by an impatient meow. "Well, this guy certainly is."

"He's always hungry."

He dumped the trash and jogged back up the stairs to find Michelle in the kitchen opening a can of cat food for the expectant Bill.

The cat fed, she stood and reached out her arms. "Okay, now give me a hug."

He wrapped his arms around her, relishing her warmth, the softness of her breasts, the scent of her perfume, the—

"God, Nick, you're cold."

He cast her a flirtatious glance. "Warm me up?"

Michelle gently disengaged herself and reached around for the wine opener. "Fat chance, bucko. Say 'hello' to your buddy while I pour some wine."

He looked down at Bill who'd been rubbing up against his right leg. He reached down and gave his cat a vigorous rub on the scruff of his neck. Apparently satisfied that the world had returned to its proper order, Bill trotted off to his favorite spot in the bedroom. "He didn't keep you up all night barfing hairballs, did he?"

"Nope, I spoiled him. He got brushed every day."

He edged toward her. "I could use some spoiling."

"You haven't been gone that long," she said handing him a glass of wine. "Tell me what you've been up to. I don't even know where you went."

He took the mild rebuff in stride and headed for the living room. "I've got something for you."

"Ooh, a surprise."

He handed her a small box wrapped in thin birch bark paper secured with a bow of hemp string.

"Nick, it's beautiful." She carefully untied the bow and opened her gift. "It's Hedwig."

"Who?"

"Terrible pun, Nick Parkos." She turned the carving of a great white snowy owl in her hand. "You know I love Harry Potter. It's his owl, Hedwig. Is it ivory?"

"Whale bone."

She threw her arms around his neck and kissed his cheek. "You went to Alaska? What on earth were you doing up there?"

"Can't say, but I did see a really cool shipwreck. A sailing ship from a doomed Canadian Arctic exploration, the *Karluk*."

"So, now you're a marine archeologist?"

"Hardly, but now that I think of it…"

"You're nuts."

"True enough." He changed the subject, "So what have you been up to besides watching Bill?"

"I've almost got enough hours for my associate degree from the Air Academy. I'm thinking of applying for the Airman Scholarship and Commissioning Program."

The news stunned Nick. *She's leaving?* "What's that?"

"If I'm accepted, I'll take a temporary leave of absence and go to a college that has an Air Force ROTC program. When I graduate, I'd be commissioned as a second lieutenant. The Air Force will pay for everything and even give me a stipend."

He pushed through the surge of anguish that washed over him. "What would you major in?"

"I'm not sure. I have to apply first but, I'd like to fly F-35s." She placed Hedwig back in his box. "A lot can happen."

He recovered enough to heft his glass while still trying to wrap is head around what she'd said. *A fighter pilot? Wow.* "Then here's to your success."

They spent the rest of their evening talking until Michelle set her glass down. "I've gotta go. Early wakeup. We have to prep Air Force One. The boss has places to go, people to see."

Exhausted himself, he was almost relieved. He saw her off with another hug and headed to his recliner. Bill appeared, jumped on his lap and soon both drifted off to sleep. And, unlike so many other nights, the nightmares didn't invade his slumber.

Chapter Twenty-One

NATIONAL COUNTERINTELLIGENCE CENTER
MCLEAN, VIRGINA
MONDAY 28 JANUARY

Two new index cards with the names, Lam Huifeng and Devon Gant, occupied prominent places on Nick's cork board. He'd added them despite his conflicted feelings about Lange. The guy's information was solid, but he sure could be a real pain-in-the-ass.

He hadn't found anything specific from his discreet inquiries to suggest Lange was anything more than he professed to be, an investigative reporter with a score to settle. He dwelled on the problem, concluding Lange just rubbed him the wrong way, but…

He glanced at his watch and eased back into his chair. Austin wasn't due for another twenty minutes. With luck, he'd have more on Huifeng.

He turned back to his computer and the five detailed spreadsheets and associated hyperlinks he'd spent the weekend creating. These new files incorporated the data from the Venn diagrams scattered across his desk and the maze of string and index cards pinned to the corkboard. The new data bases were clean, integrating assumptions with hard facts all set within the context of the broader issues at play. He wouldn't add Huifeng's name to the new spreadsheets until Austin confirmed Lange's findings.

He massaged his temples while reviewing the results filling the columns of his last spreadsheet. His eyes drifted to a framed scrap of yellow legal paper affixed above his desk. He read the quote he'd saved from his days as a criminology major at Ohio State.

Dans les champs de l'observation, le hasard ne favorise que l'esprits préparés.

In the fields of observation, chance favors only the prepared mind.

Louis Pasteur.

He set to work, Pasteur's words resonating. *Trust yourself. Trust your instincts. And get Lange out of your head.*

He compartmentalized his thoughts about Lange. He understood himself well enough to know that too much thought became an impediment, leaving him hesitant and too cautious about what he must do. But as Lange had suggested, he'd circled back to validate his presumptions.

A mouse click took him to one of the new file directories. He hit the print button, retrieved the copy from the tray, and laid it on his desk. Covered with algebraic expressions, the printout represented hours of work introducing multiple variables into a logic expression syntax.

Few in his department understood the power of those imports. They gave him the ability to reference external data and apply it to a variable, in this case, an assumption of motive. While there were still too many gaps in the sentinel logic operations he'd entered, they would help him prove or disprove the validity of his assumptions.

He nodded, pleased with the cryptic expressions detailing Devon Gant's motivations for approaching Moore. He picked up the phone, and playing a hunch, dialed his friend, Mark Arita, at the Treasury's Department of Terrorism and Financial Intelligence. Arita picked up on the second ring.

"Arita."

"Mark, this is Nick. Got a minute?"

"Ah… sure. What's on your mind?"

Humm, probably having a bad day. He dismissed the hesitance in Arita's response. "Have you been following the Russian and Chinese backed companies bidding for Emmons-Powell Mining?" He knotted his eyebrows, his instincts alerted when another pause ensued. *What the hell? Is there something going on I don't know about?*

"Ah, yeah. I've talked to Austin several times about Olympic's bid, but we only touched on the Russians. I really haven't kept up. Should I?"

"We have to stop them. If either of their proxies acquires that company, they'll control almost our entire supply of rare-earth elements."

"Oh? What do you have?"

He again detected something in the tone of Arita's guarded reply. He replied simply. "Questions."

"I'll bite. What are they?"

"For starters, I need to know if the Emmons-Powell takeover is being addressed by CFIUS."

"Funny you should ask. I don't know the specifics, but something crossed my desk yesterday about possible malfeasance by a company named Trident Metallurgics. What struck me was how a small Utah startup could come up with the funding, let alone engage a big D.C. law firm to represent them."

"Do you know the source?

"What? Who reported the issue?"

"Yes."

"The name in the memo was redacted."

"Are you on secure voice?"

"No."

He paused to consider the risk, then asked. "Do you know Devon Gant?"

"Gant? Not personally. He's one of the senior staffers for the Secretary. What does—?"

"I'd rather not go into details on the phone." Gant wasn't simply a mid-level guy as Lange had implied. A senior staffer would have access to very sensitive information. This changed the playing field. Lange needed to contact this guy if he hadn't already done so. "You free Wednesday night? Say about seven. The Cork and Barrel?"

"Hang on a sec," Arita said. After a moment he added, "Yeah, that should work."

"Thanks, Mark. See you then."

He hung up and stared into space, disturbed at what he sensed, an underlying unease in Arita's guarded responses, his friend's hesitance. It wasn't like him. *What's going on?* He straightened in his chair, recalling an aphorism once quoted by his criminology professor: *Don't believe everything you think.*

He shook his head, determined not to become a brooding specter, suspicious of every shadow. *Stop it! He's my friend. What the hell's wrong with me?* He checked the time. Austin would show in a few minutes. He decided to open the online version of *The Washington Post* on the chance something might catch his eye. He didn't make it past the front page.

Prominent D.C. Lawyer Murdered. The front-page header was accompanied by a blurry black and white security camera image of the suspected assailant. The headline and picture weren't what drew him in, though. The name of the lawyer did. Dexter Merriman.

Merriman was...*or had been*...a founding member of the

Firm of Duxtun, Luwan and Merriman. Merriman also happened to be the lawyer representing Trident Metallurgic's bid to acquire Emmons-Powell Mining.

"Whoa."

He studied the image of the alleged assailant. Hoodie, dark pants, sneakers. Look like expensive Air Jordan's. Face not visible. The perp appeared to be running down N Street, presumably after exiting the parking garage where Merriman's body was discovered. Not much to go on.

He re-read the article stopping at a quote by the D.C. Police Chief. "This tragic event was likely a random attack, but we are exploring all possibilities." He didn't believe in coincidences. *No way.* He pulled up a map on his computer detailing recent crimes in the area and located the law firm's location in a safe neighborhood near Dupont Circle. *Random? On a Sunday? Hell. This was a hit.*

"You ready for me?"

He responded to Austin's voice without looking up. "Come on in." He pointed to the *Post*'s headline before Austin even settled into a chair. "They're playing hardball. The lead lawyer for Trident Metallurgics was murdered last night."

"Yeah, I saw that. I take it, you don't believe in coincidences."

He set the paper aside and spun around. "Nope. My bet is the Chinese are sending a message. That, and they want to disrupt NBG's acquisition of Emmons-Powell while they pursue their own bid. Merriman also had his hand in facilitating Trident's financing with the Swiss investment fund, Innovel Venture Capital."

"You have anything hard connecting the murder to Beijing?"

"I'm going with my gut."

Austin noted the corkboard. "And your maze?"

"That too. So, what do you have?"

"More for your maze. Names, places of work, even Uber receipts."

He forgot about Merriman and reached for his pile of blank index cards. "You've got something on Huifeng?"

"Sure do. His name appeared several times when I ran it through our data bases. I asked the Tailored Access Operation Group's ANT… ah, their Advanced Network Technology Division to see what they had on their PRISM and X-Keystone intercepts. They linked him with Olympic, the Pan American Development Bank, Shanghai Venture Capital Fund, and Pacific Commodity Consultants, Ltd out of Hong Kong."

"You'd think he'd be more careful."

"Perhaps, but there are a couple of things to consider. Olympic hasn't made any secret of their intentions and judging from the number of intercepts, Huifeng may be having a problem with his Shanghai Venture Capital Fund."

He digested this information before going back to what Austin first voiced. "You said names."

"I came up with something while doing a bit of detective work. I got to wondering if Huifeng uses Uber."

"You found receipts?"

Austin smiled. "Sure did. To and from the Chinese embassy. An address in Georgetown. 1330 Prospect Street. I did a quick search of the city's property taxes and got the owner's name. James Wai."

Wai! Did his associate just break open his case? He rocked back in his chair. "My God, Austin. That's incredible work. Do you think Wai is his real name or an alias?"

"Don't know, but it's a starting point. Looked him up on social media. He's not very active. I did confirm he's first generation Chinese from San Francisco. Graduated from Georgetown a few years ago with a degree in engineering. I couldn't find any record of employment."

"I don't suppose his name appeared in Beijing's list of students in their Student and School Association?"

"I have to see if we even have access to that information. Besides, he's an American citizen. Why would they list him?"

"If Beijing paid for his education or has something on his parents, they'll be keeping tabs on him and want something in return. Those homes in Georgetown don't come cheap. Who holds the mortgage?"

"There isn't one."

"And he doesn't have any record of employment? Somebody had to have paid for that place."

"I'll keep digging."

He wrote a note to himself. "I'll give Jessica a call and see what the FBI can do. Maybe get a copy of his tax returns and utility bills. I just need to find a pretext to have them both placed under surveillance. Huifeng shouldn't be a problem since he's a Chinese national."

"And if you can't get a warrant to watch Wai?"

"I may have to get creative." He stood and pinned two new index cards on this board: James Wai and 1330 Prospect Street.

Chapter Twenty-Two

CENTRAL INTELLIGENCE AGENCY
LANGLEY, VIRGINA
WEDNESDAY 30 JANUARY

Nick crossed the parking lot of the CIA's headquarters building in Langley. His confident stride belied a certain perturbation and ambivalence about meeting with Taylor Ferguson. He slowed, pondering how he'd react when he saw the agent again. The antipathy he felt toward the man, whose support he'd grudgingly accepted during the al-Khultyer affair, underpinned these mixed feelings. At best, he found the man egotistical and abrasive. A probable narcissist. Ferguson also operated under a set of rules Nick didn't fully understand but would soon have to learn.

He drew a deep breath before passing under the massive wing-shaped porte-cochere designed to soften the façade of the five-story building and perhaps to offer a degree of blast protection. He made his way around the CIA seal set in the marble floor of the main lobby stopping at the security desk. The Guards verified his ID and directed him to a passageway leading to the Center for Cyber Intelligence.

A small brass plate affixed on the wall next to a closed door identified his destination. He gave a knock. No response. *More mind games?* He swallowed his anger and knocked again.

"Enter."

Ferguson didn't bother to stand, instead he tossed an impudent wave at a chair. "I've got to admit, I'm surprised to see you."

He bit back the rejoinder that sprang to his mind, and took a seat. "I don't have much choice."

"So, it appears. But then, you should always leave yourself a way out."

He cast his eyes around the sparse room. The furnishings were utilitarian. Several framed certificates hung on the walls, their contents obscured by the harsh glare reflecting back from the room's florescent lights.

His eyes returned to Ferguson, studying, weighing him. He'd changed since the last time their paths crossed. The agent's eyes gave away nothing, but his cheeks sagged in querulous discontent. His loosely-knotted tie, looking vaguely like a hangman's noose, was slung to one side of his wrinkled shirt.

"I understood you were given the lead for my SIM card."

"Coffee?" Ferguson answered.

A peace offering? "Yeah, thanks."

At one level, he could understand Ferguson's appearance and attitude. He'd likely been hung out to dry by the Agency after the operation he led went sideways. His loss of containment of the supposed CIA asset, Bashir al-Khultyer, resulted in multiple innocent deaths and his own subsequent involvement to find and eradicate the terrorist. He accepted the cup and took a sip, trying to mask a grimace. It was hideous.

"Your phone was hacked," Ferguson said, ignoring the look on Nick's face. "I won't go into details, but we followed the digital trail to the Chinese."

"How? I use *WhatsApp* to encrypt my messages."

"You and millions of others. Your phone runs on Google's Android. Right?"

He didn't respond. He had no idea.

"The Chinese are able to hack into this operating system and intercept an iPhone's audio and text messages before they can be encrypted. They're also capable of exploiting that data and avoid detection bypassing commercially available anti-virus software."

He had read accounts of this activity. *But how'd they know to go after me? They…*

Ferguson intruded into his thoughts. "I've got something else for you courtesy of your agency's Tailored Access Operations group." He opened a manila folder and extracted an intelligence assessment. "The name Lam Huifeng mean anything to you?"

His eyes widened in surprise. His coffee cup halted halfway to his lips.

"Thought so. We ran our own background and linked him to the Ministry of State Security's department which manages the front companies for elicit ventures. Got an address for him too—Interested?"

"*Interested* is one word that comes to mind. I've got the address. How did you know about him?"

"We've been collaborating with the TAO after an anonymous group of security researchers —"

"Hackers?"

"I prefer the term, researchers. In any event, they dumped a shitload of stuff in a series of blogs that unmasked the Chinese-based actors linked to the PLA's Unit 61396 and their state-sponsored hackers who are targeting U.S. companies to secure bid prices, contracts, and information on mergers and acquisitions. After the exposé, their APT3-based company went dark—Advanced Persistent Threat. Their high-level APT-10 software, code-named Stone Panda, is still active."

"You've linked these agencies to Consolidated Seabed Resources and Olympic Industries?"

"And their front companies. We detected several attempted intrusions by the Chinese into Eagle River, LCC's computers using Stone Panda. We haven't made a firm connection yet, but it appears they've also been snooping around a local business called Creekside Consultants. I don't know if there's a direct link to the other attacks."

His forced his expression to remain impassive. At least the CIA didn't know of the FBI's sting operation at Creekside and the existence of Darrell Nance. He didn't volunteer what he knew, but he did have to find out what the CIA knew about the FBI's operation. "How'd you know about Eagle River?"

"Come on, Nick. Your boss chairs the Intelligence Community's Joint Working Group. We've also been collaborating with the Defense Intelligence Agency. They're not very happy about the Chinese snooping around the proposed Ballistic Missile Early Warning System site at Cape Lisburne, not to mention their submarine operations in the Arctic."

"I'll give you that but you said *attempted* to access Eagle River."

"Firewalls stopped them. The TAO shared their information with me. Turns out the Chinese were uncharacteristically sloppy. We're looking to prosecute a vulnerability we found in their network using data we recovered from the attempted intrusion. The plan is to remotely insert our own advanced exploits into their system. We have a good IP address we believe is linked to Huifeng. We should be able to get in and out of their network without them having a clue we've been there."

"You're going to set a counter-operation and plant false information?"

"No reason why not. It'll take some time, though."

He pulled back, suspicion clouding his eyes, questions whirling through his head. Austin didn't even know about the attempted intrusions and the counter-operations. Too many agencies had their hands in his operation. Too many people he couldn't control. Too many loose ends. *There had to be someone pulling the strings. Lange? No, impossible. Who's trying to undercut me? How are the Chinese managing to stay one step ahead of me? Could they have someone on the inside assisting them? Gant might be one. Moore another. Were there others?* He made a rash decision without weighing the possible consequences. "I don't have time. I need to break into that home."

"What home?"

"Huifeng's. He's got to have something in there we can use."

Ferguson sat back. "This isn't like the movies. Why not get a warrant and leave it to the experts, the FBI? You've worked with the Special Operations guys before and know the drill. People can lose their lives."

He gripped the arms of his chair. "I've got my reasons."

The expression on Ferguson's face gave nothing away. "Word gets around."

He paused, his intuition told him they'd crossed a threshold. Ferguson understood, probably reminded that his own operation had been undercut and that he'd taken the fall. Perhaps, he too, is haunted by past memories and looking to atone. "I'm confident any words from this meeting won't travel."

To his credit, Ferguson didn't equivocate. "I gotta admit, you don't seem to be lacking in temerity. All right, tell me, what do you know about surreptitious entry? Anything?" He proceeded to pepper Nick with terms determined to shake his confidence. "How about flaps and seals? Pocket litter? Back-stopping?"

He didn't respond.

"These crafts take years to perfect and a lot of resources. What makes you so sure you can pull off this crazy stunt of yours?"

"I don't have a choice."

"I'm not so sure," Ferguson said. He gave his head a laconic shake, then acquiesced. "I'll set you up with some former associates. They can give you a primer on the basic techniques: lock picking, disabling alarm systems, reconnoitering, how to case a place without leaving traces of entry."

"I appreciate it."

"You may not."

Chapter Twenty-Three

THE CORK AND BARREL
ALEXANDRIA, VIRGINA
WEDNESDAY 30 JANUARY

Nick brightened at the sight of his friend from Treasury, Mark Arita. His meeting earlier in the day with Ferguson had gone well enough, but the ordeal had left him drained.

Arita waved his arm in welcome, beckoning him toward the corner table he had secured in the crowded bar. Nick smiled and tossed a wave in return. He worked his way around the Cork and Barrel's tables and pulled up a chair facing the interior of the room. He slipped off his coat and hung it over the chair while scanning the customers. Nobody looked suspicious and he'd taken a circuitous route to the meeting. The site was clean.

"Pour you a beer? You look like you could use one." Arita picked up a pitcher and filled an empty glass mug without waiting for an answer. "As we used to say during my Navy days, 'The drinking lamp is lit.'"

"Thanks. I think."

"You can't pass on the IPA. Local stuff. They named it Hopping Mad. Clever name and I'll tell ya, this brew packs a punch." Arita topped off his own mug, then pushed a red-plastic basket of fried onion rings across the table. "You'll want something in your stomach."

He took a sip. He wasn't much of a beer drinker but found this one surprising good. "Hey, this is pretty tasty. I'll buy the next round." He grabbed an onion ring from the basket and bit off a chunk. Across the tiny dance floor, a four-person band was setting up in the adjacent corner. He didn't recognize the group, but their instruments included a bass fiddle and a banjo. Bluegrass. Michelle had introduced him to the genre and, much to his surprise, he liked the sound. The other positive? Their music would mask his and Mark's conversation. He faced Arita. "Thanks for meeting me."

"You kidding? I'm open to any excuse to come here." Arita glanced at the musicians who'd begun testing their sound system. "So, what's so important besides the music and beer?"

He leaned forward to make himself heard. "The Chinese. They've ramped up their efforts to acquire Emmons-Powell. I think they're behind the murder of that lawyer in Dupont Circle last Sunday."

"Murder? I missed that. Who?"

"A lawyer representing Trident Metallurgics was gunned down in his firm's garage."

"A hit?"

"That's what my gut's telling me."

Arita took a slow bite out of an onion ring. "If you can tie the Chinese to the murder, that'd be significant, but why would they contract a hit? From what I've seen, their proposals to acquire the company and the mineral rights appear above board. Why kill the guy?"

"*Appear* is the operative word. They may be getting desperate to close the deal and aren't happy with the competition especially since an American company called Eagle River has just thrown their hat into the ring."

"I saw that," Arita said.

"It's a false-front op."

Arita rocked back in his chair. "No shit."

"Yeah, no shit. We decided to provide a little competition to smoke out the bad actors."

"Where does Devon Grant fit?"

"How 'bout we start with his connection to CFIUS?"

"You know, CFIUS is a complete dinosaur," Arita said. "If you're counting on that committee to stop the acquisition, I'd be looking for someplace else to place your money."

He stiffened, caught off balance by the revelation. "Really?"

"The way the current charter is written, foreign companies can exploit gaps in the committee's review process. The most egregious example is when the Russians managed to corral a big chunk of our uranium ore supply a few years back. Secretary Lum has submitted a draft proposal addressing the most glaring deficiencies. If it's passed, CFIUS's jurisdiction will be expanded to include joint ventures and sales of minority stakes that would culminate in a majority ownership by… but you know this stuff."

He swirled his beer and set down the mug. "So, I shouldn't count on anything being accomplished in my lifetime?"

"Don't be so gloomy. The proposals have actually worked their way through a bipartisan Congressional working committee and should be on the House floor for a vote before too long."

"That could be why my source was approached and told he might want to have an off-the-record talk with Gant."

"What does Gant have that's so important?"

He ran his finger through a wet ring left by the beer mug. "Insider information about possible malfeasance by Trident."

"And you have the particulars?" Arita asked.

"At the top of my list is the involvement of the hidden partner, the NBG."

"The Russians are trying another end-around play?"

"No doubt. My guess is he might have information that implicates senior officials at Treasury, State, or Interior that could expose favoritism, kickbacks, threats to reveal something unsavory."

Arita looked skeptical. "What's in it for Gant?"

"Presuming the Chinese haven't threatened him, and that's a big *if*, the usual. A self-motived insider looking to expose corruption, MICE—"

"Mice?"

"Shorthand for Money, Ideology, Compromise, Ego." All reasons for someone to want to have a talk with an investigative reporter."

"Your confidential source?"

"Yeah."

"You think Gant found something on his own or are the Chinese feeding him? Using him as a conduit for a misinformation campaign?"

He was grateful Arita didn't push to learn Lange's name, but why did he feel he was being interrogated. *What had Lange said? 'If it feels wrong, it is wrong.'* Another aphorism off his list of Moscow Rules. "Could be both," he answered. "If there are others involved on our side, I'm thinking we could use Gant to smoke them out."

Arita appeared to study him while he downed the last of his Hoppin Mad. "I appreciate what you've told me, Nick. But I need more before I can go to my boss. Has your source set up a meeting with Gant?"

Damn. He pursed his lips and leaned back in his chair. "Not yet."

"Does your guy have a relationship with the FBI?"

He replied with more certainty than he felt. "No."

"That would make it tough to use anything he provides to

justify a formal investigation. I doubt the Secretary would approve an investigation based on what you've given me so far. Have you talked to Jessica?"

"Yes, but not about Gant. She's working another aspect of my investigation." He waited for Arita to ask what that might be, but Arita responded with a nod.

The band's banjo player and fiddler rolled into a new number, Earl Scruggs' "*Foggy Mountain Breakdown,*" a real toe-tapper that charged the bar's atmosphere. He couldn't help but relax and smile at one of his favorites. He suppressed his concerns about Arita, emptied the remainder of the pitcher into his mug, and waved over their waiter to order another. "That's enough business. I'd say it's time to let our hair down."

He called it quits after the band's second set and their second pitcher of Hopping Mad. "Gotta go. Long day tomorrow. I'd appreciate any help you can give me."

"Sure thing," Arita said.

"I'll be in touch." He pushed away from the table, took a step, stumbled over the leg of his chair, managed to collect himself, and made his way for the door without looking back.

———

Intent on negotiating his way outside without wobbling, Nick failed to notice two other patrons who'd been sitting at different tables watching him. The first, the short-haired brunette from the Upper Crust, paid her tab and followed Nick. She had taken a series of pictures of Nick and Arita to pass along to her contact.

The other patron wiped the beer off his beard with the back of his hand and

pulled his Baltimore Raven's ballcap down over his forehead. He waited a moment, then made for the door, and trailed the brunette down the sidewalk.

Chapter Twenty-Four

THE WHITE HOUSE
WASHINGTON, D.C.
TUESDAY 5 FEBRUARY

Mike Rohrbaugh made his way across the street between his office in the Executive Office Building and the White House not knowing what to expect. The late-afternoon summons from Justin Brown puzzled him since they were on tap for a scheduled meeting the next morning. Perhaps Justin wanted to clarify a discussion point, but why not call? He worked his way through the narrow corridors of the West Wing to Brown's corner office and rapped on the door before entering.

"I didn't take you away from anything important, did I?" Brown asked.

"Nothing that can't wait." He settled into one of the office's black-leather chairs. "What's on your mind?"

Brown rested his hands on the desk's blotter. "We may have a situation. Bryce called with some unsetting news concerning Nick."

The statement stunned him. *Had Nick gotten in trouble with his drinking? I thought he'd been doing better. A DWI? No, hardly something to bother the DNI or NSA about.* Brown's appearance further unsettled him as did the inflection in his voice. Small lines of worry edged the NSA's eyes and he sounded subdued, both unlike him. "What's happened?"

"For starters, Nick's supervisor received a letter from a credit agency saying Nick overspent the limit of his credit card and hasn't responded to their collection efforts."

"I can't see how that would warrant your attention, Justin. How much are we talking about?"

"The card's limit is twenty-thousand dollars," Brown replied.

He gave a soft whistle. "I know for a fact Nick doesn't spend that kind of money. Hell, he still wears his clothes from college and drives a beat-up Ford Escape. I'm sure there's a plausible explanation. Did the credit agency say what he spent the money on?"

"We pressed them. Mostly electronics."

"I've been in his condo. The place looks like he furnished it from a Goodwill store. If he's bought a lot of gadgets, I have no idea what he would have done with them. Identity theft?"

"That was my first thought, but that's only part of the problem. Because of his security clearance, Bryce directed Nick's supervisor to make a discreet inquiry to Treasury's Financial Crimes Enforcement Department. They're still investigating, but the inquiry triggered a red flag for a possible violation of the Foreign Account Compliance Act. Bryce contacted me after he received a copy of their Suspicious Activities Report. The SAR suggested Nick may be concealing income from an off-shore account."

"Off-shore account? Why would…? Damn." He rocked back in his chair, staggered by the implications. "I don't believe it. Nick's rock solid."

"The personal information on the credit card, including an address for a vacant building in Wilmington, Delaware matches that of an individual with an offshore account in the Cayman Islands. The Foreign Account Compliance Act mandates that a financial institution report any income obtained by an American citizen from an offshore account. To make a long story short, they're waiting to see if Nick reports this income on his 1040."

"Then I'd say he's been compromised. Nick's specialty is transnational organized crime. There's no way he'd make a stupid mistake." He ticked off the reasons on his fingers. "First, he'd use a tax haven in the British Virgin Islands that'd bypass our financial reporting laws. Second, he'd launder any illicit income by purchasing bearer bonds through a shell company. Why he'd—"

Brown raised a quizzical eyebrow.

"He told me once how the smart guys hide their money to evade detection."

"I see."

"Who else knows?" he asked, undeterred by the skeptical note in Brown's voice.

"Mark Arita. He works at Treasury. Knows Nick. Bryce asked him to see what he could find out."

"You mean spy on his friend?" His face reddened. "That's pure crap."

"Not if he can prove Nick's been set up."

"Are you going to recommend we put Nick on ice while this plays out?"

"I haven't decided."

Mike gathered his thoughts. "Perhaps we give the appearance that he's been placed on administrative leave? Maybe even arrested?"

Brown jotted a note to himself on a legal pad. "That's worth considering."

"I—"

Brown popped out of his chair. "Mr. President."

Mike moved a bit slower, not wanting to ram his chair into

the boss. Brown gave him a subtle shake of his head. He returned an affirming nod

"I'm not interrupting anything important?" Stuart asked.

"No, sir," Brown replied, his response more guarded than he let on. The president didn't just wander around. He had something on his mind. "We were just going over a talking point for tomorrow's meeting."

Stuart dropped into the empty chair beside Mike. "Sheldon tells me China's icebreaker, the *Snow Dragon*, returned to Shanghai after completing another series of bathometric surveys north of the Bering Strait. There's no mystery as to their intent.

"We need an effective strategy to counter them and the Russians. Bryce just gave me a thumbnail and should have his recommendations to me later this week from the intelligence community's Arctic Working Group and the Arctic Executive Steering Committee. Sheldon and Bob are working their pieces at the Pentagon."

Mike agreed, recalling what he'd read in a recent Special Operations Command report. Both the Chinese and the Russians were using a combination of overt and covert operations in the Arctic, both characterized by ambiguity and misdirection to disguise the true intent of their actions. He'd like nothing better than to give them both a dose of their own medicine.

"I don't want them interfering with the activation of our BMEWS site at Cape Lisburne," Stuart continued. "And, Mike, they can't be permitted to get their hands on those rare-earth elements you and Nick saw off the coast." He faced Brown. "Justin, work with Dan and draft a Presidential Determination document for my signature. I want this on the record."

"Yes, sir."

"I'd prefer not to militarize the region, but I may not have any another options. That said, Parkos needs to keep digging and come up with a way to stop them. My Executive Order should have cleared the way for him. See if he needs anything."

"I'll touch base with him this afternoon," Mike answered.

"Good." Stuart pushed himself out of the chair and made his way down the hall toward the oval office.

"Well, that takes care of our question," Brown said. "We need to keep Nick active. I also happen to agree with you. He's been set up. But for now, I think it's best not to inform the president."

Mike made to protest, but Brown held up his hand. "My call. The president has enough on his plate. Unless Treasury comes up with something hard, we need to watch Nick's back. I'll call Bryce and Clarence Lum at Treasury and tell them to lay down some covering smoke."

"Think I should give Nick a head's up?"

Brown gave his bowtie a thoughtful pull. "No, I don't think so. Whoever's behind this could pick up a change in his behavior."

"Good point. I'll keep tabs on him to make sure he stays out of trouble."

Chapter Twenty-Five

113 TAMARIND COURT
GREENBELT, MARYLAND
WEDNESDAY 13 FEBRUARY

Nick cast an absent look out the streaked window of their commandeered utility truck, intent on reviewing what he'd been taught by Taylor Ferguson's former associates. The passing houses held little interest. He glanced at the driver. The guy's body language discouraged conversation and his expression, hidden behind a thick beard and a black Baltimore Raven's ballcap, betrayed nothing of his thoughts. The white truck, embossed with the blue and white logo of Greenbelt, Maryland's electric company would not betray the nature of their mission.

The bearded driver, Nick's controller, crunched to a stop in a dirty-gray drift of snow before a modest two-story duplex. He could only conclude that George, as his controller called himself, had picked the unassuming target at the end of a quiet cul-de-sac at random.

A burst of nervous energy coursed through his body, the incipient danger charging him. He felt alive, released from the self-imposed pedantic routine of his office. Then again, he reminded himself, this was only a test to assess his aptitude, his powers of observation and reaction to stress. If the target of their exercise had an active security system, they would choose another.

"What do you see?" George said.

He considered the scene. There didn't appear to be anything that would put them at risk. "Seems quiet enough. Nobody appears to be home in the adjoining unit." He twisted his head around to survey both sides of the street, empty except for a forlorn car with an iced windshield. The tree-lined neighborhood northeast of D.C. would ordinarily have been a picture of suburban serenity but not today. "Same with the neighborhood."

"I agree. Let's get movin'."

He avoided the front door, averting his face as he'd been taught, and approached the side entrance where there was less chance of encountering a doorbell cam. He slipped on a pair of blue latex painter's gloves and made a pretense of checking the electric meter.

"Anyone home?" George asked.

He peered through the door's windowpanes into the kitchen, knocked, then gave the door knob a twist hoping there wasn't a dog. He exhaled in relief. No dog.

"Security system?" George asked.

"I didn't see a key code box or any motion sensors."

"Good. I'll work the lock," George said. "Keep an eye on the street." A moment later he added, "We're in."

He threw a final look at the forlorn car, then followed his controller into the condo. He closed the door and proceeded across the kitchen.

"Damn it, Parkos! Watch your feet."

He glanced at his feet. He'd left a trail of wet footprints across the tiled floor.

George pointed to the counter. "Grab some paper towels

and clean up that mess. And don't throw them in the trash. Stuff 'em in your pockets. You've got five minutes."

He cleaned the floor and wiped off the soles of his shoes, stuffing the dirty Scott towels in a pocket while he scanned the kitchen. Rack of gourmet olive oils. Expensive knives. Espresso machine. *A cook.*

A small pile of mail on the counter attracted his attention. Water bill, bank and credit card statements, February issue of *Cosmopolitan.* The name on each of the address labels was the same: Kimberly Browning.

He made his way upstairs to the bedrooms. The one on the left had been turned into an office. He chose the other. Feminine decor, but not ostentatious. The bed was made, no cloths strewn about. A copy of *Women Who Run with the Wolves* lay on her bedside table. The absence of any family pictures caught his attention. Estranged? He looked at the dresser and decided not to go through drawers that would hold the woman's bras and panties. Just too weird. He crossed the room to the closet, slid open the door, and began to sort through her clothes.

She was a professional of some sort. Maybe worked for some law firm in D.C.. Next, the top shelf. Several hat boxes occupied the right side. On the left, stood a Styrofoam mannequin head topped by a dark-blue wig with light-blue and pink highlights. *Maybe she led a different life outside the office?*

He stood on his toes, stretching to snag one of the hat boxes. His fingertips inched it toward the edge. The box tipped, then toppled, the lid falling to the floor. He managed to catch the container, startled by its weight. He peered inside. *Whoa. A Barretta.*

The weapon hadn't been cared for. He lifted the pistol by its trigger guard, set the safety, unchambered a round, then pressed the release for the clip. The loaded magazine fell heavily into his hand. *God, if this thing had hit the floor...*

He left the safety on, stuffed the single round in his pocket, re-inserted the clip, and slid the hatbox back onto the shelf before exiting the bedroom for the bathroom. There were no prescription medicines. Several bottles of Joe Malone perfume were arranged on the left side of the vanity. Expensive stuff. He resisted the temptation to take a sniff and went to her office.

An iMac, phone charger, and a combination printer/copy machine were arranged across a narrow table behind the desk. A sheaf of papers stuffed into the slot of a shredding machine caught his eye. He pulled them out. *What the hell?*

The top page of the first was embossed with the letterhead of the Interior Department's Offshore Energy and Mineral Management Service. *Holy shit! This is a list of counter points to Austin's Eagle River's submission.*

The next sheet of paper was nothing but short sentences of gibberish. He picked one out at random. "You can't vada my eek. I ain't gonna squeak no palaver." He shook his head, set it aside, and scanned the third, then another.

He spread the pages across the desktop, stunned at what he'd found, then extracted a digital camera from his coat pocket, and aimed. Centered in the viewfinder was a copy of Consolidated Seabed Resource's offshore site assessment plan for a mining operation off Cape Lisburne. He moved on and snapped a picture of the second document stamped 'DRAFT', a request to designate Consolidated's bid for the offshore mining rights as non-competitive. Next, a marked-up copy of a National Environmental Protection Act analysis of the Alaskan coast off Cape Lisburne. The last, a copy of the NOAA report about the rare-earth nodules discovered by the *Healy's* scientists. *How'd she get a copy of that? Hell, I haven't even seen one.*

"We gotta go," George said through the open door.

"Hang on, I've found something."

George held his tongue, but the pucker between his eyebrows betrayed his annoyance.

"I don't have time to explain. Get downstairs and open those bank and credit card statements in the kitchen. Copy the details. Here, use this." He tossed the digital camera toward the open door.

George snatched the camera out of the air and disappeared down the stairs.

He turned his attention back to the documents and returned them to the shredder's slot, making sure he didn't activate the machine. His hand hesitated on the sheaf. He pulled out the document labeled DRAFT, folded it, and slid the evidence into his pocket hoping the woman wouldn't notice its absence.

His eyes drifted to the computer then, on a hunch, opened the desk drawers and pawed through the contents hoping to find her username and password. No luck. *Could we risk coming back here with a flash drive to copy the contents or could Ferguson's people do that remotely?*

George's voice boomed from the bottom of the stairs. "Parkos! Come on. We gotta get the hell out of here."

"Okay. Okay. I'm coming…" His voiced trialed off as his eyes fell on the trashcan tucked under the desk. *Now, what could this be?*

He reached in and pulled out a sheet of paper that had been compressed into a tight, angry ball. He pried it open and smoothed out the creases. His eye's widened as he read the contents.

He peeled off his left glove, grabbed a pen from the desk, and jotted down a name and phone number on his palm. The number looked familiar but the name didn't. Puzzled, he wadded up the note in his fist and dropped it back in the can. He spun on his heel. Time to bail before his luck ran out.

———

What were the odds of picking out a random duplex in Greenbelt and finding all this stuff? Probably way worse than winning the Mega Millions lottery.

"What'd you find up there?" George said eyeing the sheet of paper Nick had pulled out his pocket.

"Best you don't know."

He slid the paper under his coat and slammed the passenger door closed. He caught a final glimpse of the street through the side mirror before George pulled around the corner. Something else didn't feel right, but he couldn't place his finger on what disturbed him. He returned to the supposed random choice of Browning's condo. Could Ferguson have his hand in this? What if he knew about her but couldn't obtain a warrant? *Damn, is he using me again?*

He cast a surreptitious glance at George out of the corner of his eye. George appeared to be studying him, but his handler apparently knew enough not to press. That helped but who could he confide? His supervisor? Strickland had no idea what he'd just done, let alone signing off on this crazy stunt. Furthermore, he had no cover.

What he'd just done could get him thrown in jail if they'd been caught. Which raised another problem. Without a search warrant, his information would be thrown out in court or found inadmissible in a Grand Jury investigation. And why would a judge even consider issuing a warrant obtained by an illegal search. "Crap."

George shot him a flint-eyed look. "What's going on?"

"Nothing."

He slumped down in his seat brooding over his options. Ferguson was bound to learn he'd found something. That prospect didn't appeal to him, but then the asshole might be able to provide some ideas about how to proceed. *How about Lange?* Reporters are always using nonattributable sources and then claim confidentiality if pressured to divulge the name of their source. *I'll contact him.*

The decision to meet with Lange solved his immediate problem. The larger one remained. Who was Kimberly Browning and where did she fit? He held no doubt that she was channeling stuff to the Chinese. But why? Had they threatened her? That might explain the gun. And were there others in Huifeng's network he didn't know about. With what he'd discovered in that duplex, there had to be. The next question? How to flush them out?

Chapter Twenty-Six

NATIONAL COUNTERINTELLIGENCE CENTER
MCLEAN, VIRGINIA
THURSDAY 14 FEBRUARY

Nick screwed up his lips in frustration. *Too sappy.* Then again, he rationalized, Michelle's calming influence in his life had provided the stability that kept him grounded. And she'd given him support to stop his abuse of OxyContin. How could these few awkward sentences express his feelings?

He leaned back in the chair, pondering what he'd written on the Valentine card. He'd overstepped. Made presumptions. A dozen red roses and dinner reservations at her favorite restaurant. With all this stuff, she may... *Crap, I'll probably send her running for the hills and that'll be it for us. Fini. Kaput. Finalle. Pau. Done.*

Then, again, the Air Force could make the decision about their future relationship for him. Michelle's orders were pending. Her next duty station could be Joint Base Pearl Harbor-Hickam where personnel assigned to the Presidential Air Crew often rotated. But the odds favored her heading off to college ...wherever that would be.

His divorce weighed heavily on his mind. He and Marty had married young, right after graduating from Ohio State. The transition from the carefree life of college students to the responsibilities of adulthood hadn't worked out well for either of them. Remarkably, they'd remained in contact over the ensuing years, their seven-year old daughter, Emma, playing a large role, their divorce more or less amicable.

He fingered Michelle's Valentine card recalling his last conversation with Marty. "'Are you nuts?'" she'd said. "'Michelle's totally in love with you. Women can sense these things. Don't blow it.'" He sighed. He couldn't sense much of anything when it came to women, most of all what they were thinking. The fact that Marty even knew about Michelle was really creepy. *Of course.* They had talked after he'd been shot.

What insight he had into his own capricious behavior and what he soon planned to do urged him to exercise caution. He couldn't drag Michelle any further into his screwed-up life, despite the major points he scored with Hedwig the owl. He set the card aside, placing it on top of the one addressed to his daughter and turned his attention back to business.

He also couldn't afford to place Austin in a compromised position within the Agency by telling him about the break-in of Kimberly Browning's duplex. If his own actions were discovered and he was reprimanded, or worse, fired, Austin would be provided the cover of plausible deniability.

With that decision made, he turned his attention to Mike's call the previous week. A meeting with Justin Brown on tap for the coming Monday topped his 'to do' list. He jotted down a note to notify Strickland. Mike had also asked if he needed any additional resources which he'd declined without elaborating. He already had more than enough *help* cluttering his investigation and his mind. His preference remained to keep those few he had to rely on, and those whose motives he didn't entirely trust, at arm's length. There were a few notable exceptions including his assistant who, at that moment, announced his arrival.

"One down. One to go," Austin said.

He scrunched up his face consternation. "What are you talking about?"

Austin pulled up a chair, his eyes falling on the cards. "The Russians appear to be self-destructing. At this rate, I doubt they'll be able to continue their efforts to acquire Emmons-Powell."

He turned Michelle's card upside down. "What makes you think that?"

"I'll start with their two major players in Moscow. You'll recognize the name of the first guy. Vladimir Suslova, NBG oligarch and a member of President Srevnenko's inner circle. The second is Sergey Nikolaev, chairman of Bank Rossiya. Nikolaev has been charged with trying to bribe Suslova."

"How much?"

"Something in the neighborhood of sixty-million rubles."

"About a million bucks. Too low. That would be an acceptable amount to entice a provincial governor, but not a member of Srevnenko's inner circle. Nikolaev should have known better."

"You'd think, but it was enough to be considered an act of provocation against a State official. He's been placed under house arrest," Austin replied.

"That's the pretense. My bet is he's been set up. My sources in Moscow say Nikolaev threatened to create *obstacles* for the NBG when Suslova approved the purchase of a fifty-percent stake in another State controlled mineral company."

"Hedging his bets?"

"Yup. And Nikolaev made another mistake by failing to observe the accepted rules of service to the State. That made him enemies. He's become an embarrassment."

"You think Suslova leveraged his connections within the FSB for his power play?"

"No doubt. We know there's been an ongoing struggle pitting State control against privatization and personal enrichment. I suspect Suslova is trying to preserve the precarious balance of power of the various factions within the Kremlin as well as his own position within Srevnenko's inner circle by eliminating Nikolaev."

"You think he would have concluded there's too much risk in continuing to back Nikolaev's pet project, the Trident/Newtech consortium," Austin said. "Why would Suslova go against the interests of his own organization?"

"There are a number of things that come to mind. First, the rumor of malfeasance by Trident leaked by Devon Gant. The second, infighting concerning the degree of involvement in any potential deal for Emmons-Powell by the Emirates Investment Authority and Innovel Venture Capital. All told, he didn't want to risk the embarrassment and being ostracized if the project fell through."

"In any event, I'm sure these struggles are known in Beijing. The good news is these latest developments will free us to focus on the Chinese."

"And if the Chinese are behind Merriman's murder, their intent to ferment turmoil in Moscow succeeded."

Austin rubbed his chin. "Something just occurred to me. Presuming the NBG/Trident Venture has unraveled and we block the Chinese from snapping up Emmons-Powell, then the Board of Directors is left holding the bag."

He suppressed a barbed retort not wanting to play *Guess what I'm thinking*.

"What's your point?"

"We should throw our hat in the ring and have Eagle River submit a bid."

He paused while he sorted through the implications of what Austin proposed. When he spoke, his voice bordered on the incredulous. "Are you seriously proposing government ownership of a strategic resource? I can already hear the howls from Congress."

Austin nodded an affirmation to both. Undeterred, he continued. "We have a precedent with Amtrak."

"Sort of. That's a quasi-public corporation. The National Railroad Passenger Corporation."

"Then what about the Postal Service? We couldn't do any worse."

"Austin, you're either completely out of you mind or a genius. Though I suppose both compete for dominance in that head of yours."

"If nothing else, we could leverage Eagle River's bid for a plan to restructure Emmons's debt and throw in a waver for Interior's fine for environmental damage."

He massaged his temples, then faced his partner. "Talk about rolling a grenade into a room. Okay, I'll float your idea when I meet with the NSA on Monday. He'll probably throw me out the door."

"Thanks. And while I'm on a roll, there's something else I'm chasing down."

"I'm probably going to regret this. Go ahead."

"I happened across a company during my research. Outfit named Lengkok Holdings allegedly based out of Singapore."

"Allegedly?"

"There's no company by that name registered by the Singaporeans. The address given for the company is an abandoned building and there's no listed phone number. They had an old web page that's been taken down. I sent a message to the embassy and our guys checked it out.

"Lengkok's office turned out to be an unmarked door on the third floor. And this is the odd part. There was a stack of mail piled up in the hallway. The guys bagged everything and put it on a courier flight. I got it yesterday."

"You've looked it over?"

"Some. Most of the stuff was in Chinese. I sent that to the

translators. What I did find…" Austin stopped himself. "No, I'd better finish with the background. Since the Singaporeans came up empty, I checked the WHOIS database."

He cocked his head at the unfamiliar acronym.

"They track website ownership. Turns out our fictitious Lengkok Holdings itself is probably a front for another company named Pacific Commodity, Ltd based out of Hong Kong. And Pacific Commodity is a known front for Chinese intelligence. I did some more digging and came up with a name for the alleged owner of the website. Turns out the guy also happens to be the director and a major shareholder in three companies located in the States."

He gestured toward the corkboard. "What's the reveal?"

"I may have stumbled on a connection to the Secretary of the Interior."

His jaw dropped, his mind reeling at the implications. *That might explain what I found in Browning's trashcan.* "Sylvester Poad? Who else knows?"

"Just you."

"Keep it that way."

Chapter Twenty-Seven

THE NICHOLAS
GEORGOETOWN, WASHINGTON, D.C.
FRIDAY 15 FEBRUARY

Edmund escorted Nick upstairs to what had become his usual seat in front of the fireplace. He settled in, grateful for the warming fire and set a manila folder on the coffee table, his eyes straying over the room. He doubted he'd ever tire of the oak wainscoting, shelves of books, red leather chairs, the imposing desk set in the far corner. A pair of antique bronze sconces cast subdued light across several oil paintings that adorned the walls flanking him.

A subtle aroma of leather and cigar smoke completed the library's tone of dignified ambience, of restrained wealth. He focused on the depiction of the Continental Marines on the thirty-two gun frigate *Alliance* set over the mantel. Warriors. A Few Good Men. The total effect felt right, epitomizing the ultimate Man Cave. *I could get used to this.*

The naval scene also reminded him that the Coast Guard Cutter *Midgett* was still on station near the Bering Strait. The captain he'd met in Juneau, St Claire, said if they found anything of importance, he'd pass it along.

He sunk into the chair, his mind at ease. An innocent question worked its way into his consciousness. He'd never seen anybody else in the room. Did anyone else ever use this elegant study or was this Lange's personal domain? His thoughts drifted. And the deference Edmund accorded Lange? Could he be one of the directors of The Nickolas? Or fabulously wealthy? Could he—

"Would you care for something to drink or something to eat, sir?" Edmund asked. "Mr. Lange called to say he's running a bit late and for you to make yourself comfortable."

He started at Edmund's voice. *How long had he been standing there? He just snuck up on me like some special ops guy.* "Ah, maybe just a glass of water."

"Very good, sir. A sparkling? Perhaps the Perrier?"

"That would be fine. Thank you."

He returned to his musings adding yet another layer of questions to those he already had about Lange. There had to be something more than what the background check revealed. What was it?

Unable to solve the riddles surrounding Lange, his thoughts drifted to Michelle. Their evening together had ended with a gentle kiss at her front door, but no matter. Tears had filled her eyes and she'd reached for his hand when she read the note he'd written in her Valentine's card. The look in her eyes left him dazed, leaving him unsure of his own emotions. Could they—?

"Your Perrier-Jouët, sir." Lange handed Nick a flute of the French champagne. "I believe you requested the sparkling."

Good, Lord. Does he know? Jarred from his thoughts of Michelle, he stared at the bubbles emerging from a twist of lemon at the bottom of the flute. He recovered and managed to blurt. "Champagne?"

"Sure, why not?" Lange said. He glanced at Nick's folder

before setting his briefcase on the floor. If he had any clue of what underlay Nick's muddled reaction, he didn't let on. "I upgraded your order. Edmund's putting together a selection of shrimp and yellowtail sushi. They pair wonderfully."

He tried not to make a face. He couldn't stand raw fish. Growing up in central Ohio, his idea of seafood was Mrs. Paul's Breaded Fish Sticks.

"I take it sushi's not your favorite?"

"I'll be fine." He pulled out his digital camera, selected the photo of the gibberish, and handed it over. "Any idea what this is?"

Lange set a pair of smudged halfmoon reading glasses on the tip of his nose. He expanded the photo, analyzing the contents. "It's anti-language."

"You can read that?"

"Only bits. It's a type of dialect. The origin's obscure, maybe in England more than a century ago. It gained a bit of notoriety in Stanley Kubrick's seventies movie, *A Clockwork Orange*. You've seen it?"

"I've never even heard of it."

"Nowadays, anti-language is still used by a few underground groups operating on the fringes of society. They replace a common word with another elliptical word to disguise the meaning." He pointed to the screen. "Take this one; Palaver. It's a tale told to avoid blame for a crime. And this. Squeak. It means, 'to confess.'"

He recalled Kimberly Browning's blue and pink colored wig and the name scribbled on the wadded-up paper from her trashcan. Alternative lifestyle. He lifted his hand intent on retrieving the camera. "Any idea what they're talking about?"

"No idea. I need to spend some time on this. Can I keep it?"

He hesitated, then withdrew his hand. There was nothing else on the camera that Lange didn't already know or couldn't surmise. "Go ahead. You'll see some other documents that were lifted from the Department of the Interior."

Lange scrolled through the pictures. "Where'd you get these? Gant didn't mention any of this."

Damn. The break-in. Lange had honed right in on this minor detail. He hedged. "Doesn't surprise me. He leaked information from Treasury, not Interior. I didn't find anything to connect him with what I discovered."

"In other words, you don't want to say how you got this stuff?"

"No… Yes."

"Which is it?"

"It was a black bag op."

"Who authorized it?"

"Nobody."

Lange tightened his lips and shot him a knowing glance over the top of his glasses. "You went outside your agency? Are you nuts?"

"Probably."

Lange changed tack. "Did your friend at Treasury get anything more on Gant?"

"He said he couldn't provide any documentation to back up his claims."

"He may have served his purpose."

"Who? Gant?"

"Yeah," Lange affirmed.

"What about him?"

"Aren't the Russians out of the picture now?"

Lange's response surprised him. *Lange knew more than he professed.* He opted not to pursue the importance of this development. Instead, he addressed Lange's question. "Now that Gant's played his part, the Chinese will dump him. We need to focus on them."

"Then I've lost a great story."

"Not necessarily." He handed over the two sheets of paper

in his folder. While he hadn't told his supervisor about the break-in or how he obtained the material from Browning's apartment, he had said he'd come across some information that might prove critical to his operation. Much to his surprise, Strickland said to share what he had found with Lange.

Lange adjusted his glasses and studied the document.

"A little something I came across during the op."

"I'd say this is a bit more than *a little something*. Lange reached into his briefcase, extracted a notebook, a small magnifying glass, and a pencil flashlight. He backlit the paper and resumed his analysis, scrutinizing both sheets of paper while flipping through several pages of his notebook. Several minutes later, he held the paper up to the light and pointed to a faint mark centered on the page. "This is a digital watermark. There's also a unique digital string code. This copy came from a specific printer at the Department of the Interior, a Xerox Ducocolor Model #54, Serial number 29535218."

Nick stared at him, incredulous that he could identify the copy machine and its location with such certainty. *Who is this guy?* "You just happen to carry this stuff around with you?"

"Tools of the trade. I've got a source at Xerox who services Interiors' copy machines." He handed the sheets back. "Who's the source?"

Trade? What trade? Who is this guy? He made a quick decision, deciding that Lange would learn the details of the break-in soon enough. "Kimberly Browning. She works in the Mineral Management Division at Interior."

"We'll run a barium test meal to isolate her and identify any others working with her."

His eyebrows rose, so unexpected was Lange's response. "Do you really expect me to understand what you just said?"

"It's a spook term we lifted from the medical folks. We'll change the sequence of a single number or a word in the original document to prove Browning's the source of the leaks. If we can get access to her work and home phones, we'll also set up a 'tap and trace' to determine her contacts."

"I don't recall seeing a land line."

"Can you get back in?" Lange asked.

"Shouldn't be a problem."

"Good. We'll access her computer and run an analysis of her on-line posts. I have someone working for a cybersecurity firm who can run a backdoor op, but I'd prefer to use your Tailored Access Operations group."

I have someone? And Lange had repeatedly used 'we.' Who is this guy? He struggled to keep his face impassive despite the turmoil rolling in waves through his mind. What agency could run this kind of op? The FBI? Doubtful. Hell, even with the NSA's backing, the 4th District hadn't ruled on the warrant to put Moore under surveillance. And Strickland? His supervisor would be apoplectic if he discovered the true extent of what he'd done. He'd been given permission to pass certain information to Lange, but—

"Something the matter?" Lange asked.

"Naw, just thinking. I can't go with the TAO guys. I haven't got anything hard on the Chinese to prove they've done anything illegal let alone probable cause to start implicating American citizens."

Lange appeared circumspect. He reached for a cigar and clipped off the tip. "Not yet anyway. So, we have to be creative and look for a way to entrap your Ms. Browning."

He gazed over Lange's left shoulder fixing his eyes on the French musket hanging on the far wall wondering how he'd managed to get pulled into this morass. He hadn't willfully ignored Strickland's advice to not engage with Lange, but… Lange's voice intruded into his thoughts. *Browning? Wait. What did he just say?* He struggled to pick up the lost pieces and make sense of what Lange was saying.

"…using a web reconnaissance tool that will link us to our target's computer by inserting a remote script that will execute if, for instance, anyone visits the web page for Eagle River or Creekside Consultants. We'll construct the script using a Scanbox framework to…."

His mind reeled, swirling around just two words. Did Lange just drop the name, Creekside Consultants? How-in-hell does he know about the FBI's operation? What else did I miss? *Damn.* He struggled to cover his confusion while trying to think of something, anything to say. "We're going phishing?"

Lange smiled and struck a wooden match to light his cigar. He whipped the match with a flip of his wrist extinguishing the flame. "Never use a lighter. You can taste the hydrocarbons." He took a deep draw, slowly rolled the cigar in his fingers, and studied the whirling smoke rising from the cigar's ashen tip "Yeah, we've scored a win here."

Nick looked away. He didn't know about hydrocarbons. More to the point, he also wasn't so sure about the *win*. He decided it was time to do a little fishing himself. "Did you send it?"

"Send what?"

"The encrypted email I got in November. 'It's Not Over.'"

Lange set down his cigar. "Yeah, I did."

"Why?"

"You're here, aren't you?"

Chapter Twenty-Eight

USCG HELICOPTER GOOSE 21
POINT HOPE, ALASKA
SATURDAY 16 FEBRUARY

Lieutenant Sarah MacAuley tilted her head to reduce the glare from the distant ice pack. With that brief motion, she acknowledged what lay below her aircraft. Open water. In past years, the mass of jumbled pack ice would have extended well south of the Bering Strait.

The rugged peaks of the De Long mountain range dominated the eastern horizon, but her thoughts returned to the ice-flecked water stretching for miles off the headlands. That expanse, seemingly devoid of life, is what drove today's mission.

NASA and NOAA scientists had discovered that the remaining ice was actually thicker—a finding so counter-intuitive it compelled further investigation. The formation of this thicker ice also held a number of implications for the Navy. The denser, saltier water beneath the ice pack impacted the navigation, sonar, and communication systems of the country's submarine force.

She keyed the aircraft's intercom system. "Jamison, you guys set?"

"Yes, ma'am. We've got good data on the uplink."

"How's the new guy?"

"Less green now that we've got smooth air."

She smiled. The dude had taken one for the team. The NOAA engineer's presence reflected her helicopter's slow metamorphosis into a scientific platform studying the impact of global warming on Arctic oscillation—the combined effect of precipitation, wind, and temperature patterns on sea-ice formation.

NOAA engineers had also installed a sophisticated instrument package on the helicopter's undercarriage to measure the thickness of the ice. This data would then be matched for accuracy with the information relayed by the European Space Agency's CryoSat2 satellite to NOAA's Command and Acquisition Station in Fairbanks.

The second piece of her mission profile linked to the first. The maximum depth of the channel here varied from ninety-eight to one-hundred and sixty feet reflecting the land bridge known as Beringia that had connected the Kamchatka Peninsula with Alaska eons ago. That made the strait a chokepoint for submarines transiting to the deeper waters of the Arctic Ocean. The Arctic's strategic resources and the expansion of global trade routes across the northern sea routes mandated the nation contain the threats posed by Chinese and Russian submarines.

To this end, the Coast Guard was revisiting a plan first floated in 2011 that would expand the scope of the service's mission to include anti-submarine warfare. The mission wasn't new. The service had played a crucial role during World War II protecting critical commerce against German U-boat attacks spanning a distance from the coast of Greenland to the shores of the Gulf of Mexico.

Several of the service's National Security Cutters

including the *Midgett* were subsequently outfitted with a rudimentary anti-submarine warfare suite modeled on that being installed on the Navy's new frigates. She noted all the gear crammed into the small crew compartment aft of her, longing for the larger HH-60j aircraft.

She stowed the thought and assumed a new course along pre-set navigation points, then passed control of the aircraft to her co-pilot, Lieutenant (junior grade) Brian Fields. "You have controls left seat."

"Roger, I have controls left seat."

"Left seat has controls." She settled back in her seat.

Much to her surprise, she'd come to appreciate the austere beauty of the Arctic and stole a moment to admire the multi-colored blue striations of the ice pack. Her enthusiasm, however, did not extend to their extended deployment in support of Arctic Shield. She longed for the warmth and sun of Oahu.

The good news? They were scheduled to return to the Valdez Coast Guard station in a week. Not exactly Honolulu, she mused, but better than being cooped up in a small stateroom with another officer from the ship's company. She also had another reason for wanting to return to port. Much to her chagrin, she noted that Fields appeared to have read her thoughts.

"Got a big night planned at The Rampaging Moose?" Fields said.

She feigned innocence but failed to suppress her smile. "Busted."

'The Moose', as the locals referred to it, was one of four bars in the town of thirty-six-hundred souls. A ramshackle, one-story affair boasting two pool tables and three dart boards, it attracted a mix of patrons from young Coasties to locals and a few down-on-their-luck adventurers. On a good night, a discordant pick-up band replaced the music that usually blared from an antiquated juke box. And truth be told, there wasn't much rampaging in Valdez. The residents and transients both were beaten down by the brutal struggle for survival in this isolated outpost of civilization.

The Rampaging Moose aside, Valdez had little to hold her interest with one notable exception. She'd met a really cute guy seeking his fortune after tiring of his job in corporate America.

"Got some action lined up," she replied. "A rematch with an innocent chasing his money."

"How much is on the line?"

"Ten bucks. He choked on a money ball after I took him down with a cross-side."

Fields didn't blink at the terms. He knew from first-hand experience not to challenge MacAuley in Eight-ball. "Big stakes. You need backup?"

"Nah, I can take him down."

"Roger that." His eyes flashed with amusement. He knew she had something going with this guy.

She shifted the conversation to something safer. Unlike the harrowing experience they'd encountered in November, they had excellent flying weather. *At least for now*, she cautioned herself. The horizon portended something else. The distant sky had an ominous appearance, heavy with dark, leaden clouds dropping close to the horizon, the sun diminished to a dull disk. "The weather is looking pretty crappy over there."

"Yeah, I noticed," Fields concurred. "Back to the barn?"

"As soon as we wrap up this run."

She judged the threatening clouds on the horizon. "If the weather permits, I'd like to run a calibration check on our new gear and record some baseline data."

"Sounds like a plan."

Jamison's voice sounded over her headset. "The NOAA guy just finished his data pull, ma'am."

"I got it," she said, taking back the aircraft's controls from Fields. "Looks like the weather may grant us another fifteen minutes."

"Judging from the surface chop, that's what I'm thinking.," Fields added. "We should be able to work in the calibration checks."

She moved the cyclic, nosing the helicopter closer to the western edge of the ice pack that covered the remainder of the strategic Bering Strait. Settling in on the new course, she could just make out Little Diomede Island to the southwest. Two miles due west of that tiny spec, the haze-gray silhouette of Russian controlled Big Diomede thrust out of a low-lying fog bank.

These two small islands served the useful purpose of delineating the agreed upon maritime boundary separating the United States and the Russian Federation. Only forty-seven nautical miles separated Point Hope and the Russian Chukotski Peninsula at its narrowest point and within five minutes they were over Little Diomede's eastern flank .

She swung around the 1,600-foot granite peak topping the island and swept across a small village, population one-hundred-thirty, perched on the western shoreline. "Man, those have to be some rugged folks down there."

"I'll say," Fields confirmed. "I'll be sure to check that village off my bucket list of places to visit."

She slowed her airspeed so she wouldn't drift over the notional line separating the two islands, then circled back to assume a hover two miles off the eastern edge of the island. "How's the gear, Jamison?"

"I've got something," Jamison said.

"Say again?"

"There may something down there."

"What? Where?"

"Zero-three-zero."

She scanned the water from starboard to port, then back. And stopped. *Was that a wake?* "Brian, do you have anything on the FLIR? Heading zero-three-zero."

"Standby. Yeah, There's something out there. I've got a feather. Hold one. We're registering a faint signature."

"Let's take a look." She tapped the anti-torque pedal and pulled more collective, nosing the helicopter to close the contact. She maintained a steady hand on the cyclic, mindful of the distance to the unknown entity and Russian territorial waters.

"I'm visual," Jamison announced. "Got a couple masts. Judging from the wake, I'd say the contact is making about six knots."

Fields peered through his window and caught sight of the pair of black masts piercing the surface. Below them would be a submarine's sail. "Hell, we don't even know if it's one of ours."

"Could be. Jamison, get some pics."

"On it."

"I'd figure the Russians would keep to their channel west of those islands."

"You think it could be a Chinese Shang class just cruising along with no idea we're up here?"

She stared at her co-pilot. "How do you know that?"

"Wild-assed guess. It's the only one I've ever heard about."

"What else don't you know?"

"I've read all of George Wallace's books, his *Hunter Killer* series. If you want to know about a fast attack, you—"

"Brian, get to the point."

"That sub's commander may be using the chop to hide the wake from his masts. One could be a SATCOM to verify his course and not run aground. The other, a periscope so he can see what's out there. Ice, surface or airborne threats."

No sooner had those words left Fields' mouth than the two

masts disappeared below the surface. "He went sinker. Damn. I think he made us."

"Sure did. "

We need to call it in."

"Ya' know, the skipper will probably contact the District in Juneau. By the time he gets their guidance, the sub will be long gone heading to God knows where."

She pondered her options "We just stumbled onto this thing and now we've lost it."

"Affirm."

She checked their fuel status. Safety mandated they return to the ship. She made her decision. "*Midgett.* Goose 21."

"Go for *Midgett*, Goose 21"

"Request switch frequencies to secure voice."

"Goose 21, *Midgett*. Push magenta."

"*Midgett*. Switching. On magenta."

"Goose 21, you're secure."

"We have a contact east of Little Diomede Island. CERTSUB (Certified Submarine). Course 030. Speed six knots. Spotted a couple masts poking out of the water."

"Goose 21. Confirm CERTSUB. Course 030. Speed six knots."

"Brian, make sure you mark the contact's position in the GPS. The Navy's gonna want to know about this. I suspect that sub is up to no good."

"Copy. I'm on it." Fields depressed the "MARK" soft-key button on the Dolphin's GPS interface. The vessel's latitude and longitude illuminated in the display. He copied the coordinates to his kneeboard for redundancy and de-briefing on the *Midgett*.

MacAuley scanned the empty ocean, then turned her head to face the crew compartment. "Jamison, you can stow your camera. It's gone."

A gust of wind accompanying a series of brisk snow

showers buffeted the helicopter signaling the arrival of the storm front. *Time's up.* There wasn't anything else she could do but let the unknown submarine slip away. She raised the Cutter. "*Midgett*, Goose 21. Breaking contact and heading home."

Chapter Twenty-Nine

THE WHITE HOUSE
WASHINGTON, D.C.
MONDAY 18 FEBRUARY

Nick fingered the White House visitor's badge dangling from the lanyard looped around his neck. He'd been in the West Wing enough times over past year that he was no longer awed by simply being here, yet his sense of unease puzzled him. He glanced at his friend, Mike Rohrbaugh. The SEAL walked beside him, striding confidently through the narrow corridor leading to Justin Brown's office. Rohrbaugh's presence helped assuage his foreboding.

He could count on Mike. And that, he realized, defined the problem. He had not told him about breaking into Browning's condo. Worse, he hadn't confided in him about what he planned for tomorrow night.

He despised duplicity in others, so what happened? While he clearly was about to commit another illegal break-in, he couldn't place his friends in a position to suborn perjury, lie under oath or, worse, implicate them in his act. He rationalized by telling himself that he had to protect both of his friends. Yet, he continued to confide in Lange. Why was that? Could the reporter simply be a means to an end, to be used and then discarded at the end of the day? The thought unsettled him but there had to be something else going on he didn't understand. Something darker.

Mike glanced at him. "You okay?"

He stopped fiddling with his security badge and answered with a half-truth. "Yeah, just thinking."

Mike slowed at the sound of the president's Chief of Staff's, voice. "Hold on a sec. I need to touch base with Dan." Rohrbaugh ducked into Dan Lantis' office without waiting for a reply.

He welcomed the moment to gather his thoughts for the upcoming meeting with the NSA. He pondered how to approach a topic not on the agenda and how to leverage another new development to his advantage.

He'd received a message from the Tailored Access Operations group before he left his office. They had detected another attempted intrusion into Creekside Consultants computer system. The FBI's point man at Creekside, Darrel Nance, had also reported a suspicious email he'd seen to the National Counterintelligence Center. The spurious email represented another spear-phishing operation targeting the company's email accounts to entrap an unsuspecting employee into revealing his passwords. The good news? Neither Creekside, nor Eagle River, LLC had real employees.

He held no doubt about who was behind the effort and this knowledge only firmed his resolve to take down the Chinese network. The absence of any sense of ethical behavior on their part provided what rationale he needed to justify his own actions. By this time tomorrow he'd have his proof.

Mike popped out of Lange's office. "Ready to do this?"

A tight smile crossed his face. "Lead on."

Justin Brown looked up at the two men standing in his doorway, his pen poised above a yellow legal pad. "Mike. Good to see you again, Nick. Have a seat."

Nick took the left-hand chair, his eyes drifting to an open folder next to Brown's legal pad.

Brown caught Nick's eye and closed the folder containing the Treasury Department's Suspicious Activities Report and placed it face-down on his desk. The Financial Crimes Enforcement department had tracked three deposits in Nick's name to an obscure bank in the Cayman Islands, Banco Investment and Trust. The SAR detailed evidence of possible malfeasance, enough to make a viable case against Nick including share transactions and bearer bond purchases through a fictitious shell company.

Much of the information the FCE obtained remained circumstantial. Not enough to indict Nick, but considering his security clearance, enough to recommend that the Justice Department obtain a warrant to search Nick's condo. Brown pushed the report aside, tapping the report several times with his index finger before picking up a paperclip and bending it open.

Nick glanced to his right. Mike's body appeared rigid; his hands clasped, lips compressed.

"I've read your and Mike's trip report on Alaska," Brown said. "We don't need to review it unless you have something to add."

"Not to the report, sir, but there are a number of developments I'd like to discuss."

Brown set the paperclip aside. "What do you have?"

"For starters, the Russians appear to have stopped their efforts to acquire Emmons-Powell."

"I thought an American firm was competing against the Chinese? Where do the Russians fit?"

"They were in the mix as a hidden partner. They were attempting to undercut the review process for foreign investment in our critical infrastructure." He paused at a discreet nudge from Mike's elbow. "I can go over the details if you wish."

Brown glanced at Mike, then the SAR folder, before focusing on Nick. "Give me the short version."

"Trident's partner in their bid for Emmons-Powell is a Canadian company, Newtech Resource Development. The Novorossiysk Business Group, in turn, was leveraging that partnership by submitting an offer to obtain a controlling interest in Newtech. Recent developments within Premier Srevnenko's inner circle ultimately led to the NBG withdrawing their offer. Srevnenko's action was predicated on maintaining the balance of power between the rival factions within his government, those advocating State control, and those pushing privatization and personal enrichment. Nick's voice trailed off when Brown began to fidget with the paperclip.

"Are the Canadians still in play?" Brown asked.

Nick nodded an affirmative, holding on to a modicum of hope. The NSA hadn't dismissed him outright.

"Suppose the Chinese fill the void and look to partner with Newtech?" Brown continued.

Crap. He managed to keep the consternation that swept over him from showing on his face. Any sense of temerity he had vanished. He hadn't considered that Beijing might try to make a bid for a controlling interest in Newtech. *Or another company I don't know about? Now what?* He cycled through his options before settling on Austin's scheme. It might just work if he could pitch their plan.

"Nick?"

He tensed at Brown's voice. The NSA's and Mike's eyes were both fixed on him with inquiring looks. *Well, here goes.* "I have an idea that will thwart Beijing's plans whether they partner with Newtech or not."

Brown's gaze remained fixed, but he raised an inquisitive eyebrow. "What do you have in mind?"

He spent the next several minutes outlining Austin's plan for a government bail-out of Emmons-Powell. He ran his hands through his hair after he'd finished, clasping them on the back of his neck before letting them fall to his lap. He couldn't read Brown's face and had no idea how his proposal had been received.

"I can't promise anything." Brown wrote something on his legal pad. "I need to consider the ramifications of your proposal and discuss them with Dan before running them by the president. The response from the Congressional leadership is another matter entirely. They'd correctly view this as an unprecedented attempt to nationalize one of our critical industries. Who'd be next? Alcoa?"

He didn't answer the rhetorical question.

"At this point, I can't even come up with the name of a Congressman who'd be willing to stick his neck out to sponsor such a proposal."

He suppressed his frustration at Brown's response, but then, the NSA hadn't dismissed his idea outright. That was a start, but could he finesse the proposal and provide Brown some room to negotiate? "What if we stir things up just enough by floating the idea to convince the Chinese we're serious? Anything to keep them off balance and force them to make a mistake."

"Perhaps, but this proposal of yours is so…" Brown's eyes fell on the folder on his desk, then caught Mike's eye. "We have a number of delicate negotiations working in committee that we don't want to derail by causing a distraction. The president would be risking a lot of political capital."

He suppressed a shudder at Brown's abrupt change. *What's in that folder?* "I'd appreciate whatever you can do."

Brown appeared to take his response as ending the meeting and made to push away from his desk. Nick realized he had to act quickly or lose what little leverage he still possessed. There were several other sources of frustration nagging him that he needed to address. He hadn't heard anything back from his friend at the FBI, Jessica Caudry, and Taylor Ferguson hadn't provided any updates on tapping into Moore's electronic devices. He tried not to read too much into their silence, but he couldn't help but wonder if he wasn't being stonewalled.

"Sir, if I may. The Chinese—"

"You have something else to offer?" Brown said.

He chose to ignore the edge in Brown's voice. "Our best bet to thwart the Chinese is to smoke out their mastermind. I have the name of a Chinese national, but I believe he's reporting to someone else, possibly an American citizen."

"If that's the case," Brown said, "I don't see why we couldn't put Mister…"

"Wai."

"Put Mr. Wai under surveillance by the FBI and if they find something hard, indict him under the Foreign Agent Registrations Act."

"May I ask a question. sir?"

"Certainly."

"Have you had any feedback from Justice on the FISA warrant for Jason Moore?"

Brown hesitated. "It's still being worked. The Forth District denied our initial request. We failed to meet probable cause."

He pondered whether he should drop what he discovered in Kimberly Browning's condo and Austin's information suggesting a link between Sylvester Poad and the Chinese. He knew this information was dynamite, especially if he were to accuse a member of Stuart's cabinet of possible collusion.

Short of that, he wondered if he could use Lange to force

an FBI investigation of Moore and Browning by penning an expose detailing what he knew? Lange could always fall back on a reporter's right to protect his sources. *More than I'll be able to do if I'm asked how I acquired my information. No, I need to keep my mouth shut.*

Mike interrupted the uncomfortable silence following Brown's response about the FISA warrant. "Thank you, Justin. We'll stay in touch."

Nick didn't make a pretense of masking his anger when they left Brown's office. He pulled up short as they set off down the corridor. "Mike, why do I have the sense there's something I'm not being told?"

"There's been a development."

"What the hell's going on?"

"I can't say."

He made to protest, but Mike hardened his voice. "You'll just have to trust me."

Chapter Thirty

3110 PROPSECT SPTREET NW
GEORGETOWN, WASHINGTON, D.C.
TUESDAY 19 FEBRUARY

Nick could have sworn he'd seen someone. He ducked into a narrow driveway sheltered by a high wall and pressed his back against the cut stone, exhaling vaporous plumes that hung suspended in the cold air before being carried away by the wind. He blew out a longer breath through pursed lips to release the tension in his shoulders, then peered through a chilling drizzle at the darkened houses lining Prospect Street. Nothing. *I must be seeing ghosts.*

He puffed into his cupped hands to warm his frozen fingers and stuffed his hands into his jacket's pockets. Nobody in their right mind would be out on a night like this, but for his purposes the weather was ideal. With a bit of luck, he could wrap up his operation before sunup and have enough on the Chinese to shut down their operation.

He did his best to ignore the cold and rain. He had to be patient, to pick the right moment to slip into the target's home. Rather than going in blind, he'd gone to several realty sites and learned as much about the residence as he could. Two rooms stood out. A wood paneled library and a carriage house. He'd search those first.

He focused on his plan and settled in to wait. A cold fog replaced the drizzle, suffocating the neighborhood in its misty embrace, dulling the lights, muffling any sound of life. He checked his watch before chancing a look down the street.

He caught sight of a man on the opposite side of the street walking toward him, a cell phone pressed against his right ear. Another, further down on his side of the road, had a dark ballcap pulled low over his forehead. The second hunched against a doorframe, sheltering from a blast of wind that drove a page of sodden, newspaper tumbling down the sidewalk.

A solitary black sedan appeared out of the mist. Nick tensed, backing into the shadows. The vehicle slowed as it passed the second man, then accelerated. The car's high-intensity beams were diffused by the fog. Nick averted his eyes ruining any chance to catch the license plate number. He refocused. Both men had gone. The muffled sound of their footfalls fading into the darkness.

Four o'clock. He tightened the collar of his Navy pea-coat and made his way down the street to a narrow alley separating his target and a neighboring home, heedless that he'd just violated two of Lange's cardinal rules: 'Only approach a site when you are sure it's clean,' and 'If the target has surveillance, then the operation has gone bad.'

Under his self-imposed pressure to break open his case against the Chinese, Nick had assumed the first and ignored the second.

A dog barked breaking into his thoughts. Startled, he pivoted on his heel, spinning toward the sound. A white and red flash exploded behind his eyes just before he crumpled to the ground.

He woke to darkness, disoriented, unable to conjure any sense where he was, or any memory of what had happened. The last thing he could recall was a black-clad figure looming over him and a lancinating pain over the back of his skull.

Silence engulfed him, the void cracked by his own short, rasping breaths. Awareness slowly returned, overlaid by a pounding headache. A dank, moldy smell, heavy and thick, suffused the air. Somewhere to his left he heard the muted splashes of dripping water. He rolled toward the sound, pushing himself up to a sitting position. He shivered in the cold, struggling to gain some idea of where he was imprisoned.

Where am I? A basement? Another sound, a deep rumbling, felt more than heard. *A truck?* He yelled. "Hey, is anybody out there?" A mistake. His voice pounded off the walls of the enclosure slamming back against his skull. He winced in pain and grasped his head with both hands.

His head throbbed. He tested his skull, using his index finger to probe a large lump behind his right ear. He winced in pain and yanked his hand away. A solitary light shown in a corner, the bare bulb illuminating a galvanized bucket. He detected a faint odor strangely out of place among the others. *Cinnamon?*

He cocked his head, sensing he wasn't alone. Then he heard something. A sucking sound like air being pulled through teeth. Annoying. A bank of halide lamps burst to life. The blinding light drove him to the floor, searing his brain. He curled into a ball, trying to turn away. A groan escaped his lips.

A figure loomed out of the darkness. Faceless.

"So, we finally meet, Mr. Parkos."

The disconnected voice, hidden by the glare of the halide

lights continued. "Unfortunately, our time together will be brief so we must make the most of this opportunity, yes?"

He suppressed the wave of terror flooding his mind. *Are they going to torture me?"*

"What? You have nothing to say?"

He struggled to a sitting position, but didn't respond. Not so much from defiance but from bewilderment and the malevolence in the man's voice. He heard the sucking sound again and focused on the source. A quat, heavy set Chinese man. White shirt. Black pants and vest. The man glared at him, his face skewed by a smile-like grimace that displayed a large gold tooth. *Odd Job?* At least the guy wasn't sporting a black Bowler hat.

"I'm surprised you were so careless," the man continued. "Did you not have backup, Mr. Parkos. Or shall I call you Nick? After all, I know you so well."

"You're not Huifeng," Nick managed to say. "You have an American accent."

"Very astute."

"Who—?"

"I will be the one asking the questions"

"I'm not telling you a damn thing."

"Admirable, Nick. But perhaps you have not considered the well-being of Ms. O'Brian?"

He struggled to his feet. "You bastard."

The man motioned to *Odd Job* indicating he should remain in place. "Ah, so you do. An admirable quality, Nick, however sentimentality is a fatal flaw in our line of work. But then, every man has his vulnerabilities. Yes?"

The man made a pretense of looking at his watch. "You have kept us up. We will continue our conversation later." He gestured to *Odd Job*.

A plastic water bottle landed at Nick's feet.

The two men spun and thumped up a set of wooden stairs, slamming a door behind them.

The halide lights and the single bulb went out plunging Nick into darkness, leaving him alone and overwhelmed with a mix of despair, guilt, and dread of what was to come. There could be no excuse for his incompetence. He only had himself to blame if Michelle was harmed. *If those bastards dare touch her.*

The room spun as a sharp pain cut through his head. He reached out for a wall, his arms flailing in the darkness. His legs gave way in a wave of nausea and dizziness

0420 HOURS
WEDNESDAY 20 FEBRUARY

Geoffrey Lange deployed his crisis intervention team along predetermined surveillance points lining Prospect Street before making his way to the alley beside their target. He stopped at the rear door of an old carriage house, drew his Glock pistol, and turned to his bearded partner positioned opposite him to the left side of the door. "You set?"

George slid his Baltimore Raven's cap around, so the bill faced backwards, then extracted a penlight and a K-tool kit from his pants pocket. Penlight clenched in his teeth, he peered at the lock for a moment, then set to work dismantling the cylinder. "Won't take a minute."

In less than the minute, the cylinder mechanism dropped to the ground. He pushed the door ajar, checking for evidence of an alarm system. "We're good."

Lange grasped his pistol in a two-handed grip, stepped around him, and entered a well-lit room. He came to an abrupt halt, startled by an elderly oriental woman with a long-braided queue clutching an empty rice bowl. *A mama-san? Harmless.*

He lowered his weapon and lifted his index finger to his

lips. "Shhh." Her pupils widened in terror, but at least she didn't scream or drop the bowl. "Sit."

The old woman collapsed onto her haunches, without questioning Lange's emphatic command.

"Stay."

He scanned the room, satisfied she wouldn't pose a threat. Throw rug. Couch. Several chairs. End table. Bookcase. He detected the faint scent of incense.

"Looks like the place Moore described," George said.

"Dead ringer." He turned to the woman, fixing her in his gaze. "American?"

She pointed a trembling finger toward the far corner of the room and the open steps that presumably led to her apartment.

"Check it out while I watch this one."

George crossed the room and placed his foot on the first tread.

The old woman shook her head and pointed again. He stopped and looked down through the gap between the steps. "There's a trap door set in the floor."

He ducked under the stairs, threw the heavy dead bolt, and lifted the door, shining his flashlight into the void below. "Looks like an old root cellar." He descended the stairs swinging his flashlight in slow arcs through the void below.

"Parkos. Nick? You in here?"

Nick responded to the familiar voice. "George?" He tried to stand, but only made it to his knees and hands. "How—?"

"Never mind that," George said. He pulled Nick to his feet and yelled up the stairs. "I've got him."

Lange strode across the room and helped Nick up the final steps into the main room.

"Geoff?" Nick said.

"Who else did you expect to come and save your sorry ass?" He grasped Nick's shoulders, held him at arm's length, and ran his eyes over him in a quick assessment. "Looks like you're gonna live."

Nick wobbled but managed to stay upright by wrapping his arms around Lange in a bear hug. Overcome with relief, he thumped Lange's back three times. The gesture elicited a loud guffaw from his rescuer.

Nick recoiled. "I was about to get killed and you find that amusing?"

"Sorry. Another survival skill I didn't get around to teaching you at the Upper Crust. The three pats are code for 'I'm not gay.' Gays just give a hug. No back slapping."

Nick's knees gave out in another wave of dizziness before he could offer a retort. George managed to catch him before he crashed to the floor.

"Time to get you the hell out of here."

George glanced at the old women, centering the barrel of his weapon on her forehead. "What about her?"

"Leave her. No sense taking her out." He placed his finger against his lips and looked into her eyes. "Shhh."

George holstered his pistol and together, the two men half carried, half dragged Nick to the alley where they shoved him into the back seat of a black sedan. They scrambled in after him, Lange pounding on the back of the driver's seat. "Go. Go. Go."

Lange turned to Nick to assure himself that he was indeed okay, then said. "Do me a favor and don't do that again."

"They've been watching her," Nick said.

"Her? What-the-hell are you talking about?"

"Michelle. They've threatened to hurt her."

"Shit." He pulled out his cell phone and entered a seldom used number from his file. "Mike? This is Geoffrey Lange … Sorry to wake you … Yeah, it has been a long time. Listen, I need your help."

Chapter Thirty-One

WHITE OAK APARTMENT
CAPITAL HEIGHTS, MARYLAND
WEDNESDAY 20 FEBRUARY

A distant thudding jerked Michelle awake. The pounding resumed, rattling the pictures on her wall. She sat up, hugging the bed's thick blanket to cover herself. *Fire?* She dismissed the thought. There weren't any shouts of alarm from her neighbors or wailing sirens and she couldn't detect the smell of smoke. She rubbed her eyes and read the blurred digits on her iPhone. *Five o'clock?*

She climbed out of bed wishing she had a gun. The insistent pounding began again, shaking the front door. She hesitated, put on a robe, and made her way to the living room. She overcame her fear and pressed her right eye to the door's peephole. A fish-eye image of a man loomed before her, fist raised, ready to pound again. She pulled her head away, terrified at the sight.

"Michelle."

How does he know my name? She chanced another look. A second man had replaced the first.

"Michelle. It's Mike Rohrbaugh."

She recognized the voice and flicked on the porch light. "Mike?"

"Michelle, let us in. Nick's been injured."

"Oh, God." She flipped the lock, slid back the deadbolt, and swung open the door.

Nick hung limply before her, ashen faced, supported under his arms by Mike and the other man. She moved out of the doorway to allow the three to enter. Behind them stood another man in a black ballcap, his back to the door. He swung his head side-to-side scanning the parking lot.

"What's happened?" she asked, not yet able to comprehend why they had brought Nick to her apartment instead of a hospital.

Mike gestured to the stranger next to him in way of an answer. "This is Geoff Lange, a friend of Nick's. He'll explain."

The trailing man in the ballcap entered the room, closed the door and without a word approached the living room window. He pried apart two horizontal slats of the wooden blinds, peered outside. "Team's in place."

Lange looked at the man with the ballcap and gave his head a jerk toward the door. "Give Cade an assist to secure the grounds."

She ignored the encounter, focusing instead on helping Mike guide Nick to the living room couch. They eased him onto the cushions, lifted his legs off the floor so he could lay down, and placed a pillow under his head. She brushed her hand against Nick's cheek scrutinizing his face. Her inspection stopped at the swollen bruise on the back of his skull. "What happened?"

Nick's glazed eyes caught her imploring look. "Fell down the stairs."

"He did something stupid," Lange added.

She stood and headed to her kitchen not ready to learn about *something stupid*. "I'll get some ice."

———

Lange turned to Mike. "We've got to get them both out of here until this blows over while not bothering to elaborate on 'this.' We've got a safe-house outside of town even the Agency doesn't know about." He studied Nick a moment. "We have to keep you under wraps until we can figure out the amount of damage you've caused."

"Damage?" Nick tried to push himself up on his elbows. "What are you talking about?"

"Do you have any idea what you've done?" The blank look on Nick's face provided all the answer he needed.

"I've … I've got stuff to do. The …" Nick dropped back onto the pillow, unable to continue.

"If I were you," he interrupted, "staying alive would be at the top of my 'to do' list right now."

Mike attempted to break the tension. "You'll need to call in sick. We'll work your cover story."

Nick appeared to consider what he wanted to say, then asked. "What did I do besides try to break into that house?"

"For starters, you've blown our counter-intelligence op."

"What?"

"You heard me. We tolerated your investigation because you'd uncovered some useful information and were distracting the Chinese."

Nick appeared confused. "We? What are you talking about?"

He filled in the blanks. "My team. You've become a liability."

"Liability? I'm the one feeding you information for your damn stories."

He gave his head an exasperated shake. "You—"

"How did you know about toni…?" Nick's right hand darted toward his mouth.

Lange took a step forward. *"Crap, he's about to get sick."* He spun and pointed to a trash can. "Get that can. Quick."

Nick dropped his hand and took several gulps of air. "My God, you've been tailing me."

"Let's just say we needed to protect our interests and leave it at that."

Nick gazed at Lange. "You keep saying *we*. Did the DNI sign off on your op?"

He affirmed Nick's question with a nod. "But your supervisor hasn't been brought in."

"And Ferguson? He's part of this?"

He nodded again.

"I was set up. What about the break-in at the condo? How does that fit?"

"We thought Browning might be compromised but couldn't get a warrant. The evidence you found in her condo validated our suspicions. We've linked her activities to several other individuals in the State Department."

He studied Nick waiting for a response. The kid looked stunned at the revelations.

"Who-the-hell *are* you?" Nick demanded. He shifted his attention. "You're part of this? I thought you were my friend or was that all show? What about our trip to Alaska? Was that to just get me out of the way?"

Mike shook his head and made to answer, but Lange interrupted. "He didn't know. I'll explain when you're ready to listen. Right now, we have to remove you and Michelle from circulation."

Nick made to protest but couldn't. "I think I'm going to be sick." His head fell back on the pillow.

Lange turned to look for Michelle. She stood in the kitchen doorway holding a *Ziploc* bag full of ice cubes, her face a cloud of confusion. "I'm sorry you had to be dragged into this mess. You're not safe here. We've got a place. You'll need to pack some stuff."

"But we're scheduled to fly the president to Chicago this afternoon."

"We can't allow you to go." Lnage glanced at Nick's inert form. "He needs you."

"We?"

"Mike will notify your command. I'll explain later."

Michelle crossed the room to kneel by Nick's side. She gently pressed the icepack against his temple.

"Concussion," he said. "We've got a doctor who will take care of him until he's back on his feet."

Michelle grasped Nick's hand then lifted her head, searching Lange's face.

He recognized the look. He'd seen it in Iraq. Bewildered. Pleading. He extended his hand to help her up. "He'll be fine. You both will."

"But—"

"We gotta go." He nodded toward Mike. "We'll watch Nick while you pack."

"You have to get Bill," Michelle said.

His forehead wrinkled in consternation. "Bill?"

"Nick's cat."

"Right."

He waited until Michelle had gone to her bedroom before pulling out his phone to contact George. "We'll move in five minutes. You set? ... Good." He looked at Mike. "Can you swing by Nick's condo and grab the cat?"

Chapter Thirty-Two

3100 PROSPECT STREET NW
GEORGETOWN, WASHINGTON, D.C.
THURSDAY 21 FEBRUARY

Lin-Wu could barely contain his rage. He set his jaw. Esteemed Mother cowered at the far end of the table. Huifeng and Yixing were seated on either side of her, their faces expressionless while awaiting their fate. He clenched the ivory handle of his letter opener fighting the disordered thoughts festering in his mind and glared at the two men.

How did Parkos find me? Could it have been a simple error? Perhaps. But by whom? Moore? Huifeng? Yixing? Huifeng had eschewed the use of their small sedan instead relying on Uber for his trips to the Embassy to meet with his contacts from the Enterprise Division. Yixing rarely left the premises. Esteemed Mother remained above reproach. Perhaps their operating systems have been compromised? The possibilities were endless. In any event, retribution from the Ministry of State Security would be swift. *But only if they hear of my failure.* He would speak with Yixing privately. There would be no misunderstanding. The guard's fate would be worse than his own if he reported the incident.

His analysis settled on Parkos. The American could not have been operating by himself. That would account for his rescue, but why allow himself to be captured? Such carelessness from a professional prompted reflection. More to the point, though, Parkos' intrusion exposed fundamental flaws in his operation. With that truth, he loosened his grip on the letter opener and set it aside.

He took a sip of the calming chrysanthemum tea infused with valerian root, closed his eyes and leaned back in his chair, focusing on his breathing, relaxing his muscles. His mind and body calmed through the relaxation techniques of Qi Gong.

How would he contend with adversity? A passage from Sun Tzu came to him. *First of all, we must measure adversity from where we ourselves are standing.*

"Esteemed Mother, tell me what you remember of the two men who defiled your home. You will not be harmed."

He noted her try to suppress a shudder at the memory and, presumably, what he might do to her for failing. In a halting voice, she recounted the assault on her home. Her description of Lange matched that from the pictures taken at The Upper Crust: Cool, focused, piercing blue eyes, dangerous. He pulled several photographs from a folder, selecting one. "Is this the man?"

She nodded in affirmation.

"And the others? The intruder with the black ballcap?" he asked.

She shook her head, avoiding eye contact by focusing on his neck as was proper.

He concluded the other man was an operative in the mold of Yixing. He knew nothing of the third man she'd seen and moved on. "Did you hear any names spoken?"

Esteemed Mother raised her little finger, pointing it

outward to indicate her knowledge was poor. "I cannot be certain."

He ventured a guess. "Moore?"

"Moore? Yes. I heard the other say that name."

"*Zhēn de ma.* Excellent. You have done well, Esteemed Mother. You may go."

He waited until she left the room before turning to Yixing. "Kill him."

Yixing's opaque eyes betrayed nothing but a twitch of his mouth conveyed his understanding. The assassin slid his chair back.

"Stay, we are not done." He addressed Huifeng. "Our contact in their Interior Department, Ms. ..."

"Browning."

"Has she strayed?"

"On the contrary. She has completed her work. She also provided confirmation that Parkos is about to be indicted."

"Oh? How did she come to acquire this knowledge?"

Huifeng slid a folder containing surveillance photographs across the table. "At my suggestion, she befriended a close acquaintance of Parkos."

He examined several of the photographs. They appeared to have been taken at a local nightclub. "Who took these?"

"The cross-dresser. The one who calls herself Annie Goodlay."

"Is there any indication that..." His lip curled in distaste. "Can she be trusted?"

"Yes."

He tapped another picture, the face of the man sitting across from Parkos. "Is this the man?"

"His name is Mark Arita. He works in the Treasury Department's Office of Terrorism and Financial Intelligence."

"This could be very useful. Can he be compromised?"

"He already is."

Lin-Wu's brows knitted. He had not been informed. "How?"

"Arita has demonstrated a certain lack of discretion for a married man. Miss Browning beguiled him with her charm and expertise in the arts of the bed chamber. If he becomes suspicious, we will confront him with the compromising photos and texts. I believe the term that applies is 'in flagrante delicto'."

He couldn't have expected a better outcome considering the debacle of the day before. *But what of Parkos?* If Browning's information were correct, he would be indicted. Why not let the American's investigation take its course?

"Thank you, Lam. You both may go."

Left to his own thoughts, he sipped the last of his tea, releasing the remnants of his anger. Time remained on his side, but only if he moved quickly. And if Parkos manages to block approval of our mining operation? No less a personage than the Vice Chairman of the PLA, General Zi Zhao had made it clear to him that if China could not possess the riches of Cape Lisburne then neither would the Americans. The General had declined to say how he would deny the Americans, but that was not his problem. He pondered these thoughts deciding what Zi would do. A smile crossing his face. He would take a page from Parkos' previous adversary, Bashir al-Khultyer. The risk of a war with the Americans never crossed his mind.

Chapter Thirty-Three

THE OVAL OFFICE
WASHINGTON, D.C.
FRIDAY 22 FEBRUARY

President Randal Stuart scanned the thirteen-page report titled, *U.S. Strategy for the Arctic*. He dropped the binder on his desk. "That's it?"

Bob Lawson cast a sideways glance at Justin Brown before he reached into his briefcase to extract another binder.

"This one provides the specifics," Lawson said. "I can sum it up in a six words. We are a long way off."

He accepted the second report. "Who put this together?"

"The J5 shop."

"Did Justin have input?" he asked, still curious about the exchange of glances.

"I ran the general outline by him."

There had to be more, but he moved on. "Where do we begin?"

"For starters, our command structure."

"How's your plan lash up to the Coast Guard's *Arctic Strategic Outlook?*"

"They're complementary and we've reached consensus on prioritization. Both plans provide estimated costs to fill the gaps in maritime domain awareness, infrastructure, and new ship construction. The Navy, in particular, has to address modification of our current vessels. Hull hardening, insulation, and steam de-icing systems to be able to operate in first-year ice one-foot thick with sixty-percent coverage and broken ice up to two-feet thick."

He understood the significance of Lawson's summary. The cost would be in the billions. "That leads us to the broader question. Who, then, is the primary advocate for our national security requirements in Alaska? DoD, Homeland Security, both?"

"Correct."

He shook his head at the answer. He leafed through the first folder searching for a sentence that'd caught his eye. He stopped on the eighth page. "'Persistence' is the operative word."

"Yes, sir," Lawson affirmed. "We have no permanent home ports, air stations or supporting facilities north of Anchorage. Kodiak is the closest suitable port that won't take a considerable investment to upgrade and it's 1,600 nautical miles from the Bering Strait. Provided we can get Congress to appropriate the funds, and that's a big *if*, we're looking at a good five years."

"Not good enough," Brown said.

He cocked his head at Brown's remonstration. *Could that be…?*

"I concur," Lawson said. "Our report also addressed the recommendations of *The Alaska Deep-Draft Arctic Port System Study*. This study recommended we take a look at Nome. The basin would have to be dredged and—"

He handed the folder back. "Do you have anything positive, Bob?"

"Matter of fact, I do," Lawson replied. "We achieved a

significant milestone yesterday."

"And that is?"

"We awarded a 'Detailed Design and Construction' contract for the lead vessel of a new class of Polar Security Cutters."

"That's a step in the right direction," Brown said. "Sylvester must have twisted some arms."

"He didn't have anything to do with it except sign off on the draft," Lawson said. "The project is being managed by our Integrated Program Office. NAVSEA is the lead contracting authority."

He suppressed a frown at the mention of the Secretary of Interior's name and Lawson's rare condemnation. For the most part, Poad's strategy of Constructive Ambiguity was just that, ambiguous. At best, it was predictably unpredictable and that just might keep the Chinese off balance.

He checked himself. That wasn't entirely accurate, but he had to direct Sylvester and the Director of Homeland Security to go to the chair of the House Coast Guard and Maritime Transportation subcommittee and present their case. DHS did their job. The problem was, he shouldn't have had to direct Sylvester. He expected his Secretaries to take the initiative.

"They're coordinating with Homeland?"

"Yes," Lawson answered, "but a fundamental problem remains. Aside from the environmentalists, it's safe to say this country hasn't come to grips with the realization that we're an Arctic nation. We have to design a campaign to increase public awareness and pressure our friends on the Hill."

"True enough." He released an exasperated sigh at the thought of dealing with the Congress. He'd have to come up with a plan that reconciled the often contraindicatory needs of national defense and those requirements addressing the EPA's role on the Arctic Council. "Can you get on that, Dan?"

Lantis looked up from his notepad where he'd been typing

a summation of Lawson's and Brown's comments. "Yes, sir. I have a number of ideas on who to approach. On a positive note, Sylvester is making progress with the Russians to regulate the Asian industrial fishing fleets."

"Can we take a step back?" Brown asked. "Congress continues to bicker over the United Nations Convention for the Law of the Sea treaty. As things stand, we can't even file a claim with the International Seabed Authority for the rights to seabed mining beyond our continental shelves in the Beaufort and Chukchi Seas."

"What happened?" Stuart asked.

"The bill stalled in committee again."

He noted the sour look on Gilmore's face as if the DNI had read his own thoughts about the House. The DNI had been keeping his own counsel to this point but stirred at mention of the United Nations. He also knew Gilmore shared one opinion in common with the Russian President concerning the role of this international body in the governance of the Arctic. Srevnenko stated that the Arctic was an unalienable part of the Russian Federation and dismissed any suggestion that the Arctic be placed under the jurisdiction of the international community. And last week, Gilmore had stated in no uncertain terms that the U.S. should declare a similar unequivocal stance. "You have something, Bryce?"

"Forget about UNCLOS and the Arctic Council. The Chinese are pushing for a foothold in the Arctic. Their strategy is being driven by their 'Polar Silk Road' and 'Made in China 2025' initiatives. The first pertains to international trade, the second to industrial expansion, particularly in the technology sector. The latter, in turn, is driven by access to rare-earth elements and obtaining a controlling interest of our own critical infrastructure via shell companies."

"Like snapping up Emmons-Powell Mining and developing the rare earth element deposits off Cape Lisburne," Brown said.

"Precisely," Gilmore said.

"If I'm not mistaken, Beijing's push to acquire Emmons-Powell should be locked up in Treasury's CFIUS review process," Stuart said.

"*Should be* are the applicable words," Gilmore added. "Beyond the questionable effectiveness of that committee, I've been in receipt of intelligence that suggests an individual in Interior's Offshore Energy and Mineral Management Service and perhaps another person in State have been muddying the waters."

What the hell? He darted a piercing look at Gilmore.

Gilmore continued undeterred. "The bottom line is that under current international agreements, we have to legitimize the extension of our seafloor beyond the two-hundred-mile Economic Exclusion Zone, an area called the Extended Continental Shelf. Countries making ECS claims are required to undertake scientific surveys and present their data to the United Nations Commission on the Limits of the Continental Shelf."

"Haven't we submitted the appropriate documents?" Brown asked.

"The short answer is, Yes."

"And the long answer?" Brown said.

"A Chinese company, Ocean Resources Management, has positioned itself to circumvent our requests to UNCLOS, the Arctic Council, and CFIUS to procure mining rights off the Alaskan coast. Nick suspects that Chinese mini-sub the Coast Guard located discovered the REE deposits."

Brown appeared to ponder the implications of Gilmore's statement, then shifted the conversation. "On a positive note, both the Congress and DoD have recognized the implications of Beijing's predatory economic practices and their impact on our supply of rare-earth elements."

"And those are?" Stuart asked.

"The Senate has a bill in committee entitled the

Onshoring Rare Earth Act that will mandate we secure our REE sources and require DoD to obtain those elements domestically."

"Bob."

"We've drafted changes to the Defense Production Act to increase the spending caps for REEs. That'll allow us to implement what the Senate is working."

He jotted down a note as a thought occurred to him. "I haven't seen anything from Parkos. What about that other Chinese company he's mentioned? Consolidated Seabed Resources?"

Gilmore prefaced his answer with a surreptitious look around the room. "He's close to completing his report, but got sidelined by the flu."

He noted Brown's right eyebrow rise, studied both men, and again decided there must be more. He turned to Lawson. "Bob, I think we're done with your piece. Why don't you compare notes with Dan? Bryce, stay a moment. You too, Justin."

———

Stuart waited until the room cleared. "Okay, Bryce. Out with it."

Gilmore took a deep breath. "You're not going to like this. We're in receipt of intelligence from Lange's group that suggests a number of employees in Interior, Treasury, and State have been compromised and are assisting the Chinese."

Gilmore continued before Stuart could recover from his surprise. "For example, the Chinese possess knowledge concerning the status of Alaska's Bureau of Land Management and Interior's Mineral Management Service approval processes for our Eagle River initiative. They have no legitimate reason to possess this information. They also have specific counterpoints to Eagle River's submission for mining rights off the coast. One of our operatives went through normal channels and asked for information on the Chinese applications and discovered that a lawyer in State's Planning Office had designated that information as a protected document."

"You have names?"

"Yes."

"And enough to justify an Intelligence Community Assessment on Chinese interference?"

"Yes."

"Is Justice in the loop?"

"I spoke with the AG," Gilmore said. "Galvin has assigned an agent from the FBI's National Security Branch to Lange's group. You may recognize her name from Nick's previous operation, Jessica Caudry."

"Caudry?" He gave his chin a thoughtful rub. He knew of her reputation first-hand from her work on the al-Khultyer affair. Solid. He also had no reason to doubt Galvin Ruckert's choice. "What's next? Indictments?"

"Not yet, there may be others involved."

"Have Deputy Secretary Oakes and Milt Lum from Treasury been brought in?"

Gilmore hesitated and glanced at Brown who nodded. "They've been informed of our concerns, but not the specifics."

"How deep does this go?"

Gilmore tightened his lips and looked out the window over Stuart's shoulder. "Sylvester may be involved."

Stuart felt the color leach from his face. The sound of the mantel clock hammered at him from across the room. That could explain Sylvester's odd behavior at the cabinet meeting back in December ... and perhaps Kathrine's. Could she be entangled with the Chinese as well?

Poad would become a distraction. Or worse. He stiffened, angered that he'd procrastinated, not wanting to deal with the consequences if he'd fired him. And now? The vultures in the beltway would be circling looking for a way to… "What do you have?"

"Nick's investigation into a shell company that is a known front for the Chinese Ministry of State Security turned up Sylvester's name. The website owner of this company, Lengkok Holdings, also happens to be the director and major shareholder of three U.S. based companies in which Sylvester holds a considerable interest."

"How much is considerable?"

"Nearly half a million. That in itself wouldn't have been a problem except that Sylvester failed to disclose his financial interests in these companies during his confirmation hearings. We also couldn't find any records to indicate how he managed to acquire these assets."

"Maybe his wife's family?"

"There's no indication she even knows."

Stuart leaned back in his chair, stunned by the revelations. "Can this get any worse?" He looked at Gilmore and Brown's faces. Their somber expressions confirmed his fears.

"I'm afraid so," Gilmore said. "I got a heads-up from Galvin this morning. Nick's about to be indicted."

"What on earth for?"

"He's been accused of setting up an offshore account and not reporting the income."

"Hardly enough to get indicted."

"The problem is where he got the money."

Stuart struggled with the ramifications of Gilmore's disclosure. "Any thoughts that Beijing is behind this?"

"Wouldn't surprise me," Gilmore responded. "My cut is Beijing is prepared to play hardball. Hell, they already are, but they may resort to other measures if—"

"Good, Lord, Bryce. Are you implying military action?"

"We'd be well advised to consider all possible outcomes, Mr. President."

Chapter Thirty-Four

THE SAFE HOUSE
STAFFORD COUNTY, VIRGINA
FRIDAY 22 FEBRUARY

Nick paced around the five-room cottage's living room like a caged animal railing against his confinement. His fists tightened in exasperation. What could have been. What should have been. He kept replaying the past few days burdened by influences and distrust that only existed in his mind. He stopped pacing by the room's picture window wearying of the effort to confront his useless speculation.

The northeast facing window offered a panoramic view of the wooded Virginia countryside and glimpses of a small lake. The rustic cottage, sequestered within fifty rural acres near Minerva, Virginia, lay hidden at the end of a rutted, crushed-stone track that branched off county road 665 seventy-two miles south of Washington. A heavy lock secured a rusted linked-chain strung across the driveway that added another measure of security to the safe house.

A short distance from the cottage stood a smaller cabin for the security detail and a metal roofed shed housing two ATVs.

George told him that Lange had purchased the safe house and grounds with funds from a black account and only his team knew of its existence. *Impressive.*

Bill the Cat choose this moment to appear, announcing his arrival with a series of loud meows. He made his way over to Nick and rubbed against his leg. He leaned over and gave his pet's neck a good scratch. In response, Bill cast him an imploring look. He recognized the signal and the meows. "Didn't Michelle already feed you?"

He stood, intent on going to the kitchen, then stopped to massage the knotted muscles in his neck. At least the dizziness and nausea were receding as the doctor had predicted and he no longer stumbled around like a drunk.

"If your symptoms haven't worsened, then you're better," the doctor had said.

Made sense. His headaches were decreasing in severity and he felt marginally better. He had turned down the OxyContin. He could manage with Tylenol.

The sound of Michelle's humming and the aroma of frying bacon wafting from the kitchen prompted him to turn. He crossed the room and looked through the door, his buddy, Bill the Cat, forgotten. He watched her a moment before speaking. Just the sight of her in worn jeans and loose-knit sweater, red hair in disarray, softened his heart. "I'm going down to the lake. Wanna come?"

"I'm right in the middle of making breakfast, silly. The bacon's done and I'm about to start a batch of blueberry pancakes for the crew. Besides, it's freezing out there."

The crew? He fought down a wave of jealousy. Were they protecting him, ogling Michelle, or just keeping him out of Lange's way? Probably all three.

"You need to eat something," she said.

He pointed to an open pizza box on the kitchen table. "I had a couple pieces when I got up."

Michelle rolled her eyes. "You're completely hopeless."

Her comment elicited a rare smile. "Guilty as charged." He stepped through the door. "Last chance."

"You go ahead. I'll save some batter. And wear a coat so you won't catch your death of cold." She grabbed a whisk and turned back to her cooking.

He lingered before Michelle shooed him out of the kitchen with a wave of the whisk. "Now get before the weather turns."

He slipped on his coat and made his way down a narrow path through a tangle of low scrub, barren oaks and maple trees. The soggy ground gave way under his feet with a wet squish, the brown Virginia mud coating the sides of his sneakers. His eyes happened on a solitary robin perched near the top of a large maple. The overcast sky above the bird portended more snow.

He continued down the slope, stooping to pick up a small rock before happening upon an old duck hunting blind set to the right side of the trail. An AR-15 assault rifle lay propped against the woven reed wall of the blind within easy reach. The solitary guard stationed there glanced at him before swinging his binoculars back across the lake that defined the northern barrier of the safe house.

Other men patrolled the grounds. That should have reassured him.

He nodded to the man and continued on his way, his journey ending at the cottage's ramshackle pier and made his way to the end.

He tested the weathered, gray planks, then took a seat letting his feet dangle over the dark water while tumbling the rock in his hand. The solitude of the lake, broken only by the sound of an occasional bird call, quieted the turmoil raging in his mind.

He tossed the rock, following its path until it disappeared beneath the surface with a soft plunk. The concentric circles spreading across the water's surface reminded him of one of his Venn diagrams. If only he could find the answers in one of them. At the moment, he couldn't even define the unanswered questions that befuddled him. He sighed and stared across the water.

He almost succumbed to the tranquility of the lakeside but with his mind freed, his pent-up emotions again gave way to anger. Anger born of the terror, the helplessness he'd felt during his captivity, the stupidity of the attempted break-in that compromised Lange's mission, the guilt of endangering Michelle.

He gripped the raw-edged boards of the deck to prevent his hands from trembling. An uneasy premonition stuck him, but before he could pursue the thought, voices sounded from up the path. He recognized one as George's. The other probably belonged to the guard. He spun in annoyance at the intrusion.

"How ya doin'?" George said.

"I've been better."

George studied him, weighing Nick's response. "Understood. We'll have a clearer idea of when you guys can return to D.C. in a couple more days."

"Couple days? Where's Lange?"

"Cleaning up your mess."

He stared across the water fixing his gaze on the distant shore.

"I'd suggest you take advantage of your time here to recover," George continued undeterred by Nick's asperity. "Even the guys who've had Escape and Evasion training need time to get their heads right."

"Yeah."

The two men turned at the non-response and walked back up the trail leaving Nick to brood. George spun back. "You know what's the mat—" His voice cut itself off, strangled by his anger.

"No, what?" he finished for him.

"Stow the fuckin' attitude."

He stiffened at George's tirade but feigned indifference.

George couldn't contain his suppressed rage. "Get your head out of your ass and focus. You're so full of shit right now you can't get beyond your own self-pity. Hell, you've even managed to screw up your relationship with Michelle."

George's mention of Michelle penetrated the fog in his mind.

"Yeah, hot shot," George continued. "Right now, you're failing on multiple levels."

He faced his tormentor, his eyes flashing defiance.

"Good," George said. "That's the first appropriate response I've seen since you've been here."

"Go to hell."

"Yeah, I probably will. In any event, I'll give you this. Your bungled break-in may have smoked out your marks."

"What's that?"

"You heard me. The TAO guys repelled a wave of cyber-attacks yesterday targeting the cloud computing services of Creekside Consultants and Eagle River. If I were to place a bet, I'd say your Huifeng guy has panicked." George turned and took a step up the path.

"But, he's not—"

George halted. "Lange'll fill ya in tomorrow." He terminated the conversation and continued up to the house and breakfast.

He toyed with the idea of remaining on the pier after George disappeared, but pushed himself up when a snow flurry began to dust the bleached wood of the deck. He shuffled back to the house and dropped down on the tattered living room couch, elbows on his knees, staring at the floor. Shards of disjointed thoughts continued to pierce his soul. The intrigue, the answered questions, his failures, his self-doubt left him too exhausted to think.

"Nick?"

He swiveled toward Michelle's voice. He needed to talk, to explain, but the words escaped him. "I …"

"Say something, Nick. I can't … No, I won't leave you."

His head dropped, weighed down by the burden of his despair. He spoke to the floor. "I'm just …"

Michelle set the plate of pancakes and bacon she held on the small dining table. "Nick, you need time."

"But …"

"You can't keep blaming yourself."

"I guess."

Michelle appeared about to offer a word of encouragement but changed her mind and picked up the plate of food. "I'm getting some coffee. Then we'll talk."

———

Michelle threw herself on the bed burying her face in a pillow to stifle a sob. Her interaction with Nick had left her emotionally exhausted, coping with a toxic mix of frustration, guilt, anger, impatience. She'd dealt with these same emotions before during her father's gut-wrenching descent into the dementia of Alzheimer's disease. Her father had been admitted to a chronic care facility when her mom could no longer cope, and she hadn't been there to help. She'd escaped by joining the Air Force.

She rolled over and reached for a box of tissues. She could wipe away the tears, but not the memories. *Not again.* Nick had been there for her, just listening while she purged her soul, coming to grips with the turmoil that raged in her mind. He'd even gone with her when she returned home to visit her dad and mom. He understood when others hadn't. She would not abandon him as it appeared some were prepared to do.

Chapter Thirty-Five

THE NICKOLAS
GEORGETOWN, WASHINGTON, D.C.
SATURDAY 23 FEBRUARY

Geoffrey Lange acknowledged he had to bring in the FBI and, by extension, the Justice Department, but… He took a sip of Darjeeling tea and studied the newest member of his team. Tall, almost five-eleven in heels, athletic. He appreciated her unadorned beauty but concentrated on those attributes that would contribute to his team.

Senior Special Agent Jessica Anne Caudry conveyed an aura of self-confidence, assured of her place and competence despite not knowing the extent of the multifarious, clandestine nature of his team's mission. Alert, intense brown eyes judged her surroundings.

"Care for something to drink?"

"Water's fine," Caudry answered "I…" She darted a piercing look across the room.

He turned to see Taylor Ferguson appear at the top of the stairs.

Ferguson acknowledged Caudry's inimical reception, his

upper lip curling in a sardonic smile. "Nice to see you again, too, Jessica. I heard you were joining the team."

He cringed. Caudry's response didn't escape him nor did the quivering muscles of her clamped jaw. If looks could kill, she would have dropped Ferguson in his tracks.

They had a history. He'd heard the rumors. Anything could derail the working relationships within the team. One positive note? It appeared Caudry wouldn't back down from a fight. The encounter also dredged up his own encounter with Ferguson months earlier. He'd confronted the CIA agent and made it abundantly clear who was in charge of the operation.

"If you two can't be civil, I'm going to throw you both out on your asses." He paused to judge their reactions. "Good. Now we can get down to work."

He directed his attention to the fourth person in the room who'd been examining the study's large collection of leather-bound books lining the far wall. "George. Time to start."

The agent responded to his nom-de-guerre, slid the volume he'd been reading back on the bookshelf, and crossed the room. He stopped in front of Caudry and extended his right hand. "George. Counter-Intelligence."

Caudry gave the pro-offered hand a quick shake. "Caudry. FBI."

Lange directed his first question to George. "Where's Moore?"

"We haven't been able to contact him. I drove back from the safe house this morning to coordinate the search."

He kept his facial expression impassive while contemplating the implications of this unpleasant news. He had no need to elaborate what needed to be done. "Keep me informed." He addressed Ferguson. "What's your take on Nick?"

"He's clean."

"You sure? Treasury's Financial Crime Enforcement Department laid out a compelling case against him in their

SARs report," he countered, then faced Caudry. "What do you think?" He watched her eyes. If the question about Parkos startled her, she covered well. *How much did she, the FBI, and Justice know that he didn't? Or perhaps it was his mention of Moore?*

"No doubt. He's been set up," Caudry answered. "I suspect the Chinese tapped his personal information from the millions of Equifax accounts they hacked last year. It's also likely the MSS managed to bypass his personal computer's or iPhone's authentication protocols to reveal his passwords. It'd be easy enough to set up the offshore account and rely on Banco's requirement to forward details of the account's earnings to Treasury."

He cocked an eyebrow. He probed her with another question. "What about the cash and documents in his condo?"

"He wouldn't be that stupid," Caudry replied.

Damn. Did she have something solid or …? He stopped himself. "Does Justice have any exculpatory evidence?"

"None that I know of," Caudry said. "The indictment's sealed and is being reviewed by the Deputy Attorney General's office."

"Are you in a position to block his arrest?"

"No."

"I wonder if we should just let this play out?" George said.

"Maybe. The Chinese might get careless if they believe they've taken Nick out of circulation. That brings me to another loose end. Arita."

"We've got him under surveillance," Ferguson answered.

Caudry's eyes widened. "Mark Arita?"

He ignored her. "Can we set up a backdoor?"

"Already done," Ferguson answered. "The pen register, tap and trace programs we placed on his work phone didn't capture any suspicious incoming or outgoing calls."

"What about his influence nets?"

"He's been careful," Ferguson said. "We got nothing from

his phone records or computer. No implicating emails or texts."

"Can we use him?" George asked.

Ferguson's face hardened. "No. Let him burn. He turned on his friend. We tracked down the name and phone number Parkos found on that wadded up piece of paper in Browning's condo. The name's an alias, but the number is Arita's."

"What the hell's going on? I don't know a thing about this." Caudry demanded "And who the hell is Browning?"

"A suspect."

"Did you get a FISA warrant?"

"No," Lange answered, wondering how much she knew. Judging from her reaction, it couldn't be much. "We're operating off the grid."

"Under whose authorization?" Caudry countered. "You have no authority to investigate an American citizen."

"The president's."

"Does the Attorney General know any of this?"

He addressed George, intent on cutting off any further discussion of surveillance. "What else do you have?"

"We discovered a stash of steamy instant print photos in Browning's condo when we went back to place our taps."

"I take it they weren't of the family pet," he replied, ignoring the look on Caudry's face.

"Hardly," George answered. "We got Browning with another woman, both decked out in black-leather lingerie. Pretty saucy. Got one with Arita too. He—"

Lange cut him off. "You have an identity on the other woman?"

"Yeah," Ferguson said. "Ashli Thompson, a lawyer in State's Planning Office."

"Seems Ms. Browning gets around," Caudry said.

"Apparently," Ferguson added.

"Nick didn't say anything about lingerie," he said.

"Not surprised," George answered. "He's a novice. Likely didn't care for pawing through her dresser drawers."

"Are they lovers?" he asked.

"Who? Browning and Thompson?" Ferguson responded.

"Yes," George answered.

"Could be a threesome," Ferguson offered.

He heard Caudry mutter, "*Creep*," before George handed him a manila envelope.

"You'll find these interesting."

He glanced at the instant photos of Thompson and Browning before pausing at another set.

"I took these at the Cork and Barrel when Parkos met with Arita the end of last month," George said.

He examined the surveillance photos. Several were of Arita and Nick. He stopped at the third. *Damn*. He seldom forgot a face, even from a random encounter. The face staring back at him belonged to one of the two who'd been sitting next to Nick at the Upper Crust. He handed the pictures back. "Got an ID?"

"She goes by the name of Annie Goodlay."

He suppressed a smile at her name choice. He knew some real characters in the transgender community, and she'd fit right in. "I'm thinking it's time to have a conversation with Ms. Goodlay. Bring her in."

"Is there a common link between all of these actors?" Caudry asked.

"It's beginning to look like Sylvester Poad," he said.

Caudry rocked back in her chair. "Good, Lord. The Secretary of Interior?"

"The same. It appears he's gotten in over his head, but we don't have enough to indict him."

Caudry's voice reflected her incredulousness. "We?"

He ignored her. "The AG floated the idea of offering him a plea deal if he'd resign and offer evidence to a Grand Jury. We want to bring the entire network down."

"Have you touched base with Nick's assistant?" Caudry asked.

"Austin Mack?"

"He's been talking with Arita." Caudry said.

"How do you know that?" Ferguson said.

"Arita told me."

"No, shit," Ferguson responded. "Well, I guess that follows since you and Arita have worked together. What'd he have to say?"

"Nick's been fishing for information about a guy at Treasury that Mack identified, a senior staffer named Devon Gant."

"How does that link to the Chinese?" Ferguson asked.

"He thinks Gant's on their payroll," Caudry said. "Gant's being squeezed and is on the verge of exposing a messy network of favoritism, kickbacks, and indiscreet behavior by one or more executive level employees at State, Interior, and Treasury, all with possible ties to the Chinese."

Ferguson leaned forward and whistled. "Damn, this thing is way bigger than we thought."

Lange suppressed a frown. *God damn it!* Nick hadn't shared any of this. On the other hand, he only had himself to blame for not bringing him in on the operation earlier. A lot of this current mess could have been avoided. "Any indication that Arita is going to alert Gant?"

"Not yet, but we're keeping tabs on him," George said.

He changed tack. He didn't want to reveal any more to Caudry about his team's surveillance methods or the horizontal escalation of cyber-attacks by the Chinese following Nick's bungled break-in. "George, what have you learned from Mack?"

"He's been tight lipped, but I managed to persuade him we're working with Parkos. He dropped Poad's name and a Swiss investment fund that Poad may be using to hide his money."

"I'll get that to the right people," Lange said. He resigned himself to Caudry's presence despite his wariness of involving the FBI. "Taylor, have your people turned up anything on their intelligence community assessments?"

"The Chinese intrusions at Eagle River have..." Ferguson stopped and addressed Caudry. "Yeah, we know about Darrel Nance. Couldn't be helped."

She took a drink of water to stifle her retort giving Ferguson an opening to continue. "Our advanced exploits of the attempted intrusions identified a good IP address for Huefing. We breached their network. Money laundering. Links to Ms. Browning. All sorts of crap, but the best? We confirmed the full name of Beijing's man: Jai Lin-Wu Tai and his alias, James Wai."

"There enough to take him down?" Lange asked.

"Not yet. We're still setting up our counter-intelligence op to prosecute the vulnerabilities we've uncovered. There's lots of chatter pertaining to Consolidated Seabed Resource's proposed venture off Cape Lisburne and their efforts to acquire a controlling interest in a company vying to take over Emmons-Powell. That's something we can exploit."

"See what you can do," he said. "I'll deal with the fallout from Nick's problems. Anything else?"

"We might have something," Ferguson said.

"I'm listening."

"An intercept."

"Could you be more specific?"

"We've seen several references to a Chinese operation with the code name, CALAMUS and the PLA. We haven't been able to link it with anything we have on file."

Ferguson laid his pen down. "Maybe. We've got to run the diagnostics. I can't say much about the PLA. The references where pretty vague but had to do with an operation in the Arctic. Could be anything."

"Can you get what you have to our contact at the DIA?"

"Yeah, Defense might already be working it."

"Could it pertain to Nick?" Caudry asked.

Lange stiffened. *Damn, Caudry may have something.* He'd have to pursue the clue but decided this wasn't the place. "I'll set up another meeting for later this week."

He glanced at Caudry out of the corner of his eye. Her face gave away nothing. She presented more of a threat to the team by being misinformed and drawing the wrong conclusions. He had to bring her in despite his misgivings. "Jessica, would you stay a moment?"

Chapter Thirty-Six

THE SAFE HOUSE
STAFFORD COUNTY, VIRGINA
SUNDAY 24 FEBRUARY

Nick lay on his back grappling with yet another jumble of nebulous questions, a fetid bog in which he'd become mired. His internal deliberations lacked substance without reason or rebuttal, stacked like so much decaying cordwood within his mind. George's stinging remark about his relationship with Michelle topped the pile. He didn't think George's observation had veracity, but overcome by inanition, an undercurrent of doubt lingered in his mind.

He sighed in frustration and eased himself out of bed. How could he doubt the sincerity of the one person he should hold on to?

Michelle stirred, her right arm thrown across the rumpled sheets of her twin bed as if reaching out to him. He recalled her mom saying her daughter had always been a rescuer, picking up strays in need of care. That explained a lot. As did something else her mom had said. She recounted a story from her husband. He would always warn Michelle about venturing out onto the thin ice covering their pond in the depths of winter. She could fall through and drown. Nick succumbed to another wave of guilt. *Will I push her through the ice? She deserved better.*

He slipped out of his bed, walked to the room's single window, and pulled back the curtain releasing a dam of chilled air seeping in through a crack under the sill. He shivered, more from worry of what the future might hold than from the cold. A patch of clouds moved across the three-quarter moon, casting fleeting shadows across trackless new snow. The vista prompted another of Lange's Yogi'isms to pop into his brain. "If you don't know where you're going, you might wind up someplace else." He turned away from the window. *Yeah, no shit.*

He made his way to the bathroom intent on downing a couple of extra-strength Tylenols to ease his headache. He flipped on the light, freezing at the sight of the haunted image facing him in the vanity mirror. The apparition's eyes were sunken, encircled by dark bruises set above a three-day beard. Racoon eye's the doctor had said. Basilar skull fracture. He studied the face ravaged by injury, stress, and fatigue staring back at him that reflected the answers to the questions he asked but had suppressed. The room spun. He stumbled and grasped for the door frame, struck by a wave of vertigo.

"Nick?"

The sound of Michelle's voice penetrated the fog enveloping his mind and propelled him out of the bathroom. He staggered toward his bed and dropped down on the edge of the mattress.

Michelle stood and grasped his right hand. "Are you okay? You look like you've just seen a ghost." She shifted her grip to check his pulse. "You need to lay down. You're probably dehydrated. Have you been drinking your water?"

"Hey, Parkos. You decent?"

Michelle dropped Nick's wrist at the sound of Lange's voice booming from the hallway.

"What the hell is he doing here?" Nick said.

Michelle reached for her bathrobe and jammed her right arm into the sleeve. "He's sick. Give me a minute."

He struggled to stand, but Michelle pushed him back. "You're not going anywhere. I'll take care of him."

———

Lange sat on the tattered couch pondering how the sequel would go. Michelle had stormed out of the bedroom, grabbed his arm, and marched him to the living room before going back to Nick. Her reaction to his unexpected appearance brought a wry smile to his lips. *Don't mess with a mama bear protecting her cub.* He'd underestimated her love for Nick. A mistake he wouldn't repeat.

He took a sip of black coffee he'd grabbed from the kitchen and sorted through his options. Weighing on his mind were the details of the FBI's investigation that Jessica Caudry hadn't revealed in the group meeting at the Nicholas. Information from the FBI's Criminal Investigative and National Security Units. She confirmed the Justice Department would indict Nick the moment he returned to work, information he couldn't share with him without compromising the team's mission. The operation had to remain clean—no leaked conversations, no compromising emails or texts, no blunders.

Leaked conversations? He considered the implications of what he knew. Perhaps it was time to revert to his cover as an investigative reporter.

His thoughts transitioned to another concern. Jason Moore. Where the hell was he? He'd simply disappeared. No, *simply* was the wrong word. Was he dead? Had the Chinese flipped him? If so, why would he disappear? Lange massaged his chin. He had no choice but to stow the conjecture and wait to hear back from George.

His thoughts turned to Nick. *And what should I do about you?* He'd been provided assurances that Nick would be protected. He shook his head, not at all sure of those assurances. Nick would be expendable if his alleged malfeasance and subsequent arrest were somehow tied to the DNI or the president— or to him.

Michelle's appearance in the doorway halted his conjecture. Jeans and a sweatshirt had replaced her bathrobe, but the fire in her eyes remained. He set the coffee cup on the floor and stood buying a few seconds to consider what George had told him about Nick's fragile emotional state. The guy could tip over the edge if he didn't play things right. He motioned her to sit. "How's he doing?"

"Better."

"Is he well enough to return to work?"

"He needs more time."

Lange nodded. "How about you? Do you have to get back?"

"I need to stay. I'll work it out."

"Can I talk to him?"

Michelle crossed her arms over her chest. "Hasn't he been through enough?"

"Been through what?" Nick said, barging into their conversation.

Michelle pivoted at the sound of Nick's voice. "You shouldn't be up."

Lange started, shocked at Nick's appearance. "My, God, Parkos, you look awful. Do you feel as bad as you look?"

"I doubt it."

He paused and decided to leave well enough alone. "Michelle, I have to talk with Nick."

She didn't move. He didn't want to risk alienating her but had no choice. "Alone, please."

"It's okay," Nick said. "I forgot George told me that Geoff might be here today. I need to hear what he has to say."

Michelle didn't appear convinced but took a step towards the kitchen. "I don't want to hear any shouting from you two."

He waited until Michelle disappeared, then waved Nick to a chair. "How's your head?"

"Better than it deserves to be considering the thump it took."

"No. How's your head?"

"I'm good. Just got some stuff to work out."

He scrutinized Nick's face. *Stuff? No shit, Sherlock.* He decided to skip what he'd prepared to say and went directly to the highlight reel. "The Chinese are getting desperate."

"What's going on?"

"We've just repelled another wave of cyber-attacks exploiting vulnerabilities in the cloud computing services of Creekside Consultants' clients,"

"They use Cloud Hopper to seek a backdoor?" Nick asked.

"That's the current thinking. NSA has also been monitoring a horizontal escalation of attacks targeting employees of Emmons-Powell and Eagle River. Spear phishing, password spraying, credential stuffing."

"But Eagle River doesn't have any employees," Nick said.

"They do now. Austin created a fake personnel department. We used that account to entrap the Chinese hackers by having his *employees* use weak passwords. The hackers employed techniques to unmask the commonly used ones. 123456 and QWERTY–"

"Qwerty?"

"The top left letters of the keyboard. The Chinese were trying to insert malicious code to conduct wiper attacks."

"Were they successful?"

"I don't know, but the Tailored Access Operations folks are prepared to mitigate the damage and repair any vulnerabilities. Our Advanced Network Technology guys traced the attacks back to the hackers. They employed a QUANTUM attack suite to exploit a compromised router."

"Anything else?"

"Yeah. The hackers also targeted an outfit called The Capital Group. You know anything about them?"

"That's the Hedge Fund we set up to provide the funds to buy out Emmons-Powell."

"Hedge Fund. Impressive. Austin's done great work."

"He has," Nick acknowledged, "but I need to get out of here."

"Understood. Let's shoot for Tuesday." He stood. "I'll tell the team to steer clear of the house and give you two some privacy."

"Is it that obvious?"

"Yes."

———

Nick slumped on the couch in the silent house. Lange had kept his word and cleared out his team giving him and Michelle some space, but he had retreated to the bedroom right after Lange left.

Michelle understood these moods of his, the undercurrent of emotions that racked him. He longed for affection, but she knew that within him lingered the fear of rejection, of being abandoned again. He'd been orphaned when his mom died and his dad had disappeared from his life. She studied his face looking for the subtle signs that reflected what lay buried within. She reached out to grasp his hand.

He pulled away, running his hand over the stubble on his chin, and looked down at the floor. "I know I haven't been much fun to be around lately."

"Were you ever any fun?"

He sat upright, twisting to face her. "Seriously?"

Michelle's face relaxed into a smile, eyes softening. She leaned over and kissed his cheek. "Well, you may have had a few moments." Her words broke the brittle emotional barrier between them.

He circled his arm around her shoulders, and whispered into the tangle of her red hair. "Maybe we could have one of those moments."

Michelle reached up and removed his arm. "Later hot shot. Right now, we've got to get you cleaned up." She stroked his cheek. "Beginning with that awful beard. Then I'll cut your hair."

Chapter Thirty-Seven

NATIONAL COUNTERINTELLIGENCE CENTER
MCLEAN, VIRGINA
WEDNESDAY 27 FEBRUARY

Nick shut out all external distractions, concentrating on updating his spreadsheets and associated hyperlinks. Austin had brought him up to speed on the status of Eagle River, LCC and now he was piecing together all the events since his botched break-in. Not even a week had passed since he returned to his desk, yet it felt like a month.

He glanced at the cork board cluttered with green index cards and the maze of string not satisfied with the results. He stood and walked over to the board and ran his finger over several of the strings, pausing on the one connecting the new cards for Arita and Lin-Wu, his thoughts conflicted. *Why?*

He dropped his hand, deciding instead to focus on an article Austin had copied from the *Los Angeles Times.* The article addressed widespread environmental destruction of Chinese farmland and the subsequent protests by Chinese farmers whose lands had been destroyed by their government's quest for rare-earth elements. The article detailed how various government sanctioned companies had peppered the farmers' lands with gaping excavation pits. These pits were now filled with contaminated wastewater tainted by the toxic chemicals used to extract rare-earth elements from thousands of tons of excavated ore. Not unlike Emmons-Powell.

While he doubted the central government would do anything to address the farmers' grievances, he understood Beijing's rationale. They were concerned their stranglehold on the world's supply of REEs was in danger from other countries developing their own supplies. A case in point: the threat posed by Eagle River to buy a controlling interest in the old Emmons-Powell mine.

Austin also had his faux company float a proposal to expand its operations to the Arctic. The reports he'd received from the DNI indicated the leadership in Beijing was becoming even more confrontational. What would they do?

He let his mind drift. In a moment, his thoughts snagged on a distant memory, the mysterious email he'd received months ago. While he knew where the message had originated, the three words Lange sent still resonated. *It's Not Over.* Of that, he had no doubt. Something troubled him but he couldn't place the source.

He stared into space, lost in thought. *So, what would the Chinese do next if their efforts in the Arctic were thwarted?* He picked up Austin's report and re-read the article from the *LA Times*. Environmental destruction, contaminated water … *My God. His old nemesis, al-Khultyer's dirty bombs. They….*

Without finishing the thought, he typed in a search for prevailing winds, then a map of Alaska. The old base at Cape Lisburne, the Inupiat village of Werok, and the Noatak National Park caught his eye. Not only would the hundreds of the indigenous people living in that small village be at risk and one of the nation's largest national parks would be… He opened a new document and began to outline an inconceivable scenario.

A faint shadow crossed the computer screen. He stopped typing, hands suspended over the keyboard.

"We expected you yesterday."

He stiffened at the sound of his supervisor's voice. *A "How are you doing?" would have been nice.* He spun the chair around. "Good morning, sir."

Strickland pulled on his nose and peered at the faint bruises under Nick's eyes.

"I heard you got the flu then fell and cracked your head."

The inflection in Strickland's voice suggested a perfunctory statement of fact rather than any sense of concern. He remained at the door, his body poised as if wanting to bolt. His eyes flicked several times toward the hallway before he continued. "So much for the flu vaccine. I've never been much of a believer. Gives you the flu." He pulled on his nose again and stole a furtive glance down the hall.

"Is anything wrong?" he asked.

"No."

He thought Strickland's body language said otherwise and his supervisor's cryptic answer didn't do anything to assuage his sense of unease.

Strickland backed out of the doorway. "There are some gentlemen here to see you."

He cocked his head at the unexpected announcement. Before he could respond, two men dressed in dark-blue suits entered the room. One, sporting a red tie and wearing an earpiece, stopped just short of him and flashed a badge.

"FBI."

What-the-hell are they doing here? He gripped the arms of his chair and jerked upright.

"Special Agent Gunnar Vanatsky," the man said. He motioned to his partner. "Agent Tyreke McCall."

He stared at the agents. *Lange hadn't said anything about bringing in the Feds. This has to be a mistake.*

Vanatsky interrupted Nick's thoughts. "Mr. Nickolas Parkos?"

The menacing tone in the agent's voice and his penetrating, opaque eyes sent a chill down his spine. He could only nod.

"You are being charged with violations of the Foreign Account Compliance Act."

"What?"

"Please stand and place your hands behind your back."

He managed to shut down his computer erasing his memo about the Chinese, then stood, a look of disbelief on his face. He heard Vanatsky recite his Miranda Rights, the agent's voice, distant, the words muffled by the confused fog of disbelief, enveloping his brain. The handcuffs tightened around his wrists, the quiet of the room pieced by a dull Click, Click, Click. *At least he said 'please'.*

"Do you understand your rights as I've explained them to you?" Vanatsky didn't wait for an answer. He grasped Nick's elbow and lead him out the door.

Strickland stepped aside, shaking his head in disgust. Several employees chatting in the hallway aborted their conversations and stared. Nick recognized one face. "Jim, tell Austin Mack what just happened."

<hr>

Nick stared out the tinted rear window of the black SUV as they swung around the Lincoln Memorial and headed up Constitution Avenue. He guessed he was being taken to the Federal District Court building. His guess was confirmed when they pulled into the building's basement garage where another agent met the car and escorted him to a barren interrogation room.

"Make yourself comfortable," the agent said. The door closed behind him with a dull thud.

He scanned the room. Typical setup. Two-tone gray walls, bare table, two wooden chairs, video camera mounted in the upper corner of the ceiling. He dropped into a chair facing the room's one-way window, unclenched his fists, and laid his palms on the table. He stared at the far door handle determined not to lose his cool. The handle turned. The door swung open.

Vanatsky entered without a word, crossed the room, and settled into the chair opposite him. The agent made a pretense of arranging several unmarked folders on the table, then shoved a blank piece of paper and a ballpoint pen across the table.

"What's this all about?"

Vanatsky leaned back in his chair. "I thought we established that in your office."

"I don't have any foreign accounts. I haven't done anything wrong."

"You may want to reconsider."

Reconsider? The response baffled him. "What the hell is going on?"

"You've violated a trust. That in of itself is reprehensible, but that won't land you in prison." Vanatsky's eyes hardened. "You're being charged with the unauthorized disclosure of national intelligence and espionage."

His pupils widened at the revelation. *Espionage?*

Vanatsky didn't pause. "Your violation—"

He pounded his fists on the table. *Arita? He had to have known. That bastard.*

"I've been set up. That—"

"Save the theatrics, Parkos. I'm not finished. We obtained a warrant and conducted a search of your condo. Perhaps you'd like to confirm what we found." Vanatsky opened one of his folders and leafed through the contents. "Photographs, cash, bank statements. Shall I go on?"

"I wouldn't be that stupid."

"Well, it appears you are." Vanatsky slid a document across the table. "Perhaps you would care to explain this?"

He scanned the header and flipped through several pages of a credit card statement under his name. *$28,301.58 in charges, mostly for electronics.* Then he saw the billing address. Downtown Development District, Woodston Street.... *Wilmington?*

He stared at the address, a vague recollection surfacing. *Oh, shit.* The supposed junk mail with the unknown address that he'd thrown in the trash unopened? He recovered and formulated a retort, hoping his face hadn't given him away. "I've never even been to Wilmington, North Carolina."

"Look again. We're talking Delaware, but then you know that." The agent pushed a folder across the table. "Open it. The Grand Jury will have something to say about this, so you can stop the charade."

Grand Jury? Nick scanned the document from Banko Investment and Trust, dumbfounded at what he read before blurting. "This isn't mine."

Vanatsky retrieved his folder. "That's an impressive offshore account you set up, then laundering funds through your fake business in Wilmington."

Nick's mind reeled. He had to buy time to figure out what was going on. "I want my call."

"Soon enough."

"I'm not saying another word until I have a lawyer."

Vanatsky gathered up his folders and stood. "Suit yourself."

Nick forced himself to think, cycling through his options. He couldn't call Lange and compromise him. Michelle had already been through enough. Austin may already know the charges, but the agency would shut him out as a possible co-conspirator.

He had to trust that Austin had started to place calls. *What about Mike?* He recalled the meeting with him and Justin Brown at the White House back in February. He had a sickening feeling they knew something and had hung him out to dry. *What had Mike said?* "There's been a development. You have to trust me." He stared at the barren tabletop. *Can I?*

Vanatsky reappeared and handed Nick a phone. "One call."

He waited until he was alone again then punched in Mike's number, almost wishing he wouldn't answer. The damage was done. The FBI would trace the number.

"Rohrbaugh."

"Mike?"

"How are you doing?"

So, Mike already knew. "How do I answer that?"

"We're going to fix this," Mike said. "You know that? Right?"

"Make the calls, Mike. I've been framed."

"Understood. We'll do everything we can."

He ended the call and looked at the ceiling. *Do what we can? A Grand Jury? So, I'm on my own?* He adjusted his thinking to address this reality. *Where do I start? With what I know.*

The array of agencies arrayed against him was formidable. The FBI's Criminal Investigative Unit, the National Intelligence Center, NSA's Internal Affairs Division, Treasury's Financial Crimes Enforcement Department. And the revelation that incriminating evidence had been found in his apartment? That'd explain the weird stuff like losing his checkbook. He'd underestimated the Chinese. Again. *And my friends?* That was another matter entirely.

Chapter Thirty-Eight

**NATIONAL COUNTERINTELLIGENCE CENTER
MCLEAN, VIRGINIA
WEDNESDAY 27 FEBRUARY**

Bryce Gilmore stood facing the window in his office, hands clasped behind his back, staring at the stark late-winter landscape. His lips compressed into a tight line. The conversation with the president, such as it was, hadn't gone well. Stuart had cut him off when he broached the topic of Nick's indictment. While the president voiced understanding that Nick might well be innocent, he wouldn't allow his administration to get pulled into the morass of alleged accusations and counter arguments that could go public. The bottom line? He wouldn't intervene.

He turned from the window and settled into his chair, tapping out a staccato rhythm on the green-leather desk blotter. He'd developed a liking for the young analyst and agreed the evidence compiled in the folder on his desk supported his supposition the kid was innocent and had been framed. Most likely by the Chinese.

So what were the options? Lange? He couldn't do

anything without blowing his cover or risk giving the kid the impression he had been marginalized. The best of the remaining alternatives to gain Parkos' release was to figure out a way to leverage the Attorney General. And, that would be difficult. He set aside Nick's folder and picked up the thin dossier containing Galvin Ruckert's biography from his inbox.

Principled, strong-willed, shrewd. A graduate of Northwestern University's Pritzker School of Law. First government job? The Justice Department's Office of Legal Counsel. One portion of Ruckert's work history did intrigue him, though. There had been brief reference to another government job buried within the report. Before he entered law school, Ruckert had worked at the CIA. *Why didn't I know that?*

He picked up his secure phone. "Wendy, get me the Attorney General." He punched the speaker button then opened the top drawer of his desk to reach for a pack of Marlboro cigarettes. He'd always identified with the brand's iconic masculine image, the rugged, self-sufficient, western cowboy. *Come to Marlboro country.*

His hand stopped above the dose pack of Nicorette gum. He paused. Last fall he'd had a near miss. His internist had ordered a routine chest x-ray because of his eighty pack-year smoking history. The follow-up CT scan confirmed the presence of a suspicious mass.

The subsequent bronchoscopy and an open lung biopsy had shown the mass to be benign, but the episode had shaken him. He extracted a piece of gum, gave it a couple chews, and tucked it away in the corner of his cheek while lamenting the loss of the Philip Morris company's image of the indestructible American male, his image.

A self-deprecating snort escaped as he recalled what he'd told his deputy years before when the government banned smoking in the workplace. *It's none of their damned business if I want to kill myself.* With that, a favorite quote came to mind. "The lucky man is one who knows how much to leave to chance." He wasn't a man to leave things to chance, not with his work, and, now, not with his health.

Ruckert's familiar voice sounded through the speaker. "Good afternoon, Bryce. What's on your mind?"

He didn't mince his words. "Parkos has been set up."

"You're presuming I know what you're talking about."

"You know."

Ruckert countered. "Your man is in a great deal of trouble. What proof do you have of his innocence?"

He darted his tongue into his cheek to retrieve the wad of gum. How much could he reveal without compromising Lange's operation? He gave the gum a couple intense chews, a poor replacement for his Marlboros. "Are you familiar with the word, CALAMUS?"

"Calamus? Isn't that the name of a plant? Narrow sword-shaped leaves?"

"Correct. But more-to-the-point, we have intercepts to suggest it may be the Chinese code name for the operation to frame Parkos."

"What else haven't I been told?"

He countered. "What else do you have on Parkos?"

"I can't divulge that."

"And if certain information from the Grand Jury just happens to be released to the press?"

"You've got a damned plant in my office?"

"I've got my sources. None of whom I'm going to divulge." What he also didn't reveal was the information he held from Lange's intercepts of Browning's and Arita's encrypted texts. Arita had sent Browning sensitive information from Treasury's Financial Crimes Enforcement Network which she, in turn, had probably passed along to the Chinese. He planned to use this exculpatory evidence from the FinCEN to wrestle a deal from Ruckert.

"Parkos' indictment will hardly be news," Ruckert said. "Even if it makes it to one of the national TV shows. The average American's attention span will guarantee the story will be conveyed to the trash heap and forgotten within hours."

He tapped his index fingers together. Ruckert had seen through his bluff and the implied threat. "I'll give you that. But the Chinese—" He paused for effect.

"I'm listening."

"I'm looking for solvency."

"That's a financial term."

"True, but I have a cure."

"What do you want, Bryce?"

"Release Parkos on bail. He's the key to our operation to take down a Chinese operation endangering our national security. I need him."

"You're playing that card?"

"Yes."

"And if I accept your plan, you understand nothing will change in regard's Parkos' indictment and the Grand Jury."

"Understood."

"What's your cure?"

"I'll begin with the premise that Justice's focus is on obtaining a conviction."

"True enough," Ruckert said. "So, what do you have that will impact our case?"

"We can penetrate Banco's computer network." Gilmore's statement was met with a moment of silence.

"How do you know about Banco?"

His jaw relaxed but he couldn't reveal too much. "Trade secret, but I can tell you we've already begun the process."

"Give me something."

"Fair enough. We're working to access Banko's Contract Management System."

"To trace the origin of the deposits into Parkos' account."

"Correct again."

"What about the evidence we collected in his condo?" Ruckert asked.

He didn't have a good answer and hedged. "We're looking through the security camera footage."

"You think the Chinese would be that sloppy?"

He decided to raise the ante. "Perhaps."

"Then you've got more than you're telling me."

A tight smile crossed his face. He would provide just enough information to raise doubt in Ruckert's mind. Enough to make him question the validity of the DOJ's charges against Parkos. It was time to apply what he liked to call his Fourth Law of Thermodynamics. *When the heat is on someone else, it's not on you.*

"Perhaps you'd be interested in something that is newsworthy." He could almost hear Ruckert thinking in the silence that followed, then he drove home the knife.

"I have the names of two individuals operating out of an expensive Federal style home in Georgetown who are affiliated with the Tianjin State Security Bureau of the Chinese Ministry of State Security. They've been targeting and infiltrating the managed service providers of multiple American firms to steal intellectual property and confidential business data. These compromised MSPs also perform IT services for patches to various cloud services. The damage they've already done is incalculable. We've got enough for you to indict them."

"In exchange for releasing Parkos," Ruckert said.

"Yes."

"I'll consider your proposition."

"Good doing business with you, Galvin. I'll touch base tomorrow." The line went dead.

He leaned back in his chair. Ruckert had provided the opening he'd been seeking. *Or had he?* He took several more chews on his *Nicorette* gum as several possibilities unfolded in his mind. He flipped open a small leather notebook, located a private number, and placed another call.

Chapter Thirty-Nine

Geoffrey Lange took a sip of the *Inchmurrin* 18 year, an inspired whisky crafted by the Loch Lomond distillery. The whisky's finish was long and warming with hints of oak and ginger. He tilted the Glencairn glass toward the fireplace amplifying the glow of the golden-hued scotch. A bottle worth adding to his private collection.

He emitted a snort at his summation of the whisky's finish, recalling a wine critic's description of a new Washington State cabernet, "Opulent with a reticent power," questioning whether he wasn't also burdened with the pretentiousness of an oenophile. Fortunately, there was nothing reticent about the *Inchmurrin*. He also admitted to himself that he lacked the educated nose of a professional whisky sommelier, the size of his own prominent nose notwithstanding.

He set the glass down and tapped the ash off a top-rated *Cohiba Spectre* cigar as his thoughts drifted to The Upper Crust Tap and Grill. It'd been weeks since he'd set foot in the place.

He rationalized that he'd been too busy. Within his heart, though, he knew he wasn't prepared for another failed relationship. That, and he didn't want to risk encountering his old partner. He studied the glowing tip of the aromatic cigar. Robert understood, at least on one level, but—

"Mr. Parkos is here to see you, sir."

Edmund's voice, coming from the head of the stairs, cut through his thoughts. They were late. He suppressed a surge of anger before recalling George said he would take a circuitous route to make sure they weren't trailed by the Feds—or the Chinese. A prudent measure, but not of much use to throw off the marshals since Nick wore a GPS tracking bracelet. He stood and motioned Nick to the empty chair facing the fireplace before addressing the other two men. "Thank you, Edmund. George, why don't you grab something from the bar."

He took his seat after the men were out of sight and studied Nick. Dark rings of fatigue rimmed Parkos' sunken eyes. He leaned back and took a thoughtful pull on his cigar, concluding it'd be best to stay with his plan and open with something neutral, something Parkos could handle instead of delving into the treacherous waters of his arrest. That said, he wondered how Nick would handle the surprise he was going to drop on him. He blew out a thin stream of blue smoke.

"That son-of-a-bitch betrayed me," Nick said.

He jerked the cigar from the corner of his mouth. "Excuse, me. What? Who?"

"Arita."

He rested the cigar on the edge of the ashtray. *So much for easing his way into what he'd needed to discuss.* "Yeah, he did. We're looking to leverage that to bolster your defense."

"Who else is there?"

"There aren't any new players." He leveled his eyes at Nick. "We're still stringing the pieces together. That said, we did come across something in our intercepts that'll interest you."

Nick's eyes narrowed. "I'd say I have more than enough going on that interests me."

"A code word."

"Okay, I'll bite."

"CALAMUS."

"Doesn't mean a thing."

"It will. It's the name of the Chinese operation to frame you."

"Does Justice know?" Nick asked.

"I've spoken to Jessica."

"What about her boss?"

"The AG? He's holding his cards close to his chest."

"What did you offer?"

"I didn't offer him anything. The DNI did. Gilmore told him that he has enough to implicate James Wai as an unregistered foreign agent and to deport Huefing."

"I'm listening."

"You remember the attempted intrusion into Eagle River's computer network designed to entrap their faux employees? The TAO guys were able to identify a vulnerability in the Chinese network and plant false information. Huefing bought it. The team extracted his IP address and has been tracking him with PRISM and X-Keystone for the past several weeks."

Nick nodded. "Ferguson said his team had infiltrated the Chinese networks during our January meeting. That may be enough to expose the Chinese operation, but not enough to protect me."

"I wouldn't be so sure." He paused to pull his briefcase onto his lap, removed a photograph, and handed it to Nick. "Recognize her?"

Nick studied the photo. "That's the Cork and Barrel."

He leaned over and pointed to a woman sitting at one of the tables. "And that would be Annie Goodlay."

"Goodlay? You gotta be kidding. What kind of name is that?" Nick took another look. "She looks familiar."

"She should. She's one of the women who sat next to you at the Upper Crest when we first met. She's been tracking you for months."

"How'd she even know about me?"

"Good question. In any event, after you left your meeting with Arita at the Cork and Barrel, George followed her to her apartment."

"He was there too?"

"Yeah. Your counter-surveillance techniques suck, but that doesn't matter at this point. What does matter is that we brought her in for a little chat."

Nick made to reply, but he cut him off. "Aren't you interested in what we learned?" He didn't wait for an answer and proceeded to outline what he'd discovered about the Mark Arita/Ashli Thompson/Kimberly Browning threesome and how that relationship, in turn, led his team to Sylvester Poad.

"What about Wai? Do you have enough to link him as the common denominator?"

He understood Nick's focus on the Chinese and chose not to elaborate on what he knew of the American threesome's connection to Wai's network or his apparent dismissal of Poad. Both understandable considering the circumstances. "Not yet. He's remained in the background pulling the strings. What we did uncover is Wai's use of *LinkedIn.*"

"*LinkedIn?* Wha—"

"I'm getting there. The National Counterintelligence Security Center fed us intelligence detailing the Chinese Ministry of State Security's efforts to recruit naïve American academics and scientists with lucrative investment and research deals too good to be true. Wai tapped into one of these bogus international corporate recruiting firms that fronted for Lengkok Holdings."

"So, that's how they subverted Poad?"

He rolled his cigar in his fingers, studying the tip. "My cut is they ensnared Poad with a series of layered traps for the purpose of identifying and turning a member of the president's inner circle. Wai waited for the right moment to exploit him."

"What did you find out about Jason Moore?" Nick asked. "Justice never did get an approval from the FISA court to put him under surveillance."

"Moore? He works for me."

The revelation appeared to rock Nick. "What the—?"

"Jessica verified that the FBI did submit a FISA warrant to the Federal District Court to track Jason's iPhone, Google, and email accounts. Gilmore intervened and asked the presiding judge to prolong the approval process. We couldn't afford to have Jason's cover blown. That would have exposed our entire operation."

"Makes sense." Nick drew himself up in the chair. "I've got something else."

"About Moore?"

"No."

He braced himself. "What do you have?"

"I'm thinking the Chinese might resort to something extreme if their efforts to set up a mining operation off Cape Lisburne are thwarted. While they'd like to exploit those resources, they may be more interested in blocking our access."

"And you have an idea what those extreme measures might be?"

"Contaminate the entire area with an RDD."

Lange rocked back in his chair. "A radiologic dispersal device? Like al-Khulyter? That's sheer madness. If it were anybody else, I'd conclude you were nuts but you seem to have this uncanny ability to divine the future."

"I'd say that's a bit of an overstatement."

"No, you can connect a bunch of random dots. See what others can't."

"It'd be worse. They'd use cesium-137 or strontium-90. They're desperate and this action would serve the additional purpose of taking out the Air Force's plan to replace the obsolete surveillance radars of the old North Warning System at Cape Lisburne and block a critical piece of our ballistic missile defense system."

"That would be an act of war. What have I missed?"

"The DNI warmed me to tread carefully," Nick responded. "He said the senior leadership of the PLA is becoming more aggressive. Less predictable. If they perceive what they believe is a direct threat to their national security. Well…."

"Go on."

He turned away after Nick finished, summarizing his reaction with only a single word from his sulphuric vocabulary. "Shit." Then he calmed as another thought occurred to him.

Nick caught the change in expression on Lange's face. "What?"

He took a draw on his cigar. "Interestingly enough, we have an op in the works that may solve our problems."

"Is this op something I should know about?"

"As a matter of fact, it is. You're going to Lakewood, Colorado."

Nick rocked back in his chair. "Colorado?"

He motioned to the bottle of *Inchmurrin*. Nick had every right to be startled. "Pour yourself a couple fingers. You look like you could use a stiff drink."

Nick did just that and took a swallow. "Why?"

"You're a keynote speaker at a symposium."

"Symposium? Keynote speaker? What-in-hell are you talking about?"

"The Responsible Management of Alaska's Mineral

Resources. You're attending as the government's expert in rare-earth mining."

Nick finished off his remaining scotch in a gulp. "You can't be serious."

"We took the liberty of submitting your CV, Dr. Miller."

"Miller? That's my old alias."

He tried to suppress a smile. "I'm told your performance at the University of Hawaii got rave reviews."

"You know that's pure B.S.," Nick replied. "What if someone recognizes me?"

"We looked over the list of attendees. You should be good."

"Should be? That's quite the leap of faith, don't you think?"

Nick looked at his empty glass, then reached down and pulled up his pants leg to reveal the black GPS ankle bracelet. "Besides, I'm grounded by this damn thing. I can't leave the city."

"Nice try. Ferguson's one step ahead of you. One of his guys that looks a bit like you will be here any minute to remove the tracker. He'll wear it and mimic your daily routine. We're thinking it'll be some time before your watchers from Justice figure out that something's amiss and by then you should be back in town."

"Should be? That's the second time you've said that."

He continued as if he hadn't heard Nick's protest. "Ferguson's guy will stay in your condo and take care of the cat." He paused to judge Nick's reaction. "You okay?"

Nick didn't answer.

"Mike's going with you," he added trying to assuage Nick's distress.

Nick turned away, brow furrowed in thought. "How am I going to get there? I can't exactly book a flight on Delta."

"Not to worry," he answered while typing a text on his iPhone.

Nick didn't appear to notice. "You do recall that I am paid to worry."

"You'll do great."

"Yeah, right." Nick expelled a long sigh of resignation. "When do I leave?"

He set down his phone. "Wheels up in six hours. Check-in and registration for the symposium is Sunday."

"I've got to pack."

"We've got that covered."

"Wha…

George appeared in response to Lange's text and dropped a duffle by Nick's chair. "Everything you'll need."

"You broke into my condo?"

"We wouldn't be the first." George thrust out a tight bundle of fifty-dollar bills. "No credit cards."

Nick eyed the bundle. "How much is this?"

"Enough."

Nick bit off his response when he caught sight of Ferguson's man. The guy nodded at George and approached. "Let's see that bracelet."

Nick cocked is head in thought, then addressed the new arrival. "I don't suppose you could clean up my place while you're staying there?"

The guy snorted his response. "Fat chance."

Chapter Forty

CGULFSTREAM G500
DENVER, COLORADO
FRIDAY 1 MARCH

Two hours into their flight to Denver, Mike Rohrbaugh handed Nick a black-bound folder. "The team took the liberty of preparing the talking points for your presentation tomorrow, Dr. Miller."

Nick's head jerked up. *Miller?* He'd been savoring a second Manhattan, engrossed in a novel he'd been reading on his Kindle. "What are you talking about?"

Mike held out the folder. "You've been a bit distracted of late. The team decided to give you an assist."

He looked with suspicion at the proffered folder, not caring for the direction his day had just taken.

Mike flashed a smile. "Come on, take it. It won't bite."

He set down his book and accepted the folder with a frown.

"Trust me."

He answered with a skeptical "Harrumph," then turned his attention to the talking points and hard copies of the presentation's slides. He recognized Austin's input and had to admit the package wasn't bad. That said, there were a number of discussion points that didn't fit with the narrative he wanted to present. "I don't suppose I'm allowed to edit these?"

"If you must, but Geoff cautioned you have to resist the temptation to freelance and go off script."

"Me?"

"Yeah, you."

The chartered Gulfstream G500 touched down at Denver International at 1644 hours. The distant snow-capped mountains were tinged a light rose by the setting sun. Nick thought he could get used to this sort of travel. No check-in, no TSA, no cattle-call boarding process, competing for space in the overheads, weird seatmates. If only he were a multi-millionaire and could afford—

His fantasies were aborted when the aircraft braked to a stop at the private jet terminal. He took a final look around the wood-paneled cabin, gathered his things, and followed Mike onto the tarmac. They were escorted to a waiting SUV, then headed west for Lakeland.

He'd dozed off during the twenty-six-mile trip, waking when they pulled in front of a Fairfield Inn, not the squalid motel that he'd feared. Better yet, the Fairfield was the host hotel and Mike said he'd put their room on a credit card that Lange had provided. That action negated any possibility the Feds would track his own or Mike's personal or government issued cards to Lakewood. He patted the wad of fifties in his coat pocket and emitted a snort. He should have used the fraudulent card the Chinese had set up in his name. That would have set them off.

Mike turned at the sound.

"Just thought of something funny," he replied to Mike's quizzical look. He made his way through the lobby without offering any further explanation, pausing to look at a glossy poster advertising the upcoming meeting, questioning why he'd been sent here. *What have I been roped into?* He slowed by the well-stocked bar, reading the labels before moving on, intent on finding the conference rooms and registration desk.

He recognized a familiar face at his destination, University of Hawaii geology professor, Willard Diekam. *Damn, I'm busted.* He pivoted, looking to escape. *So much for Lange's assurances that there wouldn't be anybody here who could recognize me.*

He saw Diekam turn in his direction. He ducked around the corner into the hallway leading to the main lobby, then bolted down the empty corridor slowing his pace as he encountered another guest exiting a conference room. The guy made eye contact and nodded but showed no signs of recognition.

He entered the lobby, exited the front door to the parking lot, and walked to the side entrance near his room.

———

FAIRFIELD INN CONFERENCE CENTER
LAKEWOOD, COLORADO

Nick took a deep breath, not pleased with the scientists' reaction to his presentation. He saw several drop their jaws and take deep yawns. They were distracted, bored, focused more on the upcoming break. He needed to go off script. Dismissing Mike's cautionary note about freelancing, he released his thumb from the slide projector's remote and started over.

"This morning we've listened to several thought-provoking presentations on global warming and the impact on the Arctic environment, but we must also focus on the immediate threat—the danger to Alaska's fragile ecosystem from poorly regulated mining operations.

"Permit me to take a moment and provide an example, the quest for rare-earth elements. Specifically, I want to address the threat posed by unregulated foreign firms, those companies whose mining claims are shrouded in obscurity by our nation's laws governing such issues as incorporation and reciprocal rights."

He caught sight of Diekam seated in the last row of the room. *Damn.* He had no choice, but to continue. "Let me provide a specific example of the dangers we face.

"If Chinese-owned Consolidated Seabed Resources is granted permission to mine rare-earth elements off the Alaskan coast, it is prepared to deploy a 250-ton excavator. This machine is benignly called a Seabed Mining Tool in their prospectus."

He clicked through several slides and projected a picture of the behemoth. In point of fact, this 8x17x13 meter excavator will scour the ocean floor generating in excess of one-thousand tons of sediment per hour. I'll let you come to your own conclusions as to the damage this would cause to the aquatic life in the migration routes of the Chukchi Corridor."

The assembled scientists' eyes swiveled from the picture of the mining tool toward him, his statement met with consternation and an undercurrent of murmurs. Now he had their attention but he caught himself and checked what he was about to say. He had almost blundered by revealing too much. If this assorted collection of well-intentioned, but naïve geologists, climatologists, and oceanographers had any idea of the secret he harbored, they'd be aghast, disbelieving. This greater threat posed by the Chinese would be against all precepts of their conscript of ethical behavior.

He scanned his audience, suspicion hooding his eyes as Diekam and a number of attendees flipped open their registration packs, presumably looking for his bio. Could one of these men be a Chinese agent? He knew of Beijing's concerted efforts to subvert American scientists and academicians by enticing them with certain *inducements*: sex, money, access to advanced research projects. He studied the faces of the scientists, several of whom returned his gaze with an inquiring look of their own.

Which of these men would sacrifice his country to advance his own career, his greed, his ego? His eyes settled back on Diekam. The professor's expression suggested he had worked out the deeper implications of his interest in Consolidated, his subterfuge, and the reason of his visit to the University of Hawaii.

Should I bring Diekam in? And for what purpose? Could he be counted on to be discreet? No. He may have guessed what agency I work for. Nick wavered. Should he take the risk and confide in Diekam, swearing him to silence knowing that promise wouldn't hold?

"Excuse me? Doctor Miller?" someone called out.

He scanned the audience and spotted the questioner. The guy looked like a throwback 60's acid-head from Haight-Ashbury. Long unkept hair, scruffy beard, worn retro threads. A carefully crafted, and in Nick's opinion, an expensive look. All he was missing was the headband. Where was he from? Cal Berkley? "You have a question?"

"I understand you may have an active interest in Eagle River, LCC's application for mining operations off the coast of Alaska," the man responded. "Isn't that a conflict of interest?"

How-the-hell did he know that? Had the Chinese turned him? "I'm sorry sir, but I don't have the privilege of knowing you."

"Professor Ron Hopkins. Cal Berkley."

He realized he needed to negate Hopkins' question before his own narrative went completely off the rails. He also made a mental note to send Austin an encrypted text to have him run a background check on this Hopkins guy, if that was his real name. He focused on Hopkins. "I'll answer your question with a lyric. 'You don't need a weatherman to know which way the wind blows.'"

"Bob Dylan," Hopkins responded. "I'm impressed. But to answer my question."

He leaned on the podium, his eyes focused on his inquisitor. "Have you ever watched an episode of the reality TV program *Bering Sea Gold?*"

"Ah, no. I haven't."

"I'd suggest you should. I believe you'd find it enlightening. And frightening. Thanks in large part to this program, the Alaskan Department of Natural Resources has been swamped with requests for strip mining operations and offshore dredging. These are the very types of operations that present an immediate threat to the environment we all seek to protect.

"Do you think these folks, or the Chinese for that matter, who are applying for mining permits in Alaska possess a heightened social consciousness underpinned by a desire to preserve the environment?" He swept his eyes across the room. "I'll answer for you. NO."

Hopkins stood. "How do you propose we move forward?"

"I submit that we draft a position paper endorsing a moratorium on all mineral exploration in Alaska to provide the time to develop a cogent plan to protect this national treasure."

"Then I presume you would also oppose the reactivation of the old Distant Early Warning radar site at Cape Lisburne?"

"That is beyond my purview."

"Don't you—"

The conference's moderator cut off Hopkins. "Thank you, Professor. We need to move on to our morning's last speaker. Thank you, Doctor Miller, for a most stimulating presentation. I presume you'll make yourself available for questions at the break."

At the break, Nick stood to one side of the lobby sipping a

diet Coke not the least bit interested in making himself available for questions. He spotted Diekam staring at him and gave the professor a half-hearted wave. Diekam returned his gesture with a nod before making his way across the room.

"Very impressive performance," Diekam said.

"Thank you."

Diekam's voice took on an edge, the malign intent obvious. "My statement wasn't meant to be a compliment, Dr. Miller. I'm not sure who you are, but you aren't who you profess to be and I take great offense at being used."

"There's more going on here than you realize."

"No doubt. And you—"

"I have my reasons." He turned his back on Diekam, then spun. "I'd say, watch the news, but you'll never"

He caught himself and held up a hand fending off another question from Diekam. He should have held his damn tongue and stayed with the script as Mike had advised. *Oh, well.* Now he'd have to deal with the consequences, hardly feeling like the agent provocateur that he'd imagined before his presentation.

The encounter, bad as it was in retrospect, did serve several purposes. The first? He couldn't bring in Diekam, although he felt the chances of the UH professor having been turned by the Chinese were low. The other positive? He may have unmasked that asshole from Berkley. He paused again, chagrined at his characterization of Hopkins. The guy may have had legitimate reasons for his position. That is, before he'd been corrupted.

———

Mike looked up from his laptop when Nick entered their room. "How'd it go?"

"You remember Diekam from UH?"

"Sure, what about him?"

He's here," Nick replied.

His brows knotted. "Crap."

"Yeah, and that's not all. I may have identified another Chinese asset."

"Oh?"

"A guy from Cal Berkley. Guy named, Ronald Hopkins. He peppered me with questions during my presentation."

"And those were?"

"My connection to Eagle River's bid for mining rights in Alaska and a presumed conflict of interest. There's no plausible reason he could have known about my connection to Eagle River except for the Chinese feeding him information."

He set down his pen and swiveled the desk chair to face Nick. "We may be screwed if Hopkins is working for the Chinese or if Diekam opens his mouth."

"I'm going to contact Austin and have him run a check on the guy." Nick hesitated. "There's more."

He tensed, his response not lost on Nick. He didn't want to know the next surprise "What'd you do?"

"I blew it by going off script. I gave Hopkins an opening."

His jaw tightened. "I can't say you weren't warned."

Nick stared at the floor. "I screwed up and made too many wrong mistakes."

"You just used a malapropism."

"A what?"

He cut off what he wanted to say. "Never mind."

Nick decided it best not to pursue his mistakes, flipped open his laptop, and scanned his emails. He stopped at a secure message from Lange. "I've got something from Geoff."

Mike buried his anger and stood to look over Nick's shoulder. "What'd he say?"

"There's been another wave of cyberattacks. Dozens of small utility companies serving critical infrastructure were targeted. Ferguson's folks traced the attacks to an obscure site in Hong Kong."

"The Chinese again."

"No doubt," he said. "Their APT41 organization is using a variant of the APR-10 Cloud Hopper to rout their attacks through multiple layers of anonymous servers. They're also ghosting, using other hacked firms' accounts as drop boxes for data stolen from previous hacks. That, and they've targeted vulnerabilities in our ability to exploit cloud computing and networking apps."

"You're getting pretty good at this stuff."

"Naw, I'm just parroting what Geoff said. The FBI and NSA are providing an assist to the affected companies, scanning their networks for firewall intrusions and malware-laced emails. So far, sixty-percent of the targeted sites' email servers are reporting malicious code. The problem is, the cloud companies are stonewalling."

"That doesn't make any sense."

"They don't want their customers to know the extent of the intrusions into their networks."

"This could be the Russians," Mike said. "Not too long ago they hacked the Iranians to make it look like they were behind a recent spate of attacks."

He stood. "I've gotta get back to D.C."

"D.C.?"

"An email from Jessica. There's been a botched attempt to abduct Darrel Nance."

"Remind me. Who's that?"

"An FBI asset in a false front op. Business named Creekside Consultants we've been using to entrap the Chinese. Ferguson's guys are involved."

"Your buddies from the break-in?"

"Yeah," he answered. "The Chinese have been trying to penetrate Creekside and turn Nance for months. They gotta be getting desperate if they tried to abduct him."

Mike tilted his head back trying to digest this latest twist. "Let Geoff handle it. You need to contact Jessica and tell her to touch base with him."

"Good idea, but I've—"

"You're not going East, Nick. We're going another direction. Northwest. Seward, Alaska."

"Excuse me?"

"Things are heating up off the coast. With what you've just told me, we've gotta move to stay ahead of whatever the Chinese are planning."

"Heating?" He dropped onto the bed ignoring Mike's inadvertent pun. "Alaska? This have anything to do with what I told Geoff?"

"Ferguson's folks and the DIA got a few intercepts that provide some credence to your theory. Your worse-case scenario appears to be backed up by the intercepts. Geoff's been directed to focus on Beijing's intentions, possible outcomes, and what lengths they'd go to achieve them."

"Oh."

"We've been directed to rendezvous with the *Truxtun*".

"Our old friend from the last op?"

"The same. We'll leave first thing in the morning. I just have to firm up a few details with the rest of the team."

Nick dropped flat on the bed just missing Mike's briefcase. "Team?"

Chapter Forty-One

SEWARD MILITARY RESORT
SEWARD, ALASKA
SUNDAY 3 MARCH

Nick grasped the wing strut of the single-engine Maule M6 and swung himself down to the tarmac grateful to escape the cramped rear seat of the plane. Cruising along at a sedate hundred-and-forty knots, he thought the flight from Anchorage to Seward would never end. He felt as if he'd been crammed into the rear seat of a minivan instead of the aircraft that Lange's group rented from a local outfitting company.

A four-wheel drive jeep Wrangler idled on the tarmac, white exhaust curling heavily in the frigid air, ready for the next leg of their trip. He studied the vehicle. Tire chains mounted on the Wrangler's wheels were not a good sign.

Mike nodded a thanks to Lange's contact who'd delivered the vehicle, motioned Nick to the passenger seat, and hopped in behind the wheel.

He climbed in, shivering in the bucket seat while he eyed the dreary surroundings of this isolated section of the airport.

A recent snowfall had smothered the buildings and tarmac with tones of dull white and muted gray. Not the pristine landscape he'd envisioned. "Damn, it's cold. What is it? Zero?"

"Come on man, it's Alaska," Mike replied. "What did you expect?" He gunned the engine and took off, exiting the bleak airport and turning left onto State Route One.

The scenic road paralleled the north shore of the Cook Inlet before heading southwest down the Kenai Peninsula toward the Seward Military Resort.

Fifteen minutes later, they pulled into the driveway of the Seward Military Resort. Several pairs of tire tracks criss-crossed the open expanse. One set led to a beat-up Land Rover parked in front of a flagpole and a set of broad stairs leading to the resort's office. Otherwise the place appeared deserted.

Mike pulled to a stop in front of a two-story clapboard building adjacent to the office. "What do ya' think? Great, huh? We're in unit three."

He grunted a response, sprung from the vehicle, followed Mike into the unit's living room, and dropped his duffle with a heavy thump. A faint aroma of coffee lingered in the air fighting for dominance with an underlying damp, musty odor. A pile of clothes was strewn over the back of the living room couch and several camouflaged tactical deployment bags were stacked against the far wall. The folks from Joint Base Elmendorf had already made themselves at home but were nowhere to be seen.

Mike flicked a wall switch. The gas fireplace whooshed on. "Homey, don't you think?"

He spun at the sound of two men coming through the unit's front door before he could answer. He stared at the new arrivals. They looked like something out of a L.L. Bean catalog.

"You're early, but glad you made it before night set in," the nearest man said, extending his hand toward Mike. "Major Rich Carlson. Air Force. Ops."

"Mike Rohrbaugh," Mike replied.

He assumed the two men had been briefed on whom they'd be meeting and would first approach the Navy captain instead of some spook from the NSA. Fair enough.

Carlson turned to Nick. "Welcome to Alaska, Mr. Parkos."

The second man, African-American, about five-ten, muscular with a rugged face and short cropped hair stepped forward. "Lieutenant Commander Treyvon Berg." He paused at the look on Nick's face. "You weren't expecting a man of color?"

"Ah, no. I wasn't expecting a fish."

Berg laughed and held up a huge flat fish. "It's all good man. I go by Trey. And this would be a halibut. Figured we'd take advantage of the open time before you arrived to charter a boat. Try our luck catching dinner."

He cast a skeptical eye at the halibut. He had no idea what to do with a real fish. "You're going to cook that?"

Berg cocked his head. "What else would I do with it? They've got a cleaning table and all the gear in the main building. All you need to contribute is cut up and fry the potatoes."

"Ah ..."

"I'll handle it," Mike responded.

Nick woke to the aroma of breakfast and subdued voices. It seemed Mike and the others had been up for a while and had let him sleep. By design or not, he appreciated the extra rack time. He swung out of bed and padded to the bathroom, his stomach growling in anticipation of breakfast. Dressed and shaved, he headed to the kitchen.

He came to an abrupt stop at the sight of Mike and Berg

sorting through a stack of cold weather gear piled in the middle of the living room. "That's a lot of stuff for just two of us."

"Ah, you've decided to join the living," Mike said. "Trey's coming with us. He's a kindred spirit."

"Oh, Lord. Another SEAL?"

"Sure enough. You missed the secret handshake," Berg said. "Grab yourself something to eat and we'll get started."

He sipped coffee out of a white ceramic mug after downing a huge plate of scrambled eggs and sausage, judging the reaction of the two officers from Alaska Command. He'd just gone over his thoughts of how a worst-case scenario might play out at Cape Lisburne.

Berg shifted in his chair. "ROE?"

"Depends on what we find," Mike answered. "If there are Chinese assets at the site intent on rendering the installation inoperative, we're authorized to use deadly force."

"This Nick's 'worst case' scenario?" Berg said.

"Yeah."

Berg shook his head. "Since they'd have no business being there, I suspect Beijing won't react if their team just happens to disappear."

"At least not immediately," Mike said.

"Prisoners?" Nick asked, surprised at Mike's response. They hadn't discussed in detail on how they'd respond to each of his "What if" scenarios. He wondered who Mike had talked to in Washington.

"If the opportunity presents." Mike stood and made for the kitchen to refresh his coffee. "I'll go over the particulars of our rules of engagement once we're settled aboard the *Truxtun*. I don't want to get ahead of ourselves." He looked over his shoulder at Carlson. "Can you bring Nick up to speed on what the Chinese have in the area?"

"On it. Nick, you ready to receive?" Carlson didn't wait for an answer. "They've assembled a force that's out of proportion to any reasonable requirement they might have, no matter what they intend to accomplish. Stealth certainly hasn't factored in as one of their planning factors. There's no doubt they're testing us."

"What are we looking at?"

"A Dalao-class submarine rescue ship, the ice breaker, *Jidi*, and the *Zhong Jian*, an oceanographic research ship. A Global Hawk overflight deployed from Grand Forks Air Force Base picked up what appears to be a shelter for a Special Forces delivery vehicle on the *Zhong Jian's* aft deck. Escorting the flotilla is a Type-054 Jiangkia class frigate, the *Ma'anshaw*."

"Impressive."

"Yeah. And two more ships are heading around the north coast of Hokkaido, the coast guard cutter *Haijing* and a commercial fishing ship, the *Lu Yon*. A minor point of interest, the *Lu Yan* is the sister ship of a trawler sunk by the Argentine Navy in 2016 for violating their fishing grounds."

Mike reappeared and settled onto the room's couch. "Nice precedent. So, what do we have in the area?"

"Not much. Our core response at sea is centered around the *Truxtun* and the *Midgett*."

"Subs?"

"We're working a fast attack out of Bremerton and diverting several assets from ICEX20."

"Any other Coast Guard assets?"

"They're doing what they can considering Kodiak is their closest base to the Cape. Three small Cutters and several aircraft."

"Not much they can do except run interference," Berg said.

Nick stiffened, at a loss as to explain what the Chinese were up to and whether his assessment of their intentions was completely off base. *And if he were wrong?*

"Something on your mind?" Mike asked.

"No, I'm good." He nodded to the two open deployment

bags set in the center of the room. "I'm just wondering about that pile of cold-weather gear Rich is digging through."

"We need to fit you out." Carlson balanced on a knee and held up a hooded, camouflaged parka. "I checked today's weather forecast for Cape Lisburne. High of two, dropping to minus eighteen."

He turned to judge Mike's reaction. *None.*

"What you are beholding is one piece of the Army's new Extended Cold Weather Clothing System," Carlson said.

"And the rest of the system?"

"Ah, inquiring minds want to know. The ECWCS has twelve pieces that can be combined in seven different layers depending on the operating environment." Carlson dropped the parka and held up a shirt and a pair of long johns. "These go on first and are designed to wick away moisture. We'll add another insulating layer and top you off with the parka and trousers. You'll be nice and toasty but still able to move. The parka's designed to decrease your infrared signature."

"Nice touch in case someone wants to shoot me." His attention shifted from the prospect of freezing to death to what else they might encounter.

Mike left his perch on the couch, reached into one of the deployment bags, and pulled out a rifle as an answer to Nick's silent question.

He recognized the weapon in Mike's hand. A M4A1 short-barreled carbine. "Good Lord, Mike. What are you expecting us to run into?"

Mike handed him the carbine. "Best to be prepared considering what you've told us. You'll need to familiarize yourself with this piece of gear."

"That a thermal-imaging device mounted on the barrel?"

"To be precise, it's an enhanced night vision goggle system. Combines image-intensifying and thermal-imaging. The sight and the helmet mounted binocular goggles communicate wirelessly."

Mike extracted a helmet and attached the goggles. "Here, try this on for size. You can aim your weapon without raising it to your eye. Even shoot around a corner without exposing your head. Pretty neat piece of gear."

He donned the helmet, then hefted the carbine. Both weren't as heavy as he'd expected, and he liked the idea of not exposing his head. None-the-less, he wasn't thrilled. "Ah, maybe I overstated the risk."

"I doubt it."

"And there'll just be the three of us?"

"We've got backup."

"Backup?"

"Not to worry, Nick." Berg pulled out a handful of full thirty-round clips from the bag at his feet and started to insert them in the pockets of a tactical vest. "You'll literally be dressed to kill."

"Great." He gave Berg a pass on the lame joke and kept the rest of his thoughts about the SEAL's sense of humor to himself. Berg couldn't possibly know what he'd been through with the al-Khultyer affair unless Mike had provided the details. He glanced at Mike who just gave a subtle shake of his head.

Berg looked at his watch and cut off any further discussion about cold weather gear or armament. "We've gotta go, Captain. The *Truxtun* should be tying up at Seward's cruise ship terminal. We don't want to keep her waiting."

Chapter Forty-Two

USS TRUXTUN DDG-103
CHUCHI SEA
MONDAY 4 MARCH

"We've got something, Captain."

Mike Rohrbaugh pulled his eyes from the flat screen he'd been watching and swiveled toward the *Truxtun's* CIC watch officer. The ambient light of the Combat Information Center cast an eerie blue glow across the lieutenant's face, adding a surreal feeling to the tense atmosphere in the compartment.

"The Chinese may be making their move," the officer continued. "We just received a video link from a NOAA ship, the *Oscar Dyson*. She's been monitoring a webcam attached to a wave buoy off Cape Lisburne and spotted something funny."

He scrutinized the video feed. The object moving across the buoy's camera field could only be a Chinese dry combat submersible. Similar in design to the Navy's new S351 Nemesis, the vehicle was capable of transporting eight special forces operators. But why was it making its approach on the surface?

Tactically, that made no sense. Why would they risk detection? Could they be using the buoy as a way point, not trusting a problematic GPS signal this far north?

"What can you tell me about the *Dyson*?"

"She's purpose designed as an ultra-quiet vessel to monitor fish populations and study marine ecosystems. Spent the past week cruising off the coast. Makes me wonder if the Chinese even knew she was in the area."

"Can you run that again?" He studied the Chinese vessel. Perhaps they'd experienced an engineering casualty but didn't want to abort the mission? "Do you have the coordinates of the buoy?"

"Yes, sir. Just a sec." The lieutenant typed a search for the GPS coordinates into his keyboard. "68.88.11 North. 166.21.00 West. About eight-hundred yards off the beach. The Chinese must be looking to land their team before the weather hits."

He replayed the short clip. They were getting knocked around by the waves. "Solid call, Lieutenant, even if they continue, the shore break might be too treacherous for them to effect a landing."

"Sir, there's also something else they may be contending with, something the early explorers called ballycadders." He noted the look on Rohrbaugh's face and continued. "It's salt water ice along the shore that forms between high and low tides. Can make for a hazardous approach."

"When are the tides?"

"Let me check." The officer tapped in a command on his keyboard. "Low's at 0356 hours. High 0949. It could explain why they're on the surface. Making a run for the shore."

"Could be," he acknowledged. *But why else would they risk the approach on the surface?*

The lieutenant's statement confirmed his supposition that the Chinese would never abort. He held no doubt that he'd soon be facing off against the Sea Dragons, their commando unit equivalent in capabilities to the SEALs. These guys were tough, but thermal protection notwithstanding, their final wet approach through thirty-seven-degree water would be brutal. That would take some of the fight out of them.

He sorted through the possibilities, searching his mind for something he may have overlooked about Chinese Navy tactics in littoral warfare. After a moment, the answer registered. "Lieutenant, do you have the tracks of all the Chinese vessels for the past twenty-four hours?"

"We should."

The lieutenant looked over his right shoulder at a line of manned consoles. "Chief, can you bring up what we have on the Chinese ship tracks for the past twenty-four hours?"

"Do you want them overlaid, sir?"

Mike nodded.

"Affirmative," the lieutenant acknowledged. "Send what you have to our monitors."

"Roger that, sir. I'll have them to you in a minute."

The tracks of the four Chinese ship appeared in just over a minute. Two of them stood out, particularly the trawler's. The vessel traversed about a mile off the coast making several passes paralleling the shore. Their actions were consistent with what he read about "Assassin's Mace," their mining plan for shallow-water operations. "You see the pattern, Lieutenant?"

"No, sir."

"Make a nice minefield."

"Whoa. That'd account for the presence of the frigate."

"Or the fishing trawler. We've documented the Chinese equipping trawlers with mine laying racks. I suspect that's what the trawler has hidden under that canvas tarp on her stern. My guess is there are a couple racks for their ME-32 magnetic moored mines. They could have also dropped some of their drifting mines on the lucky chance we'd run into one."

"That's why that mini-sub is on the surface. They don't

want to run afoul with one of their own devices. They're using the buoy as a way marker. Damn, I've gotta notify the skipper."

"Roger that, Lieutenant. This changes the game."

———

Nick stood on the *Truxtun*'s lee weather deck at the fore edge of the flight deck, sheltered from the worst of the wind, bundled in the layered cold-weather gear he wanted to test. Mist engulfed the ship, the chilled air penetrating down the top of his zippered parka. He wasn't hopeful.

The whisper of water rushing down the side of the destroyer and the isolated cries of several seagulls whirling above the destroyer's wake were the only sounds. And the far horizon? The color of gunmetal in the Arctic sun. He widened his stance to compensate for the destroyer's movement.

The Arleigh Burke class destroyers were the Navy's best hulls for the Arctic, but they weren't ice-hardened, nor did they have the modifications like de-icing systems that allowed them to operate safely in the extreme weather conditions of the region. He wondered how long they could remain in the area with the barometer dropping or how they'd transfer to the *Midgett*. The last thing he wanted was to repeat his prior performance and be hoisted up to a hovering helicopter. Once was more than enough.

Keeping station some thousand meters off their port quarter were the Chinese Coast Guard cutter, *Haijing* and the commercial fishing ship, *Lu Yan*. Beyond them, he recognized the oceanographic research ship, *Zhong Jiam*. The Chinese could construct a legitimate cover for the research ship's presence, but he knew the ship's true mission—the transport of their special operations mini-sub.

A fourth vessel had joined the flotilla during the night.

Probably the frigate they'd been briefed on. The ship dug its bow into a large wave. He wondered if the Chinese would also have to alter course and head for safer waters.

His musings were interrupted by the sound of muffled footfalls. Mike and Trey Berg joined him at the rail.

"Thought we might find you out here," Mike said.

"Yeah, I wanted to clear my head."

Mike didn't respond, instead he studied the Chinese vessels, his face set, assimilating.

They each had the same visual perspective, but he understood that Mike had a different focus on what the vessels represented. Unsettled by that realization, he glanced at Berg. The guy's expression matched Mike's.

Mike broke the silence. "The skipper told me the DoD needs to designate the *Haijing* as a combatant. She's essentially a gray-hull that's been painted white. She outguns anything the Coast Guard has up here and all that gear on the *Lu Yan?* That has nothing to do with fishing. In fact, can you see that mount for a heavy machine gun? Probably a W-85."

He didn't comment on the machine gun. He'd been distracted by a cluster of men spilling on to the *Truxtun*'s flight deck. He recognized the leader of the embarked Explosive Ordinance Disposal unit. They appeared to be setting up a small gantry crane on the fantail.

He'd been told the detachment from Explosive Ordnance Deposal Group One had joined the ship the week before as part of a previously planned Arctic Expeditionary Capabilities Exercise. They were to test a flyaway communication system designed to address shortfalls in connectivity and linkage to the new SeaFox unmanned underwater vehicle.

"Wonder what's up with the EOD guys?" he asked.

"They're our backup if our op heads south."

"We're going south?"

Mike suppressed a chuckle. "Lordy, Nick. You know. Things turning bad."

"Oh, man. I'm—"

"You're good. We're ramping up. My guess is the Chinese weren't expecting us and we just forced their hand. The EOD guys are deploying the SeaFox to seek out and destroy any mines the Chinese might have laid."

"Mines?"

"I'm heading to the bridge," Mike responded. "You need to pack your gear."

He digested this latest development. "How soon are we leaving?'

"As soon as I can confirm my plan with the skipper."

———

Mike headed up the ladder to the bridge, formulating the final pieces of his plan. Nick's worse-case scenario could be playing out, but even if his hypothesis was off base, what were—"

The blast of the ship's horn halted him in mid-step. Four more blasts followed in quick succession—the international signal for an imminent collision. *What the hell?*

He scrambled up the remaining steps, pausing only to rap on the doorframe. "Permission to enter the bridge."

The skipper turned in annoyance before recognizing Mike and motioning him to join him. "We've got a situation."

He nodded. The Chinese coast guard cutter was just fifty yards off their port bow, maneuvering to cut them off.

"Hard right rudder."

The *Truxtun*'s bow swung away from the Chinese cutter, giving the skipper a brief reprieve.

"Hoist the 'Restricted Ability To Maneuver' ball-diamond-ball' and establish a VHF link to that damn ship." The captain turned to Mike. "We also just lost our RADARSAT-2 link."

"What happened?"

"Don't know, but nothing good. They're clearly in our

territorial waters. My guess is they're running interference for that special op delivery vehicle that's making a run for the beach."

"Anything else down?"

"The Air Force's Tactical Air Control team at Cape Lisburne has gone silent."

He stared at the jumble of broken ice the *Truxtun* was pushing through. Marginal conditions. "Captain, I need to transfer to the *Midgett.*"

The captain paused, judging the danger from the Chinese cutter, then spoke. "Concur. The *Midgett* isn't ice hardened either, but she and her helicopter detachment have more experience operating in this environment. That, and I need to ride herd on the main Chinese force. Based on our relative positions, we can affect a transfer in a little over an hour. I've also ordered the EOD detachment leader to reconfigure the SeaFox for an attack mode and arm it. We can raise a little hell if you need a diversion on the beach."

"I'm thinking we'll be needing your help. I'll gather my team. We'll be ready to cross-deck whenever you give the word."

"Skipper?" The OOD broke in. "They're changing course."

"Yeah. We're in for an interesting afternoon. Sound general quarters and get a flash message out to PacFleet."

Mike left the bridge to the sound blaring from the ship's 1MC's. "General Quarters, General Quarters. All hands man your battle stations. This is not a drill."

Chapter Forty-Three

USCG CUTTER MIDGETT
CHUKCHI SEA, CAPE LISBURNE
MONDAY 4 MARCH

Nick leaned against the weather door and pushed it open. He plunged into the howling wind swirling across *Midgett's* aft deck. The door slammed behind him with an ear-piercing clang. He bent into the wind, his parka whipping around his chest, grateful to be standing on steel. Anything beat what he'd just done. Dangling like some wind-blown spider being winched up, once again, to MacAuley's helicopter during the transfer from the *Truxtun*. At least this time he didn't have his ego bruised by using the basket.

He staggered across the deck, his short quest leading to the sheltered overhang of the boat deck. He spotted Mike at the portside rail and gave a yell, his call ripped away by the wind. He realized the futility of hollering again and made his way to Mike's side.

Rohrbaugh greeted him with a knowing smile. "Mighty sporty this afternoon."

"That's one word for it." He took his place by the rail and scanned the distant horizon. The sea was furrowed by white-capped rollers and dotted by growlers. The string of low-pressure systems roaring in from the northeast offered no relief. "This keeps up, we may have to abort our mission. I can't see the Chinese making it ashore."

Mike shook his head. "They're already there and will be extracted in a few hours. We can't abort. You ready?"

"As much as I'll ever be."

A massive wave exploded against the Cutter's starboard side, spray enveloping the ship in an incandescent cocoon of spindrift. He grasped the ice-coated cable of the safety railing as the Cutter rolled.

Mike grabbed his arm and led him toward the hatch. "That one had a bite. We gotta go inside."

"No kidding." He took a final glance at the deteriorating weather. The waves were stacking up, the wind churning swirls of white water, the sea a dull, forbidding gray. He felt the deck vibrate under his feet.

Mike answered his unvoiced question. "The captain just increased our rpms to stabilize the ship."

"Can we make it ashore?"

"Depends. MacAuley will have the final call. If she says it's too dangerous to fly, we sit."

"We don't have any say?"

"Nope."

Mike followed him through the hatch of the aft bulkhead into the safety of the boathouse. "Nick, I've reconsidered. You need to stay behind."

He set his jaw. "No way. I've come too far."

"It's my call. You're not trained for this kind of op. The risks are unacceptable."

———

Lieutenant Sarah MacAuley searched the horizon searching for a break in the dense bank of clouds rolling toward her aircraft wondering if she'd made the right decision. The blurred mass of the polar ice pack that loomed in the distance added to her sense of dread. The mammoth system left her with no choice but to plow through the weather or abort. This mission left no openings for the faint of heart. On a positive note, the latest meteorological report suggested the worst of the system would pass to the west.

"Let's make this happen."

Brian Fields tightened his shoulder harness as their helicopter yawed to starboard. "It's a beautiful day in the neighborhood."

"I'm pretty sure this isn't what Mr. Rogers had in mind." Mr. Rogers notwithstanding, the flight conditions would only worsen as they descended into the stronger surface winds from the colliding weather fronts. She backed off on their speed and turned a few more degrees into the wind to lessen the turbulence and the additional risk of a retreating blade stall that would drop them into the ocean. "Man, this is brutal."

"No shit," Fields answered. He looked toward the shore, catching a glimpse of land that abruptly disappeared in a snow squall. "White out."

The helicopter bucked again despite her best efforts as their visibility dropped to near zero in a dense mix of snow and fog. She keyed the mike. "Captain."

"Can you put us ashore?" Rohrbaugh asked.

"Maybe." Until that moment, she hadn't had time to spare a single thought to the three men she'd been tasked to deliver to the abandoned base at Cape Lisburne.

"I'm marginal VFR."

"You have the coast in sight?"

"Glimpses. I'm beginning our approach. We may—"

Her voice cut out as the helicopter encountered the

leading edge of the multidirectional gale force winds sweeping down the slopes of the thousand-foot ridge that abutted the far end of the base's gravel runway. Extending away from the top of the ridge was a long snow banner formed from the snow whipped off the mountain by the winds. "Hang on back there."

She worked the cyclic and anti-torque pedals to account for horizontal drift and continued her descent. She looked up from the altimeter and caught a glimpse of white water pounding over the runway's seawall. She came to a hover, the altimeter registered ten feet. "Brian?"

"I've got visual of the runway."

"Jameson?"

"We're clear left."

She glanced at Fields.

Another cloud of wind-driven snow obscured the brief glimpse Fields had of the runway. He leaned forward in his harness straining to catch sight of any landmarks through the helicopter's windscreen. "Clear right."

She eased up on the collective and descended the remaining ten feet through a blinding cloud of snow kicked up by the aircraft's downwash. She felt the wheels touch, then settle on solid ground. She lifted her visor and swept her gloved hand over forehead monitoring the status of her aircraft. As near as she could determine, they hadn't received any incoming fire. Her crew chief might have caught sight of something. "Jamison, you see any tracers?"

"Negative."

"Keep your eyes peeled. With any luck we may have set down without being detected."

She unbuckled her shoulder harness and rolled her shoulders to ease the tension in her back. She glanced at Fields who only shook his head, then turned her attention to her passengers. "Captain, you're good to go."

"Affirmative."

She reached up to massage her neck pondering what was next in store for them. *Of course, hot shot, you've got one other problem. You may be stuck in this God-forsaken place.*

Chapter Forty-Four

LONG RANGE RADAR SITE
CAPE LISBURNE, ALASKA
MONDAY 4 MARCH

Mike Rohrbaugh waited until the mix of swirling of snow and spicule fog of Goose-21's rotor wash settled. The weak northern sun had dropped below the horizon, leaving a solitary dark-purple streak just visible over the blurred horizon, the only remnant of daylight.

He faced forward and grasped the straps of his tactical gear pack as MacAuley's crew chief slid open the leeward door of Goose-21. A blast of subzero air howled into the rear compartment.

"Damn, that's nasty," Jamison said.

He edged his way past Jamison and stuck his head outside. The fierce wind had exposed black, mottled patches of the gravel beneath the snow incrusted runway as well as what was known as marbled crust—patches of extremely hard iced-up snow that the winds had carved out over the landing strip.

The bulk of the vehicle storage building located down the eastern side of the strip was just visible. The fog released its grip revealing the adjacent power plant. Beyond those, shrouded in darkness, was the headquarters building.

His lips tightened. He had no idea how the Chinese detachment might have deployed. Could the entire team have already made their way to the upper site dotted with its scattering of support buildings, radar dome, and the communication center? He would have preferred to set down there, but MacAuley had nixed the idea. Way too dangerous.

He refocused. If it were me, I would have left several men behind to neutralize any potential hostiles intent on disrupting his operation. One known? The EOD guys were prepared to play hardball. They'd been tasked to arm their SeaFox and take out the Chinese delivery vehicle. If that worked, the Chinese special ops detachment would have no way to return to their ship. He also assumed they wouldn't know that, which provided the first key to his plan to determine their likely extraction point and snag one or more of them. In any event, things were about to get very interesting.

This is as far as his own assurances went. Time constraints had prevented him from securing a SEAL team detachment and he'd been left with no choice but to place Nick in an untenable position. He'd developed a close bond with the young analyst and that factored heavily in his decision. Nick had no training in urban warfare and would be exposed to obstacles even an experienced team found daunting. Limited views, interlocking fields of fire, concealment, snipers...

He'd been left with no choice but allow Nick to board the helicopter and assigned him the task of locating the missing Americans. Working in his favor, Nick had proven himself in Somalia during the raid on the terrorist base camp. He'd become part of the brotherhood following the raid, having taken out an al-Shabab terrorist intent on killing both of them. With those trailing thoughts, Mike hoped he hadn't errored in relenting and then have the mission deteriorate into a total goat rope.

He addressed MacAuley. "You'll need to find a place to bed down if you can't make it back. You equipped with cold weather gear?"

"I'm not going to chance a cold start. We've gotta return."

"Be careful lifting off. Goose's heat signature likely attracted their attention. You have a weapon?"

"Ah, no."

He reached for his kit and pulled out a 9mm Sig Sauer pistol and several fifteen-round magazines. "Here, in case there's a need." He kept his newer Glock 17 for close-in work.

MacAuley accepted the weapon and gave it a quick check. "Understood."

He gave her a 'thumbs up' and gathered his gear. He inserted the front ballistic plate into a carrier vest and handed it to Nick, tapped Berg on the shoulder, and spun his right index finger in the air. *Time to get this show on the road.*

Berg nodded and followed him out the door, trailed by Nick.

Chapter Forty-Five

LONG RANGE RADAR SITE
LOWER CANTONMENT AREA
MONDAY 4 MARCH

Nick leapt out the door of Goose-21 and braced against the wind. He cinched the sling of his carbine to secure it muzzle down across his chest and hurried after Mike and Berg. He glanced back. A dense ice-fog mixed with snow hung above the crushed rock runway, blurring the outline of the helicopter as it lifted off.

A fierce gust of wind ripped off the top of a nearby dune. He closed his eyes as sand peppered the skull image embossed on his face protector. In that instant, he slipped on a patch of black ice and stumbled over a block of concrete. "Damn it."

He collected himself and continued down the runway toward the vehicle storage building determined to locate the missing Tactical Air Control party. At the corner of the sheet metal structure, he dropped to his right knee. Something sounded out of place. Like someone flicking a piece of paper. *Was that a rifle shot?*

A sharp crack tore the air by his head followed instantly by a dull *thwack*. A ragged hole was torn out of the wall beside his head. "Shit!"

He scuttled backwards seeking cover, his chest heaving at the encounter. He edged the barrel of his carbine back around the corner, then pulled back. Not a good move if someone just tried to kill you. *Now what? The radio.* "Mike?"

"Yeah."

"I just took incoming. Where are you?"

"About twenty yards to your right. You see a muzzle flash?"

"Negative."

"They're set up on the roof of the power plant. The shooter and a spotter. Watch yourself."

"Yeah, no shit."

"Say again."

"Nothing."

"I spotted a hostile behind a pile of gravel to my right. They've set up to pick us off once we clear this building."

He screwed up his lip. *Pick us off? Great.* He tightened his grip on the carbine. "Got it."

"Trey's working his way up the slope to the upper cantonment area. I'm going to flank my guy. You keep the ones on the roof occupied."

"Works for me."

"Use your scope. When you get a heat signature, take your shot. Change your aim points and use three-round groupings to keep the target occupied. And keep you damn head out of sight."

"Copy that," he replied, trying to sound more assured than he felt.

He slid down the side of the building landing on his butt, his heart jumping around in his chest like some crazed trapped bird. *This is nuts.* He took several deep breaths, swallowing his fear. *Okay, you got this.*

He'd had a chance to do some familiarization firing while

still aboard the *Truxtun* and shot the hell out of a block of ice floating down the side of the cruiser while using the optical system, a small consolation now that he flipped down his binocular goggles to activate the device.

He stuck the muzzle of his carbine around the corner and swung the barrel and the mounted optical scope in a slow arc trying to locate a target. Something appeared in the upper quadrant of his goggles. *What-the-hell?* He shifted his carbine's barrel. Nothing. He decided to trust his own eyes and stuck his head around the corner to confirm what he'd seen in the googles. *Is that a mini-quadcopter?* He chanced a longer look.

He set the carbine to full automatic, chambered the first round, and edged around the corner. *There.* He centered the thermal site of his scope on the hovering drone. *Deep breath, let it out, steady.* He squeezed the trigger, emptying the entire magazine. He thought he saw several sparks as he dropped the clip and slammed in another to resume firing at the roof. Mike's voice came over his headset drawing him back around the corner to safety.

"Three-round bursts."

"I spotted a mini-drone. I may have hit it."

"Then there may be three of them on the roof."

Berg's voice came over the net before Nick could respond. "Alpha-One, I've got a verified target."

"If you've got a clean shot, send it," Mike answered. "Nick? You good?"

"I'm still vertical."

"Target down," Berg said.

Rohrbaugh confirmed Berg's transmission. "Charlie Mike."

Nick paused before rounding the corner thinking the order to 'Continue Mission' also applied to him. *Should I weave or just run like hell in a straight line?* He opted for the latter and took off. Struggling to run in the bulky cold weather gear, feet sinking in the snow, he gasped his way through the final six yards to the power plant. He dropped to the ground, relieved he'd actually made it. He rose to a crouch, then stood upright. He pressed his back against the south wall trying to catch his breath and collect his wits. *Now what?* Mike's voice filled his earbuds.

"Nick, you taking fire?"

"Negative. I'm at the power plant."

"Secure the roof, then locate the Air Force team."

Roof? He did another gut check before proceeding to inch his way along the front of the two-story building, halting at the front door blown ajar by the wind. He stood rooted in indecision for a moment, then slid the barrel of his carbine through the opening. No heat signatures registered on his goggles.

He gave the door a push with his boot and entered the building, spotting a stairwell on the far wall. He crossed an administrative area, his footfalls thudding, unnaturally loud in the empty space. He took a deep breath at the stairwell and began his ascent fully expecting to hear the clunk of a frag-mentation grenade skipping its way down the wooden steps to blast him to oblivion.

He paused at the top before another door that had been left ajar. He kicked it open, lunged forward, and dropped, expecting a burst of gunfire. *Nothing?*

Where the hell were they? His hand felt something when he pushed off to get his feet. A shell casing. Next to it were several more abutting a dark stain in the snow. More stains created a blotched trail. *Blood?*

To the stain's right, he spotted the toggled control box for the quadcopter. Could a lucky shot from his wild barrage have caught one of the commandos? Time to pass on what he'd found. "Mike?"

"You on the roof?"

"Yeah. There's nobody up here. I may have…" He cut off what he was about to say, his eyes following the bloody trial to a lower leg protruding from around the corner of the building. "Hold one. I got a body."

He pulled out his flashlight and made his way to the corpse. On the hunch he might find something useful, he searched the commando's pockets. He worked his way down to a thigh pocket. *Got something.* He reached in and pulled out a folded piece of paper, his eye's widening at what he'd discovered. "Mike. I just found a map. The Comm facility's circled."

"The device?"

"That's my thinking."

"We'll start there. See if you can locate the Air Force team. The other Chinese you spotted are likely headed to the extract point. Stay alert."

"What—?"

"Gotta go."

Chapter Forty-Six

LONG RANGE RADAR SITE
UPPER CANTONMENT AREA
TUESDAY 5 MARCH

The ambient light from the cloud-shrouded first-quarter moon enabled Mike Rohrbaugh to catch sight of his adversary a split second before the first shot rang out.

"Gotta go." He dropped behind a jagged boulder, cutting off Nick in mid-sentence. He didn't have time for questions. He had his own problems. Nick would have to fend for himself.

A second shot ricocheted off the top of the boulder, the impact sending a spray sharp rock fragments whizzing through the air. He flinched as they peppered his helmet and ballistic goggles. Not a bad shot considering the distance and swirling winds.

Thanks to Nick, he had the probable end point, the communications building.

He'd taken out one hostile. Berg another. Nick had identified two, maybe three, killing one of them. That left three, one of whom had just taken the shot at him. Presuming an eight-man team, three, maybe four max, remained to place the device.

The domed radar building and the communication facility with its billboard antennas were perched along a narrow ridge limiting access. Taking the narrow road to the site was a non-starter. The steep terrain would offer some protection.

He spoke into his headset. "Alpha Two."

"Alpha Two," Trey responded.

"Status?"

"Making my way up the gully we identified in the pre-brief. I'm a couple hundred meters from the summit looking at a steep assent over open ground. I may have to reposition."

"He looked toward Trey's probable location. "I'm taking sniper fire. The shooter's between the main buildings."

"Wait one … Yeah. Got him. Just stuck his head up."

"Keep him occupied."

"Roger that."

"Hold one," he said, thinking better of his order. "He may not have seen you. Keep moving. I'll keep him distracted."

The crack of another shot rang out. Staying put was out of the question.

He edged around the boulder, then darted across the barren terrain, taking what cover he could in shallow depressions.

His progress ended at an expanse of open, wind-swept ground well short of the ridge. He slowly raised his head to pick his next position. 'No negative thoughts' percolated through his brain, that impulse had been driven from of him during BUDS training at Coronado. He didn't see his adversary and slow-crawled across the desolate terrain before stopping to assess his status. One hundred meters remained.

He spotted a concealment spot and sprang to his feet, sprinting across the open ground, abruptly changing directions before hitting the deck. Dropping to a prone position, he shifted to his left side, rolled into a firing position, and swept his scope across the ridge. He couldn't detect a heat signature, but he did see something else. A deep snow drift flowed from the lee side of a rocky escarpment.

Special ops trained, the Sea Dragon would expect him to zig-zag. That is, if he'd seen him. *Right or left zags? How would the Chinese think?* He calculated the odds, popped up, sprinted forward twenty meters, and dove into the snowbank. His action effectively negating any minimal heat signature that would betray his position. *First objective.*

Chest heaving, his breath hanging in frosty clouds in front of his face, he reassessed his status. The top of the ridge was mere meters way. *Time to contact Trey.*

"Alpha Two. Status check."

"Alpha One. I'm at the southern edge of the comm building. Nobody in sight."

"Hold in place and watch for my fire. I'm going to smoke him out."

"Roger that."

He checked his surroundings. Not much cover. He calculated his next move.

Slow is smooth. Smooth is fast. Now!

He leapt from the snowbank, firing a sustained burst at the commando's last position. Sprinting to his right, he fired again, releasing his empty magazine, inserting another while on the move. Maneuver. Fire. Disorient. *Again.*

The third burst found him prone at the lip of the ridge covered by a small snowslide. *Second object.* He dug himself out and slowly raised his head, scanning the far edge of the comm building. *There.*

"Alpha Two. I have the sniper tucked around the corner of the far door. He's swinging his night scope across the ground I just covered. Hold one. He's back in the building. Wait for your shot."

Berg waited until he saw the muzzle of the Sea Dragon's rifle poke around the doorframe. The target's forehead emerged. He zeroed in his IR laser and popped him with a clean shot.

"Alpha One. Target down." He didn't wait for a response and advanced to the open door.

The commando's body sprawled through the opening. *Not good.* The other two hadn't noticed their fallen comrade. *Yet.* He grabbed the sniper's gloved hands and dragged him out of sight before taking a cautious look through the door.

Before him were two Sea Dragons, one holding a large burnished canister. From what he could tell from their gestures, they were discussing where to place the device. There was no option but to take them out. *Target One, the guy with the canister.*

It was almost too easy. He pulled the trigger, dropping the first. The canister dropped from his target's hand, hit the floor with a loud CLANK and rolled to a stop against a table leg. He changed his aim point and fired again before the second commando could raise his weapon. His target spun to the floor, dropped from the three shots impacting his neck and head.

He lowered his carbine and took several cautious steps toward the inert bodies, leaning over to pick up the canister on the way, examining it for breaches. His exhaled his relief. "Thank, God."

Time to contact Rohrbaugh. "Alpha One. Targets are down. Canister secured."

Rohrbaugh appeared a moment later, weapon at the ready, his eyes scanning the room before they came to rest on the commandos. "What about them?"

"Dead."

"Okay. We'll figure out what to do with them later. We've got to check the rest of the compound. There may be one

more we haven't accounted for. We've got to work our way
back to the beach. Nick's gotta be dealing with at least two
of 'em."

Chapter Forty-Seven

LONG RANGE RADAR SITE
LOWER CANTONMENT SITE
TUESDAY 5 MARCH

Nick worked through the possibilities in the silence following Mike's abrupt signoff. If Mike and Trey didn't make it or the guys on the roof reappeared...? He wasn't visualizing good outcomes and his options on how to proceed were few. Staying put, though, wasn't one of them. *Gotta move.*

He made his way back down the stairs and headed for the headquarters building praying he wouldn't encounter the missing Chinese. He kept his back to the wall edging along the building's front until he came to a door. He turned the handle and shoved it open, pressed the carbine's stock against his shoulder, and swept the room only to be greeted by silence. *Now what?*

He couldn't see a damn thing even with the googles. He scanned the pitch-black lobby. A gust of wind rattled the windows, but something else caught his ear. *Voices?*

Suppressing the urge to yell out, he took several steps only to collide with a chair. It clattered to the floor and he staggered, trying to catch his balance. *Crap.*

A thundering burst of gunfire from a Sea Dragon's Type-76 submachine gun shredded the air where he'd just stood. The ear-splitting noise of the automatic weapon filled the confined space. A spray of bullets whizzed past his head punching a jagged line of holes in the wall behind him. *The guy's firing blindly.* Another long burst followed.

He swung his carbine toward the muzzle flashes, but before he could fire, several bullets slammed into his ceramic vest. The sledgehammer blows sent him reeling backwards, the air expelled from his lungs with an audible grunt. The impacts caused his finger to tightened around the trigger loosening a burst of 5.56mm rounds. He fired again on the way down, his mind registering a scream as he impacted the floor. The firing stopped.

Dazed by the encounter, he struggled to stand. A paroxysm of pain enveloped his chest. He emitted a strangled gasp and dropped to his knees, willing his breathing to slow, willing himself to continue. *You can do this.* Gritting his teeth, he rose to a knee, then to his feet. His nostrils flared at the acrid bite of gunpowder.

He approached the body sprawled on the floor, keeping his weapon centered on the fallen Chinese. He kicked the man's stubby submachine gun away and kneeled, stretching out his hand.

A ragged hole existed where the commando's upper neck and right jaw should have been. He jerked his hand back, his eyes fixed on the horrific wound. "Oh, damn. Oh, damn."

He tore his eyes away, trying to block out what he'd seen, refocusing on what he had to do. *The airmen must be close.* He'd heard them. There wasn't much sense in keeping quiet any longer.

"H—" He gasped, clutching his chest, the pain strangulating his voice. He wrapped his arms around his chest, bracing himself, embracing his weapon. "Hey. Is anyone here?"

"Here," echoed a muffled voice.

He struggled to his feet, stepped around the body, and made his way toward the sound, his ears still ringing from the weapons' concussions.

"In here."

He stepped into a small office. The four Air Force men were clustered in the far corner of the room, their hands and feet bound with zip ties.

"Man, are we ever glad to see you," the nearest airman said.

He leaned his carbine against the wall and used his knife to cut the ties off the closest airman. "Who's in charge?"

"I am," the man said. "First Lieutenant Eric Nielsen."

"Are there any more of you?" he asked, his voice an exhausted rasp.

"Just us," Nielsen said, shaking the blood back into his arms. "We—"

He held up his index finger silencing Nielsen at the sound of a voice in his headset. "Mike?"

"What's your status?"

"I've located the det. They're good."

"Can you get to the beach?"

"Yeah."

"Make your way there and keep an eye on the area just beyond those two fuel tanks at the edge of the runway. Alert me if you see anything. My bet is that's their extract point. Trey and I are making our way down. Do not engage."

"Got it." *The Air Force guys would have to take care of themselves.* He faced the four. "Until we secure the area, you gotta stay put. You good?"

Nielsen nodded.

He started to head outside, his vision blurring from the pain of his first steps. He clamped his jaw, trying to block the throbbing pain in his chest. A dull thud that sounded like it came from beyond the breakwater stopped him.

He swung toward the sound, grimacing in pain. *The EOD guys?* Had they managed to disable the Chinese submersible? He doubted the sound from the detonation of the SeaFox's small warhead would have traveled this far. More likely, the Chinese submersible may have hit one of their own drift mines trying to evade the UUV. He spoke into his microphone. "Mike?"

"What's wrong."

"Nothing … yet. I think I heard an explosion offshore." Something caught his eye. Two figures, one supporting the other, darted from cover heading toward the beach. *My missing Chinese?* "Hold one. I've got something."

He didn't wait for a response and flipped down his goggles, centering the barrel of his carbine on the figures. He selected the guy on the left. The FLIR's target acquisition system lived up to its name, the image of the commando lighting up on his heads-up display. He braced against a low retaining wall and tightened his finger on the trigger, ignoring Mike's order.

"Hold fire! Hold fire! Don't shoot."

He started at Mike's voice coming from behind him. He relaxed his finger, slowly releasing the trigger as Mike and Trey appeared at his side. "Damn, Mike."

Mike shouted toward the beach. "Give it up. It's over. *Fàngqì!*"

The Chinese staggered forward several more steps, then halted and turned.

Mike stepped around Nick and approached the men holding up a polished aluminum canister. "*Jiéshùle. Fàngqì!*"

The commandos hesitated, then dropped their weapons and raised their hands. "*Bùyào kài qiāng.* Don't shoot."

He stared at the canister, then at Mike. "You know Chinese?"

"Mandarin, actually. Sit tight, we'll handle this."

He held back while Trey kept his weapon centered on the two remaining Sea Dragons only too happy to oblige. Mike advanced, commanding the men to kneel before securing their weapons. He zip-tied their arms behind their backs. They weren't going anywhere.

"What happened up there?" he asked when Mike returned to his side.

"We retrieved the canister." Mike looked as if he were about to say something more, but caught himself. "Let's leave it at that."

He recognized the tone in Mike's voice. The warrior's ethos. He looked at the two men kneeling in the gravel and nodded. They would be deemed dispensable, their very existence denied by the government who'd sent them. *What would*—?

He coughed and dropped onto the edge of the retaining wall, grasping at the throbbing pain welling up from his lungs. He tasted blood in his mouth. He tried to splint his chest and coughed again. Blood tinged sputum covered his glove.

Am I dying? Lange's mysterious message, "'It's Not Over,'" that had appeared his computer months ago worked its way to the surface from his subconscious. *Could it finally be over?* He fought the thought. *I'll be damned if I'm going*—

Mike approached. "What's wrong?"

"I took a round." He made a weak gesture with his right hand. "Same damn place as the other bullet."

"Let me see." Mike pulled the ceramic plate from Nick's tactical vest. He eyed the shattered plate. It had absorbed the impact. "Your lung's been bruised by the impact. Chances are good you've also fractured a couple ribs."

"Oh."

"We're getting you out of here," Mike said, keying his radio. "Goose-21, Spinner."

"Spinner. Goose-21."

Trey nodded at the exchange, darted a glance at Nick, then glared at their defiant prisoners, daring them to move.

He made to stand, but Mike grabbed his shoulder holding him down.

"Belay that. You're in no position to move."

Undeterred, he clenched his jaw, pushed Mike's hand away, and rose to his feet. "Give me the damn canister. Those Air Force guys have to be wondering what the hell's going on. See to them."

Chapter Forty-Eight

3110 PROSPECT STREET NW
GEORGETOWN, WASHINGTON, D.C.
THURSDAY 13 MARCH

Senior Special Agent Gunnar Vanatsky watched the FBI's Special Weapons and Strike Team slip into their assigned positions. He chafed at his command vehicle being parked so far from the objective, but he couldn't take the additional risk of alerting an early riser on the quiet Prospect Street neighborhood.

The men of the assault force, in full tactical gear and armed with MP5 submachine guns, appeared as stealthy shadows in the pre-dawn darkness. In several minutes they would be in their assigned positions preparing to breach the target.

He'd also had to accept the last-minute addition of another team to his operation. A decision in which he'd had no say. "Compartmentalized, need-to-know," he'd been told. *SEAL Team 6? Army Delta Force? CIA Special Operatives?* Who the hell knew? He sure as hell didn't. What he did know? They weren't FBI.

He'd acquiesced to the order, his objections overridden by no less a personage than the director. To their credit, the other team had kept their distance after he relegated their involvement to taking down the carriage house. Their leader, face covered with a Bravo type skull mask favored by the SEALS, didn't object to his assignment. He'd also hesitated when the man's steel-blue eyes locked onto his. This guy wasn't someone to screw around with. Relenting to their involvement, he couldn't help but harbor a suspicion this mysterious three-man team were the same ones who'd rescued Parkos.

And Parkos? Another mystery he'd failed to crack. The man he'd arrested several weeks before appeared to have friends in very high places. Parkos had also managed to evade the Federal Marshall surveillance team to their and the Bureau's great embarrassment. Hell, he'd even heard rumors circulating within headquarters that Parkos had been wounded during a top-secret operation in Alaska.

A hand touched his shoulder. "Sir, the units are in place."

"Are the power, internet, and phones lines cut?"

"Yes, sir."

"And we have verification that Alert Alarm has been notified?"

"Yes, sir. The company deactivated the home's system before we cut power."

There would be no piercing wail of a motion detector or an intruder alarm. Vanatsky's jaw tightened. "All right, let's do this." He spoke into his headset. "All units. Execute."

Special Agent Anthony DiMaccio's breaching team's thirty-five-pound battering ram slammed into the home's white-oak front door just above the doorknob. The splintered door flew open at the second impact, the double locks shattered. There was no need to use explosives for a ballistic breach.

"Go. Go. Go."

His assault team poured into the foyer, the first man of their conga line sweeping the entryway with his MP5. "FBI. FBI." An instant later, the members of the single file team peeled off to secure their assigned sectors. "CLEAR, CLEARs" resounding room-by-room. He followed them in and made his way to the dining room to begin his search for incriminating evidence. Others targeted the computers.

"FBI! Drop your weapon!"

He yanked his hand from the rosewood credenza at the sound of the command. He spun, weapon drawn. Before him stood a man clad in a traditional Chinese dark-blue silk sleeping gown festooned with an embroidered Imperial five-toed dragon. The man's right hand clutched an ornate, curved letter opener. He recognized the face from the surveillance photos. James Wai. Behind Wai stood one of his agents, his MP5 centered on the center of Wai's back.

The agent repeated his order. "Drop it."

Wai hesitated, took a step, then froze.

DiMaccio leveled his weapon. "Don't do anything stupid."

Wai dropped his hands to his sides, the opener falling to the floor.

"On your knees. Hands behind you head." DiMaccio kept his weapon on Wai and addressed the other agent positioned at the room's double doors. "Cuff him and read him his rights."

A defiant scowl crossed Wai's face. "I am Jia Lin-Wu Tai, a Chinese citizen. You have no right to violate my home."

DiMaccio ignored him.

"I—"

He held up a handful of documents including a folded-up map of Alaska he'd extracted from the credenza's middle drawer. "Shut up. You are James Wai, an Amer—" Before he could say more, another agent appeared at the door.

"The house is secure, sir. We have Huifeng. There's no sign of the other guy."

———

"Go," Geoffrey Lange ordered when Vanatsky's execute order came over his earpiece.

George tightened his grip on the two handles of his battering ram and swung it at the carriage house door. There was no need for finesse this time around. The door's right panel splintered at the blow, but the locks remained intact.

Lange thought he heard a shriek. "God, we're making enough noise to wake the dead."

George wound up and swung, landing a violent strike that created a small opening at edge of the doorframe. "They must have reinforced the damn thing."

The third member of Lange's team stepped forward and gapped the door with his breaching tool exposing the dead bolt. "Man, you're losing your touch. You gotta get back to the gym."

"Screw you, Cade." George shifted his grip and swung again. The weakened door flew open at the impact.

Lange shoved the door aside and advanced, weapon leveled, prepared to engage. By design, Cade hung behind his left shoulder. If he went down, Cade would take out the shooter. Prepared for the sound and impact of gunshots, he was confronted by an ear-piercing shriek. The housekeeper. He held fire and pivoted right toward the open staircase. "Clear."

"Geoff!"

He whirled at Cade's shout, at first only seeing the old woman standing frozen in place in the center of the room. *What-the-hell?*

A muscular forearm swept out from behind the house-keeper, sending the wizened old woman tumbling to the floor.

In her place stood Wai's squat bodyguard. Tao Yixing, legs braced, clad only in a pair of black skivvies, holding a vicious machete-like Chinese dadao.

Undeterred, he leveled his Glock pistol, centering the laser sight on Yixing's heart. This bastard had probably killed Jason. Maybe in the dungeon-like root cellar where they'd found Parkos. His finger tightened on the trigger and challenged himself more than Yixing. "Give me a reason." Then louder, not knowing if the Chinese even understood him. "Drop it!"

Yixing looked down at the red dot centered on his chest, grimaced, emitting a loud sucking sound through a gap in his front teeth. He raised his head, fixing his coal-black eyes at the skull-masked intruder. He set his legs and deliberately raised the lethal sword in a double-handed grip, preparing to strike.

"*Mēigué húndàn!*" The Mandarin expletive spit from Yixing's mouth as he lunged forward, the dadao slashing through the air in a vicious arc.

He didn't hesitate. Three centered 9mm rounds struck Yixing, sending him reeling backwards, sword clattering to the floor. He lowered his weapon, smoke still curling from the muzzle, and approached Yixing's inert body. "Don't ever carry a sword to a gun fight, asshole."

He looked at George, ignoring the blood pumping from the three tightly spaced holes in Yixing's chest. "Check the cellar and see if you can find anything that can lead us to Jason."

A whimpering sound caught his attention. He cast a glance at the housekeeper. She was curled up in a ball on the floor only feet from the blood pooling next to Yixing's body. "Cade, secure the old woman. I'm going to have a look around."

Chapter Forty-Nine

THE NICKLOAS
GEORGETOWN, WASHINGTON, D.C.
FRIDAY 23 MARCH

"Good evening, sir." Edmund stood aside to admit Nick and his guest into the club's foyer. "And this must be Ms. O'Brian. It's a pleasure to welcome you to The Nicholas, madame." He flashed a smile and switched to his native Scottish brogue. "An' tis a good name you have too, lassie."

Michelle answered in Scottish Gaelic, her green eyes sparkling with mischief. "Tapadh leibh, Edmund." She judged his reaction to this unexpected twist and knew she'd won his heart.

"If I… Edmond stuttered. "If I may, I will take your coats. Mr. Parkos, you will find the other guests gathered in the drawing room."

"Wow, nice place," she said as they made their way toward the stairs.

Nick barely registered the sound of her voice. A thousand thoughts swirled through his mind as he tried to process all that had happened during the past thirty hours.

Bryce Gilmore had started the clock the previous afternoon when he'd personally briefed him on what had transpired while he'd been recuperating from his wound. The most significant? The Justice Department had dropped all their charges against him.

As for the Chinese, the DNI said that Federal Agents had arrested James Wai, aka Jia Lin-Wu Tai, for violations of the Foreign Agents Registration Act and that Wai's remaining associate, citing both Diplomatic Immunity and fingering Yixing as Moore's killer, was deported. *"What about the other guy? Odd Job?"* he recalled asking. Yixing had been killed resisting arrest.

And the traitors? Gilmore touched on all the names he'd written on his blue index cards pinned to the cork board in his office. Sylvester Poad resigned "to pursue other opportunities" after cutting a deal with Federal Prosecutors to implicate the others that his and Lange's investigations had unearthed: Devon Gant, senior staffer at Treasury, Kimberly Browning, Interior's Mineral Management Division, Ashli Thompson, lawyer for Department of State's planning office, and Mark Arita, his supposed friend.

Deputy Secretary of State, Kathrine Oakes, elected to retire after a distinguished career. Gilmore said the jury was still out, but for now, Justice didn't have enough to send her case to a Grand Jury.

On a final note, Gilmore said he'd left it to Justin Brown, Admiral Lawson, and the State Department to deal with the diplomatic fallout from the Chinese incursion at Cape Lisburne. The two Sea Dragon commandos they'd captured remained under wraps and State hadn't heard a word from Beijing demanding their return. The PLAN ships had departed the Chukchi Sea, presumably returning to their home port, shadowed by the *Truxtun* until they were well into international waters north of Japan.

Michelle cast him a knowing glance. "Are you all right?"

"Just thinking."

"That usually leads to trouble."

"Not this time." He placed his hand on the small of her back guiding her up the stairs. A rare smile crossed his face when they reached the top. "This is where it all began."

Michelle looked around the small assemblage scattered about the elegant room presumably waiting for the arrival of the guests of honor. "I thought you hatched your crazy plans at the office."

"Mostly, but this is where Geoff introduced me to some great Scotch and notable cigars. I even tried sushi."

"Really? You actually ate some? I thought you hated raw fish."

"I do. I took a bite to be polite."

"And the cigars?"

"One of the advantages of a private club," he said, spotting Geoff who was attired in his maroon smoking jacket, seated comfortably in his favorite chair by the fireplace. He was pleased to see him conversing with his friend from the Bureau, Jessica Caudry. Geoff rose, excused himself, and crossed the room.

Michelle followed Nick's eyes to Lange, Glencairn glass outstretched in his hand.

"Michelle, welcome to our secret lair," Geoff said. "It's so wonderful to see you. Sure beats the other times our paths have crossed. Can I get you something?"

"A Manhattan would be great."

"Edmund?"

Edmund gave a small nod of approval. "Certainly, sir."

Geoff handed Nick the glass. "I presumed you'd want to try one of our new Speyside scotches.

"And Nick, my friend," he continued with a wide grin,

"you're sporting a great metrosexual look. I'm impressed. Did Michelle dress you?"

Geoff's remark earned a snicker from Michelle and quick denial from Nick.

"No, she did not."

"Gotta say, you're looking good. Button-down gray shirt, designer jeans, all pulled together by a red handkerchief in the breast pocket of a dark-blue sportscoat."

"Metrosexual? Geoff, what-the-hell are you talking about?"

"It's a neologism."

"That doesn't help."

"Webster's would define a neologism as a newly coined word determined by artifice."

He groaned and turned, relieved at the sound of another voice coming from behind him. *George?* But he didn't recognize the man's clean-shaven face. "George?"

"None other."

Michelle leaned over and gave George a peck on the cheek. "Thank you so much for all you did for us at the cottage."

"I figure it was the least I could do considering all the trouble I got him into."

Nick scanned the room, declining to comment. "Is Taylor coming?"

"Couldn't make it," Lange said.

"Can't say I'm disappointed," Jessica said as she joined the group. "But enough of that." She turned to Michelle, a dazzling smile erasing the frown that had appeared on her face at the mention of Ferguson. "I finally get to meet the wonderful woman who's kept this guy grounded."

He reached for Michelle's hand, giving it a gentle squeeze. "You have no idea. I'm amazed she's put up with me."

"Well, I've been saving some good news for us to celebrate," Jessica said. "The FBI raid on Wai's place in Georgetown uncovered a trove of documents including ones labeled *Operation Hoya Saxa and Calamus*. Calamus provided the specifics on how you were targeted."

"So, that explains all the weird stuff that happened in your place," Michelle said. "You weren't nuts. Well, not about that anyway."

"Justice also unsealed the Grand Jury testimony pertaining to Wai's American accomplices."

"What about that guy from Cal Berkley?" Mike asked.

"Hopkins. We don't have enough to indict him yet, but the raid on Wai's house found his name along with about two-dozen others on documents pertaining to their Foreign Experts Recruitment program. We may have him on wire fraud and failure to disclose the Chinese money on a federal grant application."

Jessica continued before Nick could reply. "All that's to say, Nick Parkos, you're free and clear."

Michelle tightened her grip on Nick's hand. "It's really over?"

He felt the last of his doubts fall from his shoulders, all the burdens he'd carried, gone. "Appears so."

Geoff gestured toward Mike Rohrbaugh who was chatting with Austin Mack. "Michelle, have you met Austin? Nick's partner in crime?"

"No, I haven't, but Nick's told me all about his family business."

Geoff guided Michelle toward a long table set with an impressive spread of cheese and hors d'eouvres. "Then I'd say it's time to introduce you to some of Wisconsin's finest arti-sanal cheese."

"Wow, where do I start?"

Mike hefted his plate and took a bite of the bacon-wrapped oyster he'd selected. "Anywhere you'd like. It's all great."

"Austin, you've got to open a catering business. This is just amazing," Jessica said.

A gleam appeared in Nick's hazel eyes, a gleam that'd been erased by the stress of the past months. "Naw, we've got something else in mind for him."

Geoff and Mike stared at Austin, parroting the word Nick so often tossed at them. "We?"

"Yeah, 'We'," Nick said. "He's moving up to take my spot."

Geoff appeared completely nonplused. "What?"

He held up Michelle's left hand to display a sparkling engagement ring. "I'm taking an extended leave of absence."

"Say again?" Geoff said, alternately eyeing the ring and Nick's face.

Jessica recovered first. "You've set a date?"

"Maybe the second week of June," Michelle said. "I've been accepted for the Airman Scholarship and Commissioning Program. I'm enrolling at Texas A&M. The fall term begins mid-August. We're moving to College Station."

Geoff almost dropped his glass of Scotch. "What—?"

Mike anticipated Geoff's question about Nick's job and turned the subject. "We're looking at the future Second Lieutenant Parkos? Wow. Congratulations."

"Wait, wait," George interrupted. "Why don't Aggies call nine-one-one in an Emergency?"

Michelle placed both of her hands on her hips, widened her stance, and shot a defiant glare at the man towering over her . "Oh, no you don't buddy. We're not doing Aggie jokes."

"I want to be the first."

Michelle relented and smiled. "You're allowed one."

"Because they can't find an eleven on the rotary dial."

"Pretty lame, buddy," Nick said. "You're going to need to do way better than that."

"Why do Ag—"

Jessica held up her hand cutting George off. "That's it. The lady said *only one*."

Geoff reached for his humidor, then stopped. "In deference to the ladies present, I'll refrain."

"Not me," Jessica said, holding out her hand. This news calls for a celebration."

Nick turned to Michelle. "I've got a surprise for you."

"Oh, another gift from Alaska?"

"How'd you guess?" "I've been thinking. How'd—"

Michelle cast him a skeptical look. "Uh, oh. Thinking again?"

"No, really. I'm serious. How'd you like to go to Seward for our honeymoon?"

"The Army camp in Alaska you told me about?"

"It's beautiful up there."

"Just don't expect him to cook," Mike said.

"Give me a break, Rohrbaugh. I can cook," he protested.

"Back to Alaska. Isn't that a song?" George asked.

Michelle let out a sigh. "No, silly. The song is *North to Alaska*. Johnny Horton. And, Mr. Nick, I'd love to go. I'll also have you doubters know, that if all else fails, he is quite capable of opening a soft pouch of tuna. We'll survive."

"At least his cat hasn't died of food poisoning," George said.

"What about you, Geoff?" Nick asked, not wishing to talk about his cooking skills.

"Oh, there's no shortage of opportunities for the team stacking up in the queue."

"You're not thinking of including me … are you?" he asked.

"Not yet, anyway," Geoff said.

"Good."

"But you might want to consider joining the team. The offer's open."

Michelle held up her left hand displaying her sparkling diamond for all to see. "Nope. Not gonna happen."

"Sorry, Geoff," he added. "The boss has spoken."

His eyes caught Michelle's emerald-green ones, embracing them. "At the end of the day, she is what matters. Everything else can wait."

Nick Parkos' head jerked up from his notebook, his concentration broken by the sound of his iPhone singing out the first bars of Aerosmith's "Dream On." Dressed in a tattered pair of tan shorts and an old T-shirt, he'd been working on his latest project, his family's genealogy. He slid his finger over the answer bar without glancing at the phone's screen expecting the call to be from his wife, Michelle. "Hi there, kiddo."

"Please hold for the director.

His hand clenched the phone at the sound of the male voice. "Director?" he said to the empty apartment. *What the hell?* He only knew one *Director*. The Director of National Intelligence. Bryce Gilmore came on the line before he could gather his thoughts.

"Nick, we need you," Gilmore said without preamble.

He stiffened at the sound of the DNI's voice, the voice dredging up a tumult of suppressed emotions. He'd heard nothing from the Agency for three months. His last contact? A frustrating call to HR about his benefits. And now? A personal call from the Director? Nothing good would come of this.

His jaw tightened at the intrusion, his mind clouding with foreboding, his stomach filling with dread. Since moving to

Texas, he devoted his time to forgetting, puttering around the apartment, struggling to keep his mind occupied. A man without a cause.

His few outings into the community included several visits to the local range where he maintained his proficiency with his M9 Beretta, never figuring he'd ever have to use it again. He glanced at the stack of Thank You notes he'd just finished for his and Michelle's wedding. He'd left his previous life behind or so he'd thought.

Gilmore filled in the silence. Does the name, Petr Hájek, mean anything to you?"

"No, sir," he replied, struggling to ignore the churning in his gut.

"We thought it might. Things are going to hell in the Balkans."

"What about Austin?" When he had worked in the Analytics Department specializing in Balkan Transnational Crime Organizations (TCOs), Austin Mack had been his assistant. When he'd left the agency, Austin had moved up to replace him.

"Mack's the one who suggested we call. We've got a hiring freeze and couldn't backfill." Gilmore stopped. "I'll reset. You could give a damn about my personnel problems."

"I care about what happens to Austin," he answered, while silently agreeing with the DNI's assessment.

"Fair enough," Gilmore continued. Mack's swamped and you've got field experience."

He shook his head in disbelief. "You want me to go to the Balkans?"

"I can't overstate the importance of what I'm asking you to do. You're the only one I trust to get the job done. Mack—"

He eyed the plate of cooling leftovers next to his notebook, put his phone on speaker, and laid it on the table. He flexed his fingers preparing for the worst. "What's happening?"

"I can't say over an open line," Gilmore said confirming

his fears. "Talk things over with Michelle. If you agree, I'll arrange for a plane."

"Is Geoff involved?" he prodded, ignoring the offer. Geoffrey Lange led The Curators, a black ops unit of the NSA's Special Operations Center. Buried within the Special Operations Group, the unit's mission paralleled those covert direct-action groups within the CIA. The Curators operated under deep cover, conducting clandestine operations the government officially distanced itself from and which were not suitable for Delta Force or SEAL Team Six. And if a mission failed and the operators were captured? The government would disavow any knowledge of them. The Curators were not listed on the organization chart or even acknowledged.

"Lange can be if you want him on your team."

He cocked his head at the DNI's response, imaging in his mind Gilmore's eyes peering over the top of his half-glasses and down the length of his nose like sighting a rifle. *My team?*

"Call Strickland with your answer." Three tones sounded on his phone. Gilmore had terminated the call.

He stood, then dropped back into his kitchen chair and stared at the refrigerator door pasted with a scattering of notes and pictures of his new life. "Crap."

———

Where you are sets your reality. And for Nick? His new reality centered on two things, a notebook on the small dinette table pushed against the wall of his apartment's kitchen and Gilmore's call. Deep in thought, he tapped out a syncopated rhythm on the black-leather cover of the Le Vin spiral notebook Michelle had given him the day before.

He settled on a way to cope with Gilmore's call, opened the book, and scribed PARKOS/PATYKOVIA in large caps at top of the first lined page. His pen halted at the cross of the last 'A,' his eyes settling on the needlepoint Michelle had finished celebrating their marriage that hung on the wall by his head. His attention drifted to their small living room with its seldom watched flatscreen and the mix of Midwest décor from their old apartments. She'd explained the look was *eclectic*. And the new recliner? Michelle's wedding present. She insisted he trash the ancient, stained chair, burdened with its memories of the dark times in his life.

Why would I even consider Gilmore's request? He's playing the damn guilt card. He dropped his head trying to wrap his mind around what had just happened. He wanted a drink. Another demon he'd battled.

His mind settled on something the FBI's Agent-in-Charge of the Miami Field Office said years before that speared his consciousness. "It's always complicated with you guys." Nick agreed. The complications, the unanswered questions. That realization forced him to think. He grabbed a pen and began to jot down the pros and the cons, settling on what would happen if he agreed to return.

Topping the list? He'd demand that his old supervisor be sidelined. Marriage hadn't been the only thing that prompted his departure from the Agency. He'd been burned. Become a persona non grata. He suspected Strickland. Perhaps leaving was fortuitous, his career likely maxed out as an analysist. Of medium height and bone with brown hair and hazel eyes, he hardly stood out as a leader destined for an executive service or even a GS-15 level position despite Gilmore's expressed confidence in him. Those positions were beyond his reach.

He picked up the spiral notebook and wrote "Petr Hájek?" on the blank page below his own name. He'd intended to use the notebook for his research to trace his family's genealogy prompted by the ancient keepsake box discovered in his grandparent's attic. He studied the box, its oak burnished with age. The joinery was exceptional, made from contrasting woods. The filigreed latches and lock were of bronze. On the lid he could make out a Coat of Arms with the faded image of a white lion. Without a key, he dared not try to open the lock, to literally unlock the secrets inside.

He'd have to place both projects on hold if he returned to Washington. Until the call, he'd almost begun to feel normal, although he had no firm concept of what *normal* was after nine years at the Agency. He looked up at the sound of the apartment door opening. Michelle. And on the wall to the door's left? Their crucifix. He'd been raised in the church, but Michelle's faith was much stronger…perhaps strong enough for the both of them.

"Hello sweetie."

Her voice pushed the annoyance from his mind. He set the pen down and looked at his bride of two months. The greeting, meant for his pet and not him, had become a private joke between the two of them when they first began to date. He'd name the stray he'd adopted years before, Bill, after the frazzled feline featured in the Bloom County and Opus comic strips.

He smiled as Michelle swept up their limp, purring cat who'd been asleep by the front door, waiting for her. "How were classes?"

She set Bill down and dropped her backpack by the kitchen table. Weighted down by books, it landed with a heavy thud. "Fun, Newtonian Mechanics. I gotta go back for lab this afternoon."

He shook his head, marveling at her drive. She was now deep into her Aerospace Engineering studies at Texas A&M working toward a commission in the Air Force courtesy of the Airman Scholarship Program. "That can't possibly be fun." He stood and accepted her hug.

Michelle detached herself from his embrace and looked at the leftovers. "Whatcha eatin?"

"Red beans and rice. Want some?"

She picked up his fork and gave a bean a suspicious poke.

"They won't poison me?" she teased, her emerald eyes sparkling with mischief.

"Geez."

Michelle's eyes drifted to the sheet of paper covered with his scrawled notes filling the columns under the headings of 'Pro and Con.' "What's that?"

He made to cover the paper, then pulled his hand back, not knowing how to break the news. He couldn't lie. "I got a call from Bryce Gilmore."

She dropped the fork. "What on earth for?"

"He wants me to come back."

"To D.C.?"

"Yeah."

"Oh." She wobbled and reached for the table. "What did you say?"

"That we'd talk. I didn't commit." He reached for her hand. "I won't do anything you're against."

"Do you want to go?"

"Truthfully, I don't know. There's a lot of broken glass left on the ground."

"Strickland?"

"And others. I need to call Geoff."

"Good idea. Think about it and we'll talk this evening."
***
Nick scrolled through his contact list after Michelle left for the A&M campus. He picked up his phone not knowing where the conversation would lead, and tapped in the number of a burner. All he knew at the moment was that he needed to talk to a trusted friend. He answered on the second tone.

"Lange."

"You know what's going on?"

"Well, it's good to talk to you, too," Geoff Lange, the chief of The Curators responded. "How's Michelle?"

"She would be a whole lot better if it weren't for Gilmore's call.

"He called her?"

"No. Me. He wants me to come back."

"What the hell for?"

"I hoped you'd know. He asked if the name Petr Hájek meant anything."

"Never heard... No, wait. Could be the Hájek Group. I hear they're making a move in Czechoslovakia."

"Gilmore did mention that the Balkans were going to hell."

"He wants you to clean things up?"

"Can you test the waters?"

"I'll check around."

Acknowledgments

Once again you've come to the end of another novel, but as Nick's mysterious message said, "It's Not Over." Indeed. I could not have published the third book of my five novel "The Defenders" series without the advice, support, and assistance from many people. Writing and publishing a novel is a daunting task made no less easier because of the difference between reality and fiction. Fiction must make sense and with that in mind, I strove to make both the plot and characters in my novel believable. You, my readers, will be the final judge on whether I succeeded or not. So, with those few words, I want to acknowledge those friends, peers, and source experts who provided the assistance to bring *Arctic Menace* to fruition.

First, I would like to thank and send a 'Bravo Zulu" to the U.S. Coast Guard Motion Picture, Television, and Author Program Office in Los Angeles and specifically to my Project Officer, Chief Warrant Officer-3 Michael Lutz. Mike was, and still is, always available for questions and walked me through the processes to ensure I navigated the necessary requirements to ensure I met the Coast Guard's requirements for the specific chapters pertaining to the United States Coast Guard.

He also reviewed those chapters pertaining to the Coast Guard and I am indebted to him for his advice and guidance. On that note, it was a privilege for me to highlight the Coast Guard's contribution to our nation's defense, particularly the services' work in the Arctic. With those thoughts in mind, my supporting character, Lieutenant Sarah MacAuley, USCG, highlights the role of women in the Coast Guard as well as those other women in service to our nation.

Next up, Major Brian Spillane, United States Marine Corps. A pilot, Brian flies the CH-53E heavy lift helicopter and he provided invaluable insight and suggestions to ensure the multiple chapters featuring the MH-65 Dolphin helicopters were both accurate and realistic. Commander George Wallace, USN Retired, past commanding officer of the fast attack submarine *USS Houston* SSN713, and author of the acclaimed "Hunter Killer" series of novels kindly provided his insights and knowledge reviewing those chapters featuring submarines to ensure they were credible. And finally, I must recognize former Navy SEAL, Lieutenant Jake Zweig, for running a 'sanity check' of the final action chapters of Arctic Menace for accuracy and credibility.

I remain indebted to my "Primary Reader," friend and fellow author, Mr. Rick Ludwig. Rick spent countless hours reviewing my manuscript for content and flow, making innumerable suggestions that greatly improved the work. Primary Readers providing a second set of eyes and are invaluable, trusted assets who provide an honest evaluation of an author's work. The final manuscript would not have come to fruition without the editing and formatting skills of Ally Richardson. I never cease to be amazed that no matter how many times I reviewed my draft to see how many errors she discovered and noted for me to address, particularly those cursed "dangling participles."

The old adage of: "You can tell a book by its cover," is true. Think of how many times you'd glance at a cover and decide to pick the book up for a look or take a pass and choose another. Ms. Maria Novillo Sararia, BEAUTeBOOK.com, has again done a masterful job in portraying the essence of my third novel. She has carried the theme of each cover through the series that includes major thematic elements including the subtly rendered flags of the major participants. This brings me to my publicist Ms. *Sharon Jenkins, Sharon@ mcwritingservices.com.* I am indebted to her for her expertise, guidance, and patience while dragging me into the world of social media. Her design and outreach on my web and Facebook pages has been truly outstanding.

Finally, I must again thank my friend, mentor, and publisher, New York Times best-selling author, Mr. William Bernhardt, Publisher, Babylon Books. He has spent numerous hours guiding me through all the hurdles that have to be negotiated, literally, to release *Arctic Menace.*

In closing, I did manage to exercise a bit of restraint and not take a page from the producers of the movie "Hot Shot." A spoof of the 1986 hit "Top Gun," they inserted into their movie's credits two recipes and a final comment that if you'd actually stayed to read all the credits as they rolled by, "you would have been home by now." I suppose that if you are listening to the audio book and stayed with my credits, you too, might be home by now.

Cheers, Ken

About the Author

Kenneth Andrus is a native of Columbus, Ohio. He obtained his undergraduate degree from Marietta College and his doctor of medicine from the Ohio State University College of Medicine. Following his internship, he joined the Navy and retired after twenty-four years of service with the rank of Captain.

His operational tours while on active duty included: Battalion Surgeon, Third Battalion Fourth Marines; Brigade Surgeon, Ninth Marine Amphibious Brigade, Operation Frequent Wind; Medical Officer, USS *Truxtun* CGN-35; Fleet Surgeon, Commander Seventh Fleet; Command Surgeon, U.S. Naval Forces Central Command, Desert Shield/Desert Storm; and Fleet Surgeon, U.S. Pacific Fleet.

His webpage can be found at: www.kennethandrus.com

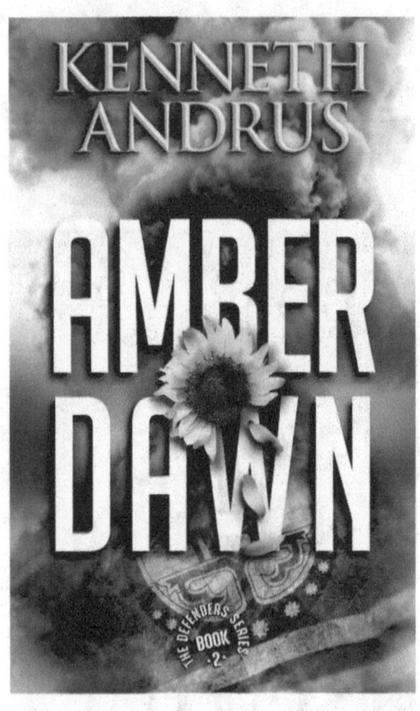

Nick Parkos is a low-level intelligence analyst when a shocking twist thrusts him to the forefront. All at once he's the man best qualified to deal with a dire threat to the stability of the entire world. Bashir al-Khulyter, seeking revenge for his family's deaths by Russian paramilitary troops, detonates a dirty bomb in Moscow's Red Square—and threatens to deploy four more bombs in the near future. With the world's capitals on red alert, Parkos must find and stop al-Khultyer before thousands are killed and entire cities are contaminated.

While dealing with powerful personal demons, Parkos follows a cryptic trail across three continents and eleven cities, hoping he can somehow prevent additional brutal and merciless deaths. But Bashir has more lethal surprises planned than Parkos can anticipate. The first bomb killed thousands—and the next could destabilize fragile peace in the world's most treacherous regions.

Publisher's Note

Babylon Books is a division of Bernhardt Books, a family-owned publishing house founded in 1999 that specializes in showcasing emerging authors and compelling fiction.

Editor-in-Chief: Alice Bernhardt
Marketing Director: Ralph Bernhardt
Chief Financial Officer: Harrison Bernhardt